Gross, Martin L.
(Martin Louis),
1925-

Man of destiny.

$24.00

DATE			

ER & TAYLOR

MAN OF DESTINY

Nonfiction by Martin L. Gross

MAN OF DESTINY

MARTIN L. GROSS

AVON BOOKS  NEW YORK

This is a work of fiction. Names, characters, places,
and incidents either are the product of the author's
imagination or are used fictitiously. Any resemblance
to actual events, locales, organizations, or persons,
living or dead, is entirely coincidental and beyond
the intent of either the author or the publisher.

AVON BOOKS
A division of
The Hearst Corporation
1350 Avenue of the Americas
New York, New York 10019

Copyright © 1997 by Martin L. Gross
Interior design by Kellan Peck
Visit our website at **http://AvonBooks.com**
ISBN: 0-380-97417-7

Library of Congress Cataloging in Publication Data:
Gross, Martin L. (Martin Louis)
   Man of destiny / Martin L. Gross.
      p.   cm.
   I. Title.
PS3557.R587M36   1997   96-47657
813'.54—dc21   CIP

First Avon Books Printing: July 1997

AVON TRADEMARK REG. U.S. PAT. OFF. AND IN OTHER COUNTRIES, MARCA REGISTRADA, HECHO EN U.S.A.

Printed in the U.S.A.

FIRST EDITION

QPM   10   9   8   7   6   5   4   3   2   1

To my wife, Anita,
for her concern and companionship
and to Thomas Jefferson,
from whom all liberty springs

ACKNOWLEDGMENTS

To my editor, Tom Colgan, and my publisher, Lou Aronica, who had faith in my ability to tell a political story as well as investigate one. For my agent, John Hawkins, with appreciation for his patience.

A special acknowledgment to my good friends, Ray and Dee Justus, who encouraged and critiqued this novel as it was being formed. And to Betsy Hulick, whose dedicated editorial advice has been invaluable over the years.

A nod as well to various federal government agencies, which—however reluctantly—provided some of the information that enabled the novel's hero, Charlie Palmer, to show the errors in the politics and structure of our democracy that first plagued, then finally enhanced, him and the nation.

—Martin L. Gross
June 1997

PROLOGUE

The pacing usually helped to clear his thoughts, but tonight he found it tiresome.

Peering down, he carefully followed the path of his heavy black shoes across the antique Herez carpet in the family quarters of the White House—wondering if he was damaging expensive public property.

This wasn't the first eccentric thought that had overtaken him this second day of his administration. Usually, he was portrayed by the press as slightly manic, full of vinegar with surges of energy that friends found exhilarating and political enemies feared.

But tonight, as President, he was more anxious than exuberant. The reason was the upcoming near-midnight rendezvous. Would it upset his plans for the nation, a vision that filled notebooks but that he hadn't fully shared even with those close to him?

Those lofty aspirations had now been pushed into the back of his mind. All he could think of was tonight's business, a nocturnal escapade that was personal and selfish, if absolutely necessary. Still he feared that someday it might explode into a national political tragedy.

Already it had upset his pressing routine. The reports he had meant to go through lay on the table, unread.

He glanced at his watch: 9:49 P.M.

Staring at the awkward half-circular window, he could see the

1

January storm pressing up against the triple-layer glass, which he heard was bullet-proof. Swirls of snow powder tumbled in the cold air like acrobats, some of it sticking aimlessly against the oversize window. For a moment, he played a child's game, piecing together the spare profile of Jefferson out of the snowflake patterns.

The thought of Jefferson, his mentor, made him laugh as he looked down at his outfit. All this time, he'd been dressed only in blue boxer undershorts and a white crew-neck T-shirt. Brooks Brothers' best.

Had anyone seen him in this state of undress? Did the Secret Service, the CIA—or some arcane intelligence outfit unknown even to him—maintain television surveillance of chief executives? Did it include voyeurism, especially sexual? That hardly troubled him tonight. He was alone, almost painfully so.

Abruptly, he halted his pacing and picked up the wine silk bathrobe, a birthday gift from his mother, which had been carefully laid out for him by the valet. As he placed his arms into the sleeves, the rehearsed details of the sortie flooded his mind. The ETA? 11:30 P.M.

A surge of adrenaline moved him swiftly across the room. Again he checked his watch. Time had outpaced him. 10:13 P.M.

Reaching a large closet, he opened it, stooped, and groped awkwardly through its bottom. Without looking down, he could feel his fingertips brush up against a hard-shell piece of luggage that had been delivered to the White House just that afternoon. The "messenger" was a trusted aide with top secret clearance who had circumvented the usual probing.

He lifted the case in a trial move. He found it heavy, but swung it back and forth as if to prove to himself that it could be handled easily without arousing excessive curiosity. All was quiet, a peculiar stillness that only exacerbated his anxiety. At 10:24 P.M., he walked through the sitting room of the family quarters and opened the outside door. Cautiously, he stepped out onto the carpeted hallway, the lush piling giving him a slight sense of confidence.

Surely, he was an odd sight. The day-old President, dressed only in a silk robe covering his underwear, with exposed long black socks, and carrying a piece of hard luggage, paraded down the hall, looking neither left nor right for fear of appearing less than presidential. He knew he was being watched by curious, inwardly smiling Secret Service agents. All the aplomb he had picked up in a short political career rushed to his defense as he walked nonchalantly, just as if this charade were part of his normal evening routine—something those around him would just have to get used to.

He might fool others, but not himself. His plan for the evening was unprecedented—filled not only with trepidation, but with inordinate risk. Still, all other options were closed to him.

From the corner of his eye, he could make out two agents poised against the wall. One was immediately to the right of the doorway. Directly ahead of him, near the private elevator, was a tall, beefy man. The President smiled, thinking that stereotypes are often correct. He looked like a White House Secret Service agent.

"Think I'll go to my office," the President said, his voice falsely casual. "I've got some important work to get through tonight."

"Good, Mr. President. I'm on duty for another twenty minutes, so if I don't see you again, good night."

He smiled at the professional indulgence of the agent, who hadn't even blinked at the sight of the President of the United States in only a robe on his way to work, carrying an oversize case obviously not designed for the tools of government.

Entering the paneled self-service elevator, he descended to the main floor, casually nodding to another agent. He hadn't seen him before, but with ear plugs and a Smith & Wesson .38 bulging against the suit, his occupation was self-advertised.

The President said nothing, then smiled—he hoped warmly enough—and began the short walk from the mansion to the Executive West Wing that held the Oval Office, a journey that now seemed interminable.

In the interregnum between election and inauguration, he had been given a private tour of the mansion and was surprised to learn that when Teddy Roosevelt built the wing in 1905, he'd failed to add an enclosed passageway between the White House and his new office. The only connection had been the open, roofed, and columned portico often seen on the television news. Behind the portico had once been John Kennedy's swimming pool, but the space had since been converted into a press room.

Family members of Presidents had pleaded with the government: Close in, or at least glass in, the passageway. But the White House Historical Society had always shot down the idea.

In 1987, fearful of terrorism, the Secret Service had finally built a tunnel between the mansion and the West Wing. Beginning in a storage closet in the basement of the White House near the president's private elevator, it runs fifty yards until it reaches a staircase up to the Oval Office, exiting in a secret sliding door next to the President's restroom.

Should he take that simple route? He decided against it when he learned that the tunnel was covered by a closed circuit monitor. Using it might instantly expose his nocturnal adventure.

He decided on the outside passageway as safer. Despite the rawness of the weather, the President's plan could not include an overcoat.

Dressed only in the flimsy silk robe, he braced for the brief, frigid walk under the outside portico, chilled by a twenty degree wind.

Setting out on this solo mission without the knowledge or presence of the Secret Service was not only daunting but embarrassing. Still, he had been given strict instructions by the other end. He was to make the journey alone.

Immediately, he had rebuffed the demand, citing his need to protect the office of the President. He offered to send an emissary with full powers to negotiate for him, but that had fallen on deaf ears. No one but the President himself would do, and no one was to accompany him. Those waiting at the rendezvous warned that someone would be watching. If he was escorted, observed, or guarded, everything they had agreed on would instantly be canceled. Not only would he have to face the inevitable consequences, but he would have to accept the full blame for the plan's failure.

The time frame was equally inflexible. It had to be on the night of his second day in office. Delay would not be tolerated, and he was in no position to argue.

Once inside the West Wing, the President hastily glanced around. No one was in sight. An agent was surely around the bend, perched in front of the Oval Office, but his path tonight would bypass his own executive suite. He made a fitful dash in the opposite direction, onto a hallway leading to a cluster of small workplaces.

Within twenty feet, he came upon a white painted door. In impressive brass lettering was the legend: "Colonel Timothy Lescomb, Air Attache."

He turned the knob. As he hoped, the door wasn't locked. Once inside, he moved quickly to the closet. Opening it, he mumbled a prayer. Yes, his target was still there: the spare uniform of the air attache, clean and neatly hung.

He hadn't chosen Colonel Lescomb by chance. The mission was too vital for such innocence. Days before, at the request of the outgoing President, he had met briefly with his military attaches, walking from office to office, introducing himself. As an ex-serviceman, he chatted with each of them about the vagaries of army life, then turned the conversation to their uniforms. Did they keep an extra one on hand for emergencies?

The air force colonel was nearest to his age, height, and weight, and, most important, kept a complete spare outfit on hand in his closet.

The President now shed the silk robe, folded it neatly into the hard-shell case, and proceeded to dress. The colonel's uniform proved to be a reasonable fit, probably a 42 regular, his size as well. He put on the trousers and regulation light blue shirt and had started to tie the navy-blue cravat in his usual wide Windsor knot when he halted nervously. Did Lescomb do it that way? He brushed the thought aside as frivolous and put on the tunic.

When dressed, he glanced at the silver eagles perched on his shoulders. They seemed to be staring at him quizzically, demanding to know his intentions. Was this escapade in the best interests of the people? To that, he had no response.

Of the two coats in the closet, one was finely tailored and winter weight; the other a dark blue raincoat. He chose the lighter-weight one, which would show less wear from the snow and dampness.

Gloves? The cold would eat away at his hands as he clutched the heavy suitcase. He reached up and sorted through the upper closet shelf. Yes, they were there. A pair of blue woolen GI issue.

Now garbed as an air force colonel, the President turned up the collar of the coat, using the flaps to hide much of his face. Suppressing his anxiety, he walked out the door of the West Wing and, suitcase firmly in hand, strolled unobtrusively down the asphalt driveway toward the guardhouse at the Northwest Gate on Pennsylvania Avenue. He assumed that there was nothing out-of-routine for the air force attache to be leaving his office this late.

The previous day the President had checked out the standard security procedure by picking the brain of Pat McNulty, the White House Secret Service chief, and now had a clear outline of the situation. The President was apparently a semi-prisoner in his fiefdom, and could only come and go if covered by a Secret Service team. But tonight he had to be alone, and disguise was his only ally.

When coming into the grounds, White House employees like Colonel Lescomb had to press their four-digit PIN into an electronic panel. They each had a pass with a hologram photo, but if they were personally recognized by the guards, they seldom had to display it.

Leaving the compound, he learned, was relatively simple. He could walk down the path toward the exit, which didn't pass directly in front of the guardhouse. When he waved, and if he was recognized, the White House policeman would just press the release button, automatically opening the iron exit gate onto Pennsylvania Avenue.

Returning to the White House was more complex, but he had planned that with equal care. From McNulty, he had requested a list of the security numbers of all senior staff, including the military attaches. The Secret Service chief seemed confused by the request, but his stoic face, the product of twenty years of dealing with chief executives and their aides, revealed no surprise. This morning, the list, marked FOR THE PRESIDENT'S EYES ONLY, had been handed to him by the agent stationed outside the family quarters.

Lescomb's number was 6814, four digits that were now engraved into his memory.

In addition to his new knowledge of the security system, the fortuitous weather was also proving to be an ally. The wind had picked up and the snow was still falling. The white swirls clouded not only his vision, but that of the White House policeman at the guardhouse as well. From what McNulty had told him, the guard came on at 7 P.M. and would not have been on duty anyway when the real Colonel Lescomb had left.

The President kept his head down, walking protectively into the snow, his face almost totally hidden by coat flaps and the precipitation.

"Good night, Colonel. Put in a long day, I see," the guard called out, pressing the release button for the exit gate.

Silently the President acknowledged the policeman with a casual touch at the brim of Lescomb's officer's cap.

Stepping out onto Pennsylvania Avenue, he glanced around in a half circle, weighing the scene. A taxi was the next prop in his scenario. He needed to get to upper Massachusetts Avenue at the northern portion of the District, adjacent to Chevy Chase, the first suburb after the Washington border. He couldn't stand in front of the White House gate and try to hail a cab. Someone might recognize him, and the chances of an empty cab stopping there on this bitter night were next to nil.

Instead, head bowed, he turned down Pennsylvania Avenue toward the Treasury Building at Fourteenth Street. Built in the 1840s, it was an architectural faux pas that blocked L'Enfant's plan of an uninterrupted sweep up Pennsylvania Avenue from the Capitol to the White House.

But his worries were now more personal, and desperate, than architectural. He walked, one, then two, blocks into the cold white wind. Approaching the renovated Willard Hotel—called the "Hotel of Presidents" after chief executives who lived there awaiting inauguration—he hesitated, then halted about seventy-five feet from its door. Caution, he whispered to himself. At all cost, caution. If he was discovered, few people would understand the nocturnal wanderings of a new President, especially one garbed in the uniform of an air force colonel.

Out of sight of the doorman, he raised first his left arm, then the suitcase itself, hoping to hail a cab approaching the Willard entrance. The snow had picked up momentum and was hitting his face with a cutting chill.

A half-dozen taxis passed by him, ignoring the wave. The smallest desperation invaded him. What if all was arranged and he couldn't get a cab on this miserable night? Was he emotionally stable enough to face the consequences?

Suddenly, a small Saab taxi stopped abruptly.

"Where to, off-i-cer?" the cabbie had called out in a French, probably Haitian, accent. "I zaw a man in uniform and had to help. Where to?"

Relieved, he mumbled, "Mass Avenue, the 4400 block." He pushed awkwardly into the taxi, whose worn rear seemed to sit only inches above the snow-plated pavement. The rendezvous was actually several blocks farther up Massachusetts Avenue, not far from the D.C. border. But still exercising caution, he pushed up the coat flaps to hide his face, and decided he wouldn't draw up directly in front of his destination.

As they rode, the driver was friendly and talkative, but the more he spoke of the weather, the city, the crime, the more silent the President became. As the cab made its way past a series of foreign embassies, he sat quietly, considering this peculiar journey and its ramifications on both his life and his new job as chief executive.

It was an unfortunate beginning to his great national adventure, but he hoped that within hours it would be over and he could take on the true work of the country. In a Washington atmosphere permeated with creative political corruption on both sides of the aisle, that challenge would require even more ingenuity than he was demonstrating tonight.

The cabbie drove on, then after several minutes, turned to business.

"Mistah, in a few minutes, we'll be coming up on the 4400 block. That will be $7.70, pleez."

The President nodded, then instinctively pressed his hand into the coat pocket, searching for his wallet.

My God. The realization was crushing. This was not his coat. His wallet was back in the White House on the bedroom dresser! Panic overtook him as he realized he didn't have a nickel on him. Never had a few dollars loomed so large in a city where billions were the guts of everyday conversation. Without his $7 plus, the driver might call the police to collect the fare.

The masquerade—the President disguised as an air force colonel in the middle of a snowy night, going God knew where—would make him a laughingstock, if not a psychiatric case history, for the nation. Would he have to leap out of the taxi and flee down Massachusetts Avenue in the borrowed uniform?

"Driver," he began, staling to think of something to barter. Perhaps his watch. No, his Rolex, a gift from his former fellow workers, was back in the bathroom, where he had absentmindedly left it. Maybe the solid silver eagles of the colonel, or the hat? No, not either. The outfit had to be returned intact to Lescomb's office tonight if he was to avoid suspicion.

As the taxi suddenly braked to stop at its destination, it skidded sideways through the slush and hit the curb. The corner of the hard suitcase rammed into his knees. His first reaction was to wince at the sharp pain. But his second? Of course. What a fool. He didn't have $7, but he had $100,000!

He lifted the heavy suitcase onto his lap and opened it. Moving aside the folded silk robe, he extracted the top $100 bill.

"Driver, all I have is a hundred dollars. Hope you can change it." He needed a carrot. "And keep an extra twenty for yourself."

The driver's grin flashed through the rearview mirror.

"Usual, I neveer cash ze large bill, but I trust officers, and I can use ze extra money." The driver searched through his wallet. "Here's your change. OK?"

Without counting it, the President pressed the money into his coat pocket and silently exited the cab. Hoping to keep Lescomb's trousers dry, he waited until the taxi had pulled away, then leaped ungracefully over an uninviting pile of plowed snow.

Several long blocks remained. Head down, he pressed through the swirling white powder, watching his feet cover only inches of the wet pavement at a time.

As the incongruity of his situation struck him, he couldn't decide if it was laughable or tragic. Why had unfathomable fate led him to this icy pavement on the second night after his inauguration? Who and what manipulated life in such near malevolent ways? Was it his fault, or was he a victim of circumstances created by others, especially his political enemies who were legion?

He guessed it was about 11:15 P.M., so he should be arriving just in time for the dreaded rendezvous. He tapped the suitcase, once, then twice, for courage and swung it back and forth, as if the torque would somehow advance his progress.

Ten minutes later, on his side of the street, he could make out the address on upper Massachusetts Avenue, almost into the edge of suburban Maryland. The house was a kind of bastard brick and shingle 1930s one-story, the type that went for about $300,000 in the inflated Washington market. Set on a small knoll about eight feet above the street, it was reached by two flights of five steps each, with an iron handrail on either side. He put the suitcase in his left hand and ascended, holding on to the right rail, afraid he'd slip on the icy steps.

Once on the flagstone landing, he rested, then rang the bell. The sound echoed in his mind, reviving the beginnings, many years ago, of what had triggered tonight's mad journey. He knew that this clandestine trip was inevitable, but what if he had fought instead of capitulating? What if he permitted the truth to be broadcast to the nation, and banked on the electorate's essential goodness to interpret it intelligently? Unfortunately, that option was no longer available.

"Anybody home?" he called out when no one answered the bell. He turned the handle. The knob yielded.

He stood in the foyer, his eyes casting everywhere.

"Mr. Fairview!" he shouted. "I'm here for the 11:30 appointment."

Twenty seconds, then almost a minute, passed, but there was no response. The President walked cautiously through the living room, an unexceptional space furnished in middle-class department-store style. Directly ahead was a small corridor with a few doors off each side and a large one at its end. Moving quietly, tentatively, down the corridor, he tried the door at the far wall. It was open.

He walked into what looked like the master bedroom, with a desk at the left end.

"Mr. Fairview?" he called out, his voice betraying his growing unease. Again there was no answer. He advanced toward the desk, which faced a large glass French door, then halted.

Someone had beaten him here. On the floor was the body of a man, sprawled out on a beige rug, now stained rust-brown with blood. A short redhead, he was positioned facedown, with a long kitchen knife protruding from his back.

The President bent, removed his gloves, and felt the pulse. There was none, but the corpse's hand felt somewhat warm to the touch. Whatever had happened, it was a recent event. The bed was made and nothing seemed out of place.

His inspection was suddenly shattered by an enormous slice of fear. My God, what had he gotten himself into? The risk was overwhelming. Everything he had done lately was laced with risk, but it had all been political and transitory. This was tangible and frightening. He was in a horribly compromising position. Should he call the police? Of course not. He had to leave—no, flee—this instant.

He turned to leave, and had moved forward two paces when he halted, suddenly petrified. An amorphous mass, a kind of shadow, had sprung from nowhere, blocking the doorway. He squinted, making out the form of a large man with a drawn gun in his hand.

"Who's there? What do you want?" he shouted, now beyond panic.

"It's me, Mr. President. What in the hell's going on?"

Immediately, he recognized the shadow. It was the night Secret Service supervisor. As a name surfaced in his mind—Larry Dunn—

relief flooded his body, followed by sharp concern. His disguise had been pierced and there was a witness to his escapade, which now included the presence of a corpse.

"What are you doing here, Larry?" the President asked. The evening was proving replete with surprise.

"I went to the Oval Office to tell you that my duty hour was changed, that I'd be on past midnight. But you weren't there, or in the small study either. Then I saw an air force officer—looked like Lescomb—walking out to the gate. I knew the colonel had left early, so I followed him. It turns out it was you. God, Mr. President, what in the hell are you doing in an air force uniform with this stiff at your feet? Is he dead?"

Without waiting for an answer, the agent dropped to his knees. He removed the gloves he had cautiously donned at the entrance to the house and felt the man's pulse, first at his wrist, then at the temple, finally at the carotid artery in the neck. Placing his gloves back on, Dunn quickly rifled the corpse's jacket and drew out a wallet.

"He's dead all right, but there's no ID on the body. Did you know him?"

"No, never saw him before, and I don't know his real name. Called himself Mr. Fairview. We spoke on the phone and I came to see him on a private matter. I put on Lescomb's clothes because I was trying to slip out of the White House unseen."

The President paused, trying to steady his thoughts. "I didn't kill him. I just walked in and found him dead. What do we do now?"

"Step back, sir," was all the agent said. He opened the French doors and swung them outward. As the cold wind rushed through, he lifted the desk chair and took it outside with him.

"Close the doors from the inside, then step out of the way," he ordered.

The President did as told. Within seconds, Dunn swung the chair in a high arc over his head and crashed it into the French door, casting shards of glass into the room. The Secret Service man came back in and started to simulate mayhem. He threw over the chair, ruffled the cover on the bed, then lifted and flung around whatever was loose. He opened the wallet and took out the money—about $60. Pocketing the cash, he tossed the empty wallet onto the disheveled bed.

"Now we've got a routine Washington break-and-enter robbery-murder. Mr. President, pick up your suitcase and let's get the hell out of here. I have my Chevy outside. You can lay low in the back. They won't check my car at the White House gate."

The President started to move out of the room, then hesitated.

Sweeping the room with his eyes, he spotted a brown attache case partially hidden by a bedpost.

He stared at the agent. "If you don't mind Larry, I'd like to be alone for a moment. I'll meet you outside."

Once Dunn had left, the President opened the dead man's case and removed a file marked "Fairview." He placed it in his own suitcase, on top of the silk robe, which was covering the incriminating money.

Outside on the flagstone landing, he stared up at the Secret Service man. "Don't you want to know what this is all about?"

"No, sir. Sure don't. Not until you decide to tell me. My job is to protect your life—maybe even against yourself. Besides, I know you didn't do it. I was in homicide in Boston, and I can tell the body's been dead for about an hour. I was maybe five minutes behind you. Now, quick, let's get our asses back to the White House before the District Police arrive. I'll call them anonymously and report the murder from a pay phone on our way back."

Mumbling, "Thanks," the President turned to follow Dunn away from the now-stilled house on Massachusetts Avenue.

The blackmailer was dead, which could mean that his cherished secret was secure. But in the process of this night's adventure, he had created another, perhaps even more dangerous, challenge.

Unknown to his millions of constituents, the chief executive of the republic had become a material witness to a brutal murder.

BOOK ONE

THE MAVERICK

CHAPTER 1

Congressman Charlie Palmer stood on the floor of the convention and gazed up at the cascade of colored balloons showering down onto the sweating, thumping crowd of delegates below.

He thought he was in the middle of an exhilarating dream as every expectation of this, his first political convention, was being fulfilled, both positively and cynically. From his seat in the Ohio section at the Javits Convention Center in New York, he watched the triangular poles surrounding him—painted with the names WYOMING, TENNESSEE, CALIFORNIA, ALABAMA—moving up and down chaotically in the hands of exuberant partisans.

He could even visualize his high school history text coming alive. It was 1860 in the Wigwam in Chicago and the jubilant delegates were nominating Abraham Lincoln as the first successful Republican presidential candidate. Or it was 1948 in Philadelphia and the crowd had just roared support for Democrat Harry S. (for nothing) Truman, then hitting bottom in the polls but ready to do battle against the popular, perennial Republican nominee, Thomas Edmund Dewey.

"MADAM CHAIRWOMAN!"

Charlie could sense his words moving electronically up past the giant color portrait of the party's white-haired standard-bearer with the legend WE LOVE LAWSON woven into an enormous silk, or maybe polyester, banner, until it reached the podium.

There, the convention chair, blue-haired, solidly constructed Congresswoman Mollie Downs of Texas was trying to hold 2,306 delegates and 2,306 alternates plus some five thousand press and hangers-on from exploding into an unruly mob.

He was surprised he had opened his mouth at all. Not that he was bashful (some thought him brash), but did a freshman representative have that right? On the other hand, he was a SUPERDELEGATE, an honor bestowed on all party members in Congress, even the most junior, like himself.

Ever since graduating from Ohio State, class of '75, Charlie had been a compulsive political junkie, if a passive one. Plunking his ass down on the couch, he'd regularly taken in the circus of democracy on CNN and C-Span. Second-guessing the politicians, he immodestly thought how much more creatively—and with less rancor—the people's business could be done. Not that he was an ideologue or an embryonic statesman. Perish the thought.

But somehow he had been fashioned with little faith in either political party or anyone else's dogma. Instead he seemed to see government clearly, as Matisse saw colors, and he was less than sure that the class of "professional" politicians, with their petty allegiances, could arrive at the same clarity, even after striking the compromises that were at the heart of the American game.

But now he was no longer passive. Finally, he was on the busy side of the tube, a much less frustrating arrangement. What, if anything, could he do with that new perspective?

"WHO'S SPEAKING?" Mollie's brassy voice blared across the auditorium. "WHO WISHES TO ADDRESS THE CHAIR?"

"ME!" Charlie's voice came out thin and funny, almost an electronic squeak.

"AND WHO IN THE HECK IS 'ME'?" Mollie barked as the delegates howled in glee.

"CONGRESSMAN CHARLES PALMER OF OHIO," he responded, having found his usual baritone.

For an instant his body froze as a hand-held TV camera pointed its curious glass head at him. He was sweating. Though the Javits people claimed the air-conditioning was working, the July heat had invaded through the geometric glass roof and hung like a vaporous steambath over the floor. Charlie loosened his collar, hoping his mother in Ohio wouldn't notice.

"I RISE ON A POINT OF ORDER, MADAME CHAIRWOMAN," Charlie shouted back to Mollie. "NOMINATIONS FOR VICE PRESIDENT WERE JUST CLOSED BUT ONLY ONE NAME—SENATOR CHAMP BILLINGS OF KENTUCKY—WAS PUT IN PLACE. DELEGATES SHOULD BE ABLE TO CONSIDER OTHER NOMINEES, SO I THINK WE OUGHT TO OPEN—"

Mollie Downs stared at Charlie as if he were an errant teenager, then flexed the gavel with extra pizzazz.

"OUT OF ORDER, CONGRESSMAN! NOMINATIONS FOR VICE PRESIDENT ARE CLOSED. TAKE YOUR SEAT SO WE CAN BEGIN THE VOTE!"

"OOOHHHHH."

An undertone of disapproval rolled through the hall. Charlie knew he was out of order, but then who on this floor wasn't, at least in their heads? After Wednesday night's acceptance speech, when presidential nominee Governor Cameron Lawson had announced his VP choice, he had left many delegates confused, even paralyzed.

Senator Champ Billings as VP? The notion of the wily, pork-happy Kentuckian one heartbeat from the Oval Office had drained the crowd like negative ions. Billings? Oh, God.

Charlie knew about Billings. The senator had been brought up on ethical charges four times, but had always escaped intact. He seemed to have more electoral lives than Grover Cleveland. Defeated twice at the polls, he had been elected for three nonconsecutive terms to the Senate, where his bourbon and branch water brand of politics worked like a Southern charm.

The delegates were soured because the brass had asked them to swallow the nomination of Billings, if only as proof of their party fealty. But Charlie had no such allegiance. In fact, less than none. So if not him, who?

In some way, he was actually pleased by tonight's brouhaha. Past conventions he had watched on television had all been dull—the primary winners arriving triumphant to be crowned on the first ballot at a $13-million party, whose full tab, incidentally, was picked up by unsuspecting taxpayers.

But this convention was almost like the brokered ones of old, the stuff of political legends. Because no one had wrapped up the primaries, there was a contest. Lawson had come in with 1,070 delegate votes, while his opponent, Senator William Storch of North Carolina, had 980, both short of the 1,154 needed for nomination.

(Thank God, Charlie said. The battle had stopped convention fathers from putting on another four-day pageant of saccharine stupidity.)

This time the swing vote was the third presidential candidate, Champ Billings, veteran porker from Kentucky, whose Senate Appropriations Committee lavished government goodies on his broad constituency—the Eastern mountain states of Kentucky, Tennessee, West Virginia, and parts of Virginia. Billions in pork had gone into that barrel, and primary voters had happily scooped it out, offering their electoral love in return.

Charlie knew the VP fix was in. Champ Billings's 256 delegates had gone en masse to Lawson on the second ballot, giving the governor the presidential nomination. The deal was closed but delegate opposition to Billings as VP was still strong. Polls showed a majority of the nation against him, and the three news magazines were bawling—"No VP, he."

It was obvious that the VP choice was particularly important this election. The incumbent president was not running for reelection, and Lawson, a strong bet for November, had just passed the biblical three-score-and-ten and was recovering from a triple bypass.

An undercurrent was circulating through the convention hall. It whispered that whoever took the number two spot might end up sitting in that big leather chair in the Oval Office early in the first term.

Charlie blanched at the thought, but Mollie had officially shut him up on the "Stop Billings" motion. But why, he mused, should he take his seat like a good party soldier? Instead, he stood patiently at the Ohio stanchion, mike in hand, hoping for some kind of reprieve. What, he didn't know. But now that uncharted fate and a sometimes big mouth had brought him to this point—why not?

"LET HIM TALK!" The demand suddenly erupted as a roar from the floor.

"OUT OF ORDER!" Mollie Downs roared back, the wooden gavel moving like a jackhammer in her hands. "COME TO ORDER FOR THE VOTE FOR VICE PRESIDENT!"

From the high podium, Congresswoman Mollie Downs stared out at the crowd, wary of a mismove by the unruly mob.

The press called her "Marvelous Mollie," and it wasn't for naught. Only six years had passed since her debut as a minor official in Waco, Texas, after which she'd left competitors for a U.S. House seat in the red dust.

Women gloried in having another bright female on the congressional roster, while men admired her blend of ladyship and rawhide frontier toughness. As convention chair, she had justified the party's faith by keeping things right on rail—until tonight.

Her choice for President, Governor Lawson, had taken the nomination on the second ballot. Champ Billings, the brokered choice for VP (and she was one of the brokers), was having smooth sailing until this greenhorn congressman from Ohio had opened his big mouth, just as he'd been doing ever since the day he arrived in the House. Charlie Palmer was a natural troublemaker, but she had handled the likes of him before. All he needed was a motherly kick in the ass.

Sure there was sentiment against Champ, the old firedog, but it wasn't going anywhere without a solid sponsor from the inner circle.

And Colic Charlie just wasn't it. He made no physical impression whatsoever and had a zero power base in the party. Though he had balls and a pretty good voice, she consoled herself that he'd soon be as stale as yesterday's newspaper—especially if she could hold him in check tonight.

"CONVENTION COME TO ORDER," Charlie heard Mollie bellow.

The buzz of dissent was still moving rapidly across the giant auditorium. Why let wily Champ Billings jeopardize Governor Lawson's chance for the Oval Office?

But the floor also had its share of cynics about Charlie. Already, he'd heard whispers in the congressional cloakrooms and in the columns of the sycophantic press. Where in the hell did this upstart freshman congressman get the nerve to challenge virtually every move in the House? And now he was trying to block the party's official nomination for VP. What was his motivation? Power? Money? Or just the lure of tainted publicity, the mother's milk of politicians.

On the floor, it was a standoff between Mollie and the anti-Billings revolt. It lasted about a minute, followed by a strange silence that was suddenly broken.

By a cough. Not an ordinary cough, but a harsh, choking sound like a cigar smoker clearing his clogged throat. It came over the electronic system like an alarm, startling Mollie, who looked ready to explode out of her tight silk dress.

"YES? WHO WANTS TO SPEAK?" she queried in her powerful ranch-honed tone.

As a television cameraman picked up the voice with the cough, every head in the vast auditorium swiveled away from the young Ohio congressman toward the Oklahoma section where the Grand Old Man of the party, once their presidential candidate and at age seventy-two still the chairman of the Senate Finance Committee, stood erect, angular, tall, next to the state stanchion. His full head of brown hair, a kind of trademark, was neatly in place. Political authority was virtually tattooed on his forehead.

"DOES SENATOR LARRIMORE WANT THE FLOOR?" the chair asked.

Charlie laughed. Mollie's tone was now dripping with respect.

"HONORABLE CHAIR," Larrimore drawled pleasantly. "I see that my fellow delegates are restless—hesitant to vote just now on the vice presidential nomination. I'd like to make a motion to reconsider and—"

ZINGHHH!

The noise was abrupt and loud, like a 1930s radio blowing a vacuum tube, followed by a dead mike. Larrimore was still talking because Charlie could see his lips move on the giant projection screen behind Mollie. But the audio was gone.

"DID SOME SON OF A BITCH CUT OFF THE SENATOR'S MIKE?"

The shout from an Oklahoma delegate traveled across the room without benefit of electricity.

On the podium, Mollie was closely huddled with party officials, in deep conversation. Charlie guessed it was a contest between Robert's Rules and the risk of defying the Grand Old Man and some aroused delegates.

Suddenly, he was gripped by doubt. Who the hell was he, in the U.S. Congress only since this April, to start such a ruckus? Had he been rash in trying to open the VP nomination?

He sensed he was doing it again, much as he had all his life— moving brashly forward for something he truly believed in, then feeling queasy about pushing himself too far too quickly, suffering the embarrassment of people staring, talking, pointing, probing. He was torn between engagement and privacy. But it was now too late for doubt. He had started the rebellion against the nominee's choice of a VP, and it was gathering momentum.

Presidents had always had the option of choosing their running mates, ballot box poison or otherwise. Nixon was Ike's uneasy pick, and no one got as much flak as Bush in choosing Dan Quayle— twice. FDR's understudy, John Nance Garner of Texas, had observed that the vice presidential spot wasn't worth "a bucket of warm spit," but history had also shown that VPs could move into the limelight at the blink of mortality.

Only trivia buffs like Charlie knew that Aaron Burr had automatically become Jefferson's VP after a tie vote for President in the Electoral College, which was finally settled in the House, the system until 1804.

Vice Presidents had since moved into prominence in the political firmament. Fourteen had eventually become President, including four after assassinations. Andrew Johnson had taken over after Lincoln's violent demise as had Chester Arthur from Garfield, Teddy Roosevelt from McKinley, Lyndon Johnson from Kennedy.

Lately, the VP slot had become the steppingstone for the likes of Nixon, Ford, and Bush. Since Truman's time, five Presidents had first been VPs. So maybe he didn't regret pushing the envelope. And who knew, maybe delegates on the floor were listening.

Only once, Charlie remembered, had a nominee democratically thrown the VP choice to the floor. That was Adlai Stevenson in 1956, when Estes Kefauver defeated John F. Kennedy in a close fight. Charlie was now playing the Stevenson card. If Mollie, with a kick from Larrimore, opened the nominations, there could be a real struggle for the number two slot.

But, happily, the matter was now out of his hands. He'd retake his seat and wait for the winds of power to move it forward, or perhaps kill the idea, appeasing that side of his personality that was not radical, but accepting.

"CONVENTION COME TO ORDER," Mollie boomed. "Senator Larrimore seems to speak for some delegates, and it's not the chair's desire to frustrate anyone. So we'll have a voice vote on reopening the nominations—if Senator Larrimore will make the motion."

Charlie smiled. Power had moved the podium, but he felt a small upsurge of pride for having triggered the rebellion.

"IS MY MIKE ON NOW?" Larrimore asked.

"YES, SENATOR. I'M SORRY ABOUT THE ELECTRONIC GLITCH," Mollie answered, sugar in her Texas drawl. "DO YOU HAVE A MOTION TO MAKE?"

Larrimore whispered to an aide, then moved back to the mike.

"I DID, MADAM CHAIRWOMAN. BUT I'VE CHANGED MY MIND."

"OOOHHH!" A wail of disappointment rose from the floor, wafting into the press gallery, bringing pencils to notebooks and fingers to laptop computers.

"CAN WE GO ON TO THE VOTE FOR VP?" Mollie's face showed the blush of victory.

"NO, EXCUSE ME, HONORABLE CHAIR," Larrimore interjected. "I DIDN'T MEAN THAT I WANTED TO DROP THE MOTION. ONLY IT'S FAIR THAT IT SHOULD COME FROM THAT YOUNG CONGRESSMAN." The senator turned briefly to his aide. "YES, CHARLES PALMER OF OHIO."

Every head, every television camera, turned, switched, zoomed its focus from Oklahoma back to Ohio, from Larrimore to Charlie, who was suddenly staring at his own grotesquely large portrait on the overhead projector. He now loomed twenty-four feet tall and was being broadcast on six national channels.

Some crappo image, he wailed. No pompadour top, no tall Kennedyesque stature, no Redford features. Well, almost nothing, except Charlie's own prosaic physiognomy, as American as apple pie if one liked a mishmash of McIntosh and Granny Smith.

His medium stature, medium build, medium brown straight hair, medium-fair complexion, made him look as ordinary as anyone in a crowd. His nose was straight and his features regular but nondescript. Someone had once described his looks as "blue collar." His only outstanding characteristics, others had told him, were high cheekbones and deep-set green eyes that lit up when he spoke.

Palmer sounded solid Anglo, but on his mother's side, Knudsen, he was Scandinavian, mixed with Irish and German. His father's lineage, he had been told—for Charlie never knew him—was Anglo, but it was also mixed, this time with Scotch-Irish and Huguenot French. Charlie stared up at his image and figured that if America was the melting pot, he was the stew.

"CONGRESSMAN PALMER!" he could suddenly hear, "THE CHAIR RECOGNIZES YOU."

Me? Did Mollie really mean it? Had the tortuous path of fifty national primaries and caucuses, millions of contributions begged and extorted, political ads—negative, positive, and just plain stupid—and town meetings and talk shows, ad nauseam, finally come down to him? Even for this brief shining moment, was he the chief protagonist in the national drama?

"CHAIRWOMAN DOWNS!" Charlie shouted back. The gallery laughed at his loud call, which outdid even Mollie's. "I MOVE THAT NOMINATIONS FOR VICE PRESIDENT BE REOPENED. I ALSO MOVE THAT IF THE FLOOR SO VOTES, THE ADDITIONAL NOMINATIONS BE DELAYED UNTIL MONDAY NIGHT TO GRANT TIME TO CONSIDER."

"MONDAY NIGHT?" he could hear the delegates' anguished whispers.

Charlie realized that he was violating a sacred political Sabbath. National conventions always closed with "God Bless America" or the "Banner" on *Thursday* nights. Now was he talking about returning to New York City in the smelly ninety-five-degree heat to continue this charade? Let's nominate Champ Billings and get it done, many murmured.

"DID THE CONGRESSMAN REALLY MEAN MONDAY?" Mollie asked, her tone incredulous.

"YES, MA'AM," Charlie answered. "IF MY MOTION WINS, I DON'T THINK WE CAN HANDLE NOMINATIONS TONIGHT. I BELIEVE THE DELEGATES NEED THE WEEKEND TO THINK IT OVER."

"YES *IF* . . ." Mollie muttered. She seemed to enter a trance, her eyes sweeping the hall from Alaska to Wyoming, as if she were counting votes—which Charlie guessed she probably was.

"ON THE MOTION BY CONGRESSMAN PALMER OF OHIO," Mollie finally said, "WE'LL TALLY BY VOICE VOTE."

In official singsong, she called out a version of the auctioneer's ramble.

"FIRST, WHICH DELEGATES WANT TO KEEP NOMINATIONS CLOSED AND VOTE ON CONFIRMING THE ONLY NOMINEE, SENATOR CHAMP BILLINGS OF KENTUCKY—WHICH BY THE WAY WILL COMPLETE OUR CONVENTION WORK. PLE-EE-ZE SIGNIFY BY CALLING OUT NAY."

Mollie then raised her arms upward in a truncated V, like a glee club leader inviting the chorus. It came. The party faithful stood on their folding chairs and screamed out their nays.

"NOW," she asked in a flat monotone, "WHICH DELEGATES ARE IN FAVOR OF CONGRESSMAN PALMER'S MOTION TO REOPEN THE NOMINATIONS FOR

VICE PRESIDENT, WHICH WILL HOLD US OVER UNTIL MONDAY. SIGNIFY BY CALL-
ING AYE."

That call came quickly as well. This time, the noise reverberated through the hall, setting up a sympathetic musical note in the glass ceiling. Charlie's being tingled at first, but when he looked up at Mollie, he could see that she was still smiling. Had he already lost his biggest tussle with the establishment?

A funereal silence then settled over the room. Mollie had gone into a tight huddle with the party brass and the parliamentarian.

Still smiling, Mollie broke out of the huddle and approached the lectern. She banged the gavel with passion even though the room was already deadly still. He tried to read her, but her smile was mechanical, obviously part of a professional poker face.

"DELEGATES!" They all shot up ramrod stiff in their chairs. "AFTER CONSIDERATION OF THE VOICE VOTE, THE CHAIR HAS DETERMINED THAT THE AYES HAVE IT. CONGRESSMAN PALMER'S MOTION IS CARRIED. NOMINATIONS FOR THE VICE PRESIDENT OF THE UNITED STATES WILL BE REOPENED MONDAY NIGHT. UNTIL THEN, THIS CONVENTION IS ADJOURNED."

The whoops of the crowd were overwhelmed by the whacks of congratulations Charlie took on his back. But he was surprised by the call. Why had Mollie Downs ruled against the wishes of the party brass? Amazing. On second thought, a roll call of the delegates probably would have accomplished the same result.

Delegates from other states now crossed the aisle to shake the hands of a freshman congressman who had made history by holding up, at least for one weekend, a presidential nominee's worrisome choice of a running mate.

Charlie stared up at the giant TV screen, where he saw himself surrounded by a crowd of congratulators. He felt claustrophobic. Was this notoriety what he wanted for himself? He got up and started to move toward the exit, longing for fresh air.

He kept up the smile and modest manner as he moved ahead, touching as many outstretched hands as he could. Suddenly, he stopped as an imposing figure, almost a head taller than he, approached.

"Congratulations, young man. You've done our nation a fine service."

Senator Larrimore placed his hand gently on Charlie's shoulder, his fingertips suggesting a warm embrace.

"Thank you, sir," Charlie acknowledged the Grand Old Man. "And thanks for making it happen. It's been a happy turn of events, hasn't it? At least so far."

Larrimore opened his mouth to respond, but the two men were

quickly separated by the pressing crowd. Charlie advanced slowly, hoping he might make it uninterrupted to the exit.

He admitted that he was touched with pride, but he also feared that his private existence, what little it was worth, was in jeopardy. And he was accumulating enemies in Washington much more powerful than the adoring delegates.

He had come into the room a happy camper ready to watch democracy unfold. And he was leaving a controversial maverick who had put a roadblock in the smooth operation of the party. Once again, he had shot off his big mouth.

To what avail? That depended on whether the brass would permit one freshman congressman—himself—and a veteran senator plus a gaggle of dissatisfied delegates to stop them from putting up any damn Neanderthal they wanted for high public office.

CHAPTER 2

The next morning, Charlie was back in Washington. Seated in a 1930s swivel chair in his closetlike office in the attic of the Long-worth House Office Building, uncomfortable home to junior congressmen, he thumbed through the paper for "the story."

He hoped he wasn't getting smug or pretentious—two social crimes Charlie hated. But he did get a kick out of seeing his name in print, as long as the press was being friendly. On page three, staring up at him was a box with his airbrushed photo, headlined: THE $402,000 MAN STRIKES AGAIN.

The short biographical piece, highlighting his cost-cutting exploits in the House, ran alongside the news story of the convention hijinks of the night before. The article described the "bravado" of he and Senator Larrimore in halting the party locomotive and Billings's nomination as VP—at least for a weekend.

YOUNG TURK BLOCKS OLD KENTUCKIAN, quipped the subhead.

This was the second time in his short House career that Charlie had been touted as a minor celebrity in the national political firmament. The most junior of his colleagues, Charlie had arrived in Congress on April 20, less than three months before, after a special election to replace Aaron Kenney, the venerable eighty-one-year-old Ohio veteran who had dropped dead right on the floor of the House during an impassioned speech.

Since then, journalists and colleagues had admitted—or charged—that freshman Charlie had raised more fuss and feathers against the congressional status quo than anyone since Henry Clay. He wasn't sure if they were right, but it did strike him that politicians—himself included—had become peculiarly prominent in the public consciousness, considerably more than a quarter century ago, when as a teenager he had first been caught up in the drama of government. He presumed it was because the escalating cost of Washington (and the statehouses) focused people's attention, much as did Samuel Johnson's caveat of the awesome threat of the hangman.

Charlie had watched the story of Congressman Kenney's death on television in his corner window office at Synergy, Inc., a maker of computer software in rural Fairview, Ohio. Not as the firm's marketing chief and executive VP, but as a frustrated citizen who followed politics with the fervor his friends reserved for the fortunes of the Ohio State Buckeyes.

Word that a special election to fill Kenney's seat would be held in three weeks set his brain waves oscillating. Charlie wasn't a partisan political rooter, but he was sure he knew how to make the weakened American middle class—the much-maligned "bourgeoisie"—whole again after years of neglect (or persecution) by Washington and assorted political entities, from the statehouse to the county seat to the school board to the motor vehicles bureau.

Only in Ohio, he learned, could ordinary citizens like himself, with no real party allegiance or experience, instantly aspire to a place in Congress. Why Ohio? Because only fifty signatures were needed to place one's name on the primary ballot for the federal House of Representatives. Charlie was considered impetuous (though he daydreamed all his actions in advance), and before he had computed the full implications of his move, he had driven to county headquarters and gotten his stack of petitions.

Wisecracking his way through Synergy offices, in two days he had enough signatures to qualify for the primary ballot. George Sempel, his boss and founder of the company, had laughed.

"That's a damn fool idea, Charlie. Congress doesn't have stock options."

Damn fool idea? Sure, George was right. But if voters carped about lousy politics—and he was the master of that citizen sport—why not put oneself on the line and try to break up the monopoly of bad government? If the professional politicians of every stripe worked overtime to destroy the sense of citizen involvement, wouldn't it be nice to reverse the damage?

That evening, Charlie tossed in bed, disturbing no one. At forty-three, he was still a bachelor, but far from a confirmed one. It was just that his daydreams had trouble matching up with available women. Tolerant of people and usually nonjudgmental, he had two compulsions that drove him—clean politics and clever, attractive, near-perfect women.

His only foray into marriage, at age twenty in college, had proven disastrous, lasting only eleven months. She was smart and attractive enough, if quite dull. In retrospect, he commiserated with his young wife. She couldn't stand his babblings about politics—constantly changing the subject from vacations and dinner parties and gossip about friends and family, into insights about the wracked and wacky world of American government. MEGLO—"My Eyes Glaze Over"— she reminded him. He listened but he didn't shut up.

Since then, he had navigated from middling to ridiculous relationships with women. Hope sprung eternal, but he no longer cared about eternity.

In any case, that sweaty night in bed, he decided he'd make the run for Congress. Since politics had increasingly become marketing, and he was a marketing man, why not? And in the unlikely event of victory, he had a giant inventory of daydreams to put into place. If the status quo of American politics was the standard, then Charles K. Palmer was a flaming radical, at least in his mind, if not in his manner, which he acknowledged was sometimes quite conventional. (Though when aroused, others said, he could be a spellbinding orator.)

As he slept and woke, Charlie thought of the flood of campaign funds, the mother's milk of what passed for American democracy. To Charlie, it all smacked of begging, a combination of demeaning posture and legal bribery. *Quid pro quo.* Cash for later favors. Apparently, there was no end to the cozy arrangements that money bought in the political arena, from breakfast with a presidential nominee to a night in the Lincoln Room at the White House. Charlie concluded that credit to prostitution as the world's oldest profession had been somewhat misdirected.

That night, Charlie made up his mind not to take other people's money. He refused all donations and put $8,000 from his modest savings into ads on radio talk shows, where his thirty-second spots outdid the hosts' needles at big government. Charlie dealt in simple stories of waste in government and evoked so much cocktail party chatter that he was soon the favorite.

That wasn't hard, since there were nine—count them, nine—other candidates, all wooed by the offer of eternal fame with only fifty backers. When the primary election was held on April 6, Charlie easily won with 32 percent of the vote. The Ohio law required no runoff. Top vote-getter wins all. (On the spot, Charlie decided that if elected, he'd work for a "majority rule" in all elections.)

Once he had the nomination, his boss, George Sempel, got truly worried. "What's all this about Congress?" he asked in his fatherly tone as they sat sipping port. "You're the best computer marketing man around, and I can't afford to lose you. Maybe I'm not paying you enough. But remember, Charlie, politics is for politicians, not for real humans like you and me."

Charlie smiled, his affection for George rising.

"George, you know I'm overpaid. That's not it. I just think I understand government better than the people in Washington. I also owe this country something. Mom and I struggled without a man, working so hard that I still think anything else is abnormal. I've made it and Mom is retired in her own house. I want that success for everybody, but Washington doesn't get the picture. They need a kick in the ass, and I think I'm the guy to do it. So, George, give me your blessing. Besides, I'll probably lose the general election."

Sempel's arm warmly circled Charlie's shoulder. "Go in good health."

Despite Charlie's modesty, the general election was a breeze. A local celebrity from his radio ads, Charlie won the congressional race with 59 percent. On April 20, his name was changed to the Honorable Charles Knudsen Palmer and he was dispatched from Port Columbus airport to Washington with cheering Synergy employees waving goodbye and the female co-workers insisting on lip kisses despite Charlie's false protests of sexual harassment.

Now, seated in his closetlike office in the Longworth House Office Building, Charlie again scanned the Washington newspaper headline that labeled him THE $402,000 MAN.

That had all started his first day in office some three months before. After recovering from the shock of his miserable new surroundings, he had called in Sally Kirkland, the staffer who had picked him up at National Airport. In the brief drive, she had impressed him with her orientation lecture on Beltway manners and mores.

"Sally, could you take an important memo?"

Her head snapped. "But, Congressman Palmer," she answered, her voice a touch hostile. "You don't understand. I'm not a secretary. I'm your legislative assistant—or at least I was for Congressman Kenney. I make $79,000 a year. Your former administrative assistant, who just quit, made $102,000. We're not in the habit of taking dictation."

Charlie surveyed his outspoken assistant. "Really $102,000? That's sinful. How would you like to be my AA, but without a nickel raise?" He smiled. "If you take it, that means I've just saved $23,000 for the taxpayers. Am I right?"

Sally responded with a laugh, which seemed out of character. In the drive to the Hill, she had been businesslike all the way. Looking at her now, he noted she was dressed for Washington combat in a navy pin-striped suit with a jabot blouse of yellow linen and low-heel shoes. Not unattractive, tall, thin, with sharp features—sort of Kate Hepburn-like. But, fortunately, nothing stirred in him. He had already sized up Sally as a rare business find.

"Let's make a deal," Charlie said. "You play secretary to me for a week. Then you can become my AA and boss everyone around, including me. Meanwhile you show me the ropes. OK?"

Charlie sensed her mixed emotions: fury at the thought of playing girl Friday, yet chomping for the AA job.

Sally eyed him quizzically. "OK, deal," she finally said. "I'll fish out the steno pad I dropped in the wastebasket ten years ago."

"Good, then let's start by cutting our office costs way back. Might be a cue for my spend-happy colleagues."

When Sally returned, she brought along the House Clerk's report, a quarterly document showing every nickel spent in Congress, down to the $40,000 for pizzas, sandwiches, and Cokes for the confabs of the "whips," the enforcers of party discipline, or as one political wag had called them, "overseers of the world's richest plantation."

She started reading portions of Kenney's budget out loud.

"Good, good," Charlie repeated, as if in a mantra, as he slashed Kenney's appropriations. "We'll cut the staff back from twenty-two to thirteen. Do we have to lay anybody off?"

"No, we've only got twelve people. The rest left for other House jobs after Mr. Kenney died."

"Great. Then we'll stay with twelve. Now, on expenses, no more government-leased car for me. My boss is driving my Olds down here next week. As for salaries, your $79,000 is the max. I also want a 15 percent cut across the board in overhead—phones, supplies, etc. You see to it."

Sally scribbled furiously as he spoke, a manic touch in his voice, as his Ohio daydreams were being transformed into Beltway reality.

"No more expense-account lunches or breakfasts for anybody on the staff, including me, and no taking freebies from anyone. If my people want to play with anyone, they go dutch. Purer than Caesar's wife. Get that?"

Sally nodded frenetically as Charlie spoke.

"My God, I see that Kenney had three local offices in the district. Cut out two. We'll see if we can manage with just one plus an 800 number."

He moved on in sharp staccato, cutting every budget item 10 to 30 percent.

Charlie zeroed in on newsletters. His predecessor had sent him three every year, filling the mailbox with expensive political propaganda. "How much do they eat up in franking money?" he asked Sally.

"Well, they go out to 243,000 households in our district, and we've got a $108,000 postage budget for them. Multiply that by 435, the number of members in the House, and we're talking about $45 million, plus millions more for printing."

"Geez, that's a lot of dough. Cut out all my newsletters and save the franking money," Charlie snapped. "My constituents can watch me on C-Span."

He rose and tried unsuccessfully to pace within the cramped office. "What's that all told, Sally? How much have I saved the taxpayers?" He could feel his maverick blood tingling.

"One second, Congressman. Hold your water." He watched, impressed, as her long fingers ranged around the calculator.

"It's $402,459.83," she uttered breathlessly.

"Good. Round it out to $402,000. Get out a press release by fax to *everybody* saying that a freshman congressman still wet behind his ears has cut $402,000 from his congressional budget his first day in office. He also promises to use the same sharp eye on everything in the federal budget—all 190,000 items. Line up time on that expensive House radio and TV studio so I can record a statement. Now get moving."

Thus began the legend of the $402,000 man, a story in print, radio, and television that had made Charlie an instant Beltway celebrity, if someone less than trusted in the hallowed suites of the Washington powerful.

Now, three months later, with his "victory" at the Javits Center Thursday night, he sensed that his party's hostility against him was hardening, and was probably spilling over into the opposition as well.

He sat at his desk, closed his eyes, and wondered how the drama in New York City would play out Monday night. In two days, they would reconvene to vote for Vice President. Would the delegates support Mollie and the party establishment? Or Larrimore and him?

"Congressman, you've had a persistent caller, a pain in the neck I can't get rid of."

Sally was standing in front of his desk after lunch that Friday, consternation covering her face.

"How come you're telling me this?" Charlie asked, remembering her little lecture. "Does the AA usually handle routine phone calls?"

"No, but this one's not routine. It's from Schuyler Rafferty."

"Rafferty? The money man?"

"None other."

"What's he want? Does he want to buy the Capitol building?"

"No, he wants to talk to you. Says he'll make it worth your while."

Charlie's usually subdued temper flared. "Who does that rich son of a bitch think he is—that he's going to buy me? Put him on. I'll give him what for."

Charlie waited as Sally left, then picked up the phone. Rafferty's voice came crackling on.

"Hello, Congressman Palmer. This is Schuyler Rafferty. I'm calling from Sky Ranch in Montana. Do you know who I am?"

"I've heard of you, but I didn't know you were so crass. Did you actually tell my AA you'd make it worth my while if I took the call?

Maybe you don't know it, but I don't accept campaign contributions. So now you want to buy me? OK, what's your price?''

Charlie sensed that the laughter at the other end was good-natured, which helped diffuse his anger.

"Excellent, young man. No, I wasn't going to line your pockets. But if you'll spend a minute with me, I'll donate a million dollars to your favorite charity."

"Oh, that's a sucker play for politicians, Rafferty. Just avoids the election law but smells just as bad. No, I'll give you two minutes for nothing. I'd like to hear your pitch."

"OK, no money changes hands. Congressman, you did a good job last night at the Javits Center, but I hope you don't believe you've accomplished anything. I've already spoken to Mollie and Billings—I'm a big contributor to both parties, you know. You and Larrimore will go down in flames Monday night. Quite heroic, but quite hopeless."

Charlie was taken aback. "I don't believe your gloomy prediction, Rafferty, but what does that have to do with you?"

"That's what I'm coming to Charlie, if I can call you that. I'm impressed with the fuss you've raised in just three months, and I'd like to see a few more like you in national politics. Meanwhile, we've got Lawson with a triple bypass and that hack Billings inheriting the White House if Lawson kicks off. So I want to talk to you—American to American—at my ranch ASAP. I need sage advice and solid help, and I think you're the one to provide it. I'll send my jet to pick you up at National Airport and fly you back. You'd be away only a few days, and maybe the country will gain something. OK?"

"No, it's not OK. I don't fly on rich people's jets. You people are always looking for favors from federal agencies—the SEC, I suppose in your case. Thanks, but no thanks."

The silence at the end lasted for almost thirty seconds. Charlie hung on, then grew impatient. He was ready to crash the phone down when he heard Rafferty's scratchy voice, surprisingly tinged with a New York accent.

"CONGRESSMAN. Please don't hang up. I understand you're not a poor man, so I'll make you a bet. If at the convention on Monday night, Billings is nominated as Vice President, as I believe, then you lose the bet and you pay your own plane fare and come out here to my ranch in Montana."

"And what if Billings is defeated for the nomination?"

"Then I never bother you again."

Rafferty's tactic struck Charlie's funny bone. He laughed, seeing the billionaire in somewhat of a new light.

"OK, Rafferty, you old Irish bastard, you're on. We've got a bet."

CHAPTER 3

Karl "King" Kellogg, Washington lawyer-lobbyist extraordinaire, glanced into a mirror of the Cosmos Club on the corner of Massachusetts Avenue and Twenty-first Street and smiled at himself appreciatively.

His beige linen double-breasted $2,500 Brioni suit was sculpted to his long, lean frame, as was the Turnbull and Asser green-striped shirt adorned with a solid brown silk tie. Affectionately, he raced his right hand over the dark blond hair, slicked down immaculately with the slightest hint of pomade.

As managing partner in Kellogg and Pace, King was creative in the ways of spending money on his lobbying activities. He prided himself that he worked with reverse accounting principles. While other businesses tried to hold expenses down to a minimum, King purposely squandered as much money as possible on his target, America's politicians. Each dollar was like a seed, eventually harvesting ten times as much in fees from impressed, and grateful, clients.

The Cosmos Club was a central part of that agenda. The gray stone building, which had once been the home of Sumner Welles, assistant secretary of state under FDR, was the prestigious "intellectual" hangout for politicians, foundation thinkers, journalists, and those who prided themselves on shaping the Beltway culture. It was also, King knew, a magnet for his clients, who loved to rub shoulders and psyches with the Washington elite.

He waited in the lobby for his two guests, continually checking his watch. His wingtip shoes tapped out an impatient rhythm. King had a maxim: Promptness was more important than godliness. Time could be measured; religion and morality were arguable.

On this Friday of the hiatus in the party convention, Kellogg was waiting for Clara Staples, young *molto rica* widow of a recently deceased Houston oil man twice her age, and Andrew Tolliver, hired party campaign director. A member of the party's Executive Committee, Clara was rumored to contribute up to half of its deficit in bad years, and to unofficially run the committee with her charm—and cash.

They were already four minutes late and King was becoming agitated. His maximum leeway on waiting time was two and a half minutes and that had passed. Now there was no recourse but to simmer, slowly, and perhaps someday get even.

"Oh," he purred as Clara with Tolliver, who outweighed her two to one and was a head taller as well, arrived on the semicircular driveway. Stepping out of her chauffeured Jaguar, they walked leisurely through the door.

"Glad you could make it on time," Kellogg lied. "I've reserved your favorite table, Clara."

King's relations with both were quite good. Through his clients he had control of some forty Political Action Committees, or PACs, the lifeblood of their calling. That ever-flowing cash gave King clout that made him a celebrity, even among politicians who considered themselves celebrated.

Bipartisanship was not an idle label with Kellogg. His client list focused on no single ideology, ranging from left to right and both to foreign firms and to their American competitors. He granted campaign relief to all, then sought political help from both sides of the aisle, making him feel as righteous as it made him rich.

Kellogg was also registered as one of the seven hundred "foreign agents" with the Department of Justice under a 1930s law designed to control Americans then working for the Nazis. That registration had now been expanded to cover other nations, including Japan, and being a "foreign agent" had achieved a kind of rogue respectability in Washington. In truth, some half of all U.S. trade negotiators had been registered as foreign agents, working for the other side either before or after their official tour. What could be more patriotic? Kellogg always asked his critics.

King controlled some $5 million a year in contributions to both parties, all legal under the strangely flexible campaign finance laws, ranging from the $1,000 limit on "hard" money to candidates, to the large scale "soft" money to the parties themselves—running collectively into the millions.

Privately, King laughed at the election finance laws. Their sophistry, he felt, made existentialism look like an American prairie philosophy.

And most important, the courts upheld everything he loved. In 1976, the Supreme Court, in *Buckley v. Valeo,* concluded that *money was free speech,* so no limit could be placed on someone using his own cash to run. That gave people like him more freedom than the next guy, which he thought only right. And in 1996, the august Court said that despite election laws, parties had the right to spend any amount of money they wanted on a campaign.

(He was pleased that Supreme Court justices were political appointees. Naturally, they just loved the two parties, as he did. Besides, he didn't write the election laws. He only exploited them.)

And whatever the source of the election cash, he, Clara, and Tolliver had a mutual respect based on contributions made and favors returned, all unspoken or, if mentioned, *sotto voce,* nice as can be.

Clara herself—he guessed she was pushing forty—came to politics with a bundle of assets: money, beauty, and charm. This rare trinity in the Beltway stimulated the envy of others, who clamored to be invited to one of her fetes at Maison Grise, a turn-of-the-century French mansion in Georgetown. The Style section of the *Washington Post,* King guessed, would have to reduce its print run if Clara ever decided to hibernate during the fall social season.

Tolliver was the clear opposite of Clara. Her party's hired gun, he was obese, foul-mouthed, but unfailingly effective. Rolling in at some three hundred pounds, he dressed in ill-fitting, unpressed clothes, but had masterminded a half-dozen party wins in the past ten years. At age thirty-eight, Andy had the town mesmerized with his political acumen and reputed use of masterful—if usual—undetected dirty tricks.

Beauty and wealth were Kellogg's taskmasters. That's why he so adored Clara. Not because of her sexuality, which he had heard was considerable. Instead, King believed that sex, as Hemingway had said, drained the creative juices. He would have none of it, with women or, as yet, with men either. Somehow he guessed he'd been born asexual, not bisexual, which surely saved him a great deal of time, to say nothing of grief.

Once seated, Kellogg and Tolliver exchanged gossip, with Tolliver heavily lacing his conversation with expletives, from "fucking" to "cocksucker." King flinched because of Clara, but it all seemed to pass her by as she silently nursed a double Jim Beam while they chatted.

King spent a rewarding few seconds taking in her beauty. Large green eyes, with the slightest hint of oval, a thin nose just a delightful touch long, a milk-white complexion and a full sensuous mouth. Her hair was a startling brunette color (today) and cut full. Her makeup was perfection, something he heard that she applied herself. And, if he cared, her figure, wrapped in a tight silk blouse, was splendid, with a full bust and miniature waist.

Her face was made for men like me, he thought. And her body— well, that was for most everyone else. Maybe for Tolliver, who for all his avoirdupois, reputedly did well with the girls at party headquarters.

"So now courtesy of Mr. Charlie Palmer we've got a little competition coming Monday night on the VP nomination," Kellogg said, opening the real conversation. "What do you think, Andy. Is it serious?"

Tolliver seemed to turn the thought over as he rinsed his mouth with white wine, then finally swallowed it, all to Kellogg's chagrin. The oversize politician was noted for his eating and drinking, if far from delicately.

"I think Billings will pull off the VP nomination on Monday night anyway," Tolliver said. "But Palmer is still worth watching. If that Ohio hick had spent any time at all in Washington, he'd be ashamed to carry on the way he is. He just doesn't know any better."

"So, do you think he's dangerous?" King asked. "Before I left to come here, I got a phone call from your Congressional leader, Mike McKelvey, that old Wyoming cowboy. He called Charlie in for a little talking to, but instead of cooling down the red-hot, Palmer got angry and started to lecture him. McKelvey was cussing so hard, it was hard to catch the drift, but it seems the leader despises the young congressman, and maybe is a little afraid of him too. Charlie warned McKelvey that he was going to take action because the employees of the Democratic Caucus and Republican Conference are on the federal payroll. Charlie says it's unconstitutional. There's no mention of political parties in the Constitution, but there are over three hundred party employees in Congress sucking off the federal tit."

(King blushed as soon as the small vulgarity came out of his mouth. But Clara just smiled.)

Tolliver whistled. "Dangerous? Yes. But only if we don't slap him down, quick. It's not that the cocksucker is liberal or conservative, or even in-between. What he is is a crazy, fuckin' fanatic, a man who wants to rip up everything except the Constitution and the Declaration of Independence and revamp the whole damn system. I'm afraid of psychos—especially country bumpkin psychos. You can't predict what they're going to do. And if anybody in Washington is both a hick and a psycho, it's Charlie boy."

King turned toward Ms. Staples, who was seated silently on his right, taking in the dialogue.

"So, what do you think, Clara?" King asked, basking in the plea-sure of just looking at her. "How do you view our latest threat?"

She stopped toying with her drink. "I like Charlie."

"You what?" Tolliver's shriek startled the guests on either side, a no-no in Cosmos Club lore.

"Yes, I like Charlie because that fuckin' fanatic, as Andy calls him, is way ahead of the curve. He's even ahead of the voters who are getting fed up with our game. Lawson is about three steps behind, and Billings—well, he's rotting in the Teapot Dome era. If Palmer ever gets real power, it'll be the coup de grace for the likes of us."

Clara occasionally punctuated her remarks with her trademark grin, a disarming combination of girlish innocence, sensuality, and savvy.

"Tolliver, you'd be thrown out on your fat ass," Clara warned. "And you, King, would join the other lobbyists who'd never again make a decent buck in this town. For instance, if his bill banning ex-congressmen from lobbying their colleagues or anyone else passes, you'll be losing your best troops. *N'est-ce pas?*"

"And how about you, Clara? Does the crystal ball say how you'd fare in a Washington according to Palmer?" King was enjoying her swift evaluations.

Clara touched a clear polished fingernail to a perfectly shaped eyebrow.

"Well, let me see. Politically, I'd be a dead duck—kicked right off the Executive Committee because I'm a rich socialite bitch. Other-wise, well, I don't know. He strikes me as someone who appreciates horseflesh, and I've been known to run a good filly mile. I'll have to see."

Both men laughed, realizing that in *realpolitik,* the battle between men and women, Clara was way out front.

Not only was King enjoying the repartee, but it was leading in his direction. "I'm glad you both have Charlie pegged. A little differently, but essentially right. And that's why I invited you today."

"Really, King," Tolliver teased. "You needed a reason?"

King ignored the comment. "As you both know, the Mining Prod-ucts Institute, one of my best clients and a heavy contributor to your party, has been having trouble with guess who—Charlie Palmer. He's wangled a seat on the Interior Committee and he's hot after the mining companies out West, especially the foreign-owned ones from Canada, France, Germany, and Japan. Even though only American citizens can 'patent,' or buy, federal lands, foreigners can do the same simply by incorporating here. Well, Charlie wants foreign-controlled mining companies to pay Uncle Sam royalties on their gross income.

He's even talking about excluding them from federal lands altogether."

Clara perked up, her face showing surprise. "You mean foreign mining companies get the same deal as Americans on our federal lands?"

"That's right, Clara," King responded. "And I handle several of them as a registered 'foreign agent,' you should excuse the expression."

"Don't worry, King," Tolliver reassured him. "The SOB doesn't have a chance in Interior. Schmidt is chairman and as a Westerner himself, he knows where his bacon comes from—the mining interests. He'll keep Palmer in line."

"Think so? Well, my leaks tell me that of the sixteen committee members, Charlie boy already has seven in his pocket. Two more and Schmidt can go mountain climbing without a piton."

King continued to pick at his oysters as he spoke. "We've got to hang together on this one. If the revolution comes, and that 'hick from Ohio,' as Andy calls him, ever gains power, our Beltway experience won't mean a thing. He'll find a guillotine sharp enough to cut off all our heads with a single stroke."

"What did you have in mind?" Tolliver's fattened face took on a serious mien.

"First, I think your party would be building a dossier on him thicker than J. Edgar Hoover's on JFK. And I mean down to the size of his jockey shorts. It could be a lifesaver when the game gets rough."

Tolliver nodded agreement. "I've already got our hound dogs out. We're hoping for good hunting."

"Excellent," Kellogg responded. "And I'm working a positive track as well. Now that free lobbyist trips are no-nos in the House, we're going back to taxpayer-paid junkets. There's no limit on that. One committee chair took a whole group to the Paris Air Show for $200,000 in government money. Well, Schmidt is setting up a mining 'fact-finding' trip to the West, with stops at the ski resorts. It'll be all expenses paid for committee members, wives, and staffers—about twenty-five in all, and all legal besides."

"Are you going along?" Tolliver asked.

"Oh, yes. I'm paying my own way and I'm taking two ex-congressmen on my lobbying staff. One of them, Haskins, used to serve on the mining subcommittee, and he has good friends still sitting there."

Kellogg smiled across the table at Clara, who was still toying with her drink.

"And you, Clara . . ."

"Yes, King, what do you have in mind for me? Am I to be Charlie's jockey shorts investigator?"

"How you handle him is your business, Clara. But you are the natural insider spy on this. The man is single, lonely, and susceptible from what I hear. And what real man could resist you anyway? I do hope he's not gay. Not that I care personally, but I'd much prefer a horny heterosexual who you can manipulate."

"You put it so crudely, King. But I have been looking forward to meeting Charlie myself. At least from afar, I find him most attractive, even a touch heroic."

She softly raised two fingers to her lips, then threw a kiss at Kellogg.

"The die is cast, King."

CHAPTER 4

"Tonight is Monday, and that makes it historic," said Don Leland, network newscaster extraordinaire, pressing his pointed chin, his twenty-year-old broadcast logo, toward the camera. "I've been covering conventions of both parties and the presidential elections since the McGovern-Nixon battle of 1972. The conventions always ended on Thursday, and *never* have I reported a closing session on Monday night."

His voice was touched with sarcasm. "No one can ever script American politics, in which the exception is the rule. That happened Thursday night when a green congressman, Charlie Palmer of Ohio, tried to change the way a Vice President is chosen. Stay with us as we break for some commercial messages. Be right back."

Leland sat overlooking the floor in a glass booth, its sides decorated with an expressionist American flag—strips flowing in both directions—and peered down on the assembled mob as he opened the coverage of the second session of the national nominating convention at Jacob Javits Center in New York City.

The delegates were milling, a little apprehensively, he thought, their mood one of small revolt.

The cause? Leland was sure it was the nervy freshman congressman who had opened a can of squirming political worms. A decade his junior, Palmer had upset the timetable by forcing the reopening of nominations for VP, and now the networks, and Leland, were scrambling to make do.

The delegates had stopped milling and were taking their seats. Mollie Downs, the chairwoman, stood at attention on the podium, wearing the same blue silk dress—which Leland thought was doing a helluva control job. He could hear director Jerry Blackman's signal in his ear. In ten seconds they would be on the air.

Leland counted down, adjusted his navy-blue polka-dot bow tie for confidence, took a breath for beginnings, and smiled into the camera. In all his years, never had he seen such grandstanding as that pulled off by the greenhorn congressman. But tonight he'd show his own independence and do a little bloodletting of the Ohio amateur, right on camera.

People expected sharp opinions from him. Leland was sure it was his sarcasm, not his agent or his exaggerated diction, that brought him his $3 million salary. He checked himself in the monitor. His once luxuriant blond tresses had been replaced by an equally blond hair rug. Was he aging too rapidly? Leland was fifty-three, and he wondered if the camera eye was piercing the makeup down to the etched lines of time and *agita*.

His number one rating had slipped to number two, beaten out by a kid who had made his mark in the Gulf War. Despite his big mouth, maybe he still wasn't controversial enough, his producers had suggested. Turn up the amperes. Build the SOB image and, in this era of anti-government, a pox on both sides. He'd try it out tonight on hotshot Charlie, with a few extra groin kicks for pork butcher Billings.

For all his bravado, Palmer had probably accomplished nothing, Leland felt sure. Even with the nominations reopened, and a few names added to the roster, either Billings would still get the party's nod or they'd trot out some obedient dray horse in his place.

"Good evening again," Leland said, beginning his coverage of the proceedings. "Welcome to the final night—we hope—of the quadrennial presidential nominating convention. Thursday evening, if you recall, a tyro congressman from Ohio turned the establishment on its head by insisting that nominations for Vice President be reopened so that Senator Champ Billings—the nominee's own choice—could be opposed. His would have been a voice in the political wilderness, except that the party's Grand Old Man, Senator John Larrimore, shocked the crowd by supporting the motion, which then passed.

"You may remember that Palmer is the publicity-hungry young congressman who sliced his own House budget $400,000, as if that made any difference to a nation trillions in debt. Now, here's Mollie Downs gaveling the convention into action."

A heavy smack of the wooden hammer resounded through the room.

Downs welcomed the delegates, then introduced a galaxy of the party's stars onto the stage, beginning with the party's congressional leader Mike McKelvey, who slammed his cowboy boots down on the stage for emphasis, and going all the way back to Homer Caspers, chairman of the House Ways and Means Committee in the 1960s, when arithmetic was a solid discipline in Washington. (The press had dubbed him "Hot Homer" for his interest in a sexy model who graciously allowed him into her bed.)

Following him onto the stage was former Senator James Tallow, an impeccable Ivy Leaguer, reputed to be Governor Lawson's choice for secretary of state, while Senator John Larrimore of Oklahoma brought up the tail of party celebrities.

"The largest applause has been reserved for Senator Larrimore," Leland reminded his audience. "Now everyone's returning to their seats so that the work of this unprecedented evening—additional nominations for Vice President—can begin."

"ALASKA!" Mollie Downs bellowed with the punch of a fight announcer. "Do you have any nominations for Vice President to place before the delegates?"

"ALASKA PASSES," they roared back.

Downs went through the roster, a state at a time. Each one demurred, until she reached Massachusetts, where a young man with clipped Boston diction took the mike.

"Chairwoman Downs. This is Congressman Tom Mahoney. I want to place in nomination a great American, a former senator of our glorious Bay State, the home of Paul Revere and John and Samuel Adams, the ocean beach capital of the nation, the commonwealth of Massachusetts where all liberty began. I give you the next Vice President of the United States, the Honorable James Tallow."

The nomination was seconded by the head of the Connecticut delegation, after which Downs continued through the state roster. But every one passed until she reached Oklahoma, where that delegation's microphone suddenly came alive.

"Madam Chairwoman," a young man spoke up. "We may have a name to place in nomination, but we request that you return to us after the first roll call is completed."

Downs rapped the gavel, her sign of agreement, then continued the roster. All states passed until she reached Wyoming.

"Madam Chairlady. Madam Chairlady," a twangy voice, more nasal than resonant, raced through the cavernous room. "Wyoming has a nomination for Vice President."

"Let's hear it," Downs agreed.

The Wyoming delegate, straddling the mike like a horse, quickly warmed to his subject.

"WYOMING," he called as if it were a rodeo opening, "the first state to give our little ladies full suffrage way back in 1869, the scenic gateway through the Rockies, the state with natural air and only five people per square mile to breathe it, wishes to offer in nomination for Vice President our favorite son, our party's leader in the House, Mike McKelvey."

A giant "Yahoo" erupted from the delegation.

McKelvey, who was seated in a side box reserved for VIPs, immediately stood and waved his Stetson to the crowd. He then stepped on top of his chair, and waved again.

"I want to make sure *everyone* can see and hear me," he began, exaggerating his Western twang. "I sure appreciate the confidence of my state delegation, but I must tell this convention, that I am— 100 percent—behind the nomination of a better man than me, the senator from Kentucky, Mr. Champ Billings, someone I consider great enough to be an honorary son of the state of Wyoming. I therefore respectfully decline the nomination."

The announcement was greeted with an equal volume of boos and applause.

"Having finished the roll call, we'll return to Oklahoma, where I understand a nomination for Vice President is being offered," Downs called to the delegates.

Oklahoma? Leland wondered what possible nomination they would offer.

"This is a surprise," Leland told the television audience. "That state's only national figure is Senator John Larrimore, and after having once been the party's presidential candidate, I can't believe he would accept the number two slot under Lawson. Now let's listen to the spokesman from Oklahoma."

The cameras zoomed to the state stanchion, where a young man was eagerly grasping the mike.

"Madam Chairwoman, I have the great honor to introduce the giant of our party, a former standard-bearer and now senior senator from the Sooner State—the home of oil, ingenuity, and mistletoe— the great sovereign state of Oklahoma. I call on Senator John Larrimore, who has a nomination to place before you."

As the veteran legislator rose, the delegates cleared his way toward the aisle.

"The auditorium has hushed," Leland reported, his voice a silken underscore to the action. "Senator Larrimore is about to make an announcement, and all 4,612 delegates and alternates are waiting to hear what it is."

The amplified sound switched to the Oklahoma delegation.

"Honorable Chair," Larrimore began, "I have the honor to place in nomination for the Vice Presidency of the United States, a rising star in the party, a man who deserves the support of all my friends at this convention—a man who will, I am confident, find a great and honorable place in the history of our nation. I refer to that courageous young congressman from Ohio, *Charles K. Palmer!*"

The cameras instantly moved to the spot where Charlie was sitting. The congressman's muscles looked totally inactive, as if he were frozen in time. His face finally squeezed out a small, stiff smile. The cameras closed in further, the lens revealing that Palmer was as stunned as anyone in the auditorium.

From there, the camera moved through the Ohio delegation where delegates were frantically pumping the state stanchion, trouncing on the fragile folding chairs, stomping, yelling. "O-HI-O! O-HI-O!"

"CONVENTION COME TO ORDER!" Mollie shouted, only adding to the chaos.

"We're watching several historic moments at the same time," Leland said, regaining his voice after his larynx had shut down in surprise. "First, the nominations for VP have been opened and thrown to the floor. And second, someone has offered in nomination a green, maverick congressman, in office less than three months, as a potential Vice President. And third, that nomination has come from no one less than John Larrimore, the Grand Old Man of the party. Now let's return to the podium, where Mollie Downs is huddled with party chieftains."

"DELEGATES! PLEASE CLEAR THE AISLES AND RETAKE YOUR SEATS!" Mollie screeched over the public address system as she waited for the noise to subside.

"Our presidential nominee, Governor Lawson, has asked for a thirty-minute recess so that the nominations for Vice President, which are now closed—the remaining states having been polled in private—can be considered. I hereby declare the convention adjourned until 8:40 P.M."

As the gavel came down, newscaster Leland leaned into his mike, the wind knocked out of his script.

"From my vantage point, I can see that the new nominee, Congressman Palmer, is standing, shaking the hands of well-wishers. But if you look carefully at his face, which is usually ruddy, it has turned a gunmetal-gray. In all my years in broadcasting, never have I seen such an unexpected turn of events. This is Don Leland, signing off until 8:40 tonight when we'll tune into the next chapter of AMERICAN POLITICAL MADNESS."

CHAPTER 5

"Have you gone stark ape crazy?" Governor Lawson shouted unceremoniously at Senator John Larrimore. "Nominating that rabble-rouser to be my VP? Is that all you've learned in fifty years of politics?"

Larrimore was surrounded by a half-dozen party leaders in a hastily called conference in a rear room of the auditorium. Before he could respond, Governor Lawson continued his assault, his face turning florid as he accused Larrimore of disloyalty.

"John, you've always been a stalwart party man. It's bad enough that some grandstanding young punk comes along and throws our convention into chaos, then insults me and our VP candidate by inference. What's worse is that you've nominated him. Have you gone mad?"

The three candidates for VP were excluded from the conference, but those present were of one mind. Senator Larrimore had introduced a wild card into a traditional poker game, and they were livid.

"You've turned traitor, Larrimore," said Harry Berry, veteran senator from Nevada. "What in the hell prompted you to upset the apple cart? We need Lawson in the White House, and now you've thrown our unity into the gutter. Why, John, why?"

Berry's heavy hand hit the table in disgust, then he stormily paced around the room, shouting expletives at the walls.

They all were making Larrimore their target. They stared at the accused, who hadn't yet answered his accusers.

"You ask why?" Larrimore finally said. "That's a good question. And I have an answer."

"Yes, go ahead."

"First off, I want the same thing you do. I want our party to win, and I want our country to win, and the two don't have to be mutually exclusive. Frankly, Governor Lawson, I think you made a mistake in picking Champ Billings as VP. Perhaps you needed his delegates to get the nomination, but that's over now. Champ is an old pro—and that's part of the problem. He represents everything wrong with our system, including shadows of big contributors leaning over his shoulder. The public is anxious about their government and Champ is not the remedy. Not by a long shot."

"All right, John, maybe I didn't chose the best man," Lawson conceded. "But remember, you turned me down, and besides, Billings wasn't nominated for the top spot."

"Governor, I feel I'm too old for the White House, and you're no spring chicken either," Larrimore pointed out. "That number two position could easily become the number one. Whoever gets it could soon be humming 'Hail to the Chief.' "

"Hell, I'm not ready for Arlington Cemetery," Lawson countered, injured by the reminder of his age. "My Vice President is only going to be a cardboard stand-in, like most of them. But why a green congressman? And from what I hear, a nasty one at that."

Larrimore rose and paced the tight floor, taking the measured steps of an old marine colonel.

"To be honest, I had no intention of naming Charlie Palmer when I backed his motion Thursday night. I hadn't even met him. I just wanted to stop Billings and to give a better sense of democracy to the proceedings. And then—"

"Then you went crazy. Am I right, John?" Lawson asked.

"No, I spent a half hour with him at breakfast and I learned that he's got his finger on the popular pulse. Palmer's angry at crushing taxes; stagnant incomes for middle-class families; enormous government waste; party squabbles; campaign finance madness; expensive, failed federal programs. The people are fed up with pork barrels, election flim-flam, foreign agents, corruption, party bloc votes, ties to lobbyists, ethical charges—at the whole crazy mess we call American politics. Look at this convention. We took a check for $13 million from the taxpayers, and now we're raking in another $15 million from corporate sponsors who line our halls. We've got to clean house—and right now."

Larrimore stopped his pacing and pointed in turn at each man. "Are you . . . or you . . . or you . . . going to do it? Am I? Hell, no. We've got our nests well feathered with our million—and two-, and three-, and four-million—dollar retirement funds, which is mostly taxpayer money. And we're only waiting for cushy lobbying jobs at double or triple our salary when we retire, or even get kicked out by the voters. But the American people who are paying for all this nonsense are bleeding in every direction. They're disillusioned with the parties and need a political doctor. I think I've found him. His name is Congressman Charlie Palmer."

"But . . ." House party leader Mike McKelvey interjected.

"Don't *but* me, Mike. Can you imagine what your $135,000 salary—and a $15,000 federal bonus for being a party boss, and your chauffeured limo—looks like to a white-collar guy in the Midwest who has just been laid off from a $40,000 job and is losing his house and trying to live on $250 a week unemployment insurance that's running out? Or who's out of work because both our parties are shipping his job overseas to some Asian peasant? And he has to take a lousy $7-an-hour job in Walmart just to partially survive? What does he give a crap about Washington bullshit and fake speech making, at which we're damn good. He wants a revolutionary like Palmer. And if he wants it, we should want it too. I tell you that government that's unaccountable is one that's going to change or fall—like the Soviet and the British and the Roman empires. I don't want that to happen to America. So—"

The room hushed, his colleagues still shocked by Larrimore's revolt.

"So to try to stop it, you've nominated a kid who's been in office only three months and is after our hides," Governor Lawson responded, his breath coming in halts. "Is that your answer to our government problem?"

Larrimore turned sharply on his accusers. "Goddamn it, yes! That's why I nominated Palmer. Because he doesn't give a damn about the party, or you, or me. He's a bomb thrower for the people, and that's exactly what we need. Someone to spit in our faces and rip the place up—to bring it down to people's size, not to the fancy expectations of the bureaucrats and us professional politicians. We're fiddling while Chicago and Kansas City burn."

The Grand Old Man turned toward McKelvey, a physical giant of a man noted for his political iron hand.

"So that's why I want Charlie Palmer in the number two spot."

Again the hush, this one deeper and longer.

"What do you know about him?" Senator Berry finally asked. "What about his character? Are you buying a pig in the poke?"

"I know it's lightning-quick and I haven't had time to check him out thoroughly," Larrimore responded. "Nor has he been screened by the FBI. But I'll tell you this—he's as smart as a whip. And this morning I called his mother, the town clerk in Fairview, two of his high school teachers, and his boss at Synergy, where Charlie was executive VP."

"And?" McKelvey asked, his voice gruffer than usual.

"You'd think he was Jesus Christ with a Ph.D."

"And you believe it?"

"Yes, I do. Maybe there are a few blips in his private life. Who ever knows about a man and his women? But on politics and money, I'd stake everything."

Governor Lawson had withdrawn from the last part of the angry dialogue, his mind spinning. Some of Larrimore's argument made sense, he had to admit. He shouldn't have chosen Billings, but he had fallen into a trap laid by Satan in the form of party loyalty. Now he faced the toughest part of his dilemma. Should he go back on his pledge to Billings?

Equally important, how could he back Charlie Palmer for Vice President? Especially since, as Larrimore had needled him, his own health was problematic. The Vice President might have to take the helm, even in his first term.

So, the question really came down to this: Who would make a better President, Champ or Charlie?

The young congressman was smart and imbued with his cause. But Champ Billings, for all his pork and conniving, was smart too, a patriot, and experienced. He loved his country no less than anyone, and just might make a great president. Hadn't Harry Truman, America's reigning folk hero, come out of the crooked Pendergast machine in Kansas City?

As for the kid congressman, what do we really know about him? How in the world can we pick a Vice President—and a potential chief executive—without an FBI check? What if he's a crook, a no-good-nik, a Communist, a Fascist, a white separatist, a shill from the other party? God knows what. A wrong choice could be devastating for the Union.

He'd have to talk to Senator Larrimore, Oklahoma bulldog that he usually was—and patriot that he surely was—just one more time, alone, before they reconvened on the floor.

Charlie stood on the convention floor, the pressure rising inside his head. The pulse at his temple was throbbing and he was straining for air.

Whatever possessed Senator Larrimore to nominate him for VP? The man must be crazy. He wasn't dry behind the ears and now his composure was ready to crack. His damn runaway mouth. At breakfast, he had tried to present a few ideas to Larrimore, but as always, he had become obsessive and unstoppable, talking, talking, pouring out his guts about the dismal state of the Union.

He'd been afraid he had alienated the old politician by his avalanche of facts about waste and inefficiency. Instead, he had apparently impressed him too much. Now he was surrounded by flashbulbs and backslappers, with nowhere to run.

As soon as the convention reconvened, he could ask Mollie to remove his name from the nomination. That would put him back on track—being a freshman congressman trying to find his way through the Capitol hallways and hoping to meet a suitable woman, if he could ever find time.

Suddenly, he felt the pressure of a hand on his. He looked up. Standing somewhat serene in the midst of chaos was his AA, Sally Kirkland. She was dressed in her navy-blue suit and—he could hardly believe it—carrying her black attache case.

"I'm sorry, Congressman, I never expected this mayhem. It's great, your being nominated for VP, but I came up from Washington not knowing about it. There're a few pieces of legislation being considered next week you need the details on."

Charlie smiled at his aide, whom he was just beginning to accept, even like, as her cool exterior began a meltdown.

"Come now, Sally. You could have waited another day."

"Well, I wasn't sure when you'd be back in Washington. And besides, I was jealous being left out of your move to open the VP nominations. All Washington is talking about that."

"I understand, and welcome to Bedlam."

"So what do you do now?" Sally asked. "You look as shocked as I am. Do you have a real chance for the nomination?"

He studied his AA. Peculiarly reliable. Someone he could talk to, he decided. "Frankly, I'm shocked. I had breakfast with Larrimore, but he never said a word about this," Charlie explained. "Now I need your help."

"You? I didn't think you needed anybody's help, for anything, at any time."

"Well, I do. I feel like a lightning victim caught out in an open meadow."

Charlie was pleased that she had arrived uninvited and had finagled her way onto the floor. But the real question was still unresolved and pressing in on him. Yes, he'd put it to her, straight.

"The trouble is in my head, Sally. Am I qualified to be Vice President? Or is it just an ego trip by another power-hungry politico? Should I go for it, or just tell Mollie it's all been a big mistake?"

Sally stared at him for what seemed like a full minute. Was she in deep contemplation or, he feared, toying with him? Suddenly she spoke up.

"Congressman, you've got a lot of hangups. You're obsessive and you can be one swift pain in the ass. But qualified for high political office? There's no one within spitting distance of the Capitol who can hold a candle to you when it comes to government. In fact, if you don't run, I'll quit as your AA."

Charlie was stunned. Sally was not a glacial person, but never had he seen her so animated.

"Coming from you, Sally, that's gratifying. OK. I'll accept the chance for the nomination. Now, let's see how it plays out. Take a seat. I'll try to keep them from kicking you out."

"THE RECESS IS OVER. DELEGATES PLEASE CLEAR THE AISLES AND COME TO ORDER. THE CONVENTION HAS RECONVENED."

As Mollie Downs's call resounded through the Javits Center, the delegates retook their seats. The last stragglers were in the Ohio section, where favorite-son jubilation was unrestrained.

Mollie gave the states ten minutes to poll their delegations, then firmly stroked the gavel.

While delegates scrambled, talked, and compromised, Don Leland hit the cough button and relieved his throat before beginning.

"The voting will start in just a moment, and its significance should not be underestimated," the veteran commentator opened. "It will settle the direction of the party, probably the entire federal establishment. Either it will turn in favor of Senator Larrimore and his protege, Charles Palmer, and rough criticism of government. Or it will turn toward the status quo symbolized by Champ Billings and James Tallow, both Washington veterans.

"Rumor has it that little love is lost between the presidential nominee, Governor Lawson, and Palmer," Leland added, his trained voice gaining in intensity. "It could be a strange campaign if the standard-bearer dislikes his vice presidential candidate—although history tells us that FDR secretly hated Harry Truman. In any case, the vote is about to begin . . ."

"ALASKA," Mollie suddenly roared. "ELEVEN VOTES. HOW SAY YOU ON THE NOMINEES FOR VICE PRESIDENT?"

There was some confusion at the rear of the auditorium. Then a voice, young and resonant, took the mike.

"This is Senator James Petri, chairman of the delegation from the great state of Alaska, the Last Frontier, the land of forget-me-nots, and the energy capital of America. Alaska casts its votes for Vice President as follows: Four votes for Senator Billings; three votes for former Senator Tallow, and—" his voice rising—"four votes for Congressman Palmer of Ohio."

As the clerk feverishly recorded the tallies, Mollie went down the roster, a state at a time. The lead shifted from one candidate to another. Billings was ahead initially, until Massachusetts, whose ninety-three votes went to Tallow, moved that candidate into first place for a while. Then, suddenly, the votes of Tennessee, Virginia, and West Virginia pushed Billings back into the lead. But Palmer kept piling up votes of his own with no regional pattern, finally challenging the front-runner, Billings.

During the roll call, two states had passed, saving their vote for the end, which the chair allowed because of their key positions— Ohio, home of Palmer, and Oklahoma, home of Senator Larrimore, who had nominated Charlie.

"By my count, it looks like young Palmer should take the VP nomination in a squeak," commented Leland as the nation hung on each state roll. "Just hold your breath for three more minutes and you may be witnessing real history in the making."

"OHIO. ONE HUNDRED AND SIX VOTES," Mollie called as the state stanchion oscillated wildly. For a moment there was no response.

"OHIO. ONE HUNDRED AND SIX DELEGATES," Downs repeated. "HOW DO YOU VOTE?"

The microphone suddenly came alive. "This is State Senator Johnny Macovitz of Ohio, the Buckeye State, the land of the Scarlet Carnation and the great football teams of Ohio State, the test market of America, and now the home of the next Vice President of the United States. Ohio proudly casts all its 106 votes for the real champion of the people, Charlie Palmer!"

The auditorium went wild. A spontaneous demonstration led by Ohio snaked through the aisles, accompanied not by music but by the incessant banging of Mollie Downs's gavel.

"CLEAR THE AISLES. LET THE VOTING CONTINUE."

In the network booth, Don Leland pushed his bow tie aside, now looking more the newsman than the television reader. Only minutes before, he had been sniping at the "green congressman." His tone had suddenly turned more conciliatory.

"It's an extraordinary day in American politics," Leland was almost shouting. "Never before has such an amateur moved so rapidly into a possible position of power. It takes a majority of 1,154 votes to win the nomination for Vice President. Palmer is now only twenty-two votes short. Champ Billings, the party favorite, needs forty-eight votes to beat Palmer, which is unlikely. Only Oklahoma, whose senator placed Palmer's name in nomination in the first place, has yet to vote. Let's return to the podium."

"OKLAHOMA. FIFTY-THREE DELEGATES," Mollie barked. "HOW DO YOU VOTE ON THE NOMINATION FOR VICE PRESIDENT?"

The sound level, which had reached ear-splitting proportions, instantly dropped to the decibels of a silent forest. The only noise seemed to be the footstep of one delegate approaching the live mike.

"This is Senator John Larrimore, chairman of the delegation of the sovereign state of Oklahoma." He spoke softly, almost as a whisper, into the mike. "I have the tally, Madam Chairwoman. Shall I read it?"

"Ohhh," the gallery murmured in unison.

"Please do, senator," Mollie responded respectfully.

"Oklahoma casts one vote for Senator Tallow of Massachusetts, three votes for Congressman Palmer of Ohio, and *forty-nine votes for the next Vice President of the United States, the party veteran, Honorable Senator Champ Billings of Kentucky!*"

With that, Larrimore sat down, his face an impenetrable mask. The silence in the auditorium was penetrating.

Charlie sat stunned as Sally placed a quick sisterly kiss on his cheek. "You're lucky to be out of it."

Charlie didn't know what to say or think. He had been in politics only three months and already the disillusionment he had feared had turned into ugly reality. Larrimore and Billings? Why?

Larrimore must be crazy, first nominating him, then backing Billings at the last minute. He hadn't asked for the nomination, wasn't even sure he wanted it. But he'd been sandbagged into accepting it because of Larrimore's support, only to be betrayed at the last moment.

Was there any sanity left in American politics? And more important, was he, Charlie Palmer, in danger of losing his own mental stability in the crazy miasma called Washington, D.C.?

CHAPTER 6

PATRIOT had just the right ring as a *nom de guerre*.

If he was going to carry out underground work to ensure the sanctity and security of the Republic, he needed an incognito.

Patriot prided himself on having an intuitive early warning system. Its nervous signals were now telling him that Charlie Palmer had become more than a simple irritant to the American body politic.

Palmer had been overly active, and something had to be done before the impetuous tyro congressman went any further in tampering with the delicate balance of the nation. Unfortunately, he had caught the imagination of the public, and for the last three months, his falsely benign face had been plastered all over the television screen, threatening the status quo with tales of waste and corruption.

And now, worse yet, Palmer had disrupted the national convention. In just one evening, he had brought party discipline to a stop and managed to delay the choice of a running mate for Governor Lawson. He had not succeeded in gaining the nomination for himself, but the pattern of disruption was there. Since nominee Lawson was physically weak (much more than the media knew), the demagogue could have moved into the Oval Office after only months on the political stage.

In Patriot's intuitive appraisal, the threat from Charlie Palmer was not over.

Of course, none of this would have happened without the traitorous work of Senator Larrimore. But Palmer deserved credit—or disrepute—for having so cleverly influenced the Grand Old Man, clear proof that he was a continuing danger. Palmer was a threat not only to one party, but to the entire system of massive compromises and self-interest that held the American political system together. Sometimes with the likes of a Band-Aid, but together nonetheless.

Those like Palmer who pretended to be "reformers" were the actual villains, Patriot was convinced. Their true intent was obvious: to disrupt the status quo so they could reshape the nation. First among these was Charlie, who he believed had only shown the tip of his radical intentions.

Patriot had hoped to avoid action, but his hand was being forced. Was it too early? Not if one believed in preventive medicine, as he did.

He had no direct contact with the specialists he needed, but he had successfully used a skillful go-between, a gentleman named Stony who handled multiple matters of a discreet nature. As Patriot, he would reach him, as usual, through a personal ad in the morning paper.

He sent the ad in by mail, with a cash payment. PATRIOT NEEDS LARGE NUMBER OF SMALL FLAGS. PLEASE RESPOND.

It ran two days later, followed by a quick response.

"PATRIOT. HAVE FLAGS. MEET AS USUAL. STONY."

The closing—STONY—showed that the message was authentic. Translated, it meant that they were to meet at the usual time, 10:30 P.M. that evening, at the usual site, a deserted boat dock on the Anacostia River.

A muddy offshoot of the Potomac, the river ran through the unfashionable far Northeast quadrant of the District, an area few of the capital's elite had ever visited. There was little chance of his being recognized there.

He and Stony had never met close-up, nor did they know each other's true identity. The conversations were held at a distance of some thirty feet. This night the weather cooperated as well, unusually cool and foggy for a summer evening, especially near the water. Visibility was low.

Someone might spot his car or license plate, so he decided to dress casually and take the Metro. He left at 9:30 P.M., allowing himself a full hour for travel. Not that it took that long, but he was unfamiliar with the subway. Except to meet Stony, he had not been down there since the opening ceremonies, when he had been a guest of the mayor. He knew that riding the Metro tonight would be a distasteful, even overly democratic, experience, but he had no other option.

He entered the cavernous Metro Center station at Twelfth and G, and descended to the waffle-roofed platform by escalator. After buying a farecard, he took the Red Line, then the Green Line to the Anacostia stop. From there, he walked to the river's edge.

The rendezvous site was perfect. There were no lights, only the pale reflection of a half moon. No one else was visible in any direction. From the edge of the dock he could see that Stony was already out on the end of the slip, dressed in a navy pea jacket, with the flaps up, hiding much of his face.

Because of the fog, he could only make out that it was a man, about average height and a little stocky. One feature stood out though, even in the pale moonlight. The man had unusual milky-white skin, almost like a child's.

"Stony," he called out in an exaggerated whisper.

"Yes, Patriot. What do you have for me?"

"An extraordinary opportunity. It will bring you $100,000."

"Really? Must be something very important." Stony's voice was touched with enthusiasm.

"No sense speculating about that. I've brought the details along with me. I'd like it done within a week."

"Of course, I'll need a deposit now."

"I assumed as much. I'll leave an envelope with $50,000 on the edge of the slip. The details are with it."

Patriot walked away, pausing long enough to see Stony pick up the envelope. It was still impossible to make him out clearly. He had no idea who he was, but then again, he had no desire to know. That knowledge would surely visit him with great grief.

Now, he could retreat back into his thoughts. The Republic's new enemy, Congressman Charlie Palmer, had to be dealt with. Others might shy from their responsibility, but not he.

His conscience was crystal clear.

CHAPTER 7

The trail was blowing cold, almost frigid, Arnie Reichmann thought as he drove his battered 1983 Dodge Dart into the parking lot of the Fairview, Ohio, Town Hall, a beige-brick, turn-of-the-century public building, so common in the Midwest.

Never in his years as a private investigator had he found so little incriminating material on anyone. Life almost always produces blemishes on the surface of even the smoothest personal history, but so far—to his disappointment—this search of Charlie Palmer was coming up super-clean.

His docket showed this job as a routine check for a million-dollar life insurance policy, but he didn't believe it for a second. The subject was a local U.S. congressman, and when it came to benefits, the House took good care of its own. More than likely, this probe was financed by someone anxious to get dirt on the politician. He, Arnie Reichmann, a licensed PI in the state of Ohio, was the tool.

A willing tool, he had to confess. Not only was his fee $500 a day, plus out-of-pocket, but the "insurance company" had pledged a $5,000 bonus for evidence of moral turpitude, which proved that his real clients were politicos of some stripe. Politics was a nasty business, but what they did with his info was their business. Long ago, he decided that moralizing was a great waste of energy. He'd leave that to the windmill tilters like Charlie Palmer.

"Good morning, Mildred, you're looking your usual beautiful self."

Reichmann, who had been covering this part of Ohio for twenty years, had learned that flattery, laid on as outlandishly as possible, was his best working tool. His own appearance was no door opener. Short, at most five feet, four inches, with an oversized head topped by kinky red hair, he looked more like the stage dwarf than the dogged investigator he was.

It pained him to play the fool, but the town clerk was not only the caretaker of the records, but held two generations of gossip locked in her head. Some said that Mildred Cole was going on eighty, but you couldn't prove it by her manner—crystal-sharp and testy if you weren't on your toes.

Her domain of Fairview had once been the hub of hundreds of commercial and family farms specializing in sorghum and soybeans, interspersed with apple orchards and cornfields. But since the 1970s, the interstate and sprawling suburbs had pushed in, civilizing or ruining the area, depending on one's viewpoint. Arnie was no tastemaker, but even he felt pangs when he saw the golden "M" arch go up where there had once been an active barn.

This was Charlie Palmer's home territory. Now that he was a congressman, people were glad to talk about his childhood, even improvise excessive praise. At the Fairview High School, teachers said he had been a very good student and polite, and uninterested in sports. Not a nerd; in fact, quite popular with his peers, if a touch removed from the authorities. He acted as if he didn't fully approve of how and what the teachers taught. But he wasn't arrogant, as it might seem. More the observer.

People hereabouts had obviously expected Charlie to become something, even though he was born real poor. From what he had heard, Mrs. Palmer and Charlie were very devoted to each other. She was seventy-two and still lived in the old family house, from which she reputedly ran everything in town, from the library to the emergency aid.

From others, he learned that life for Christine Palmer and Charlie, her only child, had once been a daily struggle. Her people, the Knudsens, had come from Connecticut in 1835, and the family had been reasonably comfortable until this generation. Charlie's father had died before he was born. People were vague about the older Mr. Palmer, but he had heard that he'd been an army officer, a captain, who was killed in Korea.

Puritanlike, Christine had refused all county or federal welfare and had raised Charlie on her own, mainly by doing domestic work and clerking in the local Woolworth's. Charlie helped out as soon as he was twelve by odd-jobbing in Dodson's dry goods store. In the warm months, he cut almost every lawn within a square mile for 50 cents a trim. Everyone interviewed confirmed Charlie's insatiable appetite for work.

Fortunately, Charlie and his mother lived in a mortgage-free farm-house passed on to her by her father. The house had run into disrepair, but as soon as he was old enough, Charlie painted and maintained it as well as possible. The aging girders had strained away from the horizontal, and no amount of love could keep its joists from groaning.

After Charlie started making good money, he offered to buy his mother a new house, but she insisted on living in her place. Charlie was reputed to have put in over $50,000 to transform the old house into a spanking Victorian, with the floors *almost* at the horizontal.

In Fairview, a town of only 1,473 people, it was impossible to lose track of Charlie, Reichmann was learning. He had gone away to Ohio State in Columbus for four years, and after graduation, with honors, had joined the U.S. Army for two years, serving in Germany. On his return, Charlie was hired by a new computer company, Synergy, Inc., just four miles from Fairview. True to the town's expectations, he had first become the marketing chief, then executive VP, and was slated for the number one spot, surely the leading industrial position in the rural enclave.

Now, of course, he was the congressman, and had already pleased his constituents pink by cutting his own costs in Washington. Not that it was going to solve the federal deficit, but to locals it was proof that Fairview raised its young in the no-nonsense American way, and not in the flashy manner they associated with New York and Washington.

"Well, Arnie, I see you're trying to worm something out of me about Congressman Palmer," Mildred said, winking at the private eye. "You're going to have a little trouble because the birth certificates from 1954—that's when Charlie was born—were burned in the old Town Hall fire. That was before we microfilmed everything. Charlie's was one of them. Jake Hansen, who was mayor then, found some burned crumbs, which we keep in an airtight container in the basement. But you'll have to see the new mayor, Bill Folsom, if you want to look at them."

"Come on, Mildred, you don't need no birth certificate to know the P's and Q's of Charlie's background. I bet you've got everyone's family history engraved on that sharp brain of yours."

"Now, you go on, Arnie Reichmann, with your sweet talk. I'm just the town clerk, and like I said, you'll have to see the mayor."

What he could get, from the county courthouse, were the marriage records. Charlie had been married while still at college to Francine Laughlin, a union that lasted less than a year and ended in an uncontested divorce. Was there a story there? Reichmann wondered.

A search of birth certificates and adoption papers under Charlie's and his wife's former name turned up no offspring. So Congressman Palmer was now a childless bachelor, just as he had heard.

"Ms. Laughlin," Reichmann said after he tracked down Charlie's ex-wife, "I'm doing a life insurance investigation on Charlie Palmer. Could you tell me something about your marriage to him?"

"What?" was all he heard, then the loud click of a phone being hung up.

The mayor was on vacation, so he decided he'd return later after a trip to Columbus, to Ohio State, Charlie's alma mater. In the library, he found the 1975 yearbook, with Charlie's boyish photo.

Several professors still there remembered Charlie. "I gave him a B in calculus," his math instructor recalled, "but I sensed he could get an A anytime he wanted. He seemed preoccupied with something, but I never learned what it was."

"I remember Charlie well," said Frank Kemper, now a full professor of political science. "Like a born violinist or artist, he just intuitively *knew* politics and government. I gave him an A even before I read his final paper on the populism of the nineteenth century. If Charlie had wanted to become an academic, I swear he could have been the de Tocqueville of our time. But he wanted to go out and make money, which is a shame."

Kemper suddenly halted in his thought. "But then again, if he'd become a professor, he might have lost that magical touch, the ability to truly understand the people. Very few—if any—politicians have it, you know."

Since Charlie had been at Ohio State from 1971 to 1975, Reichmann wanted to know if Charlie had been involved in any radical student movements.

"Not really. Charlie went to a few SDS meetings and listened, but he never said anything, pro or con. He wasn't a conservative. I'd say he was a mild liberal then, but he acted more like he was going to become a historian of the movement than an activist."

His next stop was the fraternity house where Charlie had lived as a pledge who adamantly refused to go through hazing to become a brother. The frat leaders, Reichmann learned from contemporaries of Charlie's, had let him stay because his grade average helped lift the fraternity's. But mainly it was because—to pay for his room and board—Charlie ran the kitchen cutting costs and getting out good meals on time.

The only remaining staff member at the frat house was Johnnie Rice, the aging houseman-majordomo.

"Oh, yeah, I remember Charlie," he told the private eye when he was shown the 1975 yearbook photo. "Yeah, he was a taskmaster in the kitchen. But he was no slouch at playing either. Crazy about the girls. And don't fool yourself, he could raise a little hell. No drunk, but when he stopped working and let his hair down, he could handle a lot of beer. Don't know when he had time to study, but I understand he was a very good student.''

Reichmann breathed more easily. Was this the possible breakthrough? Was Charlie's halo developing cracks?

"Did he ever get in real trouble, Mr. Rice? You know—like a lot of college kids?" Arnie asked, the scent of paydirt stimulating him.

Rice shifted from side to side, entertaining the question.

"That ain't for me to say, mister—what is it?—Reichmann? I'm not a-saying either way. Charlie's a credit to the fraternity and the school, what with him being a congressman now. You can talk to other people, if'n you want. I'll leave that to you."

With that, Rice turned and walked back into the old frat house.

Reichmann weighed the old man's hints, then moved to his Dart. He'd head back to Fairview, to try his charms, and maybe more, on the new mayor, Bill Folsom.

As he drove the sixty miles, listening to a nostalgia pop station, he noticed a white car—it looked like a new Ford Taurus—trailing right behind. After ten miles the car seemed stuck to him, maintaining the same seventy-five- to one hundred-foot spread.

He tried an experiment, shifting from the center to the right lane, twice. The Ford followed close on, and after a few such maneuvers, it became obvious that someone was intensely interested in Arnie Reichmann, or perhaps in his subject, Charlie Palmer, or both. But who and why? He hadn't the faintest.

He drove on, now seriously mapping out his search for the secret life and times of Congressman Charles Knudsen Palmer, especially the $5,000 bonus for evidence of moral turpitude. So far, that seemed out of his grasp. But in his profession of snooping into the personal lives of the important, he had learned that there was one immutable law:

You never know.

CHAPTER 8

"Charlie, you would have made a great VP," a fellow member of the Ohio delegation told him—as if he had the traits of a good cigar store Indian. Great VP? No such thing, Charlie was sure.

Everywhere he went, people commiserated with him, but he was just as happy out of that fray. If he knew anything about himself, it was that he wouldn't have made a good number two man on Governor Lawson's ticket, however honest his intentions. How could he silently play along with every dollop of nonsense handed out by party propagandists? Too often he'd be going his own way on issues, which was a definite no-no for running mates.

Charlie had always chafed at authority when he thought it wrong. And nothing could be as wrong as the wasteful policies of Beltway government, most of it supported by Lawson, and even by his opposition, the other party's presidential nominee, Arthur Steadman, former governor of Idaho.

No, he didn't miss the VP nomination as long as he had his own bully pulpit—his seat in the House, and the press as a megaphone for his big mouth. The media viewed him as a little *outre*, but good copy nonetheless. And if polls of the *Fairview News* were any indication, he was assured of reelection to the House this November for a full term, if he wanted it.

What gnawed at him was the betrayal by Senator Larrimore, which wasn't going to be salved away easily.

But right now his problem was one he hadn't anticipated—the potential addiction to publicity, the Achilles' heel of all politicians. Celebrityhood was to politicians as cocaine to a drug addict.

Charlie confessed that he sometimes got a kick out of seeing his name (especially his ideas) in the papers, but too much notoriety made him want to shrink back into his cramped apartment behind the Hill, or even return to Fairview and live quietly in that miniature pond. Here in the Washington bowl, he had suddenly grown into a big fish, and he wasn't sure he enjoyed the idea.

Despite his failure to get the VP slot, he was besieged by reporters: by *Meet the Press*, Larry King, Peter Jennings, Cokie Roberts, NPR, Wolf Blitzer. You name it. They all wanted to know: How did it feel to fight the Goliath and, unlike David, fall on his face? But he had given out orders—no interviews for now.

His press secretary, Robbie Barnes, didn't agree.

"Mr. Congressman, I think you should take on all callers. You've got a big message to sell. This way the public gets to know you no matter how much the Sunday talking heads put you down."

Barnes was a small, meticulous man with a scholarly demeanor and a Phi Beta Kappa key draped on his severe three-piece blue serge suit, which had developed a worn turn-of-the-century look. A seminary dropout who later went on to Berkeley, Barnes—Charlie understood— was a very rich and guilty young man searching for a crusade. A belated admirer of Mark Rudd and Mario Savio, he bemoaned that he had missed the 1960s era of protest celebrity. But he had since calmed down and was now an establishment spokesman working for politicians.

Charlie believed that Barnes lacked humor and couldn't see the ridiculous in modern American politics—what Charlie viewed as a screwball game without precedent. But work? He made Charlie look like a malingerer.

The scion of a wealthy New England family that had made its fortune in hardware, Barnes was the Boston Brahmin manque. Though less distinguished than his forebears, he was just as Congregational Church–serious about the fate of man. Barnes had never become a preacher, but Charlie could see the fight between the Lord and Satan played out daily in the form of that one man.

"No, Robbie, no interviews for now," Charlie insisted. "Let the press speculate. They'll find out about me soon enough from my proposals on the Hill. When I'm ready, I'll talk to them all."

Charlie opened the newspaper and reread the lead story on the convention debacle, which was headlined:

VP CANDIDATE PALMER ELIMINATED BY SENATOR
WHO NOMINATED HIM. KENTUCKIAN WINS NOD.

He put down the paper and tried, unsuccessfully, to circle his closetlike office. But those few hesitant steps telegraphed his disappointment in the whole system, aggravated, of course, by Larrimore's betrayal. In just these few months, he had come to realize that politics was too often corrupted by either money or party allegiances, no matter from which side of the aisle it sprang.

He examined his own motives. Was he disappointed because of thwarted ambition? He laughed. No, he really had no ambition, either in life or in politics. In a way, he was just an efficient drifter. He hadn't asked for the VP job, and probably never wanted it, except as a chance to get Washington off its high horse.

But why in the hell did Larrimore go back on his word? What could they promise a senator reelected six times with 70 percent of the vote? Larrimore was reputedly wealthy on his own. Cattle, he had heard.

There were only two plausible reasons. Lawson, Billings, McKelvey, Berry, et al. had pressed him on his party loyalty. Or had they told Larrimore something about Charlie that he didn't like in a possible successor to the Oval Office?

But what? Charlie never claimed to be a choirboy and he had already been divorced. Surely there were other things in his past that he had forgotten. But there was one strong consolation: His real family secret was still buried in his life history. That was his to reveal or keep private, forever.

"SALLY!" Charlie suddenly shouted into the intercom for his aide, whom he'd been leaning on increasingly of late.

She came running, her expression set in anger.

"Now, Congressman, I sympathize with your disappointment with those slimy pros, but don't take it out on me! You're treating me like a gofer, bring you coffee and trying to heal your raw psychic wound. You've got to get over it, and move on. Being VP is a lousy job anyway."

Charlie stared at his trim administrative assistant, then laughed.

"You're 100 percent right, Sally, but I swear it's not disappointment over not being VP. It's disappointment over Larrimore. Sure, politics is hardball but everyone needs a hero, a model to copy. And for a while, Larrimore was it. Now who am I going to look up to?"

"I accept your apology, if that's what you made," Sally said, her expression softening. "I'm younger than you, but I've learned one thing in my eight years on the Hill. In Washington, if you want to keep your bearings, there's only one possible model."

"And who's that?" Charlie asked, impressed by Sally's attempt at motherly wisdom.

"Yourself. In the long run, that's the only one who you can control and rely on. Think about it, Congressman."

Charlie walked over and shook her hand vigorously.

"That's for setting me straight, Sally. Damned if you're not right. But that's not why I called you in. I've got to find a report over at the Library of Congress, and I want you to come along, I guess you know your way around there. I surely don't."

Sally grabbed his hand. "Come with Mama, young man. I'll make sure you get what you want."

He stared at her quizzically as they left Longworth together.

The Library of Congress is a complex of three buildings huddled near the Capitol.

Charlie and Sally headed toward the library's Madison Building on First Street and Independence Avenue, close to the Cannon House Office Building. Like his own, the Cannon was one of eight congressional office buildings. Two new ones named after Gerald Ford and Tip O'Neill had been opened to handle the enormous legislative bureaucracy, which had grown from four thousand in Harry Truman's time to thirty thousand, about four times faster than Americans were making babies.

"Why the big hurry?" Sally asked as she stretched her long stride to keep up with Charlie's fast-pumping, smaller steps.

"I have a Social Security hearing early this afternoon, and the Congressional Research Service has issued a report on the real numbers. I want you to find it and get a copy for me. It seems a half trillion dollars of the FICA tax surplus meant for the baby boomer retirement is already gone—cash taxes turned into more federal debt. Since 1983 when we raised the FICA taxes to create the surplus, it's been put into the general—not aged—fund to spend on everything from limos to farm subsidies. Both parties have accused each other of using Social Security cash as a gimmick to make the deficit look smaller than it is. And they're both right. When the budget is supposedly balanced in 2002, it'll actually be $112 billion in annual deficit just because of the 'borrowed' Social Security money—you should excuse the expression." And in a dozen years, when the baby boomer generation reaches retirement age, Social Security, Medicare, and that supposedly balanced budget will collapse. It's one of the great government rackets of all time.

Charlie shook his head, a sign that he found the whole thing incredible.

"The missing surplus money is counted on the debt, but not on the deficit, which is a classic case of 'cooked' books."

Sally whistled. She had learned to trust his numbers, as did many members, who viewed Charlie as a determined budget watchdog.

They continued walking, then stopped for a moment at the corner of Independence Avenue, in the ghetto of government.

Waiting to cross, Charlie and Sally stared ahead at their objective, the Madison Building of the Library of Congress, on the other side of the street. Then, suddenly, they looked up in unison.

A loud screech filled the summer air as a car, which seemed to be balanced on its tire edges, turned the corner in a frenzy. Curious, Charlie stepped to the edge of the sidewalk to see what was going on.

His curiosity quickly turned to fear. The car had made the turn and instead of coming down the center of the lane, the vehicle—it looked like a new White Ford Taurus—changed course. *Charlie calculated that the speeding car was heading directly for the curb—and them.*

He tried to move backward, but he felt pressure on his back. He was being pushed off the sidewalk into the street, directly into the path of the onrushing car! His feet had frozen in place when suddenly a hand reached out and grabbed his arm. It was Sally, yanking at him, trying desperately to pull him back to safety. He seemed to move a few inches rearward, but in the process, his resistance to Sally's tug dragged her off the curb. She was now in front of him and the car was bearing down.

"SALLY!"

Charlie's cry filled the street, stopping pedestrians in their tracks. He had recovered from his paralysis and was yanking at Sally's arm just as the car closed in. He pulled at her in one swift movement, as if hauling in a large fish.

The car was now upon them. It passed in a flash, missing Charlie by inches. But as he pulled Sally in, the Ford made contact with her in a nanosecond of terror, filling the air with its screech and Sally's cry. She fell to the street at his feet.

She lay there looking up at Charlie, her eyes wide open.

"Did he hit you? Are you OK?" Charlie asked frantically, dropping to his knees to examine Sally's side.

"I got hit, but I think it was a quick graze from the car fender. I was lucky—I fell slow enough to break my fall with my hands. My head never hit the ground. How's my leg?"

Charlie stared at it. Her clothes were torn on that side and there was a bloody scrape from the hip to the calf. It wasn't bleeding profusely, just oozing.

He turned around to see a small crowd hovering. "CALL FOR HELP, PLEASE!" Charlie yelled. "Call 555-3121 and tell the Capitol operator to send the congressional ambulance. *Quick.*"

He turned back to Sally, wrapping his jacket into a pillow and placing it beneath her head.

"It's a bloody scrape. Can you move the leg?"

"I think I can, but I better not try."

"Right. The ambulance will be here in a minute. And by the way, thanks for saving my life."

"Mr. Congressman, working for you has always been interesting. But now it's getting dangerous. Could you do me a favor and slow down, just a little?"

CHAPTER 9

"So miss, tell me—do you think it was an accident, or was someone trying to kill you or Congressman Palmer?"

Detective Sergeant Sam Lemoine of the District Police was standing over Sally's bed at the George Washington Medical Center, with Charlie alongside listening to the questioning.

Sally's left side, from her hip to her calf, was encased in a soft, bulky bandage. Doctors had given her a tetanus shot and antibiotics, and the prognosis was good, they said. She should be back to work in three days.

As Charlie listened, he thought the black plainclothes detective, a thin, somewhat short man with a tight white mustache and a full head of white hair, was quite professional. He was trying to be unaggressive but still get a bead on the puzzling case. A natty dresser, Charlie thought, with only one apparent eccentricity—Lemoine was twirling an unlit cigar, as if hoping for a chance to smoke.

"Sergeant, it was no accident," Sally volunteered. "That car was intent on hitting somebody, either me or the congressman. It was headed on a beeline for the spot where we were standing."

Lemoine turned toward Charlie. "How did you happen to be standing in the street instead of waiting on the sidewalk?"

"I remember. The car was making such a loud screeching noise as it turned the corner that I got curious. I stepped closer to the curb to get a better look. It was a little stupid of me, but I tend to be compulsively curious. Then suddenly somebody pushed me off the sidewalk into the street."

"Somebody pushed you? Are you sure it was on purpose?" Lemoime asked, surprised. "Did you see who it was?"

"No, I didn't see anyone special, but there was a group of people behind me. It could have been anyone. Or maybe someone pushed me by accident in the pressure of the moment."

"So how did Ms. Kirkland get hurt?"

"She stepped off the sidewalk and started to pull me back. As she did she got in front of me, and that's how she got hit." Charlie paused. "I don't think they were after her. If there was any target it was me."

"Did either of you see any details about the car?"

"It was all white, and looked to me like a late model Ford—I think a Taurus," Charlie responded. "But I didn't get a look at the license plates. As soon as it passed, I bent down toward Sally." Palmer looked up at the detective. "Did anybody in the crowd see the license plate?"

Lemoine shook his head, almost plaintively. "No, a few people thought it was a D.C. plate, but others swore it was Virginia, and no one got a full set of numbers." The detective turned again to Charlie. "Congressman, is there any reason anyone would want to kill you?"

Lemoine had finally asked the question. Never had Charlie contemplated that the political enemies he was accumulating—from Billings and others in the party hierarchy, down to a legion of special interests he was aggravating every day—were potential criminals. Politics might be sleazy, but that?

"I don't know how to answer, Sergeant. Do you know anything about politics or me in particular?"

The detective shook his head. "I don't bother much with politics. It's rotten in the District and confusing nationally. You? No, I never heard of you until Ms. Kirkland got hit, and homicide asked me to check out an attempted murder."

He stared quizzically at Charlie. "Is there anything special about you that I should know, something that would make a difference in the hit-and-run?"

Charlie was hesitant. "Well, I've only been in Washington a few months, but I was nominated for VP recently—and failed. Some political reporters say I've been shaking up the political establishment. That may be an exaggeration, but I have made several enemies. But murder? That's seems extreme, doesn't it?"

"Congressman, you leave the detective work to us. Just supply me with a list of people who you think hate you the most, and I'll look into it. OK?"

"So what do you make of it, Detective? Was it a simple plot to kill me off by a hit-and-run? One that failed?"

Lemoine's unlit cigar was being twirled again, even gaining velocity.

"Well, it looks like attempted murder, but I'm not sure it was. Does that surprise you?"

"Yes, but why do you say that?"

"Because these people are obviously pros. I may be wrong, but I think that if they really wanted to kill you, you'd be dead by now."

"But Sally saved me. She was in the way—between the car and me."

Lemoine proffered a small chuckle. "Congressman. If they wanted you dead, they'd just kill the two of you in one quick swipe. No, I think it was something else."

"What else could it be?"

"My guess—and it's only a guess—is that one of your enemies is trying to scare the bejesus out of you. I think it was a warning. If I were you, I'd be very careful."

Charlie looked at the detective and blanched. Now his suspicions were getting an official seal of approval. His paranoia, however slight and hidden, was being ignited by the Washington scene. That, more than even the attempt on his life—if that's what it was—truly troubled him.

CHAPTER 10

It was Sunday morning so it must be *Meet the Press.*

Party campaign chief Andy Tolliver watched the program faithfully, as he did all the talking-head shows. He laughed at their tired bantering of political gossip, but he considered it a lead to what people were thinking that week. Or at least what they were being told to think.

With the regular host on vacation, the slot was being filled by Roscoe Sands, a political stylesetter whose column, "Washington Eye," appeared in over three hundred papers nationwide.

Tolliver—garbed in oversize silk pajamas that a lady friend had compared to a small parachute—had watched the promos and turned anxious. Sands's guest? None other than the Ogre of Ohio, congressman and almost VP nominee Charlie Palmer, who could still stimulate *agita* in his, or any other, party.

What would the cocksucker say? And why in hell were the media offering him such a universe of listeners? If he could understand that, Tolliver lamented, he could better pick up on Palmer's attraction to the great unwashed. Personally, he couldn't see it.

Tolliver focused on the set as Sands came on and introduced Charlie as the *enfant terrible* of American politics.

"Congressman, your press man turned us down just a few days ago. Why the change of heart?" Sands asked his guest.

"Vice president or not, I'm in Congress and there's a political mess to clean up. And there's nothing like the tube to reach the people."

"Good. And are you still nursing your loss of the VP nomination? And were you double-crossed by your own party?"

"I wasn't personally wounded, Mr. Sands. I didn't ask for the nomination and, to be truthful, I didn't particularly want it. That was Senator Larrimore's idea. Then for some unknown reason, he changed his mind in mid-ballot. I never cease to be amazed by the behavior of American politicians."

"What do you think really happened, Congressman Palmer?"

"Well, I suppose we can attribute it to party discipline, which is a polite way of saying that there are sleazy back room deals corrupting the electoral process."

"So, what do you think of our political parties, Congressman?" Sands asked. "Are they doing a good job?"

Seated in his oversize bedroom armchair, Tolliver listened intently as he picked at his teeth with a tarnished gold-plated toothpick. What was the creep going to say?

"What do I think of the parties? Not much. They're getting to be trade unions for professional politicians, and sometimes crooked ones at that. Thirty members of Congress have been convicted of crimes just since 1970, which is much worse than the civilian crime rate. Still, there's less outright graft than, say, in Tammany Hall days. The crux of today's corruption is the $1.5 billion—yes billion—that politicians, from presidents to mayors, take in and spend in presidential election years. The villain is MONEY. A lot of that is really disguised favors for contributions, what I call legal bribery. And the political parties are the Svengalis behind it all."

"But isn't Congress working on campaign finance reform?" Sands interjected. "Won't that change things?"

Charlie snickered. "No way. It's just phony window dressing. According to their half-baked scheme, if a member of Congress voluntarily sticks to a fund-raising limit—which is larger than the amount most now spend—they'll get some taxpayer goodies like discounted TV time. But Congressmen can just turn up their noses, reject it, and go back to their old ways. No, instead of present so-called reform schemes, we need a real revolution in campaign finance."

"Are most politicians guilty of this legal 'corruption,' as you call it?"

"Oh, yes. A young U.S. attorney in California set out to show that much politics in America was akin to criminal bribery—quid pro quo, this for that, according to the law. He wired a lobbyist who promised campaign contributions to state legislators in Sacramento if they would vote for his bill. They said sure. He put five of them in jail, and the court of appeals has upheld the convictions. But most politicians are smarter, and sneakier. They avoid answering, or just say maybe, but it's no less sleazy.

"The public be damned is the general rule. One influential senator confessed in his diary that he gave a big oil company a multimillion-dollar tax break. Not because he liked them, but simply as a favor for a lobbyist friend. Politicians in Washington, and in the state capitals, have too many 'friends' sucking up to them. And generally they come calling with big checks in their hands. And the latest wrinkle is even worse. Since lobbyists can no longer directly entertain Congressmen, the political parties take the lobbyists' money and set up ski and beach parties where Congressmen attend and play buddy-buddy with the lobbyists. It's a corrupt, but legal, way that turns all those reforms into a giant joke."

"That's strong stuff. Do you have a solution?"

"Oh, many, and I'll be bringing them up in Congress later on. The first thing we have to do is to attract a new class of politicians. The present crop thinks winning is the only thing. We've got to kick them out and bring in citizens who won't die if they're not elected or reelected. Jefferson was a planter. Franklin was a printer. Professional politicians and democracy don't seem to go together anymore."

"So I presume you favor term limits?"

"Of course. But Congress has refused to pass it even though they touted it in the Contract With America. What we need is a constitutional amendment that won't permit *any* elected official, down to dog catcher, to serve more than two terms. That might even require a constitutional convention called by the states to go over the head of Congress."

"Will that do it, Mr. Congressman? Are you finished revamping America?" Sands asked with a touch of sarcasm.

"No, that's just the beginning. We have to put term limits on congressional committee chairmen and the Speaker, and maybe reduce the term of office for federal judges, who are beginning to act like politicians and legislators. Most important, we must cut out all retirement pensions—except Social Security—for elected officials. That'll make them think twice about a career in politics. Some congressmen have pensions worth over $4 million, and that's almost all taxpayer money, not their own contributions."

"Is that finally it?" Sands asked, smiling at Charlie's ardor. "Are you finished crucifying your colleagues?"

"Not really. We've got to eliminate several political diseases. I'll give you another one right now."

"Congressman, please do."

"One giant gimmick is that many ex-politicians become lobbyists in Washington and the state capitals, at double their public salary, when they leave office. That should be illegal. Most people don't know it, but hundreds of former members of Congress—retired or defeated—are working as lobbyists in Washington right now, cashing in big time."

"Really?" Sands asked. "But I thought we'd already passed lobby reform?"

"More smoke and mirrors. All it does is register more Beltway bandits and describe who pays them. It's meaningless. People don't know it, but former members of Congress working as lobbyists have a special pass. After only one year, they—and no other lobbyists— can walk onto the floor of Congress, even during a vote. They put their arm around their mark, and while the doorkeeper is keeping other lobbyists out, they walk right in. I've seen it many times, and it's disgusting."

Sands seemed surprised. "But it's different in the White House, isn't it? Don't they have rules prohibiting appointees from lobbying afterward?"

"That's another fakeroo." Charlie was enjoying his barbs at the status quo. "By White House rules, former officials of the Department of Agriculture, for example, can't lobby that department for five years. But from day one, they can lobby their buddies in *any other* department. Who's kidding who? No, Mr. Sands, it all stinks to high heaven. In fact, we've got to take a hard look at the power of political parties themselves—they're getting too big for their britches."

In his apartment, Tolliver was listening hard to Charlie Palmer, his mind shooting off angry sparks. He could feel the blood rising in his ample body. Suddenly, he felt the need to pee, but he didn't want a miss a second of Cocksucker Palmer's ravings. He hitched up his pajamas and held it in.

"Tell me, Congressman," Sands asked, "where do you fit on the political spectrum—left, right, or center."

"I don't."

"You don't what?"

"I'm not on the spectrum. I'm not ideological and neither are millions of Americans. They just want what works—the old American pragmatism. FDR was supposedly a liberal, but he closed all welfare except for the disabled and widows, then gave five million Americans work instead under the WPA. Henry Ford was a right winger, but he paid his workers $5 a day, twice the going salary at the time, so that they could buy his cars. That's what made America, workers moving up into the middle class. That's not happening as much these days—because of politics, taxes, and official stupidity."

"Aren't our political parties pragmatic?"

Charlie pushed back his head and laughed, almost raucously.

"God no, it's a refuge of half-baked ideologues," Charlie answered. "There's nary a practical head in the crowd."

"GOD DAMN SON OF A BITCH," Tolliver howled at the set. He lifted a glass of water off the end table and threw it at the television. Just missing the tube, it splashed water and shards all over the wall. As he did, his pajamas, pushing out against his expansive stomach, started to fall down.

He could feel his flesh vibrate. This man was the enemy of every-thing he stood for—the anti-Christ of the American political system. He had heard enough. Reaching for the remote control, he zapped *Meet the Press* and his nemesis, Fanatic Charlie Palmer, out of his life, at least for this morning.

At the same moment, the phone rang. Tolliver grasped at his pa-jama waistband and waddled across the room.

"Yes, who is this?" he barked.

"Mr. Tolliver, you don't know me."

"So how in the hell did you get my phone number? It's unlisted." Tolliver was still agitated by Charlie.

"I'm a private investigator. Just one of my tricks."

"So, what do you want from me?"

"Oh, nothing much. I just thought you might be interested in some juicy information about Congressman Charlie Palmer. I've been checking up on him for another client—and I thought we might make a side deal."

Tolliver's interest was suddenly so piqued that he forgot he had to go to the bathroom.

"What did you find out about him?"

"That's what I'm selling, Mr. Tolliver. And at a very high price. I hope your party can afford it because I have other customers waiting in line."

"How come my own snoopers haven't found out what you have? I had them out in force in Ohio."

"Probably because you didn't hire me."

"Can you give me a hint what you've learned about that son of a bitch?" Tolliver was now almost salivating.

"I like your enthusiasm. But no, I can't. Just meet me in the Potomac Bar at the Watergate Hotel in an hour."

"What's your name?" Curiosity was killing Tolliver.

"It's sort of secret. But you can ask for Mr. Fairview."

"Fairview? Isn't that the name of Charlie Bastard's hometown?"

"Exactly." With that, the caller abruptly hung up.

Tolliver did a little jig, then moved quickly to get dressed. "Hot dawg. At the Watergate," he muttered to himself.

"Maybe that's a prophecy about Charlie boy."

CHAPTER 11

Great Falls, Montana, sounded a million miles away from Washington, D.C., but the jet from National Airport put him in Minneapolis in three hours. With a change, he arrived in Montana in two more.

Now that he was out of the VP sweepstakes, would the gumshoes still be on his case? Possibly. After all, the car run-down had taken place *after* the convention. Who could be behind it all? Tolliver probably wouldn't be checking on someone in his own party. Charlie assumed it was the opposition, headed by Norm Sobel, a former academic. He hardly seemed the type, but who knew about the inner workings of the political mind?

To shake any possible tails on this trip, he had decided on an evasive action. No one, in politics or the press, should know of his visit to Rafferty, a well-known but still shadowy financial figure.

Sally had cooperated in the subterfuge. Early that morning, he had taken a cab to her townhouse apartment in the Northwest district. He stayed a few minutes, then left through the back door. Racing across the macadam parking lot, he exited onto a tree-lined side street, then walked two blocks to the main intersection. He hailed a cab and went on to National Airport, lugging only a small bag.

He couldn't be sure if he was being followed, but Charlie was learning a Washington trade secret. A little paranoia went a long way.

Now, on the highway going west out of Great Falls later that same day, his rented Mercury Grand Marquis was eating up the highway at eighty miles per hour on this cloudless Sunday afternoon in July, all quite legal in a state with no speed limit. The destination, the Sky Ranch, was sixty miles ahead. He had been told to expect another world, one in which one man owned ten thousand acres, from horizon to horizon. That man, of course, was Schuyler Rafferty.

If truth be known, Charlie had forgotten about that disembodied voice on the phone. What with the convention, Sally's injury, hearings on the mining law and Social Security, and a dozen more interventions, it was only a dim memory. But apparently he wasn't going to be allowed to forget it.

"Kid, this is Rafferty from Montana. Remember our bet?" Schuyler had brusquely come on the phone.

Bet? Oh, my God, Charlie recalled. It had been so neatly expunged from his mind, and this old goat was reminding him.

"Are you a man of your word, or are you just another four-flushing politician?" Rafferty asked.

"Remind me, Mr. Rafferty. Exactly what was the bet?"

"You said the crook Billings wouldn't be nominated as VP, and I told you that you were a naive youngster on his way up, but still with a lot to learn."

"And apparently you won. What was my forfeit?"

"Simple. Since you're so godawful honest and wouldn't fly here on my Lear, you said you'd pay your own way—I think about $1,800 round trip—and come out to Montana."

"You mean that you intend to hold me to the bet?" Charlie had considered the incident no more than a prank. "With all that's going on in Washington, you want me to fly out there to the boondocks to jawbone with you? Come off it, Mr. Rafferty. That's just an ego trip."

"So say you, young man. But did it occur to you that I got the Billings vote right on? Maybe I know something you don't."

Charlie's demeanor softened. "That's true. Tell me, how come you saw it coming? I was banking on Senator Larrimore to crush Billings."

Rafferty's laugh and that flat New York accent now came on stronger.

"You lost the bet, kid, because you were dealing in anecdotes and not in theory. That's why people lose money on the stock market. The theory was simple. What major party was going to throw away its intimidating strength and hand its power over to some schmuck kid with a bomb in his hand—no offense meant? If they wanted to maintain their internal integrity, they had to double-cross you. And they did."

Rafferty laughed again. "And also, I'm older and maybe smarter than you. Most old farts are, but they aren't quick enough anymore. But not me, Charlie. I got a head start—brought up in a Brooklyn saloon, nipping whiskey when I was two, and fighting my Italian, Jewish, and black buddies on the way to school when I was six. Now I'm sixty-nine, I've got a shithouse full of money, a gorgeous ranch, and I can outthink and outfight you and a dozen like you any day."

"And you're also very modest, Mr. Rafferty," Charlie quickly processed the information through his own youthful computer. "So you want me to come out there to talk about something. What's it all about and how long will it take?"

"It'll take three days of your time. What's it about? You'll find out at dinner over the best steak you've ever put an incisor into. Right off the Sky Ranch grounds. OK?"

Charlie had no choice if he was to maintain his own integrity, which is why he was doing eighty MPH on a Montana highway on his way to Rafferty's spread to listen to some old smartass who just happened to be one of the richest men in America.

"Welcome young man, welcome."

Rafferty was out front, standing in the cobblestone courtyard of what looked to Charlie like a cross between a large land ship and a Frank Lloyd Wright creation. His enormous castle of wood and stone was positioned a mile or so in front of a mountain peak that overshadowed it. The rolling land of the house and environs was forty-five hundred feet high in altitude, about the same measure below the peak of the purple Rocky Mountain majesty behind it.

Rafferty was dressed for the occasion, if Hollywood was directing the production. He wore a wide-brimmed Australian army hat tipped up on one end, a safari bush jacket whose provenance was probably from the days of Livingstone and Stanley, and brown leather boots with creases creased in. A white aviator's scarf, serving no real purpose, was wound around his neck.

His white Irish mane (minus not a single hair) was peeking out of the hat, matching the white beard. With his more than six feet of height, and a touch of extra girth, he looked like someone Charlie thought he knew. Of course. Rafferty was Ernest Hemingway.

Charlie parked the car in the garage, following instructions of a cowhand. He inched it next to a twelve-cylinder Bugatti, if he remembered his antique cars. The garage was also filled with a 1920s Duesenberg, a 1949 Lincoln Continental, and a dark green Raymond Loewy 1951 wraparound-window Avanti. All this next to a prosaic Buick, vintage 1996, and a Land Rover, which were probably what actually drove them around Sky Ranch. Maybe the trip was worth it for the car show alone.

"Come, Congressman Palmer. Leave your bags for Rickie. He'll set you up in your apartment. First I want you to see Brooklyn-in-Montana, one of my pride and joys."

It had as much to do with Brooklyn as did Sea Island, Georgia, but it was obviously something out of a seventeen-year-old Regis High School Catholic scholar's imagination, a secular cathedral in the Great American Rockies.

Rafferty scurried alongside Charlie with undisguised enthusiasm, showing him through the entire twenty-five-thousand-square-foot establishment. Charlie's favorite was the "Great Room," a three-story tall space complete with stained beams and the flags of all states West of the Mississippi hanging from the rafters.

The furniture was mostly built-in, sculpted to fit the body. The rugs were Orientals alongside Indian Navajo, and totems and natural cactus were laid out irregularly throughout the room. It was a young Brooklynite's surrealist fantasy of a Western landscape—all indoors.

Charlie knew more about Schuyler Rafferty than the billionaire thought he did. Calling on Lexis-Nexis, he had collected a folder full of printouts, including a long profile from *Business Week.* Charlie was intrigued with the human color, which might be fact, or just an Irishman's tall tale taken seriously by the media because of his wealth. But true or not, Schuyler told it the same way each time, so it sounded credible.

After graduating as a scholarship student at a Jesuit high school, Rafferty was hired by a Wall Street firm, where he worked first as a messenger, then as a back room clerk. Before the days of computers, his math skill made him a mainstay, then chief of the back room of McKinney and Cohen, members of the Exchange. In those days of high commissions, Rafferty marveled at the income of the "customer's men," and decided that was a logical career.

He moved from the back room to the front, and soon became the firm's leading commission broker, earning enough to buy himself a cooperative apartment in the River House on the fashionable East Side of New York at the age of twenty-four. It wasn't an effortless accomplishment. Several tenants resisted inviting in an Irishman, then almost as much a mark of ineligibility as being a Jew on the East Side in 1952.

Rafferty methodically visited with each family in the cooperative and charmed them into inaction. When he moved in, he threw an elegant catered cocktail party for his fellow residents, picking up several customers for M&C in the bargain.

Enchanted with the stock market, Rafferty decided he could make more money as a trader than as a broker. He traded only his own account at a reduced commission rate, but the emotions of the market ruffled his logical mind. After six months of harried buying and selling, he had lost 60 percent of his small fortune.

Then, in 1954, at age twenty-six, he moved his operation into his apartment and designed the methodology that had made him Rafferty. Calling himself a "junk dealer," he decided to become a personal conglomerate. He avoided large glamorous companies that attracted attention and speculators, and started to gain control of small, particularly dull public companies selling for four or five times earnings, about half the then-going Dow-Jones ratio. Over the years, Rafferty bought an electrical supply company, a firm making oxygen for medical use, a valve company in Ohio, an air-conditioning manufacturer, a large Southern trucking company, a Western bakery, a brewery in Vermont, an educational software company, and a dozen more.

He put in good management and left them alone. Rafferty knew value, but he was no worker bee. He never rode them down. If he guessed wrong on the company, he sold his controlling interest and took his losses.

Now at age sixty-nine, the financial tally sheet was in. Rafferty, said *Business Week,* was worth $6 billion, give or take a billion. Not that such propaganda was to be believed exactly, but the saloonkeeper's son had obviously done pretty well.

Strangely, none of the articles said anything about Rafferty's personal life. Charlie didn't even know if he ever married or had any children.

As they walked through Brooklyn-in-Montana, Charlie could see that the house was a dream sequence, built to fulfill the fantasy of a young man who had been brought up in a cramped apartment over the saloon, sleeping in the same bedroom as his two brothers. Now he had room to spread, indoors, outdoors, and in his spacious mind as well.

"Tell me, Mr. Rafferty," Charlie asked, "where's your office?"

"Office? Hell no, I haven't any. An office is a cage that imprisons your mind. I won't permit that."

"So where do you do your work?" Charlie was confused.

"Anywhere I want—the Great Room, the kitchen, my bedroom, the toilet. My working tool is a clipboard, and anything on it is what I'm doing at any given moment."

"Don't you have a personal computer or a laptop?"

"God no. I wouldn't know how to work one. I'm low-tech and high-minded. The only thing I allow is a fax, which my secretary keeps in her bedroom."

Once the tour was completed and Charlie had shown appropriate visual awe at the vast operation, they adjourned to the Great Room.

"Charlie—I hope I can call you that—I'd appreciate it if you'd drop the Mr. Rafferty. That was my father's name. I'm strictly Schuyler, or Sky, if you prefer."

Charlie nodded agreement. "Schuyler—fancy name for a poor Irish family. How did your parents settle on that?"

"Simple. My mother had pretensions of class, and she didn't want another Mike, or Patrick, or Joseph, or John, or F.X. At the time, New York had telephone numbers named after rich old families— Butterfield, Havenmayer, even Schuyler. So I was christened after a phone exchange, which unfortunately has since been replaced with numbers. Matches the decline of the whole civilization. The phone name is gone, but Schuyler lives on—through me."

Charlie laughed. Rafferty was the owner of a massive ego, but he didn't find it offensive. Schuyler had made a play out of his life, and Charlie was finding this act entertaining.

"Have a drink, Charlie? Join me in imbibing?" Rafferty waved his hand for an uncostumed waiter-butler who had been waiting in the far corner of the room. "Bring me a double rye whiskey and leave the bottle here. What do you want, Charlie?"

"A cold beer, if you have one."

"Have one? I own a whole brewery—Old Green Mountain—a nice tangy flavor. Bring two bottles," he ordered.

The two men chatted aimlessly for fifteen minutes while Charlie watched Rafferty down four doubles, then belch, almost politely, before pushing away the whiskey. Charlie stared at him, somewhat amazed.

"So you find my imbibing startling, do you?" Rafferty asked. "Yes, it is, especially for an Irishman. There's a myth that we can hold our liquor. No such thing, which is why St. Patrick's Day became so famous. But me? I was inoculated by drinking 100 proof from the time I was a baby."

"What about your liver?"

"So far so good. But my heart? As strong as a lion." Rafferty annotated that with a small roar.

They both seemed to be enjoying themselves, but Rafferty remembered his manners.

"Charlie boy, you've been traveling all day. Dinner will be at 6:30. So why don't you take a little nap? There'll be three of us for dinner—you, me, and my daughter, Jenny, who runs this whole damn place. See you then."

Daughter? Charlie had no idea Rafferty had a child, grown or otherwise. But now he was staring at her across the small dining table at the far end of the Great Room. On his tour, he had seen a dining room that could seat thirty, but that was obviously reserved for formal occasions.

Jenny was less expansive than her father. She exchanged a few pleasantries, asking about Washington, then confessed that she knew nothing about politics and couldn't care less.

"Our ranch is my love, and I dropped out of Wellesley to take care of it when my mom died five years ago," Jenny explained, just as Rafferty appeared. He was wearing a corduroy suit, looking quite cosmopolitan, more like the New Yorker he really was, Charlie thought.

"You're getting the royal treatment, Charlie," Rafferty observed. "Jenny is wearing a dress, the first time I've seen that since Christmas. She must be impressed by the company."

"Hardly, Schuyler. Jenny just told me she couldn't care less about politics. She's probably never even heard about me."

"Not so, Charlie. When you were on *20/20* I dragged Jenny into the TV room, and she watched—a bit impressed—as you tore into Washington wastrels in both parties. The best case for me was the Eighty-ninth Airlift out of Andrews AFB near Washington—what they call the 'Airline of the VIPs' with their plush twenty-three airliners to take politicians all over the world at $25,000 per seat per flight. That got to both me and Jenny. She likes mavericks, horses and men. Right, girl?"

"Oh, shut up, Daddy."

"And she's been listening to me rant and rave about the way things are in Washington, and the arrival of Congressman Charles Palmer, one man not afraid to take on the establishment."

"Cut out the blarney, Rafferty," Charlie said, flattered.

"It's not blarney, Charlie, I've never been more serious. And I'll prove it to you as soon as we finish our salad and start on the piece de resistance, a Sky Ranch steak, whose breeding, incidentally, is supervised by my little Jenny, who's still not thirty herself. Right?"

Jennie just grimaced, patronizingly, at her father.

Charlie stared at her for an instant. She was not unattractive, of average height, with a full pleasant face, blond hair in a ponytail, and no makeup. More like a college kid than the manager of a great spread.

The meal went on without event, except when the name of Schuyler's late wife, Angelica, came up. Sadness then suffused the faces of both Raffertys, if only for an instant. This was the first sign that the indomitable Schuyler Rafferty could be vulnerable. Charlie himself had never experienced real grief. Poverty and too much work, but not grief. He had never known his father, and his mother was alive and kicking, sometimes uncontrollably.

"NOW," Schuyler called out to the two servants—the woman, about forty, wearing a simple dress, and the man, dressed in Levi's and a cowboy shirt. In fact, it was Rickie, the one who had parked the rented car. They carried in large silver trays filled with what were varied cuts of beef—rib, Porterhouse, New York cut, filet mignon—all barbecued and rare within.

"Eat well, everybody. Who knows what fate awaits us—and our nation—tomorrow," Rafferty pontificated.

He began to speak, in his unique way. He'd take a bite of his steak, exclaim about its wonders, then talk—in bursts somewhat reminiscent, Charlie thought, of the one-minute blurbs allowed House members on the floor.

Charlie knew this was why he had been called here. He listened, not daring to interrupt.

"Charlie, Jenny," Schuyler began. "We all love our country, but I fear it's fallen on bad times. Not instant, but slow and deadly, like a company whose guts are being sold off by raiders."

Rafferty took another bite of steak and washed it down with scotch.

"Charlie, that's why I asked you here, or really inveigled you with a bet I knew I'd win. Why? Because I'm like an old Diogenes in search of an honest patriot. Not the fatigue-garbed nuts in the hinterland or the sleazy hacks in Washington who take millions from special interests. Some of our politicians are OK, but too many are egotistical, celebrity-driven men and women. Meanwhile, a lot of good people who won't put up with the system just drop out. Or worse yet, never drop in. And what's the result of all that?"

Charlie could see that Rafferty was getting more loquacious with each tumbler of Chivas.

"I'll tell you. We're killing the working middle class. The average wage earner makes 20 percent less in real dollars after taxes today than twenty years ago. I get away with murder by taking most of my money out in capital gains, but the typical family spends more for taxes than for food, housing, and medical care combined. A self-employed man in the lousy $40,000 bracket is paying 41.3 percent federal taxes—income and FICA—on top of state and local bites. Naturally, a lot of them become tax crooks and disappear into the underground economy. Many of our corporations keep cutting out workers and managers to raise their stock price so that the big boys can cash in their options. The government says there's 5.5 percent unemployment. That's bullshit. With temps, part-timers who can't find regular work, the chronically unemployed who aren't even looking anymore so they're not counted, the laid-off managers barely existing as self-employed, and welfare cases, the real number is closer to 15 percent. Even the Bureau of Labor statistics—in their unpublicized notes—says the real number is 10.8, not 5.5, percent. It all stinks to high heaven, and there's only one group to blame—our politicians."

Rafferty cut another piece of steak, then lubricated it with Chivas.

Charlie had promised himself silence, but he felt pushed. "So tell me, Schuyler, what do you think the answer is—a third party?"

Rafferty reared back his head. "I used to think so, Charlie, but I've changed my mind. I think the corruption you talked about on *Meet the Press* can only be cut out by some tough independent-minded leader. Let's look for another Teddy Roosevelt, another Lincoln, another Jefferson, another Harry Truman, someone with brains and balls—someone who can rip up the whole system then put it back together in better shape. Then I'll bankroll that person for President. So, I've deposited $100 million in cash in a special account to pull it off."

Charlie was sharply taken aback.

"A hundred million dollars? Does that mean you're going to make a run for the White House yourself—a la Perot?"

Rafferty almost choked on his steak.

"Me? No way. You couldn't find a worse president than Schuyler Rafferty. I think everyone should be up by 5 A.M. Work fourteen hours a day, ask help from no one, have no debts, never get sick, and be able to retire at forty. No, I'd have no compassion for the left-outs, the mediocres, the also-rans. I think everyone should be rich enough to piss on Washington. No, a bastard like me should never be President. But I do love my country as much as the next guy."

"If not you, who?" Charlie asked, quickly adding: "Surely not me. I'm just a novice at this business."

"No. You're a natural but you're still untested. I didn't ask you here to offer you $100 million or a nomination. What I need, Charlie, is two things: advice and selection. I need a short list of people who could be President and Vice President on a maverick ticket. I also need a list of *everything* that's wrong with the country today and how to fix it. I think you're the only one who could write it and pick the right candidate."

Rafferty paused, then asked in a voice more solicitous than any Charlie had yet heard from the old billionaire, "So what do you think, Charlie? Is it doable, and will you help me?"

Charlie's mind was whirling.

"I never expected this, so don't you expect an answer from me right now."

Charlie cocked his head back and looked challengingly at Rafferty.

"Besides, you know how I stand on money in politics. I think it stinks like overripe fruit. I refuse to take anybody's money. Now you're asking me not only to tolerate your pouring $100 million into the political pot, but you're trying to get me personally involved. I don't know."

"JESUS! You sound like a twelve-year-old, Congressman. Like me, your mind is filled with a million schemes to change crooked politics. But you're not willing to use the same tool the phony bastards have on their side—money, and gobs of it. I'm offering you a chance to become a linchpin in a real revolution, and you give me your immature whining horseshit about principles. Grow up, Charlie, and quick."

Taken aback by Rafferty's temper and a verbal onslaught he hadn't expected, Charlie hesitated.

"Like I said, Rafferty, I don't know."

Charlie could see a touch of remorse in Rafferty's mien.

"I'm sorry I blew my top kid. Just my way of showing that I want it a lot. And besides, I'm not giving you the money. It's going to whoever runs for the White House as an independent—so your hands are clean. OK?"

Charlie couldn't help but laugh at this big, bluff, conniving Irishman.

"OK Schuyler, I'll think about it. But . . ."

"But what?" Rafferty asked, concern in his voice.

"But whether I take up your offer or not, I'll give you a few caveats."

"I'm waiting."

"Well, first off, the two parties make it difficult for independents to get on the ballot, using all kinds of legal rigmarole. Secondly, if you back an independent candidate, you've got to realize that you can't control him, or her, or anything. Your money will get you a consultation on the nominee, but no veto. And just this one time. If you pull it off and a new independent President makes a real revolution, you'll be left in the backwater. Do you thoroughly, truly understand that?"

Rafferty listened and nodded, twice.

"That's exactly the way I want it, Charlie. I've got enough power with my money for ten lifetimes. I just want to change this bullshit and I think you're the only one with the political instinct to help me. If you agree to come aboard, I'll fade out like the old boozer I am. I swear."

Rafferty's expression remained conciliatory.

"Of course, Charlie, you realize that if you take this on, you'll be finished with your own party. They'll never forgive you, and maybe get rough besides."

"Thanks, but I'm already in Alaska in the winter as far as they're concerned. In fact someone's already tried to run me and my AA down by car right outside the Capitol."

Rafferty was genuinely surprised. "Really? Any idea who did it?"

"No, but the District detective thinks it was a warning to me to shut up and go away. But I won't. I'm going to keep on doing just what I've been doing. But before I give you my answer, Schuyler, I have to ask you this: Why trust $100 million to me? What do you know about me other than what you read in the paper or see on C-Span?"

Rafferty guffawed so loudly that Jenny twitched.

"Kid, I know more about you than you know about yourself. I've got the best intelligence network in the country. Without it, I couldn't stay in business one day."

"And did I come up smelling in your investigation?"

"Well, we're all human, Charlie, so I ain't a-sayin' exactly. But you're here, aren't you? And if I'm guessing wrong, I may be jeopardizing our nation. So you think about it, and please give me your answer soon. If you agree, then you're the man to work up a fighting platform and find us a standard-bearer to lead us out of the darkness."

The old geezer's sincerity had come shining through, Charlie thought. He was truly touched.

CHAPTER 12

"Look down there, Clara," King Kellogg shouted over the roar of the helicopter rotor. "That's the PPP—Pemenex Palladium and Platinum Mine. It may take only white minerals out of the ground, but it's a potential gold mine for your party."

"You really think these people are going to part with a million bucks for our national campaign?" Clara asked.

As Kellogg considered Clara's question, he realized how lucky this day was for him. As a lobbyist, he was by nature bipartisan, but was now leaning toward the Lawson-Billings ticket. If he could convince Pemenex to part with the million, he'd earn the confidence of Lawson, probably the next President, and that of Champ Billings, who had already proven himself a most accommodating politician.

The second reward was being with Clara, who made his latent libido stir. Glancing at her beside him, he marveled at her beauty and poise. Always immaculate—a trait he revered—she was dressed stylishly in a silk bush jacket and skirt, as if on an African safari. If he ever moved in either sexual direction, Clara was the only one who could push him over into heterosexuality.

Kellogg and Clara had just landed at the new Denver International Airport, where their luggage survived the computerized system. The PPP helicopter had picked them up for the short flight to the mine in the Colorado Rockies.

"To answer your question, Clara, I do think PPP will come along. They're a foreign-controlled corporation mining on our federal lands, and they're worried abut what Washington will do. They need us and we need them. Your presidential ticket has $70 million in tax money, but the congressional races are crying for cash. A million dollars will buy three thirty-second national TV spots—the real battleground in November. That's why we're here."

Pemenex, King explained to Clara, was a consortium controlled by investors in Singapore, Taiwan, and Germany. The company had mines all over the world, but the American operation was the most successful. It had a minority of American shareholders, but the majority of its profits were shipped overseas.

Clara knew her politics, but today her job was singular: to charm the Pemenex chairman, Hans Treulich, a Bavarian, and keep him receptive during negotiations.

"Clara, the reason I think they'll play ball is that Pemenex's mine is worth $40 billion. But if their application with Interior is approved, they'll be getting the whole twenty-five hundred acres for only $5,000 or $2.50 an acre under the old Mining Act of 1872, which is still the law because of a presidential veto of an omnibus bill in 1996. And even though they're foreign controlled, they get the benefit of that dirt-cheap price. And they don't pay any royalties at all on the minerals they take out of our grounds."

"Are there many foreign mining companies on U.S. federal lands?" Clara asked, intrigued.

"Oh yes. Of our top twenty-five gold mines, sixteen are wholly or partially owned by foreign interests. We're talking big money. A House committee report says we've given away $91 billion in mining land just since 1987. And it's my job to keep it going just that way."

The helicopter landed in the bull's-eye in front of the administration building, on top of which waved Old Glory.

"Velcome, King and Ms. Staples," Treulich greeted them. "An honor to have such prominent American visitors." Then with a quick aside to Clara—"and such a beautiful politician."

"Thanks, but I'm not really a politician." Clara smiled her radiant best. "Just a rich amateur going along for the ride, wherever it leads me."

Inside, Treulich showed them samples of the metals taken out of the mountain: bars of platinum, palladium, and iridium, white metals that would end up in Van Cleef and Arpels, or as car pollution catalysts, or in other high-tech uses.

"Now, let's take a look at the field of operation." Hans led them to a vintage open Mercedes, a six-seater touring car.

Kellogg could see Clara lavish the green enamel masterpiece with the same lustful eye Hans was directing at her. Surely forty years old, the car was a masterpiece. King hoped Treulich would sell it to Clara, but he didn't want to jeopardize the deal for a trinket, no matter how lovely, and no matter how much it would ingratiate him with lovely Clara.

As the Mercedes took them over acres of bumpy gravel roads, Kellogg started to feel uncomfortable, the movement and the heat upsetting his equilibrium. As Treulich explained how the ore was separated, not only was he bored, but he could see Clara's eyes occasionally flicker, then close.

"I think it's time to get back to headquarters, King," Treulich said, noticing their inattention.

Back in the conference room, Treulich introduced a young American named Hoot Jackson, the firm's governmental affairs specialist. A former congressional staffer, he had since cashed in.

Jackson, a tall, spare Coloradan, began.

"Ms. Staples, King, we're worried about legislation now in the hopper to stop foreign-owned corporations such as ours from buying federal land cheaply. It would also force us to pay double royalties. I don't think that our people in Taipei and Berlin would be happy."

Jackson paused. "We need your help to stop the new bill in the House where Congressman Palmer is pushing it."

"Charlie seems to be everywhere at the same time," Clara commented dryly.

King suddenly stood, his white seersucker suit still pristine looking.

"Mr. Treulich, Mr. Jackson," Kellogg began, "I don't know if we can stop Palmer's bill in the House, but our Western friends like Senator Berry should be able to kill it in the Senate. Should it pass there, I can absolutely guarantee you a presidential veto when the Lawson-Billings ticket wins this November. Your profits will be secure."

Treulich, who had been staring at Clara, suddenly refocused. He stood up, ramrod straight.

"A veto? King, that would be wunderbar. What can we do to help make it happen?"

"You can support the national party with a sizable contribution."

"Why, of course. Each American Pemenex executive will contribute the limit—I believe $1,000. I can safely pledge $25,000. Will that do?"

King smiled. "I was thinking of more like a million dollars. It's really a small investment for such high returns."

"A million dollars?" Treulich was taken aback. "That's a lot of money. Besides, wouldn't that be illegal?"

"It would be if it was in hard money. That's strictly limited. But not soft money."

"Soft—hard. What's the difference? It's all money."

"In America, it makes all the difference, Hans. The hard money limits apply only to candidates. Soft money is for the party, and those contributions can be much larger. You see, Herr Treulich, in America, we pass strict laws that let us feel righteous. Then we pass others with loopholes that let us do anything we want. It may sound corrupt, but it's the American way."

"Strange," Treulich commented. "But surely you wouldn't want so much money directly from a foreign firm like ours, even if we are incorporated in America. It would stand out too much."

"Of course. But there's a way you can contribute a million dollars."

"Really?" Treulich seemed confused.

"It's simple. Organize a group of forty of your wealthy American stockholders. Ask each to contribute $25,000 or so in soft money as insurance for their Pemenex investment. Have them send the money directly to party headquarters in Washington. As a private company, you can even reimburse their gift with extra stock, or options."

Treulich seemed troubled. He silently circled the large conference table, then returned to his original seat.

"But won't it look suspicious if so many of our investors give large amounts of money to your party?" he finally asked.

"No one will ever know," Kellogg assured him. "You're a privately held company, so your investor list is private."

"WUNDERBAR," Treulich called out in glee. "King, you are a genius. I was told to make sure I got King Kellogg as our Washington man." He turned to Clara. "And with such a beautiful partner, I am sure there's nothing you can't do."

Treulich paused, concern once more on his face. "So I have your guarantee that even if Congressman Palmer's horrible bill passes Congress, that President Lawson—once he wins in November—will veto it?"

"Absolutely, Hans. You have my word. And without my word, I am out of business."

"Good. You'll have the money within thirty days."

They moved outside toward the helicopter, where Treulich bent to kiss Clara's hand.

"You like the Mercedes, Miss Staples?"

"Very much," Clara answered.

"Then it is yours, a gift from a grateful firm. It will be delivered to your home—I believe in Georgetown—within the week. *Auf Wiedersehen*, my beautiful politician."

Buckled in for their return flight to Washington, first class, Kellogg poured Clara the Lafite Rothschild '82 (at $185 a bottle) he had ordered in advance.

As she sipped the wine, her eyes displayed confusion.

"Tell me, King. How could you guarantee that Lawson would veto Charlie's foreign mining bill? Don't you have to clear it with the nominee?"

"I cleared it with someone more important, your party's VP candidate, Champ Billings. He has a deal with Lawson. If they win, Billings will have authority over all domestic matters that involve large party contributions, like this one. And by the way, Clara, you did a splendid job with Hans. He's absolutely besotted."

A sudden thought struck King. "And as you saw, Clara, Charlie Palmer still has his hand into everything, even mining rights. Do you think you can make contact with him soon? He's a walking time bomb."

Clara smiled enigmatically.

"King, I have every intention of making 'contact,' as you call it, with that flaming radical. It might be the best thing I could ever do for my country."

CHAPTER 13

"How's your seat?" Jenny called out to Charlie, who had just mounted a docile pinto, speckled brown and white.

"I can't tell yet. I'm getting a little vertigo. Haven't been on a horse since college, and then I wasn't too good."

Charlie had stayed over in Montana another day, luxuriating in the mountain peace. He and Jenny had saddled up at the utility stable, where the Raffertys kept a dozen work horses used as auxiliaries to the Jeeps and Land Rovers that handled most of the cattle on the massive ten-thousand-acre spread—an expanse of 350 square miles, the size of New York City.

"This morning we'll take it easy, Congressman," Jenny explained. "End to end, the ranch is twelve miles, but you'll see a good part of the operation if we do four miles. And don't worry about the pinto. That's Bertha. We use her for the twelve-year-old kids to be safe. Daddy can't afford to lose you."

Swell beginning, Charlie thought. I'm classed with the children. But at least they value my head.

As they rode, Charlie gained confidence and Bertha accommodated him with a lazy trot. The landscape of the foothills of the Rockies was magnificent. The land held every variety of topography—mountain plateaus that ran without end, rolling hillsides, and plains suffused with tall wild grasses. In the valleys were cattle, indifferent to the humans on horseback surrounding them. The sky, dotted with puffs of cumulus clouds, spelled nothing if not tranquillity.

"Like it, Congressman?" Jenny asked after twenty minutes of silence. "Kind of different from the East. Right?"

Charlie felt transformed by the peace, except, he thought, nothing really escapes Washington's long arm. Almost thirty percent of Montana, not just the Glacier National Park, belonged to the federal government. As a member of an Interior subcommittee, he had already faced the tug-of-war on mining and grazing rights between the West and Washington, which, strange to say, owned half of everything on that side of the Mississippi, including eighty percent of Nevada.

Strange because Washington owned almost nothing in Ohio and even less in Connecticut, where his mother's people had come from. Why? Because Connecticut was there before the U.S.A. The federal government never had a chance to get its greedy grasp on it.

But the West? Washington took the land from the Indians and the Mexicans, but when the Western states were formed, from 1836 up through 1912, Congress asked itself: "Why give them the land? We'll just keep it." That clever scam was now causing no end of friction, with even county officials in the West fighting an increasingly oppressive Washington jurisdiction.

Why not give all the federal land in the West, except for national parks and military sites, an area the size of Western Europe, back to the states? Charlie thought. The people of the West would know whether to preserve or develop it, or provide an equitable environmental mix. A good point to bring up in committee when he got back to Washington.

"Here we are, Congressman," Jenny, who had ridden a little ahead, called out. "If you look straight ahead, you'll see our thoroughbred horse operation. Whatdya think?"

He figuratively rubbed his eyes in disbelief. Coming off a downward slope of wild country, lying in front of him was the largest cultivated grass meadow he had ever seen, all closed in by immaculate white fencing, outside of which had been planted an enormous number of shrubs. From where he was, they looked like rhododendron.

It was, Charlie decided, a piece of the manicured Virginia countryside transported intact to wild Montana.

Jenny, with her pork-pie cowboy hat now thrown back on her neck, raced ahead, turning occasionally to laugh at Charlie's slow progress. In five minutes had caught up to her at the elegant stables, painted glossy black and lemon, the racing colors of the Sky Ranch.

After they had dismounted, Jenny took him firmly by the hand, pressing warmly into his palm. "Come, I'll give you the tour," she ordered. They moved through the stables, where bays and chestnuts, mares and stallions were happily housed in equine luxury. Jenny walked close to him, smiling broadly every time she caught his eye.

"We breed them, raise them, train them, race them, sell them," she explained. "They're all thoroughbreds. Some go into our racing group, others are slated for breeding. Some we sell to fancy stables as riding horses for rich American bitches—the human kind, that is."

The acorn didn't fall far from Rafferty's tree, Charlie mused.

Outside, Jenny continued the tour. "Over there is the training track where our one-year-olds go through their paces. If they're fast enough, we'll race them. No Derby or Preakness champs, but as my tasteless father says: 'We've made a good dollar on racing.' They're all beautiful, so if they can't cut it in the second year, we sell them to the elegant ladies."

Charlie was enjoying the outing. Suddenly, he found himself staring at Jenny, trying to gauge his emotions. He hadn't been with a woman since he left Ohio, and the voice of desire was growing within him. All day, Jenny seemed to be subtly—and not so subtly—flirting with him. He sensed that he was attracted to her, but his discretion told him it was *verboten* territory.

Jenny was probably too young (he guessed about twenty-five), but more important, she was the daughter of his host. He concluded that friendship, not romance, was the more reasonable option.

Jenny seemed to enjoy being the focus of his eyes. She motioned to him and they moved back to their horses. They mounted and headed back toward Brooklyn-in-Montana, Charlie now a little more sure of his seat on Bertha. As they rode, Jenny smiled almost continually at him, giving still more evidence that she found what she called "a most mature man"—attractive.

He gazed at her young lithe body as it swayed on the horse and thought how delightful it would be if he were less discreet. Then he smiled back at Jenny and repressed the whole idea—at least for the time being.

CHAPTER 14

"Hallelujah!"

Rafferty was exuberant when Charlie called from Washington to tell him he had accepted the offer to be headhunter and gofer for an independent race for the White House.

"Charlie, keep one eye peeled behind your back. Your party's going to go after your hide now."

"My hide? It's going to be open season—shoot to kill."

"And your House seat is up in November. Won't the party mount a primary against you?"

"It won't do them any good. I got a 79 percent approval in the *Fairview Times* poll. My rural people cheer every time I clobber the citified Washington government."

He had turned over Rafferty's offer during the flight from Great Falls. The thought of being even tangentially attached to $100 million in campaign funds nettled him. God, much of the undemocratic nature of the American political system was based on tainted money going to candidates and the two parties. Now he was being asked to become part of the whole mess. How could he tolerate that?

But Rafferty had made a salient point. If the reformers didn't have a pot to piss in, how were they going to fight the party opposition and clean house? It was a Hobson's choice, and he didn't know which side to come down on.

He decided to sleep on it, which was a false metaphor.

That night, in his small apartment behind the Capitol, he didn't sleep on it or on anything else. He tossed most of the night, pondering his dilemma. So far in his career, he hadn't thought anything out fully. His rapid rise—if that's what you could call it—had been the result of animal instinct. He had just exercised what seemed right at the time, a reflex of his whole being, which he guessed was a reflection of his upbringing in Fairview, and the influence of his mother. But now . . .

Now, he was being asked to plumb his philosophical bowels and decide whether he should be involved in a massive money-heavy campaign that could *truly* change things. Or to retreat back into his "principles," as Rafferty had so sneeringly called them, and turn down the possible revolutionary adventure that lay ahead, with all its potential.

He had another quandary to resolve before he gave Rafferty his answer. Did he want the extra work and publicity, still another intrusion in what once had been an ordered, private existence that gave him daily satisfaction. (So, if you were so satisfied, why did you rush into the mad quest for a House seat? he asked himself, playing the smartass.)

A lot of people had him marked as an "ambitious" politician, a pushy pol who had his sights on power. God, how wrong they were. How they misread him.

He *happened* to fall into computers. He *happened* to get into politics because of old man Kenney's sudden death on the House floor. He *happened* to get a phone call from wily Rafferty, asking him to run a Presidential campaign against the entrenched two parties, including his own.

Did he want to do it? That wasn't a reasonable question. He was convinced it was tied up with his destiny. Where the script was written he didn't know, but he sensed he had to faithfully play out the role.

Charlie stared out the window at the approaching dawn, with the sun casting its first tentative light. With the same reflex (hunch?) that had guided his energies thus far, he decided he would accept Rafferty's offer. If nothing else, it was practical. He would call him with the news as soon as he reached his Longworth office.

History would decide if he was serving the national good, but he was convinced that the contemporary body politic was festering and in urgent need of cure. Perhaps his personal mandate was not as strong as was Jefferson's and Madison's at the founding, but he was convinced that these were also crucial times, and that he could play a crucial role.

His mandate was clear: to reduce the power of special interests, change the election and campaign finance system to reinstitute democracy, pay more attention to the Constitution, cut out government fat, and, most vital, rebuild the ailing, overtaxed, American middle class. In every culture, it was not the rich or the poor who maintained civilization, but the much-maligned bourgeoisie.

If he found the right man or woman to be the presidential candidate (with him on the inside), and with a little luck, he sensed they could come close despite long odds. But that was all speculation. One thing was real. That was Rafferty's last words on the phone.

"Charlie, I've opened an account in the Riggs Bank in Washington in your name, and put in $5 million for startup. You're the only signator. So good luck to you—and America!"

The next call was to Fairview, to his old boss, George Sempel, an organizational wizard. He needed to convince America, $100 million or not, that the campaign of Candidate X—whoever that would be— was a serious bid for the White House.

Sempel had founded Synergy, Inc., with $600 in 1970 and had built a profitable niche in genetic engineering software. A Ph.D. in biochemistry from Carnegie-Mellon, he had just turned sixty and was now a multimillionaire. He was also the closest thing Charlie had ever had to a father.

George was "cherubic," everyone said. An unimposing five feet, eight inches, he was in no way fat, but did carry an extra fifteen pounds. He had a round, lineless face. If one were to gauge his age by his wrinkles, he could be thirty. But the mature, if still eager, eyes, gave away some of his senior status. Most people guessed him to be about fifty, give or take a couple of years.

Sempel was Jewish but secular, just as Charlie was Protestant and equally secular, sort of first cousins, like a lot of similar combinations in modern America. They both strongly favored the moral imperatives of organized religion, if only because it thrived without them. If not, Charlie might have to go to church on Sunday as would Sempel on Saturday. Instead, a few hours on the High Holy Days sufficed for George, and Charlie paid his respects to Christianity on Easter Sunday and at Christmas midnight service.

"Have you gone crazy in just three months in Washington?" Sempel screamed when Charlie made his pitch. "You mean you want me to stop running Synergy so that I can come to Washington to help you in a campaign for President that's doomed from the get-go? Son, independent movements don't work in America. And where's the money? Don't expect me to get into the dirty world of campaign contributions. That's not my glass of hot tea."

"No, George, that's the beauty of the plan. I've got an angel with $100 million if we have a candidate and an organizer. That's where you come in."

Sempel laughed. "Well, the $100 million helps a little, Charlie. Who's backing you—Bill Gates? And please forgive me for getting angry. You know I'd do anything for you—EXCEPT THIS. It's meshuga, mad, crazy, fou, patso. Stay in Congress, boychik. You're doing a great job. Or better still, come home. We've got a slew of new competitors in genetic software, and I need you."

Charlie knew he'd have to play a trump card if he was ever to get Sempel on board the "meshuga" scheme.

"I agree with you, George, but tell me, when did your people first come here to America? And from where?"

Sempel seemed surprised by the question. "From Hungary, Budapest to be exact. In 1893. What does that have to do with anything?"

"And have they done well?" Charlie asked.

"You know the answer. Ever since we came to this blessed land, we've worked hard and reaped the harvest. My children are graduates of Harvard and Princeton. I'm a rich man, and my older brother's child is a tennis pro. What could be more American?"

"Well, that's my pitch, George. It's payback time. America's the only hope of the world, and we're sinking into a swampland, economically, politically, and morally. The political class has some good people, but too many are blowhards. They're good at raising money and getting elected, but lousy at governing. The country needs you, George. Brownstein is a programming genius and he can take over Synergy for a while. After November, you can go home."

"Are things really that bad in government, Charlie? I must admit I've been too busy to follow it enough."

"Bad? They're horrendous. Washington needs every ounce of brains and guts it can muster."

Charlie paused as Sally burst into his office.

"One second, George." He looked up. "What is it, Sally? What's the big emergency?"

"Congressman, some horrible news!" Her voice was laced with desperation. "It just came over CNN. Presidential candidate Lawson dropped dead two hours ago of a massive heart attack. He was on the twelfth hole at the Burning Tree Club."

Charlie quickly turned over the ramifications. Lawson was no political genius, but basically a good man, if too closely tied to the status quo. Who would take his place?

Sally immediately answered his curiosity. "The Executive Committee called an emergency meeting at the Madison Hotel and it just broke up. On the first ballot, they voted eleven to one to name the VP nominee, Champ Billings, as the party's new presidential candidate."

Billings? Oh, my God.

Charlie quickly picked up the phone. "George, did you hear that? Lawson is dead and Billings has just been named the presidential candidate. You know what that means?"

Sempel was quiet for an instant. "Charlie, I'm no political maven, but I do understand that. The man could be a big problem. So, you win. I'll be down in Washington to see you tomorrow. But there's one thing I want you to know."

"What's that, George?"

"Charlie, you wonderful SOB. I didn't have to hear about Billings. I knew the minute you asked that my answer would be yes. You make everything seem so logical. That's why you're the best marketing man around. But I'll make a deal with you."

"What's that?"

"I'll come down there and contribute my all, without pay. But if the independent thing falls on its face, as it probably will, I'll go back to Ohio—with you. Enough time spent on Don Quixotism. Now you need to build your fortune and find a woman so you can spend it on your family. Does that make sense?"

Charlie agreed that it did, but though he shared George's pessimism about independent campaigns, perhaps this one would be different. Perhaps destiny, which had always protected America, would confound all that had gone before and use him—and the still unchosen Candidate X—as an instrument for survival.

CHAPTER 15

The hearing room of the House Judiciary chamber was chosen for its size, but Charlie wondered about the choice, made by Robbie Barnes. The room reeked of history. It was the place where President Richard Nixon was in effect given his walking papers by then-chairman Peter Rodino of New Jersey. Charlie hoped it was not prophetic.

The marble chamber was choked with television cameras, radio mikes, and reporters hoping to witness still more history. Were they here because they took him seriously? Or was he in danger of becoming a political sideshow geek?

He was struck by the work of Barnes, a miniature machine who seemed to operate without anxiety or temper. No more than five feet, six inches and 130 pounds, Barnes had an angular face that reminded Charlie of Bobby Kennedy. Like Bobby, he exhibited a steely determination even when ordering a cup of coffee.

"Mr. Congressman." Charlie felt a tug at his sleeve. It was Robbie. "They're settling. If you begin with a strong loud sentence, they'll shut up and you can get rolling."

Charlie nodded and took a swing of Evian.

"GENTLEMAN AND LADIES. I THINK THE NATION IS READY TO ACCEPT AN INDEPENDENT FOR PRESIDENT," Charlie half shouted his opening line for the kickoff of the new presidential movement.

Barnes was right. The buzz quieted. "As you may have heard, that's why we're here," Charlie reminded the press. "I'll read a short statement, then I'll take questions. OK?

"America is living through tough times—everything from high

taxes, to huge trade deficits, to the loss of manufacturing jobs to overseas, to stagnant family incomes, to corporate downsizing, to narcotic smuggling, to Medicare and Medicaid bankruptcy, to racial unrest, to massive illegal immigration, and venally corrupt politics, among other things," Charlie began. "Some of it is inescapable, but much of it rests on the head of American politicians on both sides of the aisle. The two-party system has not produced enough good leaders, and that's why I'm here. I am the chairman of a new movement to elect an independent-minded President. End of statement."

"Does that mean you're starting a third party?" shouted Jill Mahoney, a CNN White House reporter.

"No way. It's too late to get a new party going this year. There's more leeway for an independent candidate by petition. But that's not the real reason."

"Then what is?" she asked.

"Because under our crazy electoral system, third parties are only spoilers—a wasted vote. You can get 49 percent of a state's popular tally and still not get a single electoral vote. And if you get ten percent of the vote, you could be throwing the election to someone you don't like. The whole system is manufactured for the two parties and to stop independents."

"Is that bad?" yelled a number of the ABC news staff. "Haven't they served us well?"

"They used to. But there are now more independents than people registered in either party. And a small segment in each party generally seizes control and manipulates the country. The tail is running the dog."

"What do you hope to accomplish?" asked a *Post* staffer. "You don't really expect to take the White House—do you?"

"We won't know that until November. But right now Congress can pass a constitutional amendment to close the Electoral College, count only the popular vote, and stop anyone who hasn't received a majority from becoming President. You know, that's happened twelve times in our history. People think that backing an independent candidate is a wasted vote. We have to change that, both in perception and reality, and quickly."

"How would you do that?" asked a *Times* reporter.

"I'll give you a hint. It's called a runoff of the top two vote-getters. Other countries, including France, even Russia, use it in their presidential elections. Here we do it only for congressional elections in the state of Georgia. If we adopt that nationally, no one will be a spoiler. People like our Candidate X could get in the finals, and his votes won't be wasted. The second runoff would produce a President with a majority. It's foolproof."

John Pemberton, a Sunday talking head, raised his hand.

"I suppose Charlie Palmer will be the first candidate for President in this new movement? Am I right?"

"I shouldn't be answering you. I'm needled too much on your show."

The assembled media proffered Charlie a small laugh.

"No, you're wrong. I have no interest in running for President. The last time I stuck my neck out, it got chopped off. My job is to search for Candidate X, then help run the campaign."

"So who do you have in mind for President?" Jill Mahoney of CNN asked, her camera zeroing in.

"No one. That search is just beginning."

The next questioner was the redoubtable Ms. Shirley Townsend, oldest ranking member of the Washington press corps. Dressed in her traditional gray-striped suit, vintage 1930s, with a long skirt, a small felt hat on her bluish hair, and a small red carnation in her lapel, she raised her hand—a signal always honored by America's politicians.

"Yes, Shirley, what can I do for you?"

"Just this, Mr. Congressman. The two parties have been running the country for a long time without any help from independents. So is your campaign realistic or just a harebrained scheme?"

Charlie knew he'd better come back solidly.

"I hope it's more hard-brained. The two-party idea was necessary before we had modern media. Now we don't need anybody to tell us how to vote. If we elect an independent President, the people might see they've been sold a bill of goods. Who says only two private clubs in Washington, D.C.—for that's what they are—should run our country?"

James Smart of CBS, a $2-million anchor of no little ego, jumped to his feet without being recognized.

"Congressman, where do you get the nerve to start a presidential campaign four months before the election with little or no money? The other parties will spend $200 million each, most of it taxpayer dough. Can you raise even $5 million for Candidate X—someone you don't even yet have?"

"Glad you asked, Jimmie. I didn't mention money because I was waiting for you to bait me. Then I could clobber you. Actually, we already have $5 million in the Riggs bank."

"Is that all?" Smart's voice was heavy with sarcasm. "Are you wasting your—and our—time?"

Charlie slowed his delivery. "No. First, we're not taking a penny in matching taxpayer money. And secondly, our fund-raising is completed, all in one fell swoop."

"So how much have you gotten?" Smart asked. "Six million?" His colleagues laughed.

"Try $100 million."

The buzz in the room immediately soared to high decibels.

"We have a pledge for that amount from a very rich American, someone you all know."

As hands shot up, Charlie looked for a face to recognize. Of course. Don Leland. The newscaster rose slowly, and spoke in his best stentorian tones, reminiscent of Cronkite.

"So tell us, who is this fairy godfather who's backing your candidate? Another billionaire like Perot who dreams of sitting in the Oval Office?"

"No, Don. Like Perot, this godfather loves America. But unlike Perot, he hates politics. He won't run for any office and he'll have no veto on the campaign or the candidate. For some reason, he trusts me to make the decisions."

"So what's his angle?" Don Leland asked. "Does he have his eye on the Treasury?"

"No, he's in better shape than the Treasury. They're $5 trillion in debt, and he has billions and no debt. No, his only angle is that he thinks American politics needs a radical face-lift. And I agree."

"WHAT'S HIS NAME? WHO IS IT?" a half-dozen reporters called out.

"Ah, there's the rub." Charlie was enjoying the game. "He wants to keep his identity secret. So if you fellows and girls are still reporters, try to dig it out . . ."

Charlie never had a chance to finish the sentence. Scores jumped up and raced out of the hearing room, ostensibly to begin the hunt for Schuyler Rafferty.

BOOK TWO

THE CAMPAIGN AND THE CONSPIRACY

CHAPTER 16

Freddie Boxley spit on them all. As far as he could see, this new crowd of reporters were half-ass political pundits who had never uncovered a story in their lives. They were all trying to imitate the talking heads on Sunday morning television who made a fortune but wouldn't know a story if it fell on them. The further one got away from real journalism, it seemed, the more money they made.

Pure bullshit, and only because the public felt they needed an authority to tell them what they should say and think.

Since Boxley was a real reporter, he felt lucky to even be working. After thirty years, he knew his career was going nowhere. But he still had the satisfaction of pulling off a good one now and then.

He was at Charlie Palmer's news conference that morning. It was obvious there were two good stories there: (1) What nut was going to part with $100 million for a freshman congressman to launch a presidential campaign? (2) What were the two parties going to do about upstart Charlie? He guessed they'd do more than just bite their nails over it.

Boxley's pay was miserable, but at least he was working for a real news-gathering outfit, the Metropolitan News Service. A kind of miniature Associated Press, it covered Washington for out-of-town papers without a news bureau. Occasionally, the two local dailies, the *Washington Post* and the *Washington Times,* picked up his material as well.

But what he really liked about his job was that it got him away from fashionable editors. He didn't have to worry about what some

American lit major who was playing editor thought about Charlie, or Billings, or the righteousness of welfare or abortion, or anything else. Just the facts, ma'am.

Boxley wasn't quite a Damon Runyon character, but he did wear slightly loud $80 suits from outlet shops and sported a large, fake diamond stickpin in the center of his tie.

His first stop was, naturally, the Riggs Bank, where Palmer had said the first $5 million was deposited. Within minutes, he was at Fifteenth and Pennsylvania Avenue talking to an assistant cashier.

"Tell me, Mrs. Burke—or is it Ms.?—does Congressman Charles Palmer have $5 million in an account in this bank as he claimed at his press conference this morning?"

"All I can tell you, Mr. Boxley, is that he does indeed have an account here, but as to the balance . . ."

Freddie thanked her, then got on the horn to Vinnie Russ, private investigator specializing in credit and financial reports. "Vinnie, I need to know Congressman Palmer's bank balance at Riggs and who put the money in for him."

"OK, Freddie, I'll call you back in thirty minutes."

Boxley had just walked into his office when the phone rang. "Fred, this is Vinnie. The balance is $5 million and Charlie is the only signature needed on the account. Also, the man who put the dough in is smarter than both of us. It came from an offshore bank in the Cayman Islands, and they don't talk to anyone, not even the FBI. But I'll stay on it and let you know."

Boxley turned his attention to the two political parties. Would they do anything preemptive to stop Palmer? Just intuition, but why not call the party campaign chiefs, Andy Tolliver and Norm Sobel, and see what their spin was?

"Andy, this is Boxley from Metropolitan News," he announced on the phone to Tolliver, the honcho at Charlie's former party. "Tell me, what did you think of Palmer's press conference this morning?"

The voice at the other end rose an octave. "That cocksucker? He's going to ruin the Republic if he keeps putting his hick nose in everybody's affairs."

"But what about his independent presidential bid? Will it go anywhere?"

"First, I don't think he's got any $100 million. Write this down, Freddie. Whoever he puts up to head his cockamamie ticket will get no more than eight points in the November election. And most will come from Sobel's voters. Champ Billings is the next President of the United States."

Under his breath, Boxley muttered: "God protect us."

"What did you say, Freddie?"

"I said, sounds about right. Andy, can you see me now for just ten minutes? I'd like to run an interview with you about Charlie Palmer and his new campaign."

"Sorry, Boxley. I have to take a rain check. I'm going out of town in a few minutes. Call me tomorrow when I get back."

Quickly, Boxley called Norm Sobel, campaign chief of the other party, whose nominee, Arthur Steadman, a former Western governor with a good record, was trailing Lawson in the polls by ten points. But that should pick up now that Billings had taken Lawson's place on the ballot.

Once Boxley reached Sobel, he gave him much the same answer as did Tolliver, if in a more dignified manner. Sobel called Palmer a "bomb thrower" and predicted a nine percent vote for the independent candidate, whoever it turned out to be.

Boxley posed the same question to Sobel. "Norm, can you see me now for ten minutes, a short interview on what you think about Palmer's move and his $100 million Candidate X?"

"Sorry, kid, I'm going out of town right away. I'll be back tomorrow. Call me then."

Something struck Boxley's reportorial instinct. Both party heads said they couldn't be interviewed because they were on their way out of town at the very same time. And both would be back tomorrow. A coincidence? Or could both wheels be leaving simultaneously because they were going to the same place—to meet with each other. And plan God knows what? The idea sounded screwy, but Boxley knew that sometimes the best news lead came from the most outlandish hunches.

Why not test his theory? He'd follow one of them, and see if it was more than an old newsman's twitching nose. Tolliver would be the easiest to cover. You couldn't miss his massive ass and flapping oversize clothes. Besides, his party headquarters was just a block away from Boxley's own office in the National Press Building.

Quickly, Boxley pulled a recording device with a long-distance mike out of his drawer and stuffed it into his briefcase. He raced to the elevator, puffing all the way. Within five minutes, he was standing in front of party headquarters, waiting for Tolliver—if Tolliver had told him the truth.

Hailing a taxi, he gave the driver a $10 bill. "Wait right here," Boxley instructed the cabbie. "I'm expecting someone and we'll tail him. If he doesn't show, you can keep the money. If he comes, there's another ten-er in it for you."

Boxley had time to catch his breath. He waited almost ten minutes to the side of the entrance, then decided that the whole thing had been his fantasy, born of frustration, when suddenly he noticed what looked like a small parade coming laboriously through the circular doors. It was Tolliver, briefcase in hand.

The party boss made a beeline for Boxley's cab. "Take me to Union Station, driver. There's a good tip if we can make the 4 o'clock to Baltimore."

"Sorry, man, I've got a fare. Waiting for him now."

Tolliver left the curb and frantically waved his briefcase. Within a minute, a cab stopped and he pushed his way in.

Boxley watched, then quickly moved into his waiting taxi.

"Where'd that guy say he wanted to go?" Boxley asked.

"To Union Station, to make the 4 P.M. to Baltimore."

"Good, take me there, quick."

Union Station was festooned with its new glamour of flags, restaurants, and boutiques, but Freddie's eye was focused on Tolliver, who waddled rapidly to make the train on Track Four. Since Tolliver knew him, Boxley kept a conservative fifty feet behind, not spending time buying a ticket. He could do that on the train with only a small penalty.

Carefully, he kept one train car between himself and Tolliver. The whole trip to Baltimore took only forty minutes, and by 4:40 they had arrived. In the Baltimore station, Boxley raced ahead of Tolliver and grabbed a cab.

"Driver, here's a ten. Wait here for a minute until that heavyset guy with the tan jacket gets in a cab, then follow it—kind of discreet if you can."

The two cabs in tandem wound through Baltimore, past the side-to-side old townhouses with spotlessly whitewashed steps, then through an industrial district, then to a deserted dock area, far from the revived port that had become a favored tourist site.

This section was grungy, filled with unpainted stores and desolate-looking people. Tolliver was not stupid. There wouldn't be a soul within a mile who would recognize him despite his occasional appearances on television and his telltale girth.

Now, the test, Boxley thought. Was Tolliver on some extracurricular sexual adventure, something he was noted for? Or was he, Boxley hoped, out to meet his adversary, Norm Sobel, in an unprecedented secret rendezvous? He'd soon find out.

Tolliver's cab suddenly came to a stop. He got out at the corner, next to a dilapidated laundromat, then walked to the left.

"Drive past that parked cab," Boxley barked. "Then turn and go slow. Stop when I call out."

The cab made the turn and slowed as Boxley searched for the rendezvous point. Just a hundred yards ahead he spotted it—the BALTIMORE DINER in neon lights, with the N in DINER blacked out. Tolliver was just approaching the stairs leading to the eating emporium whose elaborate chrome trim was tarnished from neglect.

"Stop the cab about two hundred feet ahead, driver. I'll walk to the diner. Here's another ten. Wait for me. I should be back within twenty minutes."

He was ready to get out of the cab when he remembered something. Boxley opened his briefcase and took out the recording device, stuffing it into his jacket pocket. He then removed that day's *Washington Post*, which had picked up his story on a robbery in Arlington. Leaving the briefcase in the car, Boxley adjusted his outsize zirconium stickpin and got out of the cab.

As Boxley walked down the street, he watched Tolliver enter the diner. He slowed his pace. He'd give Tolliver at least five minutes to get seated and meet whoever he was going to meet. That would also give Boxley the chance to sit unseen, aiming his sensitive mike to pick up the conversation. If Tolliver was having an assignation with a woman, it would be less important, but probably still worthwhile. Never know when extra information can provide leverage.

Boxley mounted the stairs to the diner, then halted in the vestibule. Hidden behind a small wall, he peered in turn at the two eating sections—tables and chairs on the left and stools to the right.

Tolliver was on the left, at the far end, already seated and reading a menu. No one was with him! God, he berated himself, had he wasted an afternoon and $75? Boxley laughed. Was he losing it? Tolliver had surely not traveled all this way just to eat alone in a greasy spoon in Baltimore.

Boxley moved to the counter section and sat at the end. He'd just wait to see who completed the rendezvous. He ordered an English muffin and coffee and kept his face buried in the main news pages of the *Post*, as if reading. He placed the small mike on the counter and laid the business section of the paper over it, leaving only a tiny opening for the sound head.

No more than three minutes had passed before the front door swung open. He peeked out from behind the newspaper. Great! It was rival party leader Norm Sobel. The old reportorial smeller was still working.

Sobel looked nothing like his political counterpart. Thin, of medium height, he looked like what he was, a former professor of political science. A New Yorker with a Ph.D. from the University of Michigan, he wore glasses, dressed in tweeds, and carried a pipe everywhere, even into territory like the diner, where it was forbidden to smoke. The pipe had become his caricature image, a symbol of the intellect he had tried, somewhat in vain, to apply to the rough-and-tumble of American politics.

Things were falling into place. There were only six people in the diner. Boxley could aim the mike right from where he was seated. It had a clear channel across, with no one in the line of sound.

He had just congratulated himself on his good luck that no one was seated near him when the door swung open. A man, wearing a black leather jacket and seeming as if he was looking for trouble, walked in and sat down two stools from him. His face was covered with what seemed a perpetual sneer. He stared in Boxley's direction.

"Have you got a light, friend?" he asked.

Boxley spoke from behind the newspaper, hoping the interloper would go away. Or at least shut up.

"No, and smoking's not allowed in the diner anyway."

The leather-jacketed man just laughed. From the edge of the paper, Boxley could see that he had already pulled out a pack of cigarettes and was lighting one up by himself.

"Oh, yeah. Who says?"

Boxley decided on silence, which he had learned was the best defense against ignorance.

Across the room, he could see that Tolliver and Sobel were now ordering from the waitress. Boxley couldn't hear a word they were saying, but with his left hand, he reached into his pocket and clicked on the microphone, hoping.

As soon as the waitress left, the two politicos began what looked like a friendly, earnest conversation, far from their usual world of spin control and angry blasts at each other. Tolliver was gesticulating with his hands while Sobel was soberly sucking on his unlit pipe.

The quiet whir of the tape recorder in his pocket was reassuring— it was all being taken down on magnetic plastic.

He'd wait until they finished, then give them five minutes to find a cab. His own transportation was waiting about a block away to take him back to the train station, then to Washington, where he'd listen to what the two campaign chiefs of the major parties were plotting—if the tape recorder had done its job.

Reaching down to fix his zirconium tie pin, he felt rewarded. This, finally, was real reporting.

CHAPTER 17

Even Charlie was surprised by the public's enthusiasm for the movement.

He had dashed off an ad—simple and surely derivative, but he hoped dramatic:

WANTED! MEN AND WOMEN TO SAVE AMERICA. PAY—ZERO, DEDICATION—TOTAL.

George Sempel had arrived in Washington and opened a storefront headquarters on Washington's "Main Street"—Pennsylvania Avenue—just four blocks from the White House. The big handpainted sign outside just said: INDEPENDENT CAMPAIGN FOR PRESIDENT, and featured a blue silhouette of Thomas Jefferson, the spiritual mentor of the campaign.

Sempel quickly spent all $5 million to run the ads in newspapers and on radio and television with a catchy phone number—1–800–555–8000.

"Charlie, we hit a giant exposed nerve," Sempel told him. "I never knew the dissatisfaction was this deep. We've gotten over a million volunteers and they're pouring in—from Seattle to Key West. You may be Peck's bad boy to the politicians, but somebody out there loves you."

Suddenly, Sempel's face fell a bit.

"Volunteers are no problem. What we are facing is a conspiracy by the two parties to keep people like you off the ballot. I'm calling in a friend, Joe Burke, the former attorney general of Ohio, to take us through those paces."

Burke arrived later that morning. A tall spindly man with only wisps of hair and a weak voice, he was impressively erudite.

"The election apparatus is purposely stacked in favor of the two parties," Burke explained to them in George's inner office. "When Bob La Follette ran for President as an independent in 1924, he needed only forty thousand signatures. Now you need almost a million—twenty-five times more. It's a racket run by state legislators of both parties.

"Your biggest problem is the early filing dates in many states," Burke continued. "If you follow the statues, it's too late to get on the presidential ballot in fifteen states. They purposely make those filing dates early, before the regular party conventions."

Charlie sighed in disappointment.

"Is there anything we can do about ones that have already passed?" George asked.

"Yes, there may be. In 1980, presidential candidate John Anderson sued Ohio because it had an early closing date, in March, for independents. The case—*Anderson v. Celebrezze*—went up to the Supreme Court, which ruled for Anderson. Justice John Paul Stevens said such early dates for independents was unconstitutional. Ohio moved it up to August 22, and George tells me you'll have no trouble making that date."

"But what about the other states?" This time Charlie asked the question. "Doesn't Stevens's Supreme Court ruling cover all of them?"

"You'd think it would, wouldn't you?" Burke responded in his slow monotone. "But a 1988 suit filed in Texas used the Supreme Court decision as an argument. Guess what? After all this time, the state court still hasn't ruled on it."

"Then what can we do?" Charlie asked, more than a little concerned.

"Simple. We forget the state courts and go right to federal district courts, first in Washington, then in the state capitals involved. Meanwhile, please get your petitions in. Without them, we don't have an argument."

"What are our chances, Joe?"

"Hard to say. Everyone follows the Supreme Court decisions except when it comes to politics. They just ignore them and the courts don't seem to care. Remember, all the judges—local and Supreme Court—have been appointed by the parties, or have run on their tickets."

George had been listening intently. "Joe, say we lose in court. How many electoral votes will we miss out on?"

"I'd say about 150 out of 538."

"That won't kill us outright," George commented, "but it's not good. So go get them, Joe, and let's hope."

After Burke left, George and Charlie had a short discussion.

"That's a real problem," Charlie echoed. "But we have another one that's probably as serious."

"What's that?" George asked.

"We still don't have a candidate for President."

CHAPTER 18

Fred Boxley closed the door to his rabbit-warren office at the Metropolitan News Service.

He had made the 6:17 Amtrak train from Baltimore to Union Station, and he was back at 7:25. It looked as if everyone had gone home, but he didn't trust the thickness of the walls. He put the player volume on low. Pouring himself a scotch, he leaned back into his chair and touched the switch.

Had the mike picked up the Tolliver-Sobel conversation?

He put his ear close to the player mike and prayed. It wasn't going to win any hi-fidelity awards, but he breathed easier as he heard the tinkling of glasses and the voices of a waitress and customer in the Baltimore Diner.

Then suddenly, there it was. Tolliver came on first.

"Norm, we meet in strange circumstances in a strange dump where nobody, thank God, is going to recognize or hear us. It wouldn't look good—campaign chiefs of the two big parties in collusion, hiding away in a greasy spoon in Baltimore. But I had to talk to you about our mutual enemy, that crazy Charlie Palmer. The phones can't be trusted and we can't be seen together in Washington except on television or at some crappy cultural event."

Norm Sobel's professorial voice came on next.

"Why do you think he's such a threat?" he asked. "He lost the VP nomination, and he doesn't even have a candidate for the presidential race. Andy, I think you're worried too much, but I came to hear you out."

"I'm glad you did, Norm. I've been at this longer than you and I've never seen anyone like Charlie Palmer. He's magic. He's a devil. And he's dangerous. His big mouth says in the open what people secretly think. When they hear him, they nod—yes, yes, yes. Norm, we've fucked up and America knows it. And now this bastard comes along and is telling the people exactly how to screw us. We've got to do something about him, and quick."

"You don't really think they have a chance this November, do you, Andy?"

"It depends on who they get on the ticket. Remember, people are pissed. I told Boxley I expected Charlie's candidate to get only 8 percent of the vote, but I was bullshiting him. If they put some hick senator who doesn't beat his wife on the ticket, they'd get 15 percent. A real ticket could pull 20 or 25 percent. But with Fanatic Charlie running the campaign, anything could happen. Norm, either your party, or mine, could be like the Whigs, on the way to oblivion come this November."

"Whooo. Andy, we fight every day but I respect your opinion. What do you think we should do?"

"Here's for starters, Norm."

The mike picked up the sound of something being slapped hard onto the table.

"This report on Charlie's personal life is the first step. If we make him look like a horse's ass, his campaign will be dead. Read it and put it in your safe. When it breaks in the news—and I promise you it will—we don't want anyone to know it came from us."

There was silence for a minute. Sobel was obviously reading.

"Boy, this is good stuff, Andy. Where'd you get it?"

"Don't worry your head. It's only the first step in destroying Charlie boy."

"What do you suggest?" Sobel asked. "Dirty tricks?"

"I prefer something more euphonious—like Special Effects Project. Each of us should put up $100,000. I've got money coming from Kellogg. You get some of your own and we put it into a joint fund. We can keep it in the Cayman Islands. I understand that's where the $100 million for Charlie is coming from. A nice touch."

Boxley turned off the tape. That's all he had to hear.

A quiet jubilation overcame him. His first instinct was to type out the story, call his editor, and see if they couldn't get the morning's page one of the *Washington Post* and *New York Times,* a double exclusive.

Then he thought better of it. This was a timeless time bomb, and it was still early in the political fray. He could explode it any time between now and Election Day. Probably later in the campaign, when it would create the greatest noise.

Now, he'd just take the tape home and put it under his pillow. Tomorrow morning, he'd stash it in his private safe deposit box at the Riggs Bank in the name of Fred James. No one, not even his wife, knew about that.

If the journalistic community was honest, this story would surely bring him a Pulitzer. For a moment, he fantasized about the glory and even saw himself at the awards dinner at the National Press Club.

Then he laughed. This story was too honest for that. Probably the only prize it would ever win was a $50 raise from a begrudging boss. But one thing he did know. It was just right for the American people.

CHAPTER 19

Veteran television newscaster Don Leland, hoping the camera was obscuring the wrinkles engraved into his fifty-three-year-old face, fingered the confidential report on Charlie Palmer as he waited to go on camera that Sunday morning.

The twenty-two-page document had come to him in the mail from some anonymous source, whose identity wasn't hard to figure. Either Tolliver or Sobel. Clearly they were both petrified of Charlie, whose independent movement for President had just taken off even though his Candidate X had yet to be chosen.

Leland had heard that their ads (which you couldn't avoid) had produced three million phone calls, a greater avalanche than even during the first days of Perot. The anti–two-party idea was in the wind, and Palmer obviously hoped to catch the breeze.

But Leland could promise that tonight would be a lot less salutary for the new American hero. Charlie would be his victim or, as the public preferred to call it, his "interviewee."

He hated almost all politicians, but especially Charlie, who had rubbed him the wrong way at the convention. Some were OK, but many were transparent phonies whom he could clobber with an easy aside or an inflection of his voice. But Charlie came on as Mr. Messiah, exuding great sincerity and believability—the politician who was going to save us from other politicians.

The plodding ones looking for perks or contributions didn't bother him. It was the charismatic types like Charlie that burned him. Smart? Oh, Charlie made the others seem retarded. But at the core he was no different, Leland was sure. Egotistical, power-mad, public-ity-driven, narcissistic. Over the years, he had seen hotshots like Charlie come and go, but the political landscape was still rotten. Charlie was just the latest of that ilk, and he wouldn't be the last. And after tonight, his demise might come sooner—much sooner—than anyone thought.

Leland cast an eye at his notes, then another at the camera. Seated in a brown leather swivel chair he relaxed in the sophisticated televi-sion setting. Two chairs were on a raised circular stage. One was for him and the other for his intended victim. It was like theater-in-the-round. Or, it occurred to him, a Roman coliseum. And Charlie was the Christian.

Charlie stared into the three cameras that had triangulated him. Suddenly, the light turned red and he heard the theme music, a piece by Berlioz.

"Today, we have a special treat," he could hear Leland's resonant tones. "We'll be speaking with Congressman Charles Palmer, he of government waste fame, gadfly at the presidential nominating con-vention, and now the chairman of a new independent movement for President—the latest in the age-old, and futile, attempt to break the monopoly of the two-party system."

Leland paused to check his blond hairpiece in the monitor. Good. It was squarely on his head.

"Congressman, welcome. That was quite an impressive ad cam-paign. Did it do as well as projected?"

"Oh, better. We've had 3.5 million calls, and they're coming in at 250,000 per day. We figure that we'll have five million volunteers by the end of the month."

"What about your budget? Did the $5 million stretch far enough?"

"Not quite. But we've gotten voter pledges of $3 million, and we've taken down $2 million more from our magical $100 million source, all of which will nicely be deposited in the Riggs Bank when we need it."

"And you can't talk about your fairy godfather—or is it godmother?"

"No, that's still a state secret. When our benefactor wants it known, he or she will announce it."

"Congressman, you've been promoting your American Manifesto, a thirty-five point program to remake America. I see that it covers virtually everything—from stopping elected officials from ever be-coming lobbyists, to eliminating retirement pensions for congress-men, to radical campaign finance reform, to closing both the Electoral College and the IRS, to eliminating six million of the twenty million public officials through attrition, to closing five Cabinet agencies, to a 30 percent federal tax cut. It all sounds good, but isn't it just too radical for most Americans?"

"Judging from our ad responses, I'd say it's probably not radical enough. We also want a public referendum on all tax increases and to close all eighty-one federal welfare programs—except for the disabled—and bring back FDR's WPA with a public job for everyone on welfare, along with health insurance and day care. That will give us full employment and save $100 billion of the $400 billion we now spend each year. Incidentally, all the welfare costs you read about in the newspaper are lies. We also want to cut out $80 billion a year in corporate and farm welfare at the same time. We want—"

"Slow down, Congressman. We get the idea. You want a *real* political revolution."

"A perfect ten, Mr. Leland. I'm pleased, and a little surprised, that you get the idea."

"Excellent," Leland responded, his tone sarcastic. "No one doubts your knowledge or ability, Congressman. But do you really think you're the caliber of person we want to lead us in this crusade for better government?"

Charlie was taken aback.

"What does that mean, Mr. Leland?" He glanced at the monitor. Surprise was etched on his face.

"What I mean, Congressman, is—are you emotionally and morally fit to lead this movement to elect a President and reform American politics?"

Charlie stared blankly into the camera. That had come out of left field.

"I think so. Why do you ask?"

"Because I have information which leads me to doubt that."

Charlie was experiencing momentary shock. What was Leland talking about?

"From what I understand, Congressman, you were married in college, then got a divorce after less than a year. Now twenty years later, at the age of forty-three, you're still unmarried. Isn't that a sign of first, poor judgment, and second, an inability to make a commitment at your age? You seem to be floating through life. You discarded one woman, never married since, and have no children. Are those the attributes of a mature leader?"

Charlie was nonplussed. What was Leland leading up to? He wasn't applying to become minister of a fundamentalist church.

"Don, I thought all this harping on the personal life of candidates and presidents was passe. Kennedy was our first Catholic President. Reagan was our first divorced President. Buchanan was a bachelor in the White House. Jefferson, Jackson, and Van Buren were unmarried widowers in the White House, and several had affairs with women. Grover Cleveland sired a child out of wedlock, then gave it his name. Me? I'm just a divorced bachelor without even a girlfriend, and I have no intention of running for President, God help me. So why this inquisition?"

"Very good American history, Mr. Palmer. But how do you explain your own history?"

Now Charlie was getting angry. "And what in the hell is that supposed to mean?"

"I'd like to refresh your memory, political moralist Palmer. Do you recall a Rebecca Hartley, a fellow student at Ohio State? Well, she's now happily married, and she's signed an affidavit that you made her pregnant when you were both eighteen. You didn't do the honorable thing and marry her. Instead, you paid for what was then an *illegal* abortion. Is that the behavior of a man we're supposed to admire and follow?"

Charlie reeled, swiveling erratically in his chair. Rebecca, of course. He had forgotten—or wanted to forget. The pain of that twenty-five-year-old incident flooded his mind. How would he rebut this unexpected revelation of an unhappy event?

"I have no real defense, Mr. Leland, but maybe none is needed. We had sex and neither of us wanted to get married. That was before *Roe v. Wade*, so I paid for an operation from someone with an M.D. Honestly . . ." Charlie found himself stammering. "We were young, and there didn't seem to be any other way out of our dilemma. I think . . ."

Why did he need this? He had given up a successful private life and had now exposed himself to ridicule? Somehow he had thought he was immune, but it had suddenly struck. Was it he or the system? His inner turmoil was relieved by only one fact. The sleuths were still ignorant of the one secret that meant everything to him, and his.

"Yes. You think what?" Leland goaded him.

"Nothing, Leland." Charlie used the newsman's last name to convey his contempt.

"Well then, let's go on."

Charlie's emotions were in turmoil. His mind searched backward in time. What blow should he expect next?

"I have in my hand a copy of a Columbus, Ohio, police report for May 24, 1975. Does that date mean anything to you?"

If Charlie had his way, he would tell Leland to shove the report, smack him in the face, then storm off the set. But he knew that any display of temper would destroy his movement. End of that history.

"Yes, that sounds like the date of my graduation prom at Ohio State. Why?"

Suddenly, Charlie remembered and winced.

"Well, I'll fully refresh your memory. You were arrested on campus for drunken driving at 1 A.M. after a beer bash and you spent a night in the tank with other criminals until your mother bailed you out. Now, does it come back to you?"

Charlie's emotions, just a moment before on a roller-coaster, were now flat, almost deadened.

"Yes, I remember now. I felt quite sober and I was driving carefully. But the meter put me just over the one-tenth of 1 percent of alcohol. It's nothing to be proud of, but now I drink almost no alcohol—just an occasional glass of beer or wine."

Charlie stared at himself on the monitor. He was ashamed that he had to undergo this inquisition docilely. If this were not politics, most people would see it as the foibles of a young man and his rite of passage. But this *was* American politics.

"Do you have anything else in your character assassination report?" Charlie asked tartly, not knowing what else to say.

The temptation to slam Leland in the face was overwhelming. Instead, as the concluding music played, Charlie got up, smashed his right hand into his left palm and walked, slowly, and falsely confidently, off the set.

The taste of humiliation was in his mouth. All he could think of was how quickly he could leave Washington and return to Ohio. Now he really felt like a geek in a sideshow—in the circus of American politics.

CHAPTER 20

Charlie kept the blinds closed and the lights low.

It was already 11 A.M., the morning after the Leland interview, and he was still in his apartment, dressed in pajamas. The two aspirins had stilled the pounding in his head, but the emotional pain had spread throughout his body.

He was obviously not as strong as he thought. Attacking his policies was one thing; that he could brush off. He even enjoyed controversy. But this personal attack had truly wounded him, even showed him up to himself as thin-skinned. Perhaps it had already defeated him.

On his lap, he held a copy of a Churchill biography, which he had been reading until 2 A.M. Without making exaggerated comparisons, he was consoled somewhat by the steadfastness Churchill had shown before his warnings about Nazism finally brought him to office as prime minister.

In Charlie's case, his enemy was not Nazism, or Communism. It was American bureaucratic and political insensitivity, the unprincipled waste of people's money, and the distortion of the campaign and election process. It wasn't democracy that was failing. It was politics.

Of course, he also had himself to blame for yesterday's debacle. He should have known his enemies would try to destroy his ideas by getting at him personally. How had he been so stupid—or so careless—as to let himself forget what had happened twenty years ago and not prepare for a rebuttal?

He supposed he had now been exposed as a phony, a moralist whose own morality was suspect. Could he excuse it because of his youth at the time? He doubted the public would let him off the hook that easily. And maybe they shouldn't. The greatest defeat was the loss of his self-confidence, without which he could lead no movement. He feared there were few, if any, who could take his place.

Was his chance to change Washington finished?

Perhaps he should chuck it all and take up George's offer to return to Fairview, eventually as CEO of Synergy. Of course, that's what Tolliver, and Norm Sobel, and Champ Billings, and the others, wanted.

He had finally decided to get dressed when his apartment doorbell suddenly rang. Sally Kirkland, his AA? Almost no one except she knew he lived behind the Capitol in Jenkins Hill Apartments, named after the original owner of land on which the Congressional home now sits. This little redoubt was his sole bit of privacy.

He rose from bed and, barefoot, padded into the hall.

"Who is it?" he asked through the door.

"Me."

Hearing a female voice, he assumed it was Sally's. He opened the door and there, indeed, stood a woman.

But not Sally. This woman's dress and appearance was as far from the style of his AA as anyone could be. Of medium height, she was wearing a thin fake fur coat with a small cloche on her head, and undersize but brilliant diamond earrings. She looked prepped for an elegant cocktail party. Her makeup was applied exquisitely to her white skin, as if by an expert. Yet somehow she didn't present an artificial or overdone look.

She was beautiful. That was apparent. But less obvious was the intelligence in her deep-set green eyes, and the resolve in her expression. Quite an impressive uninvited visitor.

"Yes, can I help you?" Charlie asked, a bit embarrassed by his pajama outfit.

"Yes, you can. My name is Clara Staples. I'm a member of the party's Executive Committee. May I come in?"

Charlie was taken aback, but after only four months in politics, he was learning how to disguise his feelings.

"Yes, please do."

Still stunned, he offered her a chair in the small living room, and a drink.

She shook her head. "I'll sit, but no drink this early, Congressman. I'm here on a political mission, or perhaps a humane-political mission."

"But you hardly look like a politician," Charlie said with a broad smile. "At least, not those I've met so far. You look more like Miss

Gotrocks, Society Hostess with the Extreme Mostest, perhaps even the Showgirl Gone Straight. Which is it?"

"All of the above, Congressman. But surely you've seen my picture in the newspaper, or heard of me?"

"Yes, now that I see you, I must admit I have. You are, if I recall, the major contributor to my former party."

"Exactly. They say I'm attractive and throw good parties, Congressman Palmer. But that's nonsense. I assure you that if my checks bounced, I'd be serving on very few committees."

Charlie laughed, finding her candor refreshing in the dim light of his personal catacomb.

"By the way, how did you find me?" Charlie asked. "I thought my little hideaway was secret."

"Yes, but not from the House Clerk. I have friends there as well."

Charlie nodded, then was suddenly embarrassed by his appearance.

"Forgive me. I forgot my manners. I'll go put on a bathrobe."

"Don't bother. You look fine. So masculine."

Charlie restrained himself. Don't get nervous, or excited, he warned. He sat down and tried to look at ease, which took a little dissembling.

"So, Ms. Staples, or is it Mrs. Staples?"

"Either one. I'm a widow of three years. My husband, Amos Staples, was a 'multi' and had no children. So after four marriages, I'm finally filthy rich. But I try to wash away the guilt whenever I can. That's why I'm here."

"So?"

"So, I've been taken by three things about you, Mr. Palmer. You obviously have the brains to understand the quagmire we call government. You've also shown the courage to fight it."

"And the third?"

"The third is that I'm afraid you were excessively wounded by Leland's attack. I could see that in your face when you walked off the set. That's why I'm here. To try to spread some cheer. How do you feel?"

"You guessed it. Pretty far down."

"Of course you're depressed. And a lot of people are angry because their idol was shown to have feet of clay. But I'm guessing it'll blow over. The public is getting more sophisticated." Clara smiled at some private joke. "Thank God, I wasn't on that interview chair. I'd make Sweet Charity look like a nun."

Charlie laughed. This woman was an analgesic. Why had she suddenly dropped into his apartment? And his life?

"That's nice of you, Mrs. Staples. But you didn't come to this unfashionable part of town just to cheer me up. Did you?"

"Indirectly, yes. I was afraid you'd think about leaving politics. I want to stop that, so I have a concrete offer to help it along."

"What's that?"

"I'll play spy for you in the party so this kind of snide operation doesn't happen again. I am a party loyalist and not a complete whore, so I won't give away any of their election strategy or political secrets. But if they've got any more dirty tricks up their sleeves, you'll be the first to know."

Clara paused and broke into a smile, which to Charlie looked incandescent. "But," she added, "all that depends on your staying around and doing what you do best."

"Why are you doing this?" Charlie was near dumbfounded. "What do you have to gain?"

"Simply that I have a hunch about you, and I always play my hunches, whether at the track or with men. I think the country really needs you. Though I can sometimes be the consummate rich bitch, I am an American. Without our free enterprise system, how could my late husband, Amos Staples, have made all that filthy money, then have given it to me just because I'm beautiful?"

Charlie laughed despite his private woe. This woman was clever.

"Well, this is a big surprise so early in the morning—or maybe it's not so early. So I presume you're here as an individual. Nothing to do with the party?"

"Absolutely not. If they found out, I'd be excommunicated. Probably shot like Mata Hari. By the way, who do you think dreamed up this whole smear campaign against you?"

"I assumed Norm Sobel from the other party."

"Hell, no. This was the work of big Andy Tolliver, your once-upon-a-time party campaign boss. He put gumshoes on you very early, even before the convention, when you started to make trouble in Congress. He's smart enough to spot a maverick at any distance. But his investigators said you were as clean as a whistle. Then he paid top dollar to some private eye who was checking you out for somebody else. I'm sure Tolliver's the one who passed the report on to Leland, anonymously. He hoped you'd do just what you've been thinking about—dropping out."

"They hate me that much?"

"Oh, much more than that. You're the most dangerous threat to everything they stand for, and enjoy. That's why I've come as Florence Nightingale. To bind your wounds and get you out of bed and back into the election business."

Charlie felt overwhelmed by the woman. Her presence and words were stimulating his senses, probably excessively. He rose and hitched up his pajamas to avoid a minor catastrophe.

"Mrs. Staples . . ."

"Call me Clara, please."

"All right, Clara. That's the best offer I've had this morning. I have to admit that I thought about dropping the independent movement. But now? How could I disappoint such a beautiful woman?"

Staples laughed. "I doubt that I'm the reason, but I hope that I have helped you make the right decision."

She moved toward the door, which Charlie opened.

Clara leaned forward. In a rapid movement that stunned Charlie, she pressed her body against his so that he could feel the pressure of her breasts and thighs through the thin coat. Then, before he could react, she gave him a surprisingly full kiss on the lips.

"Until next time, Mr. President-to-be, I remain . . ." Clara whispered, softly closing the door behind her.

Mr. President? Where in the world did she get that crazy idea?

CHAPTER 21

Freddie Boxley was chafing at the computer.

As he reread his notes on the Baltimore Diner conspiracy, he realized he had something worth more than a $50-a-week raise. After years of digging in the Washington journalistic trenches, maybe now he could go over the top. The next step up was "investigative journalist," a title worth at least $20,000 a year more from any wire outfit.

The very pinnacle of his profession was, of course, "pundit" in television land, where fees were of the Monopoly variety. He could never aspire to that. His diction was just short of atrocious. And what with two crooked teeth that had never seen an orthodontist and somewhat acned cheeks, he looked only like what he was—a big-city gumshoe reporter.

He had left the Tolliver-Sobel tape in his private safe deposit box under the signature of Fred James, his first and middle names. The first time around, he had taken no notes off it. Half panicky with glee, he had just pushed the tape into the box for fear of losing it.

Now, he was going to listen to it line by line. He packed a steno pad in his briefcase—shorthand was an old skill he had learned in high school—and left the National Press Building.

At the bank, he signed in as Fred James. A guard brought him the box in a small cubbyhole, just large enough to do his work. Removing the tape from the bank would be foolhardy. Reaching into his briefcase, he took out a small battery-driven player, then lovingly stroked the secret tape (also his secret hope) before inserting it.

With the volume on low, he listened with the steno pad open. Whenever anything seemed promising, he scribbled it verbatim in his old Pitman shorthand—man's first word processor. He wrote feverishly when the fat boy blabbed that the $200,000 dirty-tricks slush fund was going to be held in a Cayman Island bank.

He noted that the British island was the same place where Charlie Palmer's sponsor had stashed the $100 million campaign money. That was a new challenge. Learning the identity of the "Mystery Billionaire," as the press had dubbed him, would make another sure headline. Why not try for a double, or triple, play?

The tape was a reportorial gold mine. One of the things he had missed the first time around now popped out at him. It was the name Kellogg. Of course, that was Karl "King" Kellogg, chief of the Beltway Bandit lobbyists. It seemed that King was personally contributing $100,000 in to the party, funds that would end up in the two-party "Special Effects"—or dirty tricks—fund in the Caymans.

Three possible exposés in one Caribbean hot spot sent his head spinning. He'd have to tell his editor, Max Freeman, just enough to get the Metropolitan News to pay his expenses. But not so much that another hungry journalist could steal his Pulitzer. Please, right up to God's ears.

Boxley taxied to National Airport, smiling at how easily he had conned Max into this trip. Revealing nothing about the tape, he merely explained that a tipster had informed him that the $100 million campaign money was coming out of a Cayman bank.

"Here's $1,500 for travel," Max had said. "You came back with that rich putz's name and you've got a $2,000 raise and an exclusive on covering the billionaire—wherever he lives."

"Even in Zurich or Rio?"

"Even the South Pole."

At National Airport, Boxley boarded American Airlines Flight 1461, leaving at 10:10 in the morning for Miami. There he changed planes for the 1:30 P.M. flight to the Grand Cayman Island, the larger of the two Caribbean dots due south of Cuba, and one of the few British colonies left anywhere. That took $621.95 of his travel account. Scoop or not, he had no intention of spending his own money. He'd have to watch the rest of the $1,500 carefully.

From the Owen Roberts Airport in Georgetown, the Cayman capital, he took a short cab ride to town. He had gotten in at 1:53, so he could still make it to the Cayman Colonial Bank before it closed. Then he'd scoot over to the Hyatt on the beach where he had a reservation for $180 a night. With three nights' lodging, food, and an evening libation, he was about maxed out.

"Can I help you, sir?" a British type replete with Bermuda shorts inquired as Boxley approached a bank officer's desk. He got a kick out of English colonials. Each seemed to have lived a saga of hard knocks that had sent them to this hundred-degree summer clime while London basked in temperate glory. A never-achieved life, sort of like his own. The thought warmed him to the banker, about forty-five, a thin, pencil-mustached fellow—David Niven without the truly good looks.

"My name is Boxley, Fred Boxley," he began, flashing his Washington, D.C., press pass, figuring some naively mistook it for a police ID. "I'm here to trace an American bank whose depositor is financing an American political movement. Just last week a $5 million draft from that account was sent from your bank to the Riggs Bank in Washington. We believe it's a case of dirty pool, maybe even illegal. Can you—"

Before the sentence was completed, David Niven stood up, his face flushed and his voice indignant.

"Mr. Boxley, there is the door. Please use it, quickly. Cayman banks gained their reputation because, as in Switzerland, our affairs are strictly confidential. If you can produce a bona fide federal officer with evidence of fraud, we will cooperate. Otherwise, please return to Washington or enjoy yourself swimming at our beaches. They're some of the world's finest."

Boxley left, smiling at the banker's indignation. Never had he expected to learn anything in a frontal assault. Unlike the states, which had IRS restrictions on the movement of cash, in the Caymans, you could get a free dinner, or a lot more, for depositing $100 million. But history had taught Boxley that the direct assault had to be the first maneuver. In one in ten cases, some shmuck talked just because he liked talking.

He might as well check into his $180 room off the beach. Donning his plaid shorts from J.C. Penney, he headed for the water, then for a nap on the chaise. It was a lot better lounging in the Caymans with an ocean breeze than in the sweltering Washington humidity in July.

"Man," he heard through the fog of his sleep. Someone was nudging at the chaise. "Wake up and hear the good news."

Boxley looked up. The man staring down at him was of mixed race, with a delightful Calypso accent.

"I was in the bank when you were making inquiries. I have a cousin who works in the bank's back room. If you want to reach him, I can arrange it—for a small fee."

"How small?"

The man puckered his lip. "Say $50 American."

Boxley stared at him suspiciously. "When?"

"At five o'clock, right here."

Boxley looked at his watch. "It's already 4:30."

"That's right, man. In a half hour. Now give me the $50."

"Oh, no. I'll give you a $20. The rest when he comes."

The tall stranger laughed loud. "You Americans are all suspicious. OK. Give me the $20. See you right here."

Boxley now felt more at home. Money was passing hands and there was no greater sign of man's sincerity.

Punctually, the "cousin" showed, wearing a T-shirt that said "New York Yankees: World's Champions, 1956."

"What do you want to know? Give me your questions and my friend will answer them if his bank was involved. They handle most of the big money deals on the island. He'll meet you in the Hyatt coffee shop at 10 A.M. tomorrow morning."

"What will it cost me?" Boxley asked. "I'm not rich."

Both locals laughed. "You rich Americans plead poverty lately. I liked it the old way—when you were crazy braggarts. First you owe my cousin $30 more. Then I get $100."

"A hundred dollars. That's robbery."

"Of course. But it's cheap robbery. I'm sure you'll cash in better than us when you get home. Now what are your questions?"

Boxley asked him to check on who sent the $5 million to the Riggs; about the $200,000 deposited by Tolliver or Sobel, and if King Kellogg had an account at the bank.

They promptly disappeared. The next morning in the coffee shop, Boxley was approached by a distinguished-looking local, standing at least six feet, three inches, with a thin mustache, and dressed in a white linen suit, white silk shirt, and purple silk tie. He looked like nothing less than the President of the island republic—which the Caymans weren't.

"Mr. Boxley, I presume," he said as he approached the newsman reading the *New York Times*, a $3 item.

"Yes, I am."

"Man, you've hit the jackpot. I have information on two of your three questions."

Boxley smiled broadly. "Good, sit down. Have some coffee."

"No, I'm afraid I have to get back to work. Just took this break to make a quick $1,000."

"A thousand dollars? You must be crazy."

With that the tall man turned smartly on his Bally wingtips, making a loud squeak as he headed out of the room.

"WAIT A MINUTE!" Boxley called out. "Sit down."

This time, the informant turned and sat. "I'll tell you what I know, and you tell me if it's worth the thousand. If so, I want a check right now."

"How do you know my check is good?"

"I trust you because I believe you're interested in your continued good health. Do I make my point?"

Boxley nodded, then did some quick arithmetic. He'd be spending $1,130 for the information. With the hotel and the airline, he'd be out about $800 on top of his expense account. Either Max would make it up, or he'd have him take it out of his $2,000 raise if the poop was significant.

"Shoot."

"Well, first the $5 million to Riggs is part of a $100 million deposit."

"Great. Who made it?"

"I have no name, but it came from the First National Bank of Great Falls, Montana. There can't be too many people there with that kind of money."

"And the others?"

"I just found one. That lobbyist you mentioned, King Kellogg, doesn't have an account on the island. My friend at the bank says he used to, but it's been transferred to Switzerland. But your Mr. Tolliver does have one here. It's registered under a post office box address in Alexandria, Virginia. He has deposited $200,000 in an account called Special Effects. Does that mean anything to you?"

"Oh, yes. You're worth $1,000. Who do I make the check out to?"

"Just to CASH."

"Why, do you pay income taxes to British Inland Revenue?"

"Heavens, no. We'd have a revolution. I just prefer not to have our little understanding recorded anywhere."

Boxley laughed at his new friend, perhaps his open-sesame to journalistic heaven. Even Max, sour as he was, would appreciate the value of what he had just bought.

CHAPTER 22

Charlie didn't return to his congressional office till the second day after the Leland debacle, waiting until he felt secure enough to face his colleagues.

His entrance on Tuesday was surprising. As he walked into his cramped space, a few male employees rushed up to shake his hand, while two of the women kissed him on the cheek despite Charlie's friendly protestations.

Most told him to tough out the Leland onslaught. With the presidential election coming up, there was more at stake than his peccadillos as a college student. "Stay with it, man," an intern advised, offering a warm grab at his shoulder.

The most unlikely response came from Robbie Barnes, his press secretary.

"I'm sorry you didn't want me to send out a press statement explaining *exactly* what happened twenty years ago," he told Charlie in his precise diction. "I think you owe that to your growing public, and to yourself."

Charlie just smiled at Barnes's overseriousness, probably the residual effect of having been a seminarian. People accused Charlie of moralizing too much. They should hang around with Barnes.

"Thanks for your concern, Robbie, but I think the less said about it the better. When I do constructive things in the House, I hope it'll all balance out."

In the apartment the day before—no longer plunged into near darkness—Charlie had used the time (and the encouragement of that wonderful Clara Staples) to mend his psyche. He had begun his main task, working up a short list of selection for the presidential nominee. He scribbled names on a long yellow pad, then almost as rapidly crossed them off.

Now back in his Longworth office, he continued his brainstorming.

"Congressman, you're looking peaked," Sally said. "Perhaps you need a short nap."

"No, Sally, it's not fatigue, it's frustration. As soon as I come up with a name, or someone suggests someone, I find ten reasons why he or she wouldn't make a good President."

Charlie paused. "What's our mail like on the Sunday morning eat-Charlie-alive television show?

"It's mixed. Of eighteen hundred faxes and phone calls, you have 906 on your side. So you're ahead by a squeak. Some said you were a big phony like other politicians. But others said, what the hell, you've made mistakes, but haven't we all. Once the people have a chance to evaluate it, I think they'll realize that few eighteen-year-olds are fully reliable. You've had twenty-five years to grow up, and they have nothing on you as an adult. I believe that's the real test."

"Sally, that's too logical. Politics is often more emotion than anything else. Maybe that's where I'm deficient."

His AA laughed. "In fact, we got a fax a little like that. A woman agreed with your politics and wished you—not Candidate X—would run for President. But she also said you sounded too perfect, a crusader with no faults. You know, that 'St. Charles' stuff. But now that she knows you've gotten drunk, she feels better about you. She sent in $15."

Charlie smiled, aware he was mending, if slowly. Now he had to survive well enough to line up a solid presidential ticket. Perhaps he could then recede into the background, away from the sniping press.

He laughed at that thought. Everyone loved to use the press for publicity and have the public love him. But if the media zeroed in, as they did on him, they were journalistic pimps. Well, he'd been both a user and usee of the Fourth Estate, and he much preferred being the former.

"Sally, I've boiled it down to six possible candidates for the White House—good people who might consider an independent campaign, especially a well-financed one like ours. Here, take a look at my short list."

"Does that mean that you're going ahead?" Sally asked, her voice brightening. "Then you haven't lost heart because of Leland? That's great news. The people here have been talking about nothing else. Except for one or two, the staff is behind you."

"Yes, I'm going to stick it out. My wounds would never heal if I turned tail. Let my enemies crow now. You know, what goes around . . . Now, take a look at my list."

Sally picked up the single sheet scribbled with the names of possible Presidents. Topping it was Laurence Rosenstedt, former secretary of state and now a university president.

"He's as nonpartisan and as smart as they come," Sally commented. "But absolutely bloodless. No personality."

"I agree," Charlie said, crossing off the name.

"General Bernard LaCrosse. Now there's a powerful one." Sally added a small whistle. "Former joint chief and Vietnam superhero. I think he's now retired to Arizona, where he runs a military academy."

"So what do you think, Sally?"

"Reminds me of the man-on-the-white-horse ready to take over. Remember General James Mattoon Scott in *Seven Days in May* who was going to make a military putsch? LaCrosse could be that man."

"Next," was all Charlie said, eliminating the second name.

"Oh, here's someone I could warm to," Sally exclaimed. "Governor Nancy Claiborne of Iowa . . . She's every woman's role model— rich, beautiful, feminist, and issue-oriented. But . . ."

"But what?" Charlie wondered. What could be wrong with a powerful woman from another adoring woman's point of view?

"She's too trendy. Wears fashionable clothes no matter how screwy they are. Is a charity ball hound. Goes to cocktail parties in Hollywood. Has her picture in *W* every other week. Into animal rights and vegetarianism, even a touch of reincarnation. Interesting but not presidential."

Charlie got up and shook Sally's hand.

"You know, I've been wasting my time. I should clear my list with you beforehand. I've got three other names—Arthur Beaver, ex-chairman of the Federal Reserve; former Vice President Larry Stentor; and Senator Bill McCormick of Wisconsin. Even though they're distinguished men, the first two have problems. Beaver is a banker who's gotten people angry with his love of high interest rates. The former VP has been in retirement and out of the public consciousness."

Charlie got up and tried, again unsuccessfully, to pace in his cramped space.

"But McCormick is a good shot. He takes no campaign contributions and he's been my strongest ally in the Senate in cutting waste. He's well liked nationally and one of the few senators the public views as a statesman. I'll go talk to him. He could be the one."

Charlie sat, staring at his vanishing list of potential chief executives.

"You know, Sally, when I began this search, I figured it would be so easy that I could pick ten prominent Americans out of a hat and they'd all fit snugly into the White House. Now, if I don't get McCormick, I think I'll get a brain tumor. What's wrong with our country?"

Sally shook her head. "Charlie Palmer, you're an original, but we're not making them anymore. We have two kinds of wannabe presidents—those who rise in the party ranks and have the fire in the belly for the White House. No matter how flawed they are, they'll do virtually anything short of murder to get to the Oval Office. Then there are those who might make great Presidents, but wouldn't touch the present crazy campaign system with a twenty-foot pole. I wish you well, Congressman, but I can't see any potentially great President anywhere in the Beltway—maybe not even McCormick."

Charlie scribbled McCormick's name on a fresh sheet of paper, then crumpled up his old list. He threw it into the wastebasket with a perfect set shot. "Sorry, fellows and girls, you almost made it."

He stared hard at the remaining sheet. Next to McCormick's name, his pen, almost involuntarily it seemed, started to scribble another name—JOHN LARRIMORE. The senator from Oklahoma and former presidential candidate was surely the smartest and, he had once thought, the most courageous and honest of all American politicians. Until he had betrayed his word at the convention.

He crossed out the name but the pen kept writing—"John Larrimore, John . . ."

"Congressman, guess who's on the phone?"

He was still cogitating when Sally burst back into his office. "Who?"

"It's Schuyler Rafferty. He's *demanding* to speak with you."

He had kept Rafferty's role private from the world, even from most of his staff. But both Sally and George were privy to the secret. Sally obviously knew the import of this phone call.

Rafferty? Oh, my God, Charlie thought. I completely forgot to get in touch with him after the Leland debacle. He must be burning mad after that exposure. And at least seven million of his dollars have already been spent. No escape here, Charlie acknowledged, as he picked up the phone. He heard Rafferty's voice, deep and tense.

"Charlie. This is Schuyler Rafferty. I'll be arriving at National Airport on my jet at 7:25 A.M. tomorrow morning. I'll meet you at Taft Campanile on the Capitol grounds at 8 sharp. See you then."

Charlie started to respond, but the phone was dead. His rich patron from Montana had just hung up on him.

CHAPTER 23

"Charlie, glad you could make it."

He turned. There stood Schuyler Rafferty, or a reasonable facsimile thereof. His demeanor was more restrained than usual.

Charlie had been waiting at the Taft Campanile on the Capitol grounds for fifteen minutes, sweating in the humidity-soaked heat that ruined Washington summers. But in his position, this was one appointment he couldn't afford to miss.

The bell tower honoring Senator Robert A. Taft of Ohio, son of former President William Howard Taft, and affectionately called Mr. Republican, was strangely the only monument to any senator at the Capitol.

Standing there, Rafferty looked like a different man. Instead of his usual Hemingway hunting togs, he was dressed like a senator himself, in a blue pin-striped suit with a Harvard class tie. Charlie thought that peculiar, considering that Rafferty had never spent a day in any college.

His white hair and beard no longer had their characteristic freedom look. Both were carefully cut and coiffed so that Schuyler appeared to be a character out of a history book, perhaps a Civil War legislator. His "disguise" (and Charlie assumed that's what it was) was topped off by a pair of large sunglasses.

"Schuyler, how was your flight?" Charlie asked, hoping polite conversation might delay the inevitable.

"Fine."

Charlie tried to find something telltale in Rafferty's expression, but the ex-Brooklynite was playing it deadpan.

"Let's go for a walk, Charlie, down by the Reflecting Pool."

As they walked, the Montana billionaire was silent. Charlie thought it impolitic to break the mood. He felt like a schoolboy outside the principal's office. What was the principal—Rafferty—going to say?

Had he been dishonest in not telling Schuyler his whole pedigree before he accepted $7 million for the campaign? It must seem that way to Rafferty. But Charlie had honestly forgotten, or at least had trained himself not to think about the Hartley girl.

The drunken driving incident bothered him little. He hadn't gone more than two blocks, and he wasn't even drunk—just a few beers. But the abortion was something else. Why hadn't he kept it front and center all these years? God knows. He realized he didn't have a clue about himself in that part of his life.

Surely the Montanan had flown into Washington to shoot him down or, worse yet, take away his backing from the presidential race. If so, let it be. It wouldn't hurt his own reelection to Congress. Just make him look like an ass to the nation and to five million volunteers. Well, such is the nature of Judgment Day.

"Charlie, you sure made the headlines with that Leland interview," Schuyler began, breaking the tense silence. "How come you didn't call me right after?"

"I was too confused, too angry with myself. But as far as telling you beforehand—which is more important—I just didn't remember it until Leland brought it up. Obviously, I was wrong. For all your savvy you obviously sized me up incorrectly. The whole thing must have been a big surprise to you."

"It was no surprise at all, Charlie."

"WHAT?"

The congressman halted and looked up at Rafferty, who was a half a head taller than he.

"What do you mean no surprise? You expected Leland to hit me with something negative. Is that what you mean?"

"No, I meant what I said. When you were sitting at my dinner table in Montana and going horseback riding with my wild daughter, I knew everything about you, back to your kindergarten schooldays."

Charlie's mind was doing handsprings.

"I don't get it, Sky. How come you knew everything and then backed me anyway?" Charlie's voice raised as his emotions outraced his mind.

"Simple, Charlie. I hired the best investigator in your area to get me the dirt on you. I found out he was a shady character. Once he gave me the information, and I paid him an extra $5,000 for what they called 'moral turpitude,' I knew he'd also sell it to your enemies.

They'd waste no time getting it a good media play. With Leland's help, it worked out just the way I figured."

"YOU CONNIVING OLD BASTARD," Charlie shouted, which brought a smile to Rafferty's visage. "But if you knew all about me when I was in Montana, why did you give me carte blanche on the presidential campaign and $7 million? I don't get it."

"Simple, young man. I don't give a shit about your love life in college. What does that have to do with anything? I just wanted any piece of dirt on you out in the open. Then I'd see how you'd handle it. If you folded up like a wet noodle after the Leland attack, I'd fold up the campaign as well. As it is, you passed with flying colors. Now it's behind us. I doubt it'll cost us one percent of the vote—maybe some old ladies in Dubuque. Actually, you did the honorable thing. Had you married the girl, you both would have been miserable."

Charlie didn't know why, but a tear welled in his eye.

"Rafferty, you really are a sly old fox. Smart, but sly."

"I would think so, Charlie. Do you think anyone accumulates $6 billion in this cutthroat world without being sly. Kid, you're an innocent. But, of course, that's one reason I picked you. But you'll learn better as you go along. I'm betting $100 million on it."

The walk continued, with Charlie's psyche somewhat salved.

"So how's it going with choosing a presidential and vice presidential candidate?" Rafferty asked. "You know, you can't go further until you do."

"I know. I've gone through twenty names and no one shapes up. I have one possibility, Senator Bob McCormick of Wisconsin. Great cost cutter, smart, and honest."

"Yeh, but there's one small problem."

"What's that?" Charlie asked.

"McCormick's been having an affair with his AA for the past ten years. Almost everyone in Washington knows about it except you. And I suppose Sally as well."

Charlie now felt supremely dumb. "I suppose we're not into gossip."

"That's for sure."

"I had another one, a man who would make a great President," Charlie volunteered. "Senator John Larrimore of Oklahoma, who nominated me for VP at the convention. But John turned tail when the party pressure was put on."

"So what's your plan? I'd say you have to move quickly."

"Honestly, Schuyler, I have no plan except to keep thinking. Maybe you've got some ideas yourself."

Now, for the first time that morning, Rafferty broke out into his unabashed Irishness. He took off his sunglasses and grasped Charlie's shoulder, half embracing him, emitting an old-fashioned belly laugh.

"Kid, there's only one possible candidate for President. I knew that the day I called you to come up to Montana, and I haven't changed my mind for a second."

Who was he talking about? Charlie was now totally confused.

"And who is this secret leader of the people?" Charlie asked.

"Charlie, face it—YOU'RE IT. You may be innocent, unseasoned, a little compulsive and fanatic, but you're it. In fact, maybe all those so-called liabilities are the reason you'll make a great President. A total break with our recent political class, that gaggle of nobodies. Yes, Charlie, I'm afraid you're the man of the day and you'd better face up to it."

Charlie stopped in his tracks, his expression turned hostile.

"Schuyler, that's bullshit. I have no desire to run for President. And more important, I'm not going to. I just don't want it."

Rafferty nodded his head, knowingly.

"I don't doubt that. Do you think I want to part with $100 million? Maybe I can afford it, but I didn't get filthy rich by giving my money away. It's compounding that works. No, I'm not in this because I want to. It's because of destiny. We're both tied into it—up to our assholes—and we really have no choice. We do it or else."

Charlie listened, unbelieving. "Or else what?"

"Or else life will give you such a kick in the ass that you'll never recover. One thing I've learned in my sixty-nine years, Charlie. You go with the flow or you pay the price."

Rafferty kept walking, his mind obviously moving in an obsessive vein, something Palmer easily recognized.

"Charlie, you have no choice," Schuyler continued. "There is no one else. You do it, or it doesn't get done. There's a thing called a short list of selection and sometimes it's so short that there's only one person who can fill the bill. Without FDR, there'd have been no victory in World War II. Without Churchill, England would have played dead and been occupied by Hitler. Without Truman, the Communists would have taken over Western Europe after World War II."

Rafferty paused and stared at him.

"Without Charlie Palmer, as I see it, this country ain't going anywhere except down in a slow, deadly spiral. So don't give me this bullshit that you don't want to do it. What does that have to do with anything?"

This fucking Irishman was too smart, Charlie thought. Just as Georgie Sempel had told him that he'd have to leave his wonderful company because Charlie's logic was impossible to deny, so Schuyler had him beat as a marketing man—ten times over. Rafferty had taken a forty-three-year-old with only three months' experience in government and convinced himself that he was the *only* savior of the country. It was pure bullshit.

"But Rafferty, that's just not true. Who the hell knows I'm alive?" Charlie asked. "Sure, I've made some noise, but what are my recognition numbers among the public? About 21 percent. I've seen the list. Way below the Speaker, and nowhere near Billings."

Schuyler just laughed. "Kid, how many people made the Russian revolution—either the first or the second? How many colonists fought to split us from Britain? Maybe only one in five Americans even know your name, but they *really* know it. Why do you think you got five million volunteers with a few days of ads? Because they want a free booklet of Jefferson's quotes? No Charlie, strange as it seems, you've caught the imagination of a large group of disaffected Americans, and they want you to lead them. So forget your half-ass opinions, and tell me you'll do it."

"And what if I say no?"

"Then I'll just fold the operation and put the remaining $93 million into a little company in Boise I've got my eye on. If you want to continue the campaign without you as the candidate and without my cash, be my guest. You'll get some warmed-over hack as your candidate. You'll raise maybe another $10 million and you'll get clobberred by the two parties. I predict your candidate will get less than ten percent of the vote in the general election. Go try it."

"You'd really pull out if I don't accept the nomination?"

"You bet your skinny ass I will."

Charlie kept walking, his mind turning over at an accelerated RPM. They had reached the Reflecting Pool on the Mall, and Charlie stood immobile, looking into its clear water. But his thinking wasn't clear. The options were pushing up against one another without clarity. His brain was muddied.

He turned to ask Schuyler how long he'd have for a decision when he suddenly heard footsteps behind him.

A young long-haired man of college age was standing there staring into both their faces. Quickly, he whipped a 35-mm camera out of his pocket, and in the space of a second, took two frames. Before they could react, the young man pushed the camera back in his pocket and took off, racing down the path.

"Get him, Charlie!" Schuyler shouted.

He took off in pursuit, but the forty-three-year-old heart, out of shape since he had come to Washington, wasn't up to the challenge. He chased the photographer for a few hundred yards, but as the distance between them grew, he halted. Puffing heavily, Charlie walked back to Rafferty, who was standing in the same spot near the Reflecting Pool.

"I'm sorry, Schuyler. The kid's just too fast."

"Don't worry about it. More important, what's your decision?"

Charlie was still puffing.

"But, Schuyler, don't you see the jam I'm in? Even if I wanted to do it, I can't."

"Why's that?"

"Because I spent the last weeks telling every media person in America that I was not after the presidency, that I had no personal ambition, that I was searching for *someone else* to get the nomination. It was plastered all over the tube and in every damn paper in the country. Now you expect me to go back to them and say I'm going after the Oval Office? I'll look like an asshole."

Schuyler laughed his usual laugh, a kind of guffaw that could only be translated as "Fuck them all." Sure, Charlie thought. He's got the world by the tail and is used to manipulating everyone with his charm and his billions. But all he himself had was a few bucks in Synergy stock and his reputation—especially his reputation.

Besides, it suddenly reached his cortex that the $100 million of Rafferty's money would now be expended on him if he accepted the nomination. That ruffled his internal feathers. How the hell could he, a raving critic of money as the mother's milk of corruption, accept $1, let alone $100 million?

"Rafferty, did you ever think how the public is going to react to my taking a fortune from you? Some of them think I'm a straight shooter, and not just a political whore. What are they going to say if I accept your offer?"

Charlie looked down at the floor, the sense of embarrassment already suffusing him.

"I know you're sensitive about your principles, Charlie. And I respect that," Rafferty responded, his demeanor now quieter, and seemingly more sympathetic. "But look at this way. What's more important—the future of our country or your hurt feelings and temporary embarrassment? You'll survive it but maybe America won't. If you look down the long pipe of history, do you think anyone will remember or give a crap about your pride? Or more likely, won't people bemoan the decline of our country? You may think I'm bullshitting you, Charlie, but I'm absolutely convinced that without you, we're not going to pull out of our national nosedive."

Charlie stared into Rafferty's eyes. He was bluff, even crude sometimes, and of course almost pathologically acquisitive. But when it came to the Good Ol' USA, Charlie knew it came from the heart.

"So how long do I have before I give you my answer?" Charlie asked.

"I'm a nice fellow. You know that. I'll give you thirty seconds."

Charlie couldn't help but smile. Rafferty had pressed all the right buttons, the essence of a marketing genius.

"Like you say, Schuyler, I seem to have no choice. You win. The answer is yes. I'll take the nomination. But we're in a jam. We need another five hundred thousand signatures in a few weeks and that'll take a lot of money. Can you send some more quickly to our account?"

"Charlie, before I left Montana early this morning, I wired $10 million to your account at the Riggs Bank."

"You did what? How did you know I'd accept the nomination?"

Rafferty's broad smile was illuminating.

"Destiny, young man. It's written all over your face."

CHAPTER 24

The front page of the morning paper seemed to belong to Charlie and Company, for better or worse.

The second lead story was headlined:

CONGRESSMAN CHARLES PALMER THROWS HAT IN PRESIDENTIAL RING;
MAJOR PARTY CHIEFS SAY HIS CAMPAIGN IS DOOMED

A photo of Charlie and Rafferty, taken at the capitol's Reflecting Pool, ran at the bottom of the page.

$100 MILLION MYSTERY MAN REVEALED;
BILLIONAIRE RAFFERTY IS POLITICAL ANGEL

Bylined Fred Boxley of the Metropolitan News Service, the story began:

Investor Schuyler Rafferty is the man behind the $100 million backing for the independent presidential campaign, now headed by Congressman Charles Palmer. This reporter traced the money from a small bank in Montana to a secret account in the Cayman Islands, a British colony known as the Switzerland of the Caribbean.

A poll conducted yesterday by Time/CNN showed that any independent candidate for President is favored by 10 percent of

the voters. But with Congressman Charles Palmer of Ohio heading the ticket, it draws 20 percent.

Inquiries made at the Montana residence of Schuyler Rafferty
were not returned. Finally, Jenny Rafferty, the billionaire's
daughter, issued an unprintable statement filled with expletives.

Charlie laughed with gusto. Everything they did now seemed to
become instant news. Not because of him, he was sure, but as part of
the nation's anger at the debilitating status quo. At the same time—
considering that only 21 percent of Americans even knew his name—
Charlie thought his 20 percent support wasn't half bad.

Charlie was impressed by Barnes's work on his presidential announcement, which produced not just a file cabinet full of press clips,
but a video piece done at taxpayer expense in the House recording
studio.

(He scribbled a quick note. "Talk to Chairman Jack Knowles of
the House Administration Committee. Close the congressional studio,
a ridiculous perk, and save $500,000 a year.")

Now that Charlie had announced his candidacy, both Sally and
Barnes would have to leave government employ and move into the
Pennsylvania Avenue campaign headquarters. It was inconvenient,
but he intended to scrupulously obey the FEC election regulations.

He had yielded to Rafferty and taken the presidential nomination
of the new movement, but he had to admit to himself that he enjoyed the prospect of the upcoming campaign, win or lose.

Politics seemed to flow like a subterranean river through his blood-
stream. Now he needed to prove to himself that he was not just
another politician, but someone immune to the narcotic of power
and celebrity, and driven only by love of country.

Only one thing remained gnawing at his psyche. Whatever happened to that lovely woman, Clara Staples, who had rescued him
from the depths just a short while ago?

CHAPTER 25

"Charles, I have two tickets for a private Mozart concert at the Kennedy Center, my payoff for a large contribution. It's formal. Would you like to come as my guest?"

The sound of Clara Staples's voice on the phone startled him. He had thought of her from time to time, but had chalked up her uninvited appearance at his apartment as a lovely fantasy—something he had dreamed up to fill his void. But now, here she was calling his congressional office.

"You are real then, not just something out of my imagination," Charlie responded.

"Oh, yes, Congressman. Flesh and blood, and plenty of it, I've been told."

The woman was an outrageous flirt, but Charlie found that he enjoyed her patter.

"Love to, Clara, except that I don't have a tux. But I suppose I can rent one, and I'll pick you up. What time and where?"

"At my house, Maison Grise, on Third Street in Georgetown. See you at seven. Please bring along a happier face than the one you wore the day we met. I see that you're back in the political fray— big time—and that pleases me greatly. Did I have anything to do with that?"

"You sure did, but I don't yet know if I should be appreciative or not."

She laughed in her surprisingly girlish way.

On his arrival at Maison Grise, Clara looked stunning, almost like an apparition. Seeing Charlie walk up the path, she had opened the door herself.

"Good evening, Charles," she said, kissing him on the cheek, much as she would an old friend.

Charlie had a striking vision, as if he had been happily married to this woman for ten years. He had met her only once, in his apartment for twenty minutes, and now she had suddenly come back into his life. Yet he felt instantly at home, without self-consciousness. He knew such things were impossible, but he gloried in the feeling, no matter how false or transient.

Clara seemed to share something with him, if not that. She grasped his hand warmly.

"Come see my mansion, one of my ill-gotten goods. But I must tell you, I'm very proud of it."

As well she should be, Charlie thought. It was almost as exquisite as the woman. He knew little about decorating but the rooms spoke of ease. Furnished in French antiques, the entire ground floor of the mansion was elegant, yet not ostentatious.

"Come. Now that you've seen some of the place—if not my sumptuous bedroom—we should leave for the Kennedy Center."

As they left Maison Grise and drove in her chauffeured Jaguar toward the Kennedy Center, a prosaic modern building on the Potomac across from the Watergate Apartments, Clara sat silently for a moment, touching his hand.

"So now, Charles, you're running for President. That's good. I'd like to have the ultimate influence with the ultimate American, the President of the United States."

"You're ahead of yourself again, Clara. People smarter than us—like Ladbrooke's betting people in London—have me as an eighteen-to-one longshot. I think they're closer to the mark. But I'm mystified. How did you happen to mention me as the President-to-be in my apartment at the bottom of my existence?"

"Oh, I've never doubted it, and I still don't. It's all over your being. But, of course, you've got to help it along."

He didn't answer Clara, just turned to look at her alongside him in the backseat.

Her hair, now almost platinum in color, was piled up on her head, with a small coronet resting atop it like a flower. The color was surely not natural, but it suited her white skin perfectly. The woman was so beautiful that he ached. Not so much with passion—although he didn't rule that out—but as if confronted with an Aphrodite, one with a sharp brain.

Can you be in love with someone after knowing her only a half hour? Charlie asked himself. What was she, some kind of a witch?

A gorgeous, witty, sensual one? Whatever, his soul was riding on air, and she, not his political future, was the reason.

"Charles, love," she said, turning to him, "I don't want you to think I invited you because you're a candidate for President. Remember, I first came to see you in your depths. And if you hadn't announced, I was going to try to convince you to run. So I can't be accused of pure opportunism. Can I?"

"Of course not. I haven't accused you of that, have I?"

"No. But I must admit that driving in my Jaguar with a handsome man in a tux, who just happens to be seeking the highest office in the land, does give me a real thrill—you know where. Is that all right, or am I just a gold-plated hussy?"

With that Clara leaned over and gently kissed Charlie on the lips, before pulling back.

"I don't know if you're a hussy, Clara, although I suspect you are." Charlie was trying to control the pleasure coursing through his body. "But, Clara, is it possible that I'm already in love with you?"

"Oh, don't be silly, Charles. All men fall in love with me the first hour. It's the second hour that counts."

He laughed, feeling himself in the presence of magnificent womanhood, something he had never experienced in his misdirected love life. He had been with loose women, uptight women, smart and dumb women, women who acted like second-class men, beautiful if not overly bright women. But never had he known anyone remotely like Clara Staples. He was in the Elysian Fields and he had just encountered Helen of Troy.

At the concert, Clara was delightfully flirtatious. She bantered with him mercilessly. When they walked together for refreshments during the intermission, she grasped the crook of his arm, as if to hold on for life, smiling at everyone who cast a glance their way. All Washington society seemed to be milling around them.

Charlie held no brief for his own mundane—some said blue-collar—looks. But he supposed that with his newfound importance and Clara's beauty, they did make a couple. But, he warned himself, these are moments to be seized and not to be taken too seriously. On a long-term basis, life is simply not that generous.

After the concert, they said goodbye both to friends and to Charlie's political enemies and left to return to Maison Grise.

"Darling, Charles, come in for a drink." Clara laughed. "Did I say that right, dear?"

In front of the fireplace, Charlie nursed a beer while Clara sipped white wine. "Charles, if you're going to be President, you have to drop that beer-drinking business. Your Cabinet just wouldn't understand."

He chided her again for her foolish talk about the presidency. After a half hour, Charlie felt intoxicated, but not from one beer. Clara had set him off balance. He was unable to make reality out of this waking dream. Twice, she kissed him so passionately that he feared—he knew not what.

"Come, darling. It's time for you to see my bedroom. Really the nicest room in the house."

Upstairs, Charlie took in the room, like something out of Versailles.

"Now you sit here on this chaise," Clara ordered. "And don't you move. I want your opinion on something. Be right back."

Clara disappeared for a few minutes, then returned. She was now standing about ten feet from him, wearing a brassiere, long black pantyhose, and green satin high heels, with the same jewels around her neck she had worn earlier that night. Her hair was up as before, and she stood jauntily with her legs apart.

"What I want your opinion on is this, Charles. Is this nicer, I mean more exciting, than the usual nightgown that prosaic housewives wear in their boudoirs?"

This time Charlie didn't wait for Clara to make advances. He hadn't been with a woman since April, and the voices of desire were loud. Charlie walked up to her, pushed heavily into her body, his hands reaching for her breasts.

"That's nice, Charlie. I like you to be aggressive. Now I want to show you something else."

She turned. "Unhook my bra."

Charlie did as he was told, and Clara turned back to face him. His eyes were riveted on her breasts, full and high, as if there were no gravity in the room. Charlie could feel his control fall away. He moved toward her, kissing her, again fondling her breasts.

"Charlie, I don't want you to wait too long. We don't want a premature accident. I'll meet you in a minute."

Clara was true to her word. With her makeup still on, but her hair now down, she slipped naked under the covers.

"Take me, Mr. President-to-be. I'm all yours."

Charlie laughed, and was soon occupied caressing Clara's body—her breasts, her thighs, the space between her legs. She sighed, then reached for him, toying expectantly.

"Just a moment, dear." She guided him into her, and as he kissed her, more passionately than he believed possible, the pleasure became so overwhelming that he feared something untoward would happen—that Clara would suddenly vanish.

Charlie started to laugh.

"What's so funny?" Clara asked.

"Nothing, darling, just comparing my life yesterday with my joy today."

"Good boy, you're doing beautifully," Clara purred. "Whoever thought such an idealist would be so virile?"

"I'm not usually, Clara. It's just that I love you," he said, not losing a motion.

"Oh, all you boys say that before you come. Will you love me afterward?"

"Always, dear Clara, always," Charlie said just as the final thrust exploded into her.

She sighed. "Good boy. Now just rest your tired head. All the poisons are gone, and you can sleep—I hope more peacefully than ever."

CHAPTER 26

Detective Sergeant Sam Lemoine bent over the gutter of a quiet residential street in the Northwest area of Washington and examined the body. A patrol car had spotted it at 4 A.M., long before dawn, and called homicide.

"Gruesome," Lemoine commented to his sidekick, Detective Al Dennis. "The top of his head's been virtually blown away by a bullet. Looks like a .44. Death must have been instantaneous. Geez, and right out here on the street."

The victim, Freddie Boxley, was lying at the edge of the curb, in a small pool of residual rain water. He was face up, his eyes open and staring at the sky, frozen in surprise.

Lemoine bent down and checked the diamond stickpin in Boxley's tie.

"Strange, Al. It looks like a fake. Otherwise I suppose the killer would have taken it. Put it in an evidence bag," Lemoine ordered. Slowly, he transferred the cigar in his mouth to his hand, where it twirled slowly.

According to the coroner, Boxley had been murdered at about 2 A.M., apparently on his way home. A check with his employer, the Metropolitan News Service, confirmed that he had worked until after midnight. Probably he had stopped in for a few drinks. The corpse still exuded the smell of alcohol.

A check of the neighbors in this middle-class section came up empty. No one had heard a shot or had seen anyone on the street. They were almost all asleep at the time, and the killer had surely used a silencer.

Boxley had been murdered no more than fifty feet from his house. Forcing their way into the premises, the detectives stepped gingerly through a mess on Boxley's bedroom floor. Drawers were emptied and clothes were strewn everywhere.

In a small study, an old rolltop desk stood empty. Notes and manuscripts—the detritus of one man's unsuccessful life, however precious to Boxley—were scattered. Nothing they found pointed to any reason for murder.

Mrs. Boxley had been with her sister in Arlington for a few days while Freddie was in the Cayman Islands on business. When informed by the police, she became hysterical, then collapsed. District Police suggested she stay with her sister.

Dennis found the rear window of the bedroom jimmied open, obviously the point of entry.

"Al, this looks to me like a contract killing. The hired killer was probably asked to find some document or whatever."

"But what?" Al asked. "Boxley was no big shot. What could he have that anyone wanted?"

Lemoine pulled a folded clipping from his pocket.

"Look at this, Al. Front page of yesterday's paper. Boxley was a reporter and he got the scoop of his life—found the identity of that mystery billionaire who's anteing up $100 million for the presidential campaign. Maybe that's what ties this all together. Someone wanted to find out what else he knew, then decided to shut him up forever."

Lemoine walked silently around the room. "Make sure everything is put into glassine bags and marked. If anything could have prints, give it to forensic. OK?"

He didn't expect any fingerprints. There never were any in professional jobs. Maybe Boxley was up to his ears in some political deal. Maybe that was the route to follow.

Who gained from searching Boxley's house for who knows what reason? Lemoine asked himself. And who gained from killing him? Was it Rafferty, the guy who was giving away all that cash? Or Charlie Palmer, the presidential nominee who was on the receiving end? But why? He'd have to talk to them.

His only fear was that he—a mere District homicide hound—was getting in over his head.

"There's a D.C. detective to see you," Sally said in a half whisper as she walked into Charlie's inner office. "Looks like the same guy who came to the hospital when I got hit by the car."

Sally had broken his reverie, a daydream of Clara. He was forty-three and had never been truly in love before. Pickiness and unfilled fantasies had stood in his way. Never before had he been fully satisfied with his women friends. He wanted them a bit more beautiful, better dressed, more clever, a little sweeter. The result? A lousy love life, and on-and-off sexual existence coupled with a sense of incompleteness that hung over his psyche day in and day out.

But now? God—or politics—had thrown him into Clara's magnificent net, and he was thrilled to have been caught. Just after his time in bed with her, he asked himself—"How long has this been going on?" Never had he experienced such joy, not just in sex, but in love. Or at least by him and perhaps some artful portrayal of it by Clara.

Did Clara want him for his true self? Or was she a power player merely attracted to his Washington fame?

What a ridiculous question. If he had stayed in Fairview, would he ever have met a woman like Clara, a gorgeous, wealthy widow, the doyenne of the capital's social scene? And if by a fluke, say, he had met her in a hotel lobby during a software convention in Washington, would she have given him, a small-town marketing executive, the time of day? Of course not. And he wouldn't blame her.

What in the hell was our true self but the sum of our experience, including that which was new, ephemeral, and perhaps quite fleeting.

Clara possibly didn't love him. The most he could hope for was that she was infatuated with him, at least for the time being.

But he? He would go to the ends of the earth to be with her. She had devoured him, not just sexually, but in his spirit, his total being. He wanted nothing more—not even the Oval Office. Only Clara.

He smiled at the thought of her most recent invitation. She'd asked him over to Maison Grise for a quiet dinner tonight. For afterward, she had the video of a new film hit, the gift of a movie lobbyist. But don't expect super-festivities like the other night, she warned Charlie. Too much too soon would turn him into an unappreciative, jaded suitor.

But, she added, she had enjoyed herself immensely. Once again, she'd felt like Florence Nightingale, this time for breaking his four-month drought of manliness.

Now his reverie was being interrupted by a District detective. Who and why?

"I'm Detective Sergeant Samuel Lemoine of District homicide," the man, a relatively short black policeman, said for openers.

Charlie watched as Lemoine squinted. "Oh, I remember you," the detective blurted out. "Your assistant got hit by a car and we suspected attempted murder. I met you at the hospital, Congressman."

Lemoine took the unlit cigar out of his hand and placed it in his mouth, starting a slow chew.

"That's right, Detective. Did you ever learn anything about the driver of the car—I think it was a white Ford Taurus?"

"No, Congressman. From your list, we checked out all your political enemies, but they all came up clean. There are no further leads, so we've dropped the case."

"So why are you here, today, Sergeant? Am I suspected of anything except annoying the voters?"

Lemoine gave out a reluctant chuckle.

"No, not suspected of anything. But maybe you could shed some light on a murder we just uncovered."

"And who's the corpse?"

"Freddie Boxley, a newsman. Did you ever meet him?"

"Boxley? No, never heard of him. What does he do?"

"He's the reporter who broke the Rafferty story."

"No, I didn't notice the byline. By why would anyone want to kill him?"

"That's why I'm here. I spoke to Mr. Rafferty by phone, and he said he did notice the byline. But he says he holds no animosity. After all, Boxley was just doing his job. Rafferty said he respects that. Seems like a nice guy for a billionaire."

Lemoine transferred the cigar to his hand. He pushed away a small table in the cramped quarters so he could sit in the chair opposite Charlie.

"But tell me, Congressman," the detective continued. "How do you and Rafferty *really* feel about Boxley having told the world your secret? Must have aggravated you no end. Right?"

"Wrong. To be honest, Sergeant, I couldn't care less. Mr. Rafferty would have preferred to keep it secret, but I'm sure he'll live with it. And he's not the type to get involved in violence."

Lemoine nodded, got up, and moved toward the door.

"Still, there's got to be a reason why somebody ransacked Boxley's place, then killed him. You sure you have no idea, Congressman?"

"Not in the slightest. But if I learn anything, I'll call you."

The detective left and Charlie returned to his reverie about Clara.

"Could it last?" he asked himself. Then he realized that there was no answer to that self-query. Life, like politics, was up to the gods.

Suddenly, the phone rang. Sally had obviously put someone right through without asking him.

"Who is this?" Charlie asked.

"Congressman Palmer, you'll have to excuse me. Perhaps my call is not appreciated. This is Senator John Larrimore of Oklahoma."

CHAPTER 27

The bank of pay phones in the Longworth House Office Building was finally empty. The caller dialed the party headquarters on M Street and asked for Andy Tolliver. The voice was strained, sounding neither feminine nor masculine, a kind of unisex disguise.

"Who shall I say is calling?" the operator asked.

"Tell him it's Justinian, with word from Congressman Charles Palmer."

The caller turned inward so as not to be recognized by passersby. Finally, Tolliver's gravel drawl came on.

"Justinian? Who the hell are you? And what's the good word from Charlie, the Ohio psycho? That he's dead?" Tolliver laughed. "And why are you bothering a busy man like me?"

"I hope I'm not a bother. I work in the Palmer camp and I'm privy to most of what's going on. I'd like to keep you informed—in the hope it'll help you to stifle his movement."

"Are you kidding me, Justinian? And are you a man or woman? Your voice is high enough for a girl's chorus."

"That's not important, Tolliver. I just want to sign on."

"Oh, yeah? This is probably a disinformation gambit. I wouldn't put it past Mr. Self-Righteous to pull more dirty tricks than we have in our inventory. Do you have any bona fides—information I can use right now? Something to prove you're not a double plant?"

"As a matter of fact I do. Candidate Palmer just got a call from Senator Larrimore, your Grand Old Man. The congressman's going over there in the morning. I thought you might want to feel out the senator before the meeting."

"Larrimore and Charlie? How come?" Tolliver was confused. "Why would Larrimore call Palmer after everything that's happened? What did he say?"

Tolliver's voice rose after each rapid-fire question.

"Only that he wanted to see him in his Senate office. But I don't think it's just a social visit."

"Justinian, I appreciate your help and I hope we can get together personally sometime. But tell me, what's in it for you? How much do you want for your services?"

"Nothing, Tolliver. I don't need or want your money. Just doing my patriotic duty. My boss, Congressman Palmer, is moving rapidly toward destroying our political traditions, and I want to stop him before the Republic is irreparably harmed. Being on the inside, I can be of great help to you. And I'd like you to share your information with everyone on our side—if you can trust them. I've got to go now."

"But, Justinian. When will I hear from you again?" Tolliver almost shouted into the phone. But all he could hear was a dial tone. His new contact in the Palmer campaign had hung up.

CHAPTER 28

In his short time in Washington, Charlie had learned that the distance between his closetlike office in the Longworth Building and the Hart Senate Office Building, where Larrimore had his, might be short in yards, but was enormous in psychic and historic proportions.

Larrimore's Senate office was on the second floor of a building that had cost $138 million in 1982, but would take a half billion to replace. It was a marble Roman palace, much larger than those in the Forum, where the ancients were more modest (except in Hollywood films) than their modern imitators.

The Hart Building was a temple to the power of one hundred senators, whose very number added austerity to the body's reputation as a conclave of solons. Rather than be squashed onto continuous benches as in the House chambers, each senator had his or her own desk, some as old as Daniel Webster's—sought-after pieces of antiquity in this tradition-conscious assembly.

Before Charlie started his walk, he had read up on Larrimore's establishment. As senator from Oklahoma, he had forty-five employees, about ten times as many as his predecessors in the 1940s, when Congress had only four thousand employees. Today there were thirty thousand employees, and Larrimore shared in the largesse.

Congress was always attacking the presidency for outrageous waste in the executive branch, but Congress was equally guilty. The growth in congressional committees was absurd, Charlie learned. After World War II, there were forty-eight committees and subcommittees in Congress. Now there were 225 in all. In the Senate, there were more committees than members! As one wag said, if anyone yelled "Mr. Chairman" in the House or Senate mess, about half the members would stand up.

Larrimore had a suite of eight rooms, plus another set at his other fiefdom, the Senate Finance Committee in the Dirksen Senate Office Building, where he was chairman. There, another twenty-eight employees answered to the call of the Senator.

Charlie felt that the whole Hill establishment was grotesque in size and cost. The congressional budget had now reached $2.3 billion, or almost $5 million per member. Despite the publicity his own cost-cutting had received, Charlie noted that none of his colleagues had picked up on his austerity budget as a model. The talk of congressional reform was mainly that—talk.

As Charlie walked the few blocks, from Independence and New Jersey to Second and Constitution, in the heat, he wondered, What could Larrimore, who had proven to be the ultimate party man, now want from him?

Well, he'd soon find out.

"Congressman, please come in."

Larrimore stood as Charlie entered. Once again, he was impressed by the senator's commanding voice and physical appearance. The Grand Old Man looked like his sobriquet. He was tall—about six feet, two inches—spare, with sharp aquiline features. Despite his seventy-two years, he had a full head of brown hair. (Was it Grecian Formula? Charlie wondered.) Like many men from the Midwest, he favored brown in his suits as well. His face had been engraved on many a campaign button, and was almost as well recognized by Americans as the sculptures on Mount Rushmore.

Charlie looked around the enormous reception room, decorated mainly in Federal-age antiques, the period when the Capitol was built at the turn of the nineteenth century. Larrimore gestured to two oversize wing chairs and they sat facing each other.

"Charles, I know I killed your chance to be named VP at the convention, but I'm delighted by what you've been doing since. I feel the same way about you as I did when I nominated you that night."

Charlie was surprised, even a bit shocked, by the accolade.

"If you feel that way, Senator, then why did you do such a last-minute about-face? Not that I care now. I'm much happier outside the party. I'm afraid that if I'd stayed they might have made me a prisoner as well."

As soon as the words "as well" came out of his mouth, Charlie regretted it.

"I'm sorry, Senator, I didn't mean to imply that you're a prisoner of the party."

"Don't apologize, Charlie. You hit it on the head. I tried to break away that night, but I failed."

"Why?" Charlie asked, showing sincere interest in a man who had once been something of a father-figure.

"It's hard to explain fifty-year-old habits, Charlie. It's like sleeping on one side of a bed, or what you have for breakfast. I was addicted to the party. I was elected a state legislator, then a House member, a senator, chairman of congressional committees, even became a presidential candidate, all with the party's help. When I tried to break away that night, they threatened me with loss of all my power—then turned the argument against you. Said you were not only untested, but a dangerous fanatic determined to break the party."

"What exactly did they say?" Charlie asked, curious what rumors they were passing.

"Lawson said Tolliver had some dirt on you, and if you were nominated as VP, you might have to withdraw. I didn't look forward to another Nixon Checkers speech. Finally, in that crucial half hour, Lawson got me alone and pounded. And so I yielded to the party."

Larrimore stopped, apparently short of breath.

"And, Congressman Palmer. I'm humbly sorry for what I did. It was a grave mistake and an insult to the country."

Charlie was overwhelmed by Larrimore's candor.

"But why tell me this now?"

"Because despite all that silly dirt on the Leland show, you've had the courage to take that final step toward independence—courage I didn't have. The party was my home, but no more. Like you, I'm fed up. Only you did it in a few months and it took me half a century."

Charlie suddenly rose to Larrimore's defense.

"But, Senator, for many years the parties were of great service to America. The worst of the philosophical corruption is only a few decades old, heightened by television and the mad race for money. Now we need a new view and that's why I've left them."

"Exactly, Charles. Members are deserting the Senate because they're as fed up as I am. But I'm not just leaving. I hope to do something constructive about it."

"And what are you thinking of, Senator?" Charlie asked, his curiosity rising.

"Well, first off, Andy Tolliver knows about this meeting. Someone tipped him—I think a spy in your office."

Charlie was distressed by the news of a spy. This was more than the small leaks his staff had learned about.

"A spy? Who was it? What did he say?" Charles asked, apprehensively.

"I have no idea who it was. He told Tolliver that I wanted to speak to you about something important. Tolliver immediately called me. I told him about my plans and he tried desperately to talk me out of it, just as Lawson did at the convention. But not this time. I'm sticking to my guns, and . . ."

"Yes?"

"And, simply, I'm leaving the party in protest and becoming an independent. I can now do one of two things. One is to run for reelection to the Senate without the party. I think I can win that race. Or, two . . ." Larrimore hesitated.

"Or?"

"Or join you and help build an independent alternative to the parties in the presidential race."

Larrimore walked over to an antique desk and leaned over its polished surface.

"Charlie, it's hard for an old man to eat crow, but I'm going to do just that. I turned Lawson down when he asked me to be VP. But now I'd like to join you in the number two spot—to get your nomination as Vice President on your independent slate. I think I could add solidity and experience to the ticket."

Larrimore lowered his head. "I'll give you a day or two to think it over."

Charlie feared he couldn't keep up with all the change. But in the fierce tide of modern politics, he knew it was swim or else.

"I don't need ten seconds, Senator. Your presence as VP adds maturity to my bomb throwing. I'm honored to accept your offer to join me."

Charlie got up, and in a sign of respect between the generations, reached out both hands and grasped Larrimore's.

"Senator Larrimore, I think Jefferson would be proud."

CHAPTER 29

Martha Boxley feverishly opened the two large UPS boxes that had been delivered to her door.

Inside, she discovered the glassine envelopes with her dead husband's effects, originally taken by Detective Lemoine. As his note explained, none held leads to the killer of Fred Boxley.

Fred had gained a posthumous celebrity among reporters for his gumshoe work in the Caymans. That meant something to Martha, whose insolvent husband had left her almost nothing except a small insurance policy. Strange that she should have married a reporter—she a bookkeeper with a practical eye.

That eye came into play the moment she opened the UPS boxes. She didn't believe that Fred's murder was a case of random breaking and entering. More likely it was connected to Freddie's newspaper work, either the Rafferty story or another case.

Someone was obviously afraid that Freddie had evidence that could incriminate them. That's why the house had been ransacked and her husband killed, she was convinced. The last person anyone would want to rob was Freddie Boxley, who never had more than $20 on him at a time.

She started her search through his effects, one by one. In the sixth envelope she found a sheet of paper with the same signature written on it, over and over, in what looked like Freddie's handwriting. The name on it was peculiar: Fred James. Of course, they were her husband's first and middle names.

The rest of the search turned up nothing, but the name Fred James was seared into her mind. Why would her husband write down only two of his three names? Obviously, it must be part of a secret checking account, or a contract, or some such shenanigans. A nom de plume, an incognito.

What was he trying to hide? And from whom?

The first step was the Riggs Bank where they had a joint safe deposit box. In it, she kept jewelry her mother had left her, Freddie's small insurance policy, and the deed to their house.

At the local bank branch, she approached the manager. "Mr. Foster, you know that my husband was killed. I've taken possession of our deposit box," she reminded him.

"Yes, Mrs. Boxley, I know. But what can I help you with now?" Foster seemed a bit unsure.

"Well, I wonder if Freddie had a second bank account or another security box here?"

"No, Mrs. Boxley, we've already checked that. Nothing else in the name of Fred Boxley."

"Oh, I know that. What I'd like you to check is under the name of Fred James."

"Fred James? Wasn't James Mr. Boxley's middle name?"

"Exactly. The police found a piece of paper on which Freddie was practicing that signature. I brought it with me." Martha handed the worn document to the bank manager.

"One minute, Mrs. Boxley." The manager booted up his computer and typed in "Fred James."

"No, there's no account in that name. But if you'll wait, I'll go downstairs and check our safe deposit records."

Martha waited an interminable three minutes. Fred couldn't be brought back, but she was building a compulsive resolve to track down his murderer. His $20,000 insurance policy meant she could spend some time playing detective.

"My God, Mrs. Boxley. It looks like you've hit it on the head. We have a safe deposit box in the name of Fred James, and the signature card exactly matches the sheet you gave me!"

The manager was astounded, perhaps a bit thrilled to be thrust into the midst of a murder mystery.

"Good, Mr. Foster. Could you please open the box for me?"

"I'm afraid that's not possible, Mrs. Boxley. I *know* it was your husband's safe deposit, but it's not in his real name. You'll have to get an order from probate court permitting me to open it. Bring along this signature sheet, and get a statement from the police that they found it in your house. Maybe the court will go along. But until I get a court order, I'm afraid the box stays here—unopened."

Martha felt a small defeat, but only for an instant.

"I'll be back, Mr. Foster. You can bet on it."

CHAPTER 30

King Kellogg cast an approving eye over his conference room. He had taken the architect's sketch for the renovation and added touches that transformed the prosaic into the gifted.

It was eclectic but not ostentatious. He had placed a mahogany ledge around the room, and set a series of objets d'art, from pre-Columbian fertility statutes to Steuben glass prisms and miniature Giacometti-like pieces of metal sculpture, every few feet. Above them, on the wall, were signed lithos and estamps by Picasso, Mondrian, Bracque, and other post-Impressionists.

Each morning, a young assistant kept them spotless. Spores, insects, dust—any category of misplaced matter—upset his well-ordered world.

But what really disturbed his organized existence was the headline in the morning paper, staring up at him from his long teak table. He could feel a small migraine coming on.

SENATOR LARRIMORE JOINS INDEPENDENT TICKET IN VP SLOT;
PUBLIC SUPPORT FOR PALMER JUMPS FIVE POINTS

The Larrimore candidacy was the latest affront. Who would ever believe the Grand Old Man would not only leave his party, but join Charlie? *Incroyable!* He was lending distinction to what was a ragtag middle-class operation. Now it had money from Rafferty, brains and balls from Palmer, and experience from Larrimore.

Kellogg had no favorite in the upcoming election—as long as Charlie didn't win. He had befriended both Tolliver and Sobel, and vice versa. But Palmer was another matter, and thus far all attempts to destroy the anti-politician had failed. He thought Leland's exposé would demonize him, but he was wrong. It had hurt Charlie initially, but the latest poll showed he had recovered, and his prestige was now heightened by the John Larrimore defection.

Charlie's numbers were up to 26 percent. Billings was at 36 and his opposition, former Governor Arthur Steadman of Idaho, held 34 percent, with four percent for the fringe parties and all "undecideds" split proportionately.

Not quite a horse race, but troubling enough to irritate. King put a finger to his right temple, feeling a quickened pulse, his barometer of any disorder or delay.

Today he had scheduled a meeting with the Billings-Tolliver people. Norm Sobel had wanted to attend, but realized the danger. The press often staked out King's place for the comings and goings of leading politicians with their hands extended. Instead, Kellogg had scheduled a separate gabfest with Sobel and Jason Hollingsworth, their vice presidential candidate. Steadman, the ticket head, had gracefully declined.

King stared anxiously at his Patek-Phillipe watch. The other participants were already two minutes late, with just thirty seconds leeway left. At that instant, he brightened. Billings and Tolliver had just come through the door.

Thirty seconds later, Clara joined them. Her hat, a 1930s-style pyramid of faux leopard with a small feather, was almost as exquisite as she. God, why hadn't he tried out his latent manliness with her? It would be better therapy than all the sex experts who were bleeding him for $300 an hour.

Only Senator Harry Berry of Nevada—chosen by the party as Billings's vice presidential candidate—had yet to arrive. Kellogg tapped his thin gold pencil on the table, checking his Patek until Berry stormed through the door.

"Welcome, Harry," Kellogg said to the large-framed Westerner, who dressed as if his horse were double-parked. Kellogg's smile was more forced than usual as hellos were exchanged all around.

"Shall we begin?" Kellogg asked rhetorically once they were seated around his conference table.

"Good. I'm afraid that the Palmer situation is more serious than we envisioned. With Larrimore in the number two spot, Palmer now has respectability, and is no longer the head of a radical fringe group. I'm not a member of your party—or any party—so I won't discuss strategy against your friendly opposition," King reminded then. "My concern is the two-party system, the lifeblood of the political nation, and my bread and butter. The enemy here is Charlie Palmer, and now the renegade Larrimore. We need a strategy."

Kellogg turned to Clara. "Could you start by filling us in on Charlie? I understand you've made contact."

Clara opened her suit jacket. As she leaned back, her bosom caught the eye of nominee Champ Billings, who seemed taken with her.

"Oh, yes, excellent contact," Clara confirmed, "if I say so myself. We're now good friends and he trusts me."

"Good. And I presume you've gotten some valuable intelligence from him?"

He could see Clara fidget. "Well, some, but not as much as I would hope. I've gotten a copy of their 'Green Book,' their campaign strategy, but Tolliver tells me he's already received it from another source, a spy inside their headquarters. I think the name is Justinian. Am I right, Andy?"

Tolliver nodded as Clara continued, her voice still hesitant. "I've delivered a few memos to Andy on the Palmer organization, but nothing earth-shaking. To be honest, these people are too open to make much political espionage worthwhile. They don't seem to lie or even consider dirty tricks."

Kellogg listened intently. "But I suppose you've tried to talk him out of his race for the White House?"

"Quite the opposite, King. If Charlie had stayed in the party, he'd turn Congress upside down. What with new Turks coming in every two years, he'd lead that pack and you'd see a real revolution. No, right after the Leland attack I encouraged him to continue. That way if he loses the race for President this November—as everyone expects—he'll be on his way back to Ohio and out of your hair."

Billings, the presidential nominee, continued to ravish Clara with his eyes. A former banker from Lexington, Kentucky, he looked the role. Medium height, thin, with a mustache, he was almost a Clifton Webb look-alike.

"That makes sense, Clara. I'm glad we've got you on the inside," Billings announced to a small titter from the group.

Party boss Tolliver moved uncomfortably in his chair, one designed for aesthetics, not to accommodate someone his enormous size.

"Tell me, Clara," Tolliver asked. "Can we make a deal with Charlie Bastard—you know, money, ambassadorship, committee chair?"

She threw back her head and laughed so raucously that her 1930s pyramid hat threatened to fall off.

"Deal with Charlie? No, that would only super-energize him. You're dealing with a strange man. He's totally incorruptible when it comes to money or power. Has no interest in either. He hears only one drum and that's inside of him. Has no guile, no strategies. In a way, a very innocent, even naive, person."

"Doesn't he have any weaknesses?" Tolliver kept probing.

"Oh yes, I would say two. One is loneliness. He's perfectly virile but he wants everything in a woman—that's why he's not married. So I suppose until he met me, he was quite lonely."

"And the second weakness?"

"He's not as confident as the world thinks. With all his bravado, he's a small boy in a way, even a Walter Mitty character. Perhaps a Don Quixote, daydreaming up a storm, then tilting at every possible windmill. The difference is that somehow, some way, Charles seems to turn his fantasies into reality. There's a kind of destiny about him."

Kellogg stared into Clara's eyes.

"Sounds to me like you like this fella."

Clara blushed. "I never really thought about it, King, but I suppose I do. He's really very nice. Maybe a crazy bomb thrower, but a pleasant and exciting one."

"Does that interfere with your work—your hopes for the party?"

Clara didn't answer for a moment.

"I sincerely hope not, King. We've all got a job to do."

Clara listened less closely as the others droned on about their campaign against Charlie.

They had the attorneys general in states they controlled defending against Charlie's lawsuits on early filing dates for presidential electors. Norm Sobel, the other party campaign chief, was doing the same, Tolliver explained. To counter them for Palmer, George Sempel had hired the best law firms, some with partners who had been state supreme court judges.

The fifty secretaries of state were redoubling their scrutiny of the Palmer petitions, searching for minuscule errors to disqualify them. Charlie needed some nine hundred thousand names nationally, and over one million had already come in. But Tolliver expected that number could be cut back after their challenges.

"No sense having a two-party system if we can't use it to keep interlopers out," she heard Andy say.

For a few minutes, Clara tuned out the meeting completely, thinking about Charlie and their relationship.

Had she done anything that had betrayed him? What did she want for him? God, he seemed so happy, so much in love—either with her or, more likely, with his vision of her as the perfect woman. Beautiful, sensual, intelligent. Maybe. But Charlie had yet to come into real contact with her fantasies.

But he was not alone in that. Neither had she. Would Charlie help her deal with reality? Or would he drive her deeper into fantasy? She had no idea. But she did admit that as of now, her little game with Charlie Palmer was making her happy, if confused. All she could say was that she liked, maybe loved, his presence around her, in and out of bed.

Suddenly, she picked up the voices of Tolliver and Kellogg again. They were talking about Synergy, Charles's former company.

"All his independent wealth, and that of George Sempel, come from their stock holdings in Synergy, that Ohio software company," Kellogg was explaining, "That means that right now they have no money worries. I suggest we create some."

"How can we do that? Their friend Rafferty's pockets are almost as deep as Uncle Sam's," Billings pointed out.

"Yes, but from what Clara says, Charlie is too independent to take any money for his personal use. If we can hurt Synergy, we could make both him and Sempel financially insecure—and less effective."

"What do you suggest?" Tolliver asked.

"Andy, it's quite simple. Between you and Norm Sobel, you can talk to the right people and knock the props out of any government contracts that Synergy has or is pitching for. From what I hear, that's about half their software business. We probably can't bankrupt them, but we can also try to manipulate their stock and bring down its price—and their personal wealth with it. That should put a worry line or two in their faces."

Clara listened. She could feel her usual impeccable poise crumbling inside. Shouldn't Charlie know about this? Or was secrecy the price she had agreed to pay when she entered this game?

God, sometimes she wished she had never met the man. She was violating her principles by becoming emotionally involved. That alone seemed to be affecting her values. They might be distorted, but they were her own.

When the meeting ended, Champ Billings helped Kellogg usher the other guests out, then approached him.

"Could we go to your office, King," the presidential nominee asked. "I've got something very confidential to discuss."

"Surely, Senator. Come this way."

In his inner sanctum, Kellogg poured Billings a glass of Lafite Rothschild as they sat in Benjamin Randolph wing chairs from Philadelphia, circa 1770, which had cost him $300,000.

"So what's on your mind, Champ?" King asked. "And by the way, I had to make the Palmer incursion seem more serious that it probably is. I think you're as good as in the Oval Office."

"Thanks for the encouragement, King, but I don't fool myself.

There's still a threat, no matter how small. What I need from you is some personal financial advice. My bank balance is suffering anemia."

Kellogg was surprised. He had always assumed that Billings was himself a millionaire. He had visited his mansion in Lexington, a marvelous example of antebellum architecture.

"Yes, Champ. Shoot away."

"Well, I appreciate the million dollars for the party—and of course for my campaign—that you obtained from the Pemenex people. That all helps. But I've also got to look out for my personal financial security. If I win the White House, I'm secure. My God, the memoirs alone would bring in millions. But what if I lose? My Senate term is up, you know."

"How about your Senate pension?" King asked. "That should be in the six figures each year. Am I right?"

"Yes, my pension is good, but hardly enough for my style of living. King, I promised Pemenex a veto of any hasty mining bill if I win. But if I lose, I need some insurance from those foreign people. Something to tide me over, something to encourage me to keep my pledge if I win. You know what I mean?"

Having spent his life in politics, often at its steamiest, Kellogg shouldn't have been surprised, but he was. After all, he was talking to the man favored to be the next President of the United States. Still, he reminded himself that everyone was human, and not everyone was as rich as he.

"I fully understand, Champ, and I guarantee you that I'll make some arrangement with Pemenex. They have a lot to lose if you turn your back on them. So take my word for it. I'll get an airtight insurance policy from Berlin and Taipei—with absolutely no premiums."

Billings's face brightened. "Good, King. I knew I could rely on you. You're a solid American."

CHAPTER 31

"Would you please tell Mr. Don Leland that Mrs. Boxley, Mrs. Fred Boxley, is here to see him?"

"Do you have an appointment?" The receptionist at the television network asked the question with that air of disdainful importance adopted by underling guardians of the mighty.

"No, I don't. But tell him I'm the widow of the newsman who was murdered—the reporter who broke the Rafferty story."

The receptionist stared at Martha Boxley. She had no idea who she was, but there was something tragic in her face. Leland had told her to keep the public out, but he had also said to tip him to anyone who might make news. If this lady's husband was a newsman and had been murdered, maybe . . .

Helping break a story was surely the way up, perhaps even to a job as a production assistant, who were mostly young women like herself.

Walking back to the studio, she saw that the red "On Air" light was off. Through the small glass window, she spotted Leland sitting in a canvas director's chair, papers of some sort on his lap. Slowly, she opened the door a few inches.

"Mr. Leland," the receptionist whispered. "Can I speak with you?"

He looked up sharply. "Don't whisper, kid. We're not on the air. Come in. What is it?"

"There's a lady outside who wants to see you. Says she's the widow of the newsman who broke some case. He was murdered. I thought it might be a story."

Leland's expression turned cynical. "Honey, newsmen are involved in crime stories every day. Washington is the murder capital of the world. That's local stuff. Tell her to write me a letter. I'm busy checking my intro for Sunday's show."

The receptionist walked away, crushed.

"Mrs. Boxley, I told him who you were, but he said no," she informed the widow on her return. "He said to write him a letter."

The visitor's face turned so purplish-red that the receptionist became frightened.

"Mrs. Boxley, you'd better sit down. You could have a stroke."

"No, honey, that phony Don Leland will have one when I get through with him. Did you tell him everything I said?"

"Yes, I thought it sounded important but he didn't. He probably knows better than we do."

"Like hell he does." Martha Boxley's anger was percolating. "Did you mention the Rafferty name? Did you tell him my husband wrote the Rafferty story?"

The receptionist's expression turned blank. Had she mentioned Rafferty? No, she didn't think so.

"Why, is that name important?" the young woman asked.

"Only a hundred million dollars' worth, that's all. Now go back and tell Leland that my dead husband wrote the Rafferty story. Remember—Rafferty!"

The young receptionist took wing. "Mr. Leland," she said, barging into the studio. "The lady said to tell you that it involves a Mr. Rafferty and $100 million."

The newsman swiveled in his chair. "Why in the hell didn't you say that to begin with? Where is she now?"

When the receptionist pointed, Leland rose, straightened his shirt and tie, put on his suit jacket, then rushed toward the reception area.

His voice was calculatingly casual. "Madam, this young woman says you have some information regarding your husband and Schuyler Rafferty. Is that true?"

Hurriedly, emotionally, but still rationally, Mrs. Boxley recounted the tale, up to her meeting with the bank manager.

"I've gotten the court order and they've opened the safe deposit box. I found this cassette in there. I've listened to it. It's real juicy, especially for someone like you. I'm convinced this is why my husband was killed and the house ransacked. The murderer was looking for this cassette."

"Why didn't you take it to the police? Maybe it would help solve the murder," Leland asked, insincerely. He didn't want to be accused of suppressing evidence.

"I thought of that, but I want you to listen to it first, then do something big on the air. If I gave it to the police now, they might not let you play it. I want people to know why Freddie was killed. I'll give it to the police right after that."

"I understand, Mrs. Boxley. Leave the tape with me. Meanwhile, don't say a word to anyone. Leave your phone number with the receptionist."

Mrs. Boxley seemed a touch hesitant. "Only if you swear to listen to it and take it seriously."

"I swear, Mrs. Boxley," Leland assured her. "Especially if it's as important as you think it is.

In the studio next door, Leland listened to the tape.

It opened with Boxley explaining how he had got the Rafferty scoop. Obviously the reporter had dubbed the original to add his narration. That was interesting, but hardly explosive. But of course that's why he had paid attention to Mrs. Boxley in the first place.

But then the tape veered in another, fascinating, unexpected direction. Boxley was narrating the events leading up to this recording, which involved the campaign chiefs of the two parties. He described his hunch, and how he followed Tolliver to a greasy spoon in Baltimore, away from the prying eyes of the Beltway—or so the party boss thought.

Then, suddenly, other voices, surrounded by the tinkling of glasses and dishes, came on.

My God, it was a clandestine meeting between Tolliver and Sobel. Pure dynamite. As Leland listened to them conspire against Charlie Palmer, his cynicism about politicians was being confirmed in real time. The two must be crazy to meet that way. The pressure of bomb thrower Palmer had obviously pushed them over the edge. But, of course, they had no idea anyone was listening in. Still, for the campaign honchos of the two major parties to meet secretly and plot Palmer's political demise was shocking, even to an unshockable like himself.

A troubling thought nagged at him. Could the duo also have planned Boxley's murder to shut him up? Did they suspect that he had stashed away a tape of their unprecedented confab—only to have it come back and haunt them after his death?

Kellogg's name had surfaced as well on the tape. What did King have to do with this political fiasco? Or, knowing King, what didn't he have to do with it?

Boxley had done a great reporting job and might have gotten a Pulitzer had he lived. Maybe now the Pulitzer would go to Leland instead. Naturally, he'd give Boxley a posthumous plug.

He wasn't thrilled about helping super-moralizer Palmer. But with this sordid two-party gang-up, the young presidential candidate was looking better all the time.

Leland wondered what the Pulitzer Prize looked like. Did they have a statue like the Oscar? He had a spot picked out on his office mantel, where the network brass, who kept fretting about his age and his declining ratings, could see it every day.

CHAPTER 32

Clara didn't enjoy pacing around her bedroom, but Charles had forced her into a punishing self-examination.

Never had she met a man of such proportions. She could look into his soul and find nothing to hate. His politics? Well, that was something else. Lord knows she was no theorist, but her lover seemed to be seeking a revolution against the likes of her.

Still, Charles was a prize. Unlike most men she had dated (or married), he was exciting, seeking new plateaus of existence every day. In that regard, they were soulmates. For her, routine was a depressant, one that she dreaded almost as much as death itself.

Not that she was bad, but there was no denying that she strived, almost compulsively, to escape what had been an early life of struggle in a poor immigrant family in Pittsburgh. Then she was just Clara Kosmicki, the daughter of a truck driver and the victim of unwanted advances from men from the time she was thirteen.

She dreamed of exchanging that life for one that matched youthful fantasies that then seemed beyond her grasp. Finally, Clara had decided to exploit her God-given charms, and had since realized her dreams, and much more.

Now Charles was challenging everything she stood for. She had been loved by many men, in and out of marriage, including some she found almost loathsome. But never had she experienced love herself—until Charles. She wasn't sure if she truly loved him, or if it was the infatuation of a belated adolescence. But she did enjoy him immensely. He was so bright, so exciting, and in his own quiet way (except when he was horribly bombastic about politics), so reasonable.

And what was she doing in return? She was spying on him. She was in an alliance with the political establishment to destroy him, to preserve her party, her position in life.

That tore at her, but what was she to do?

After an uphill struggle in which she often held on solely by her polished fingernails, she had finally created an idyllic existence. Charles had now come into the picture, both to enhance and to upset her equilibrium. When she was with him, life was like Nirvana. His kisses, his consideration, his extraordinary place in the American firmament, made her feel like the fairy princess she had conjured up in her depressing puberty.

But when she contemplated the compromise she had agreed to with Tolliver, Kellogg, Billings, et al. against her new lover, she felt shamed, even truly angry at herself. During her whole purposeful ascent, she never once felt remorse. What she had done, she needed to do to survive, and win.

Now she was feeling shame for the first time. Why? Because Charles deserved better than deceit, even if she was rather ineffectual in her Mata Hari role.

She could not continue with divided loyalties. She sat at her desk and took out a piece of gold-embossed stationery. Yes, she would tell Charles that she could not see him anymore. She wouldn't speak of her mission of betrayal, which was causing her daily pain no matter how little she put it into practice. She would just say that their politics were diametrically opposed.

Clara picked up her pen and wrote:

"Dearest Charles. We have come to a crossroads in our relationship. We have been lovers, but we are not yet one. I don't believe that can happen because of a chasm between us that I cannot bridge. Therefore, despite the great happiness you have given me in our short romance, I have decided . . ."

Clara picked up the unfinished letter and rose from her desk. Holding it in her hand, she read it over and over, like a mantra as she paced the enormous room.

Finally, she looked out the tall windows, at the setting sun, and crumpled the note.

"The hell with conscience," she said to herself. "Where could I, or any woman, find a man like Charlie Palmer?"

With that she threw the letter into the wastebasket, knowing that she had no intention of getting rid of him. Nor did she intend to leave the party.

She would just have to live with them both as equal and integral parts of her charmed and conflicted existence.

CHAPTER 33

Don Leland stared at the Hirschfeld-like caricature of himself with the pointed chin and the blond rug and decided it'd make a good on-air trademark.

He'd asked the producer to use it on today's show, but warned him: Make sure it gave no hint that the tresses had been manufactured off his scalp. It wasn't just vanity. It was ratings, translated into dollars: $3 million a year worth.

He wondered. How much was that a hair?

As he prepared for his 428th Sunday morning show, Leland was experiencing a strange emotion for a thirty-year veteran of television. He was feeling the smallest pre-program butterflies.

Why? He had broadcast scores of exposés, converting four into Emmys. Recently, he had revealed Charlie Palmer's early life, receiving plaudits and brickbats. Yet his stomach had never before complained to his head.

The reason for his anxiety was the tape of the Baltimore diner, the guts of today's interview with party campaign bosses Andy Tolliver and Norm Sobel. Leland couldn't predict what his guests would do when confronted, and he hated the unpredictable.

With a cassette player under his arm, he moved onto the set just as the young assistant producer seated his guests. Instead of the usual bucket seats, which couldn't handle Tolliver's rear, Leland had asked for upholstered club chairs. Taking his own seat on the raised circular platform, he acknowledged Tolliver and Sobel.

"Good morning, gentlemen. We'll start in a minute. Take a little

172

water to wet the whistle," was all he said. He'd found that some of the best dialogue was wasted off camera.

The music played and Leland's voice rose gradually, from a soft confidential tone to a powerful baritone, Cronkite-like.

"Good Sunday morning, everyone. This is Don Leland, watching the capital of your world, Washington, D.C. No holds barred, no subject too delicate, no one exempt from scrutiny.

"Under the political microscope today are the hired heads of our two parties, which have always claimed the privilege of running our country because they represent the people. But that's changing as independent candidates for office, as high as the presidency, throw their hats into the ring.

"Why? Because voters increasingly associate the major parties with influence peddling, lobbying, bloated campaign financing, self-interest, egotism, favors for favors—the old Tammany Hall system.

"My guests, the modern political bossess—Andy Tolliver and Norm Sobel—are usually quite uncivil with each other. But this morning, they've agreed to appear together, civilly, to discuss their weakening role and the appearance of a joint enemy, presidential candidate Charles Palmer. So tell me, starting with Mr. Tolliver: What do you think of Palmer and his movement?"

Tolliver awkwardly shifted his weight.

"Well, Don, I disagree with every word in your introduction. From the time of the Federalists and Anti-Federalists—John Adams and Tom Jefferson—Americans have looked to the two parties for wisdom and strength. Can you imagine Abe Lincoln without the Republican Party, or FDR without the Democrats? No, the two-party system *is* America, and most people intuitively know it. As for Palmer, he's a clever showman who's caught some people's imagination. But he'll fade come this fall and, like all independent presidential candidates, end up as a footnote in the *World Almanac*."

Leland shifted his eyes. "And, Mr. Sobel, tell me, are you alarmed enough by Mr. Palmer to get together with your natural enemy, Mr. Tolliver here, and gang up on the independent?"

Sobel put down his unlit pipe. He looked quizzically, first at Leland, then at Tolliver, who was grimacing. Unlike Tolliver, Sobel was considered the intellectual of party brass, noted for ideas rather than tactics, the specialty of Tolliver.

"God, no, Don. The only communication between myself and Tolliver is charge and counter-charge. Charlie Palmer is just a radical aberration who'll soon be old news. My real enemy is sitting right there, Mr. Andy Tolliver, campaign chief of the opposition."

"You agree, Mr. Tolliver?" Leland asked.

"Absolutely. That's what it's all about."

Leland looked into the camera, leaning forward for emphasis. "Good. Then you fellows won't mind if I play a piece of this tape?"

Leland pressed the play button and smiled into the camera. He cast a side glance at his guests, who seemed anxious, shifting in their chairs.

"Listen well," Leland told his audience. The sound was scratchy, but quite audible. Tolliver's voice came on first.

"Norm, we meet in strange circumstances in a strange dump where nobody, thank God, is going to recognize or hear us. It wouldn't look good— the campaign chiefs of the two big parties in collusion, hiding away in a greasy spoon in Baltimore. But I had to talk to you about our mutual enemy, that crazy Charlie Palmer. The phones can't be trusted and we can't be seen together in Washington . . ."

The two guests looked at each other, their faces registering a combination of fear and anger. Tolliver moved his massive body from side to side, hoping to extricate himself from the club chair.

"NOW WAIT A GOD DAMN MINUTE, LELAND. DID YOU INVITE US HERE FOR A SANDBAGGING?" he exploded. "I JUST WON'T TOLERATE IT!"

Sobel's complexion turned ghastly white. He rose quickly from his chair and walked off the dais, the camera following his tweedy presence across the sound stage and out the exit door. Tolliver, having finally struggled to his feet, started to follow Sobel out, his waddle exaggerated by his speed.

But Tolliver suddenly stopped and changed directions. He walked right up to the camera, pushing his now-florid face into its eye. His expression was coldly contemptuous.

"ANOTHER EXAMPLE OF PRESS BIAS. CHARLIE PALMER IS OBVIOUSLY THEIR NEW BOY," he shouted, then left, stage right.

Leland couldn't resist a laugh. Never in thirty years had anyone walked off his set. One man had died in the chair, but no one had walked off. He was making history, of a sort.

When the guests were gone, the camera panned the empty seats. Leland stared into the camera, his sincere look redoubled.

"Folks, let me set the stage for what has just happened. This audio-tape was secretly made in a Baltimore diner where the two campaign chiefs had traveled incognito in order to plot against independent presidential candidate Charles Palmer. They were followed there by Fred Boxley of the Metropolitan News Service, the man who broke the story that Schuyler Rafferty was bankrolling the Palmer campaign. Boxley taped the conversation and was murdered soon after, the top of his head blown off by a .44 and his corpse left to rot in the gutter. His house was ransacked, but nothing was found. Then his wife located this tape in a secret safe deposit box and brought it *exclusively* to me.

"You can tell its impact by the fact that the campaign chiefs have refused to listen to their own conniving and have walked off the set. Now, let's hear some more of their shenanigans. And try not to be too shocked. That's the way the political game is too often played in this town.

"But first, a commercial."

CHAPTER 34

"Have Tolliver and Sobel gone around the bend?" Charlie asked George as he entered the Pennsylvania Avenue headquarters, accompanied for the first time by two Secret Service escorts.

"How come you've got an official entourage?" George asked.

"Well, the joint congressional committee handling campaign security finally decided that I'm a major candidate. I suppose it's a compliment."

Charlie waved a copy of the morning paper with the screaming headline:

PARTY CAMPAIGN CHIEFS STORM OFF THE TV SET,
TAPE EXPOSES SECRET BALTIMORE RENDEZVOUS;
CLAIM TAPE WAS DOCTORED, THREATEN TO SUE.

"How silly can these guys be?" he asked rhetorically.

Moments later, when the inner circle of the staff convened in Sempel's office, smiles were bright all around. The group—including Charlie, George, Sally, Robbie, and two assistants—were trying to evaluate the newspaper reports.

"They're talking about lawsuits," George commented. "They were caught red-handed and they're screaming like banshees. Couldn't happen to nicer guys."

Everyone agreed that the exposé of the two-party conspiracy against Charlie could only help. Newspaper editorialists were having a field day.

"By conspiring in a diner forty miles from Washington," commented one daily, "the two party bosses showed their fear of the voters and connived to stop an independent movement. Shame."

The group was talking this out when Barnes announced that CNN as doing an overnight poll on the campaign. The results would be out in about twenty minutes.

"Then we'll see how the Tolliver-Sobel exposé is playing with the public," Charlie said. "I hope people haven't become so cynical that they view double dealing as normal."

"I have some news as well," George spoke up. "First, the requests for the thirty-five-point American Manifesto are coming in heavily, as are orders for our booklet of Jefferson's quotes. Secondly, there's been a breakthrough in our request for a debate with the other two candidates."

"Really? When did that happen?" Charlie was obviously pleased. "They've been stonewalling us long enough."

"This morning at six o'clock. Frontrunner Champ Billings called me at home. Woke me up. Said he changed his mind about debating you. Of course, that comes on the heels of Tolliver and Sobel making asses of themselves on television. If the offer of a three-way debate was still open, Billings said, he'd accept. Suggested two weeks before election. Just a single one-hour debate among the three major candidates."

"What did you say?" Charlie asked.

"He wanted an answer on the spot, so I accepted. I hope that was all right?"

George's voice was hesitant. Though he had been Charlie's boss for twenty years, Sempel realized he was now working for someone who might become the President.

Charlie grasped his hand. "Of course, George. Whatever you say is OK with me—as long as it's free." The good cheer became contagious.

"There's another item of business we have to face—head on," George said. "We run an open campaign with few secrets, except for our strategy bible, the Green Book. There's only four copies and it's not supposed to be copied. But it has been. Yesterday morning, I came in before the trash was emptied. In a wastebasket there was a smudged Zerox copy of a page of the book."

The candidate seemed unnerved by the news.

"I hate to hear that, George," Charlie commented. "It makes me nervous that someone is working for the other side. People listening in on my conversations is not my idea of heaven."

"Do you actually mean there's a spy in our midst?" Sally asked.

"I think I have information on that," Robbie Barnes said. "Don't jump to conclusions, but the other night—it must have been after 9 o'clock—I went into Sally's office to ask her something. She had gone home, but one of her young interns, Maggie Swanson, was reading a copy of the Green Book. She had obviously opened the secure drawer with Sally's key."

"Oh, yes," Sally interjected. "I left my keys in the office that night. I remember because my house key was on the same chain. Luckily, I had a duplicate in my car."

"So what did Maggie say when you confronted her?" George asked.

"I tried not to be harsh. Just reminded her that the book was confidential. She said she was curious about what was in the Green Book. She's a political science major and had heard that the strategy was well done. Said she was sorry and that it wouldn't happen again."

"Do you think we should bring in a private eye?" George asked the candidate.

Charlie shook his head vigorously. "No way. We'll leave the snooping to the other side. It's not our style, and it'll only escalate. Sally should be assigned to find the spy, and to double-check on Maggie. We can't afford continual leaks."

They continued the conference, but it was obvious everyone's mind was on the upcoming poll. (Charlie hated polls, but like King Canute, he knew he couldn't hold them back.) The atmosphere was a little like that among relatives waiting outside the operating room of someone undergoing a triple bypass.

Barnes had left to get on the phone with CNN. Minutes later he returned, his face expressionless.

"The results are in," he announced. "In five minutes, it'll be on the air, but they gave me an advance peek." He slipped a note to Sempel. "I think George should announce it."

Sempel studied the paper for a mere second.

"HALLELUJAH!" he shouted. "We've picked up five points. We're now thirty-one to Billings' thirty-four and Steadman's thirty-two. Just three points between the front runner and the new kid on the block!"

Charlie's smile spread across his face. "As I've always told everyone: Just keep faith with the American public and they'll respond—maybe."

After the meeting broke up, George pulled Charlie aside.

"Let's talk privately in your office," Sempel suggested. "I've got news, good and bad."

"Yes?"

"First, the federal district court in Washington has turned down Joe Burke's appeal for the injunction against the states with early closing dates."

Charlie's face fell. "What was their logic? I thought the Supreme Court had already ruled on the same question in Ohio."

"True, but they said that the Supreme Court's decision affected only Ohio, and that which happens in other states is out of their hands. Sometimes I think this is a lawless country."

"So what's good?"

Sempel's face brightened. "The good news is that Burke's idea to sue in the federal courts in the state capitals is paying off."

"Hallelujah!" Charlie said in imitation of Sempel's favorite phrase.

"Of the fifteen lawsuits, we've won in nine states. They're being ordered to push back the filing dates on the basis of discrimination against independents. But Texas is still hopeless. That suit goes back to 1988 but the local federal court refuses to get involved."

"So what does it mean?" Charlie inquired. "In how many states will we be on the ballot come November?"

"If it goes as we figure, in forty-four states."

Charlie's expression soured. "Does that mean we have no chance in those six states? Will it kill us on Election Day?"

"It doesn't help, but we can still win without them. Besides, we've got an alternative—a write-in ballot."

Charlie was confused. "Aren't write-in campaigns a waste of time?"

"Usually, but remember that we've got five million volunteers. We'll blanket those states with ads showing the sample ballot and where to write in their names. It'll be a first in American politics."

Moments later, Charlie sat alone in his office. Despite those snags, he had every reason to be pleased. Polls showed him at 31 percent. That was even higher than the prior record independent vote—29 percent for Teddy Roosevelt in 1912.

Still, he had to be honest with himself. He doubted he'd win the election in November. La Follette had tried it. TR had tried it. George Wallace had tried it. John Anderson had tried it. Perot had tried it. All had failed.

He knew that was a debilitating thought. The "winning syndrome" was a key to victory, something he had taught his salesmen at Synergy. But how in the hell did he expect anyone, himself included, to overcome two hundred years of two-party politics?

But George Sempel had faith. Ladbrooke's of London had scaled down his election odds from eighteen to one to ten to one, and George had wired $10,000 to his London office to place the bet. In his inimitable, sage way, George told him: "I can use the extra $100,000. That will pay for one year at college for one grandchild."

Charlie's other doubt involved his own emotional nature. He had lived a life in which praise was routine and criticism sparse. His mother loved him and regularly let him know it. His teachers were pleased with him, and almost never offered criticism. At Synergy, it was assumed he was the heir apparent. Wherever he went, society had tipped its hat to him. And Charlie made sure it would never go to his head.

But now, the shoe was on the other foot. Oh, he still got praise, but he was also regularly beaten up by the establishment press and the party people as a "dreamer," even as a "wild-eyed fanatic." And someone had tried to run him down by car. Then there was Don Leland, whose appetite only seemed satisfied by chewing on Charlie's reputation. Washington was a world of carnivores, and although he enjoyed an occasional steak, he didn't enjoy being one.

But all that aside, his poll numbers were up, and there was Clara.

She was meeting him for lunch soon, and with just the thought of her breeziness, a kind of controlled euphoria, filled his heart. The woman was superb. Never had sex been so satisfying. Never in his life had he had such companionship, such empathy, such brightness. In the vernacular, he was in love—an emotion that had escaped him as a younger man.

Was Clara in love with him? He swore he would never ask. All he needed was the impression that she was. She laughed at his jokes, as thin as they might be. She listened to his tirades against bad government, sometimes wincing, but usually taking it well. She praised him, counseled him, steadied his frayed nerves. She was friend, amour, courtesan, and sister.

At this juncture, as the presidential candidate of the movement and lover of Clara, he felt that his daydreams and reality had come into happy confluence. He could hear the sound of golden flutes in his head. But would his luck continue?

People always commented that you needed "fire in the belly" to make the White House, a symbol of extreme ambition that separated wannabe Presidents from other mortals. He knew he didn't have that. Perhaps "fire in the head," a compulsion for his ideas for better government. But ambition for himself? No.

But equally important was his obsessive desire to hold on to Clara. He confessed that she helped pump up his sometimes lagging ambition. If he lost the race and went back to Ohio, would she follow him there? No way. He even laughed at the vision of her in Fairview. This was no small-town girl willing to live a routine life while the neighbors watched.

The reality was that if he wanted Clara, he'd have to stay in Washington. He couldn't keep his House seat, which was expiring in January. So he supposed that if life was to remain at this level of nirvana, he had only one choice.

He'd have to become President of the United States.

CHAPTER 35

King Kellogg waited in his office, quite curious about his guest, Norm Sobel. The party boss was not the type to be visiting lobbyists. Still, he had asked for an early morning appointment in King's opulent digs. What could he want?

The reverse image of Tolliver, Sobel was thin, immaculate, and reserved. He spoke without obscenities and measured his every word. Actually, Kellogg was pleased Norm was seeking an audience. Normally, he'd be more candid with Tolliver, whose attitude toward politics was as flexible as his own.

But Sobel seemed to be getting more aggressive, and more worried, as the detente between the parties against Palmer solidified. That, King assumed, was the reason for this visit. It could only help his lobby operation to get closer to Sobel.

Kellogg glanced at his watch. Sobel was not due for another two minutes. Would he arrive on time? That would start the session off well.

He needed a good omen. The Baltimore diner exposé had lifted Charlie's poll numbers to within striking distance, which was unnerving. Perhaps Sobel knew something that would lift Billings's chances. Even though he was bipartisan, Kellogg believed that (1) Billings had a better chance of beating Palmer than did Sobel's candidate, Arthur Steadman, and that (2) he could more easily do business with Billings in the Oval Office. The thought of Charlie in the White House was too chilling to entertain.

"Mr. Kellogg," his secretary called. "Mr. Sobel is here."

Good beginning, King mused. His guest had arrived thirty seconds early.

Sobel became candid the moment he was seated. "King, I need your help on something."

"Yes. What's it about?"

"It's security at my HQ and perhaps at Tolliver's as well. Documents are missing, and my guess is that someone is operating sub rosa for Palmer."

"Who do you suspect?" King's appreciation of political intrigue was endless, and Sobel was providing fuel for entertaining speculation.

"Clara Staples. I think she's the spy."

King's surprise was evident. "Clara? But she's working for us. She loves the two-party system."

"Maybe. But I believe she loves Charlie even more. I've had a little routine surveillance done. They've become a tight couple. He regularly stays over at her mansion in Georgetown and they're seen everywhere together. Even at their age, they hold hands. I'm convinced she's become a double agent."

"Double agent? Norm, are you reading too many espionage novels?"

"No, King. Our insider in the Palmer camp seems to always know our strategy. That info could only come from Clara. I also suspect that her fine hand was involved in the Boxley exposé of our meeting in Baltimore. He was just a ragtag reporter. Tolliver denies it, but I think Clara may have learned about the meeting from Tolliver, then tipped off Boxley."

Kellogg was doing mental handsprings. Clara did seem infatuated (surely, she was not truly in love) with Charlie, something he sensed at their last meeting.

King initiated a thought experiment. *What if* he were Charlie and hopelessly in love with Clara, something that was not unlikely? Wouldn't he try to seduce Clara into becoming a political ally? He had once thought her allegiance impervious to outside influence, but who knew about beautiful women?

"Norm, I'm not convinced that Clara has become a traitor, but I do hear you, loud and clear."

"What can we do to find out?"

"I'll talk to Tolliver and a few other people, including Billings. Perhaps we should conduct a close investigation."

Once Sobel had left, Kellogg mused painfully. God, he hoped Clara was innocent. Such beauty should not be tarnished by betrayal.

CHAPTER 36

The two men in the Ideal Plumbing and Heating white van, dressed in coveralls emblazoned with the company insignia, waited impatiently across the street from Maison Grise in Georgetown.

It was Tuesday, and according to their detailed instructions, Daisy, Clara Staples's maid, had that day off each week. Ms. Staples employed two in help, and the second person, her combined chauffeur-butler, was in the house. Their typed primer also explained that when madam wasn't home, the chauffeur occasionally deserted his post in favor of the neighborhood bar.

After a half hour had elapsed, the green Jaguar left the grounds. Immediately, they drove the van up the circular gravel path and parked in front of the door. The taller man inserted a key into the door lock, but it wouldn't turn.

With their tool kits, they moved to the back of the house, strolling slowly so as not to invite interest. At the double French doors on the flagstone terrace—dotted with boxes of sculptured boxwoods—they put down their tools.

From where they stood, they could barely be seen. A line of topiaried hemlocks, some six feet in height, hid them from the view of the houses behind. They opened their kits, but the tools they extracted had nothing to do with heating or plumbing.

"This is the best point to break in," the taller "plumber" said to the other. "We don't have time to play with the lock. Use the crowbar and break the door jamb. That'll just take a minute."

His prediction was right. The two men were soon inside the house.

The shorter man raced to a near wall, seeming to know the layout intimately. At the alarm console, a buzzing signal warned that there was only thirty seconds left before it went off. He glanced at the instruction sheet and pressed in the number 1789—the date of the French Revolution—which immediately disarmed the alarm.

They scampered up the stairs, halting at the landing, where the shorter man pointed ahead. "Her bedroom is off that corridor, second door to the left."

Entering, they gasped at the opulence.

"Shame we didn't come here for a real heist," the taller one said. "We could get some great pickings."

"Just do what we're paid for. Rifle the place and look for papers from any of the politicos. Our people think she may be double-crossing them. Turn the place upside down. It'll help the search and it'll look like a real break-in."

The two "plumbers" did a credible job. They threw clothes, including original designer gowns, out of the closet onto the floor, helter-skelter. Each drawer, separately endowed with pantyhose, or scarves, or whatever, was piled into a heap. The bed was stripped, as if they were searching the mattress, and the tons of well-ordered material atop the six closets was thrown haphazardly onto the green Aubusson rug.

The French antique desk, circa Louis XIV, was ransacked, and its papers also thrown about. Only here did the plumbers search assiduously for evidence.

"Here's a few memos signed by Mr. Tolliver. Let's take those."

"And look, I found a couple of reports from Palmer's people. Here's a big one. It's called the Green Book. I'll take that too."

After twenty minutes, the men gave up. The whole tally of documents was less than an armful.

"Jim, you forgot something," the shorter man said.

"What's that?"

"We're supposed to make like burglars so it'll look kosher. It wouldn't hurt to make a few dishonest bucks."

They quickly attacked several jewel boxes and vanity drawers, emptying all the contents into a black bag they had brought along.

"Now let's get out of here before anyone comes home."

CHAPTER 37

Sally Kirkland watched as the chauffeur opened the door of the dark green Jaguar and Clara Staples stepped gingerly out. The fine lady had come to visit Charlie Palmer in his campaign headquarters on Pennsylvania Avenue.

Was she jealous of Clara? She wasn't sure, but she did know that she felt like Charlie's self-appointed guardian. "Self-appointed" was the right word, for he knew nothing of her personal interest in him.

Charlie and Clara would be away for the weekend, at an old resort called Mohonk in New York State. He had left the phone number in case of an emergency. Sally didn't worry about any "emergency." What she did fear was that the trip itself was dangerous for the candidate.

No doubt the woman was beautiful and clever, but no one could mistake her four marriages as a character reference. Now she had fastened onto Charlie. Money was no longer the currency. It was power, and who could have more of that than the President of the United States?

What would happen if Charlie lost the race, as most everyone was predicting? Where would Miss Power-Mad Clara be then?

Besides, Clara was an official of Charlie's former party. Was she playing spy for the other side? Everyone had assumed the unknown leak was a staffer. But could it be Clara instead?

Clara wasn't going to learn much walking around headquarters, but she didn't have to. Tonight she would have the candidate himself alongside her (or more likely on top of her) in bed. What better position for political espionage?

Sally hadn't said a word to Charlie about Clara. That could be as dangerous to her career as she thought Clara was to Charlie.

Sally's thoughts were interrupted as Clara entered the headquarters. The door was opened by a male intern, a college kid whose libido seemed ready to explode at the sight of a woman old enough to be his mother.

"You're Sally, I presume," Clara said, breezily planting a kiss on her cheek. "Charlie tells me you keep him organized in this den of revolutionaries. Where is the man of the hour?"

Charm. Charm. Charm. Clara had an enormous inventory of it. It didn't mean she put it on. From what Charlie said, you could wake her at 3 A.M. and she'd be the same vibrant, friendly, clever, good-natured person. No, it wasn't an act, but Sally had found that the volume of charm was often in inverse relation to the amount of character. And true character, she was sure, was what Clara lacked.

At that moment, Charlie virtually ran from George's office toward the glass front doors, where he embraced Clara, his face lit as if he hadn't seen her in years. Sally politely moved away from the couple, out of earshot, embarrassed—or annoyed—at the display of affection.

"Darling, I just heard about the robbery at your house yesterday. Thank God you weren't at home at the time. Did they steal much?" Charlie asked Clara, his face displaying concern.

"No, Charles. Just some costume stuff—not worth over $10,000 altogether. I keep my real jewels in the bank vault."

"Costume jewels worth $10,000?" Charlie laughed. "I can see you're out of my league. Were they after more expensive stuff?"

"No, I don't think they were robbers at all. My bedroom was totally ransacked but they left all the silver down in the dining room pantry. I think they were after something else."

Charlie's expression showed his confusion. "If not jewels, then what?"

Clara smiled enigmatically, and opened her shoulder purse.

"This," she said, raising a tapestry-bound book, about seven by nine inches.

"Why, that's just an address book, or a diary. Isn't it?" Charles's confusion was being compounded.

"Yes, it's my dairy. I write everything down in here, and that's what Tolliver or Sobel or somebody on their side was looking for. But whenever I go out of the house, I take it with me."

"Are your musings that valuable?" Charlie asked.

"Well, they thought so." She smiled. "And you might too. It's obvious they wanted to find out if I was still loyal to the party—or if I had switched allegiance to yours truly."

"And what's the answer?" Charlie was now finding the game entertaining, if a bit touchy.

Clara toyed with the book, turning it over, then back again.

"Charlie, you'll find out when you read my innermost secrets in the diary."

"And when will that be?"

"When I know you better," she answered, giving out a small trill, her trademark laugh.

Charlie turned toward Sally, who had been standing a respectful distance away.

"Sally," he called out. "I see you've met Clara. I've got a little work to do with George before we go to lunch. Why not show Clara around the shop?"

Sally walked toward Clara and was taken aback as the grand lady took her hand.

"Please give me the tour," Clara said. "I want to see how David is going to slay the two-party Goliath. It could happen, you know. No one has a candidate like Charlie Palmer."

As they walked, Sally introduced her to a dozen people, from Robbie Barnes (he of the serious mien broke into a healthy smile) to the young female intern, Maggie Swanson, a tall, big-boned blond from the Dakotas.

Sally quickly surveyed Clara's outfit. It was a simple tight-fitting Chanel suit with matching shoes and small hat. She always seemed to wear hats, a throwback to the 1950s. Sally supposed Charlie liked that touch of tradition. For all his revolutionary zeal, she believed he was really a dyed-in-the-hinterland middle-class traditionalist, a firm believer in Victorian houses and good mothers, of which he had both.

But Clara was made in another image. She was an enigma, Sally decided, a mixture of the modern power feminist and the courtesan of eighteenth-century France. Who could beat such a combination? But weren't the two mutually exclusive? Someday, she feared, the conflict would hurt Charlie.

It was obvious why Charlie had fallen in love so readily and heavily, as had many other men. Clara was an original. A beautiful, mysterious original.

She had left Clara in the office of the assistant press man, and walked out just in time to meet Charlie.

"So what do you think of my latest acquisition? She's really something, isn't she?" he asked, almost cockily.

Sally was about to say the expected. But suddenly—perhaps influenced by Charlie's own undiplomatic candor—she blurted out what she swore she'd never do.

"Charlie, she's beautiful and charming, just as you said. But I must tell you she makes me nervous for you. I'm afraid that somehow, at some time, she's going to hurt you badly. I think it's a matter of chara—"

Sally never had a chance to finish the sentence. Never before had she seen his benign face take on such a look of hostility.

"Sally, you're a good worker and I appreciate everything you do. But when it comes to my personal life, please mind your own business."

With that, he called loudly to Clara, who was just approaching the door, exaggerating his diction.

"LET'S GO DARLING. WE'VE GOT A LUNCH DATE."

Sally stood, immobile, ashamed, as the couple of the decade walked out the door.

CHAPTER 38

Tolliver was worried. Charlie's poll numbers had skyrocketed to 31 percent following the Baltimore debacle.

He'd love to deliver a knockout blow to the SOB—if he could find one. Unfortunately, he wasn't getting what he needed from the intelligence front. After the Leland exposure, there had been some stuff from Justinian, but not enough. He had never met the traitor in Charlie's camp. His only contact with the anonymous informer had been by phone, talking to a weirdly unisex voice.

Despite Sobel's insistence on pulling off a fourth-rate Watergate, the break-in at Maison Grise to check on Clara had come up empty. He had reluctantly supplied Sobel with the house layout, the key, and the alarm number, which Clara had probably forgotten she had given him a year ago in case of emergencies.

The key had not worked, probably because Clara had changed the locks, but the alarm number succeeded in giving their "plumbers" enough time to make the search.

He didn't believe Clara was a traitor, or a double agent, and the break-in had proven that. The few memos they found were innocent. He had given them to Clara to study months ago. In fact, the only important document was Charlie Bastard's Green Book, which she had managed to pilfer from the opponent's HQ.

But it was true that Clara had been somewhat of a bust as a spy for him. She had produced a few tidbits and had helped out with Pemenex, but either she was lazy or, more likely, she just dragged her feet (lovely appendages, they were) because of her infatuation with Charlie, or at least with his presumed power.

Nor was there any further contact from Mr. Fairview, the little redhead who had brought him the first goods on Charlie. At the time, the price tag of $50,000 seemed steep, but without that exposé of tainted youth, Cocksucker Charlie's big mouth would have swayed even more people. He'd gladly pay another $50,000, or more, for explosive new information. Meanwhile, the $200,000 bipartisan Special Effects fund was rotting in the Caymans, unused.

He had already poured himself a scotch and was lying back in his oversize chaise, with several political journals filled with titillating gossip in hand: *Roll Call, The Hill, American Spectator, The Standard, Progressive New Republic, National Review, The Nation, George.* Several articles discussed the Larrimore defection, which had hurt the party and Tolliver personally.

Charlie could thank the Oklahoman for five points in the polls. So far, Tolliver hadn't heard much about the Great One, who was now Charlie's running mate, but he presumed that come Labor Day, they would trot him out like some superannuated race horse.

Tolliver was into TRB in the *New Republic* when the phone rang. Getting out of the chaise took more physical effort than he could handle on his Saturday off, so he had placed a receiver on the floor.

"Who is this? Oh, Justinian." Again that same ghostlike unisex voice. "What do you hear from the front?" Tolliver asked, expectant.

"I have a piece of important news," the voice said.

Tolliver's tongue licked his front teeth in anticipation.

"How much will it cost me?" he asked.

"Tolliver, I've told you. I don't want any money. I'm a patriot doing this for our country, not to line my pockets."

That troubled Tolliver, who was convinced that amateurs in politics were dangerously unpredictable. Money gave predictability to men's affairs. Of that he was sure.

"Tell me, what is it?"

"Palmer and Clara Staples are going away together for the weekend, to a place called Mohonk in New York State. Do whatever you want with it."

Tolliver had more questions, but he heard a click. The line was dead.

A weekend in the country for the fabulous duo? Things were moving more rapidly than he thought. This was clearly a recording job for Johnny Max, a way to spend some of the Special Effects money.

He became gleeful at the thought of the tapes that might emerge from that romantic rendezvous. The grunts, groans, and ahs of lovemaking by Charlie would find a ready market in the supermarket tabloids—not unlike the phone sex of Prince Charles and his lady friend captured by a London daily.

But Clara? My God, she would be incensed. Her cash contributions to the party might be threatened—along with his own job. She was no lady to tangle with. He *should* pass up the opportunity.

Still, it was tempting. He could edit out Clara's passion and keep her name secret. He leaned back in the chaise and smiled at how pleasant it would be to eavesdrop, and how damaging it could be to Charlie. Everyone goes to the bathroom and most everyone has sex. But few have the doubtful privilege of having it recorded for posterity.

It was surely something to think about.

He should be reserving it for himself, but he had his duty. He'd pass this lively morsel on to the rest of the "Loyalists," an informal network of all those alarmed at the threat of SOB Charlie Palmer as President of the United States.

CHAPTER 39

The Mohonk resort was ideal. The rustic wooden Victorian haven was over a hundred years old, somewhat antediluvian and absent the swinging set. The place didn't even have a bar.

All Clara and he did during the weekend was walk in the woods, do a little canoeing on the lake. They even watched old movies on television, some as early as after lunch, then played cards and dominoes.

At Mohonk, Charlie took stock of his emotions. At age forty-three, it could hardly be called young love, yet he challenged the calendar. If it wasn't youthful ardor, it was a reasonable approximation, and a happy one.

That weekend he spent an inordinate amount of time just looking at Clara, who finally complained.

"Charlie, you keep telling me how beautiful I am. I appreciate it, but you look at me so intensely that I'm afraid you'll find a blemish on my face."

"No, Clara, I'm just admiring how good you look without much makeup. Plain Clara is not so plain. Go for the natural look whenever you're out of the Beltway eye. It compliments you. But please don't get so outdoorsy that you take up golf or tennis," Charlie said, faking a frown. "All my life, I've been searching for a woman who shares my love of physical indolence. The only muscles that work in me are in my head, and . . ." He blushed.

Clara laughed girlishly.

"You know, I believe in the hydraulic law of life," he explained.

"If you push yourself in one direction—say athletics—it just cuts down your mental energy. Same is true of exercise. I think we were born with just so many heartbeats. Use them up in jogging, golf, or tennis, and they're gone forever."

Clara laughed again at his eccentric comments.

The weekend was idyllic except for two drawbacks. They were under the eye of two Secret Service men. Both tried to fade into the background, but guests who knew Charlie was a presidential candidate enjoyed picking them out by their *almost* hidden Smith & Wessons.

The other drawback was a tall, swarthy man who turned up virtually everywhere they went. But Charlie chalked that up to his political paranoia, an occupational disease of Washingtonians.

The evenings were spent in dining and watching the entertainment. Afterward, in their room overlooking the lake, the couple chatted, read a little, and—Charlie was surprised—at Clara's urging, they made love each night. He had resolved not to push himself on her. Surely, she'd been forced enough by men, beginning, she had told him, at age thirteen.

Clara appreciated his deference, and made the evenings monumental. She was not only beautiful but had a natural talent for pleasing men. Usually quiet during lovemaking, Charlie found himself suddenly voluble, talking and laughing, and carrying on like an aroused teenager.

"Charlie, you're wonderful. But can you imagine if your worshipful followers, or the press, could hear you now—babbling like a lovesick banshee while getting laid. Lordy, they'd say you're just a horny kid pretending to be a President."

"Do you mind?"

"I think it's fine, Charlie love. Loosens up your image with me as an unapproachable intellectual. You know, most people think that anyone who's good at thinking can't screw. But you're living proof that they're wrong." With that, she reached over and kissed the life out of him.

After the sex was consummated, they settled back into the bed, with Charlie's head on her ample breast.

"You know, darling," she said, "I've been very happy in spite of myself."

"Why in spite of yourself?" he wondered.

"Well you know, all the political complications."

"Such as?"

"Such as the differences between us, and the fact that I'm privy to what Tolliver and Sobel are doing," she explained. "I told you I

wouldn't betray their campaign strategies. But I also promised to
snitch to you whenever they came up with crazy dirty tricks."

"And have they any tricks in the works?"

"Oh, yeah. They're holding some back from me. They know that
we're—that way. But I do know one which burns me."

"What's that?"

"Just the other week, King Kellogg, the lobbyist, and Tolliver out-
lined a nasty scheme to make you and George Sempel poorer—to
kill your financial independence."

"How would they do that?"

"They were going to stop Synergy from getting new government
contracts, and try to cut off any old ones. I also think they're planning hanky panky with your stock. I didn't get all the details, but it
sounded rotten to me."

Charlie hugged her warmly. "Thanks for letting me know, Clara.
I understand how conflicted you are about your double life. But does
that mean you're coming over to my side—that you see the light?"

Clara's expression quickly turned from warmth to disdain. With
one swift movement, she pushed him away.

"Oh, so you're the light?" Clara's voice was filled with sarcasm.
"Is that the way it is? And I suppose I'm the soul of darkness—
Mr. Idealistic Know-It-All? Did it ever occur to you that you might
be wrong?"

Charlie was surprised how quickly her ardor had cooled.

"But darling," he implored, "can't you see how corrupt our political system can be? Some of the politicians think that lying and dirty
tricks are quite normal in a democracy."

Clara quieted, seemingly in contemplation. "Charlie, you know I
can't keep up with you intellectually, nor can anyone else. But can't
you be a little less fanatic about changing the system? It has its
virtues, you know, and it's served us well for two hundred years."

"It *had* served us well," Charlie corrected. "But can't you see we
have to change to survive?"

"I'll admit some change is needed. But so much? Charlie, please
leave us stick-in-the-muds with something we can hold on to, corrupt or otherwise. And what would I do without the party? I'd hate
to visit little brats in school or collect money for the Salvation Army.
I love my part in politics, and I'm just so afraid you're going to ruin
it all—especially if you become President. You've got me so torn,
Charlie, that I don't know what to think. One day, I want you to
win and I'll be so proud to see you in the White House. Then the
next day, I'm scared stiff you're going to kill the golden goose."

Clara's expression had now turned plaintive. "Charlie, Charlie.
What should I do?"

He couldn't help himself. Clara's brave front had collapsed and he now felt guilty. Her expression was that of a little girl who had lost her doll. He took Clara's face gently in his hands and kissed her softly.

"Clara, please stop worrying. I can't promise you I'll change, but there is great hope for both of us."

"In what way, Charlie?"

"In spite of my rise in the polls, Ladbrooke's is betting seven to one that I'll never make it to the White House, which means that nothing is going to change. We won't have anything to argue about. We can just make love and take care of each other. OK?"

Clara laughed in her girlish way. "Charlie boy, you are a dear. I shouldn't love you, but I'm afraid I do."

Never had she used the word "love" before. He couldn't believe his ears or trust his luck. What was more important to him? The White House and the chance for true reform? Or Clara?

He had no answer, but tonight he had come to a keen insight. Suddenly, he was deathly afraid he could never have both.

CHAPTER 40

"Charlie, like the primitives, I believe the weather is a good omen. There's not a cloud in the sky."

Georgie Sempel was seated next to Charlie on the dais outside Independence Hall in Philadelphia the day after Labor Day. Over a thousand people were on folding chairs, waiting for the opening salvo in the independent campaign for President.

Permission to use the historic grounds was not easy in coming. The site was now a national park, run by the Department of Interior. For openers, George was turned down by Secretary Stan Bonham. But Charlie knew that it really was a nemesis of his, Congressman James Schmidt, the chair of the Interior subcommittee, who had given it the kibosh.

During August, Charlie and George decided not to heat up the campaign for fear of early burnout. Instead, they used the time for organizational work, which was blossoming. Robbie Barnes kept pressuring Charlie to do Larry King and every other talk show during the quiet month, but Charlie was pleased that George vetoed the idea.

He did agree to appear on the *This Week* Sunday show, where Charlie told of the administration's turn down, then asked viewers to complain to the National Park Service. The calls and faxes made for a quick switch in official policy.

The mayor of Philadelphia was also less than enthusiastic, but local volunteers—sixty thousand strong—soon changed his mind. Hizzoner Jacobs was also on the dais, ready to welcome the independent candidate to history.

The press took two hundred seats up front, with every network camera at the ready. The event seemed to be self-hyped. Independent candidates for President were a staple curiosity, but seldom did they come near the 31 percent polling mark of the Palmer-Larrimore team.

Senator John Larrimore's presence as VP candidate was not lost on the press either. Everyone had started to fidget until Larrimore rose and stood at the lectern, looking, Charlie thought, a lot more presidential than he.

"Ladies and gentlemen, and the press, and that was not meant to be mutually exclusive," Larrimore began in his Oklahoma drawl to a small roar from the audience. "Today is a historic day. One hundred years from now, it might well be recorded that *two* memorable events in the glorious story of America took place at Independence Hall.

"If you look on your seats," Larrimore was saying, "you'll see a copy of our American Manifesto, that little red, white, and blue 35-point pamphlet that we believe will remake America. And now, I give you its author, and the next President of the United States, Charles Knudsen Palmer."

Charlie shook Larrimore's hand warmly while the crowd roared its approval. Then, in his own style, Charlie began softly, almost hesitantly.

"Mayor Jacobs and Americans all. I hope today is as historic as Senator Larrimore believes. Not because I'm the candidate, but because I'm an ordinary citizen like yourself, just new to politics. And once out of office, whether as congressman or President, I'll return to that position, which should be the most honored in America."

Charlie then delivered a strong blast at growing political corruption and Washington scandals, adding: "Like the oft-quoted football coach, too many politicians believe that winning is the only thing. Instead, they should be holding on to their integrity whether they win or lose. That's the best remedy for an ailing democracy like ours."

He stood at the lectern and cast his eyes across the horizon of people. In the Washington grapevine, George had heard that Tolliver and Sobel had infiltrated the volunteer corps with ringers. Some might be here. Would they try to raise a ruckus?

"Virtually all politicians belong to one of the two trade unions— the political parties who've cleverly split the American pie in half," he continued, his voice gaining in stridency. "Today, with the launching of this independent campaign, we're going to expand that pie. We're adding the slice that seems to have disappeared, the one that represents the working middle-class American citizen. If I win—"

He halted in mid-sentence. A young man standing on a seat raised a megaphone. He was shouting above the din.

"MAKE ANY MORE GIRLS PREGNANT LATELY, MR. CONGRESSMAN?"

"SIT DOWN AND SHUT UP!" someone roared back. Suddenly from the rear, another young man stood atop a chair, this time cupping his hands as he yelled.

"CHARLIE BOY! DON'T GET DRUNK IN THE WHITE HOUSE."

People surrounded the two men, joined by Secret Service men, part of an eight-agent detachment. Within a minute, the intruders had been taken away. The scene was restored to normal.

Except for Charlie. He had been shaken. Not visibly. He was learning outwardly to control his emotions, but the disorderly nature of American politics still troubled him. It even set up an internal nervousness that took hours to subside. George's advice now reentered his mind. Toughen your hide and stiffen your brain. It's only going to get worse.

Did it have to be this way? Was the conflict between the parties something like the ferocious competition in organized crime? Had the party fight over spoils, both in power and money, taken the civility out of the process? Charlie was sure it had.

"As I was saying when interrupted, citizens have lost confidence," Charlie continued. "Why? Because the process is all wrong. AMERICAN POLITICS IS CONTROLLED BY MONEY—BY BIG MONEY IN BOTH PARTIES—AND IT'S GOT TO STOP!"

Again he was interrupted, but this time by applause. The audience seemed to be having a good time. Charlie could feel his adrenaline pumping, the fear and hesitancy being transformed into confidence.

"Politicians are leaving the ship—retiring in record numbers. Even they can't stand the gaff of MONEY, MONEY, MONEY. One of my fellow congressmen tells me he feels like a beggar shaking a tin cup, not a legislator. To get elected, the average member of the House has to collect over $600,000, and many go over a million. For a senator, the average is $4 million, and some raise over $10 million. They dignify it by calling it campaign contributions. Actually, it's just legal bribery! And then the rich try to buy elections with their private bankrolls. That's not American in spirit."

Charlie's passion was reflected in his eyes. He paused and took a sip of water. He was now in high emotional gear.

"This money raising is like an addiction. The two parties talk about real reform, but don't you believe it. I've seen it from the inside and it's all baloney. They're both convinced they can raise more money than the next guy and buy more thirty-second television commercials. When all the so-called reforms are put in, candidates who spend a little less will get a few freebies from the government. That's all nonsense—Congress's way of coopting your revolution so they can continue to rip off the American public!"

A hush had fallen over the outdoor auditorium as Charlie spoke. It now slowly changed to applause, then to the rhythmic clapping of hands.

"I HAVE A PLAN!" he roared. "We should pass a constitutional amendment making it illegal for a candidate to collect even $1 from anyone—or to use any of his own money in a campaign! Nor should we use taxpayer money to support candidates as we now do for the presidency. Instead we should set up a voluntary organization like the United Way or the Red Cross. People can contribute as much as they want to this election fund, anonymously if they wish.

"The money collected will be divided up equally among all candidates for federal office, from the House to the presidency. Maybe a congressional candidate will get a check for $100,000—and that's it. Maybe $10 million for a presidential candidate instead of the present $70 million. No one can raise any more or spend any more. No more using of taxpayer funds in elections. And most important, no more whoring by public servants!"

The audience was strangely still. Charlie knew his no fund-raising plan was radical. He could sense them mulling it over.

"But what about television political ads? you ask. They take about half of all the money spent. Well, most of them are lies that distort the opponent's record. We have to stop all that phony advertising. Remember, the people own the airwaves and we've already made cigarette ads illegal on television. Let's remove the next pollutant— political ads! Instead, we'll substitute free time on radio and television as do other Western countries.

"The result? People can run for public office without having to sell their souls. The professional politicians will scream bloody murder and they'll give you a whole flim-flam of fake reforms. But I promise you this. There's no other way if we're going to have the democracy our Founding Fathers visualized."

The audience, almost as one, left their seats and began a chant: "WE WANT CHARLIE! WE WANT CHARLIE." It filled the space outside Independence Hall, then spilled over into the city of Philadelphia, and on television, into tens of millions of homes and offices in America.

The independent campaign of Charles Knudsen Palmer for President had begun in earnest.

CHAPTER 41

Arnold Reichmann was proud of his ingenuity.

He had already received $500 a day, plus expenses, for his investigation of Charlie Palmer's past, plus a $5,000 bonus from his anonymous employer. But his real coup was the additional $50,000 from a side deal with campaign boss Andy Tolliver.

He waxed proud when his work made national television on the Leland show, but he was miffed that few people knew of him. And some who did ridiculed his eccentric appearance.

But his product—confidential information on Palmer—had finally become dinner-table gossip across America. He had made a nice buck, but there was also a psychic bonus in his job. He enjoyed watching politicians, CEOs, and other assorted "winners" squirm when someone put the truth to them, truth turned up by none other than little Arnie Reichmann.

But he was still frustrated. He had an open client in Tolliver, who was willing to pay a small ransom for any further dirt on Palmer. But he had nothing to sell. That is, until his phone rang one morning.

It was Bill Folsom, the new mayor of Fairview, who had spouted info on Palmer, as did the majordomo at the frat house on Reichmann's return. Their tongues had been loosened with $1,000 each, money paid by his client, whoever that was.

"Mr. Reichmann. This is Bill Folsom. You said to call if I had any more saleable information on Palmer. Well, I do, and it's hotter than the other stuff. But it'll cost you $15,000."

"Fifteen thousand? That's robbery."

"OK, I'll sell it to Palmer's enemies instead. Of course I prefer to deal with you. I do have my political reputation—small as it is—to protect. So do you want it?"

"All right. I'll meet you at your house in Fairview."

He had made the journey and found it promising. The story had happened long before Folsom's time, but his leads were solid. If Reichmann could confirm them, he'd really have something. The $15,000 was high but he had the $50,000 from Tolliver, and his smeller was telling him he was on the right track.

This time he wouldn't sell it for a pittance. This would be his masterpiece, the culmination of a lifetime of unheralded detective work.

But more important than recognition, this would be his retirement nugget, the coup that would get him out of everyone's pajamas and into a Florida condo, for the rest of his life.

He had already set a price of $100,000—just a down payment on money to be paid, over and over, until the well ran dry, which was never. And he had the ideal buyer in mind.

None other than Charles Knudsen Palmer, independent candidate for office of the President of the United States.

CHAPTER 42

Clara Staples had just awakened.

She sat up in bed and rang, a signal to her maid, a young Irish girl named Daisy, to bring her breakfast, a frugal fare of one toasted English muffin and hot water and lemon.

Nature had so fully endowed Clara that any extra calories moved her toward fat. She valued her trademark pulchritude and couldn't afford to lose it.

She was sitting up in the elaborate bedroom of Maison Grise, waiting for her breakfast. Instead, Daisy rushed in, wildly flailing a newspaper about. Her breath was heavy, her face flushed with alarm.

"MISS STAPLES! LOOK HERE," she screamed. "THE SUPERMARKET PAPER HAS YOUR PICTURE ON THE COVER . . . AND SUCH A NASTY STORY!"

Clara jumped out of bed and grabbed at the tabloid, the *National Tattler*. The headline was almost as lurid as the baby with two heads featured in the upper corner.

SEX TAPES OF PRESIDENTIAL CANDIDATE CHARLES PALMER AND HIS
WEALTHY GIRLFRIEND. EXCLUSIVE. WORD FOR WORD, ONLY IN THE TATTLER.

"My God. My God," Clara whimpered as she read.

Clara realized that she had now been drawn into the cesspool of a presidential election. It wasn't Charlie's fault, she repeated as she read what seemed like pornography. Their words in bed at Mohonk had been recorded for the public's insatiable prurient interest.

It was Charlie's passion, one memorable night at Mohonk, put into print along with her avid responses. In context, it was lovemaking. Charlie had been delightfully youthful, even funny. But out of context? God, it sounded either lurid or inane.

Clara sat on her tapestry bench and started to cry, slowly, softly, with real tears. She had not done that since her father died, driving a truck at age sixty when he should have been retired. If only he had lived a few years more, she could have supported him.

He would have been proud of her for having reached some sort of life pinnacle. But now there was her photo, taken at the Mohonk dance, right alongside the "sex tapes," with a verbatim record of her cooing, and writhing, and more. In print, it was enough to make you sick.

What about Charlie? Would he care, or would the caveman in him emerge? Would other men be revolted, or would they applaud his sexual conquest? Who knew about the male sex drive anyway?

She had exploited it all her life, but did she really know how men felt when aroused? She sensed that it was a powerful emotion. And by glory, Charlie boy had put it into words that night. Some of it was quite graphic and other parts almost poetic. And now it was all laid out for anyone to read for seventy-five cents at the local supermarket checkout counter. Sex tapes of a presidential contender peddled right alongside baby food and apple pie. Wasn't that just dandy?

Someone had to pay for this and she was sure who it was. As Clara hurriedly dressed, her mind ran to revenge.

The secretary tried to stop her, only adding to the redness in Clara's eyes, a warning of the tempest to come.

"Out of my way, girlie. I'm going to get him."

Clara pushed her aside without ceremony and lurched at the door to Tolliver's private office. She turned the knob, swearing that she'd break it down if she had to. It opened to show Tolliver leaning back precariously in his double-size chair, a copy of the *Tattler* covering his face. Murmurs of salacious glee were coming out of his mouth.

Clara moved quickly. She raced around his desk and snatched the *Tattler* out of his hand, throwing it to the floor.

"YOU FAT SON OF A BITCH," Clara shouted shrilly. "JUST FOR YOUR FUCKING POLITICS YOU'D RUIN EVERYBODY'S LIFE. YOU'VE PLASTERED NEWS OF MY ORGASMS ALL OVER THE WORLD!"

Clara attacked, pummeling Tolliver's enormous face with her two fists. There was no science, no art, no rhythm, just an angry woman taking out her bile on her despoiler with all her strength. For a moment Clara visualized Tolliver as her rapist, if not of her body, of what dignity she had managed to garner over the years.

Tolliver tried to defend himself, but the blows were coming too quickly and from all directions. He leaned back to escape, but as his three hundred pounds shifted off center, it sent the monster chair tipping over. Tolliver hit the floor with an enormous thud. He was thrown out onto the rug, on his back, faceup.

Clara moved quickly. She grabbed a brass table lamp and stood over her victim, threatening the coup de grace.

"For God's sake, Clara!" Tolliver pleaded, his fattened arms raised upward to ward off the blows. "I know it's horrible but I didn't do it. I swear I had nothing to do with the sex tapes. I'm not crazy, you know."

Clara slowed, her breathing irregular and painful.

"What do you mean you didn't do it? Do you mean your patsy partner, Norm Sobel, did it? Same thing."

"No, Clara, I admit I toyed with the idea, but I visualized just what's happening—that you'd kill me if I taped you at Mohonk. No, I don't have the slightest idea who's behind it, unless it's Justinian . . ."

Clara turned to look at herself in the mirror. She was a mess, sweat ruining her makeup, her eyes bloodshot from crying and anger. She turned back to Tolliver.

"OK, get up. Now tell me everything you know. And don't bullshit me, Andy. Remember, my purse strings are long and my temper is short."

"Oh, really. Tell me about it," Tolliver said as he tried to get back on his feet, allowing himself a little sarcasm as the price of injured pride and a bruised back. "Just give me a hand, Clara. I'd like to rejoin the living."

Clara stretched out both her arms and entwined her fingers into Tolliver's pudgy appendages.

"OK. At three you lift and I pull. One, two, upsy daisy."

Clara gave out a little groan and Andy pushed up against the fallen chair. It took a minute, but the improvised human crane had worked. He was standing now, obviously afraid to sit down for fear of another fall.

"So who's Justinian?" Clara asked, her anger not ready to fully subside.

"He or she—the person puts on a unisex voice—is our spy in Charlie's headquarters. We needed somebody. You haven't given us very much, you know."

"Wait a minute. I would have given you the Green Book, but you already had it. Actually, there's little to spy on. Almost everything is open and these people never tell a lie. A professional spy could starve there."

"Maybe, but Justinian has given us a few things. He-she is the one who called to tell me that you were going to Mohonk. My guess is that Justinian—whoever that is—is the one who's behind the sex tapes. There's probably a vendetta against Charlie involved, maybe deeper than our little game."

Clara upended a chair and sat. Her composure was only beginning to return.

"Don't ask me why, but I believe you about the tapes. But how about that meeting of you and Sobel in the Baltimore diner? That was plain stupid. I've gotten a half-dozen calls from Executive Committee members asking my opinion—whether we should give you the boot. What do you think?"

"Clara, it's hurt us, no doubt. But it was actually the only thing the two parties could do. Despite the risk of exposure, we've got to get together and stop Charlie Fanatic. If he wins, it could mean the end of one or both of the parties. So we can hate each other some other day. Now, it's not important which of us wins. Only that Charlie doesn't."

"Does that mean that you're willing to kill?" Clara asked, her eyes suspiciously squinted. "You know that Boxley, who made the tapes at the Baltimore diner, was murdered. Did you or Sobel have anything to do with it?"

"God no, Clara. The police hounded us for days and they found nothing. So help me, Clara, I'd never go that far, even if it meant Charlie became President." He crossed himself. "God forbid."

Clara could see that Tolliver had put her in a box. She had to admit that she liked the political system just the way it was. She also liked Charlie, and every other day it seemed she wanted him to win. But when push came to shove, she didn't want the party out in the cold. And her with it.

"Look, Tolliver, I've been confused, and now I feel violated by the sex tapes. Find out if this Justianian is behind it and who Justinian is. I'll find a way to get even."

Tolliver had regained some of his composure as well.

"I'll do what I can, Clara. I'll let you know Justinian's identity, if I ever learn it. But meanwhile, what about my job? I know the committee listens to you."

Clara looked into Tolliver's mirror. She combed her hair, repainted her lips, then turned back.

"I'm sorry I hit you, Andy. You should understand how distraught I was. As for your job, I'll help you keep it, but only under one proviso."

"Tell me and it'll be done. What is it?"

"No more dirty tricks against Charlie. If we're going to win, it'll have to be fair and square."

"I agree."

"Politician's honor?"

"Well, I could swear on that, but that's not exactly a Bible plat-form. But yes, if you can believe this, I swear on my own honor as a professional. No more dirty tricks."

Once Clara had left, Tolliver sat down in his monster chair and poured himself water from his gold-plated decanter, a gift of the party on his senatorial election campaign.

He had to make that dirty-trick pledge to Clara, and he'd *try* to keep it. Only extremis at the last moment could force him to yield. Still, he was comforted by the thought that virtually every campaign was fought at the very edge of sanity.

His promise to help smoke out the spy Justinian? Well, he'd like to learn Justinian's identity himself. But tell Clara? No way. She might tip off Charlie and the cover would be blown.

The sex tapes were a slimy trick and Clara had every right to be outraged. He didn't do it himself, but wasn't he a happy camper that Justinian, or some other patriotic American, had the guts to pull it off and give it to the *Tattler*?

If he knew anything about politics, the grunts and passion of presi-dential nominee Charlie Palmer making love—all printed up in a wonderfully lurid format—would make Charlie look like either a man without dignity or someone too passionate in the sack to make a good President.

Everyone had heard the cliche that if you wanted to lose respect for an idol, just think of him on the toilet. Well, thinking of Charlie on top of a woman, carrying on like a dog in heat, could accomplish much the same.

He'd bet that the Ladbrooke odds on Charlie, which had gone to a favorable four-to-one, would drop precipitously as more of the scandal sheets played up the sex story.

Tolliver lifted a copy of the *Tattler* and raised it high over his head.

"Here's to all great journalists, wherever you are!"

CHAPTER 43

Schulyer Rafferty woke in a bad mood.

At dinner the night before, his daughter Jenny had greeted him with a copy of the *Tattler* with Charlie's sexual proclivities smeared all over the front and back pages.

"Oh, Daddy, he's such a nice man. What in the hell are they doing to him?" Jenny frowned. Then suddenly she smiled, a touch naughtily. "And besides, I had no idea he was so virile."

Schuyler read some of the transcript, then disgustedly put down the paper. Like Jenny, he had never thought that Charlie was that passionate about sex. Usually, he seemed so cerebral.

Then again, how would his own passion with his sweet Angelica have sounded to others outside the bedroom?

The whole thing was so miserable. Charlie and Clara were single, both around forty. What did people expect? That a bachelor presidential candidate would be celibate? He knew this would hurt Charlie in the polls despite the reasonableness of it all. It wasn't the sex itself. That had been going on for some time.

No, it was that it was in print. And that Charlie seemed so responsive. People imagined political leaders were cool about sex. Could one imagine Harry Truman in heated foreplay?

In any case, Rafferty turned on CNN and there it was. The new poll showed a drop of six points in Charlie's numbers, pushing him well down into third place behind Arthur Steadman, former governor of Idaho and a Western neighbor of Rafferty's. And he feared more damage to come.

The kid needed help, badly. Neither did Rafferty want to see his $30 million, the amount spent so far, go down a rat hole.

What to do?

Rafferty dressed quickly and decided to call the journalists, academics, and money managers he had under retainer around the country. Normally, they fed him business leads, but he had asked them to track down political gossip as well. He called three of them, in New York, Chicago, and Miami.

"Anything happening locally on the presidential race that hasn't been published?" he asked. Though the chats were interesting, there were no new concrete leads.

Then he remembered. One of his best seers was a Denver business editor with a nose for mining gossip. The mining people were particularly active, afraid of losing more of their taxpayer-subsidized perks on federal lands. He had heard that their contributions to both major parties were way up.

"Manny, this is Rafferty. How's the old word prospector? Tell me, do you hear anything local that's smelly and ties into the presidential race?"

"Matter of fact there is one thing that gets my curiosity up, Schuyler."

"What's that?"

"Well, two big shot Washington politicos came out to Pemenex a short while ago—a woman party executive, a real looker, and a top-flight lobbyist, a guy named King Kellogg. When I heard about it, I called Treulich. He runs the place for a foreign conglomerate. I asked what it was all about. Sounded like a good story, but he said it was nothing. He was putting together a pot of contributions from the American executives of his firm—$1,000 each, and they had come from Washington to thank him."

"What do you think, Manny?" Schuyler's antennae was activated.

"Oh, that's pure bullshit. He was talking about $20,000 tops. Those two wouldn't go to the bathroom for that, let alone travel two thousand miles. No, something stinks. But Schuyler, I hate to admit I don't know what."

"Could you please keep on it, Manny? Talk to some of your people at Pemenex and let me know."

"Don't worry, Schuyler. Your retainer keeps my little place in the mountains from foreclosure. I assure you I'll be on it the minute we hang up."

What's next? Schuyler asked himself. He couldn't ask Charlie to speak to Clara. The candidate had enough aggravation with the *Tattler* story, and he had to avoid a split between the couple. It could send Charlie into the dumps and kill the campaign.

Damn it. Who in top party circles might know something?

Rafferty poured himself an ounce of Johnnie Walker, his pre-breakfast waker-upper, and picked up his clipboard. With his Waterman real-ink pen (he loved the schooldays feeling of liquid ink), he started to scribble names, a technique he found was the best stimulus for thought. People moved the world, and each name conjured up images out of his brain.

He wrote the names of a dozen people, including the VP candidate under Billings, Senator Harry Berry of Nevada. There was also Senator Jason Hollingsworth, the running mate of Arthur Steadman, the underdog in the presidential sweepstakes.

Why not start with Steadman? The former governor was virtually a neighbor. His ranch in Idaho was just thirty miles from the Montana border. In a political gossip column, he had seen that Steadman was home for the weekend, a pit stop between speeches. Would he let Rafferty visit on such short notice?

Surely Steadman wasn't happy about his bankrolling Charlie. On the other hand, he had always given Steadman maximum contributions for his local races, from state senator to attorney general to governor. And as a former governor of Idaho, Steadman had plenty of dealings with the mining industry.

(Rafferty had also slipped Steadman business tips about firms he had his eye on, companies whose stock rose nicely thereafter, thank you. Surely, the man couldn't be that ungrateful.)

He checked his telephone book, a worn looseleaf, then dialed Steadman's private number.

"Arthur?" he asked as soon as the phone was picked up.

"No, this John Rollings, his assistant. Can I help you?"

"I don't think so. This is Schuyler Rafferty and I want to talk to his nibs—personally."

"I'm sorry, Mr. Rafferty, but that's impossible. He's taking a nap, trying to recover from last week's campaigning."

"Good for him. Wake his ass up. Tell him Schuyler's on the phone and I have no time to waste."

Rollings disappeared without comment. A minute later, a voice came on.

"Schuyler, this is Arthur. How's the old reprobate? Making much money?"

"I used to, Arthur. But as you know, these days I'm mostly spending it—trying to save the Republic."

"Good show, fellow. I sure hope your boy doesn't beat my ass. But aside from that, what can I do for you?"

"Arthur, I'm not sure what I'm after, but I need more time with you than a phone call. I'd like to drop over, say around noon. How about it?"

"Well, I've got a full day, but I'll squeeze you in. Come for lunch and take potluck."

"Good." Schuyler hung up then turned to his daughter.

"JENNY!" he screamed.

"What's up, Dad?"

"Call the Great Falls airport and get my helicopter up here. We're flying to Idaho to see a presidential candidate."

"Charlie?" Jenny asked, her face lighting up.

"No such luck, kid. But we're seeing Steadman, looking for intelligence to help Charlie. Want to come along?"

An hour later, the Sikorsky helicopter, a piece of army surplus Rafferty had picked up for a song and had renovated, was out on the heliport on the first section of the cattle range.

Rafferty was dressed in his usual hunting clothes, and Jenny was in her blouse and jeans, carrying a sweater for the mountain coolness.

They boarded the machine and fifty minutes later had landed on Steadman's lawn. Elegantly grassed in at its center, it was bordered by western wild grasses as far as the eye could see. Steadman came running out of the house, a giant faux log cabin some three stories tall, surrounded by small guesthouses.

"Rafferty, you old robber baron, come in. Jenny, you can see my horses if you'd like. They don't compare with yours, but I try."

Inside, in the all-glass sunroom, the two men faced each other in heavy wooden chairs made from still-barked tree branches. The view outside, overlooking the valley below, rivaled Schuyler's own.

Both were Westerners. Steadman was born and bred, part of the hunting culture. Stuffed trophies of bison, elk, and bear hung along the tall walls.

Rafferty, of course, was a Western fake. He had fired a gun only once in his life, as a nineteen-year-old Army Air Corps cadet. He had almost killed the captain with a wild shot from a .45, and swore never to fire a gun again, except in defense of his, or Jenny's, life. To him, hunting was barbaric, but he never shared that secret with fellow Westerners. Rafferty, who was from Brooklyn, would always be, until the day he died, a Brooklynite.

"Arthur, I'm hoping for my side to win the election, just as you are for yourself," Sky began. "But I want this election to be fair and square. And that's why I'm here. I need to learn if you've heard of any shenanigans by the Billings camp."

Steadman looked Rafferty squarely in the eye. "You know the present thinking in both parties, Sky?"

"In what way?"

"About your protege Charlie and his independent campaign. I think you got a hint of it when Leland exposed the greasy spoon confab between Tolliver and my party's campaign director, Norm Sobel."

"Meaning?"

"Meaning that the big brains think it's not important whether I win or Billings wins. As long as Charlie loses."

"Do you agree?" Rafferty asked, smelling a wedge.

"Hell no. That's pure bullshit. I didn't put my reputation on the line so that Billings could beat the kid and leave me out in the cold. No, I'm in this to win the presidency and screw the other candidates, whoever they are."

"Perfect, Arthur. That's the way I like to hear a man talk. So, really I'm here to help you. Not to beat Charlie, but to give it real hard to Billings. What I need is info on a sleazy fund-raising scheme I think his party is carrying on. I don't have a solid clue to the scam, but I know it's operating."

Schuyler filled him in on the unlikely visit of Clara Staples and King Kellogg to the Pemenex mine.

"So what do you think, Arthur?"

"What I think is that Pemenex needs a lot of help in the Interior subcommittee, especially since they're foreign-controlled and Charlie is looking for their heads. They'll pay any amount—under the table, in the dark, hard money, soft money, even an occasional bribe. My guess is your guess: that something rotten is going on in Colorado."

Rafferty tried to hide his excitement. "Arthur, can you find out what's going on?"

"I want to help," Steadman responded, "but not for you. If I can knock Billings out of the race, it'll be just me and Charlie, and I can beat that kid hands down anytime. Can I get the info? Normally maybe not, but we have a detente with the other party. Just give me a week and I'll try to have the poop. Not in writing and not on tape. Just ask Tolliver or Charlie about that. No, when we meet it'll be only the two of us out on the range, with no one but the coyotes for a mile around. OK?"

Schuyler shook his neighbor's hand.

"It's a deal, Mountain Boy. And maybe, just maybe, I'll have a stock tip for you coming up soon. I've got my eye on a sweetheart of a genetics company in Boise."

CHAPTER 44

Patriot felt somewhat better since he'd heard the news of Charlie Palmer's precipitous drop in the poll numbers courtesy of the so-called sex tapes that revealed him to be as horny as he was over-bold politically.

But that was still not assurance that Palmer's quest for the White House was dead. Just since Labor Day, the candidate had advertised in virtually every newspaper, offering free copies of the American Manifesto, his catalogue of future national mayhem. Patriot heard that they had received four million responses in just one week. Tragic.

Not content to intrude on the prerogatives of the two parties, Palmer had promised that if elected, he would put in a "no subsidy" law, which would wipe out all corporate and business welfare, whose cost had been estimated at some $85 billion a year.

On Charlie's long hit list were the below-cost sale of timber from the Forest Service to lumber companies (including $200 million in free roads for access), even the Export-Import Bank, cleverly developed to loan taxpayers' money to foreigners to buy American products, whether they could afford it or not.

Always eager to rub somebody's nose in it, Palmer had reprinted the paragraph in the federal bank's annual report that projected a *40 percent default rate*, or some $6 billion that taxpayers would have to shell out for just one year's defaulted loans. What amateurs like Charlie didn't want to understand, Patriot thought, was the cost of visionary government.

He had tried to be a patient man, but apparently Palmer was too stubborn to know when he was defeated. Personal revelations had brought some disgrace to Charlie, but had not worked well enough to stop him. Now was a time for more extreme measures.

His best instrument was that loyal, if expensive, someone from another world.

He drafted his usual "personal" advertisement: STONY. NEED STILL MORE FLAGS. PATRIOT.

In a few days, he anticipated an answer and a meeting at the usual place, usual time—10:30 P.M. on the deserted dock on the Anacostia River.

This move, he hoped, could well write "finis" to Charlie's game.

CHAPTER 45

Rafferty's smile was almost smug.

That was one of the luxuries he permitted himself after a victory, which he had just accomplished by uncovering the facts of the Pemenex campaign swindle.

His second reward was two hours of total relaxation. He visited the stables with Jenny, who now was as interested in Charlie as in the birth of a foal sired by their best stud, Skytop. Surprising everyone, Rafferty took a half-hour nap, his first in years. His doctor had prescribed that as a daily regimen, but the doctor had since died, and at sixty-nine, Rafferty felt as chipper as ever.

He attributed his longevity (he planned to live to one hundred with a fortune of $100 billion) to his leaving New York City. The cultural loss was made up by better air. Instead of murky bus effluent, the air at Brooklyn-in-Montana seemed to have been processed by God himself, as it surely was.

Jenny, not he, was the real Westerner. To her, a sick horse was worth thirty humans. To him, from childhood in Brooklyn, horses were animals who pulled vegetable wagons and defecated in the street. He paid for the Big Sky stables and enjoyed the victories—not the losses—in the races. But the setup was really for Jenny, who would someday (he figured she would be fifty-three) inherit the whole shebang. God protect her.

In any case, today's victory was a sweet one. Manny had done an intrepid job of espionage and faxed him the details on Pemenex in a coded document, which his receiver digitally translated. Steadman had scored as well. But instead of a private mountain rendezvous on a moonless night, they had met in a civilized environment—in armchairs under a stuffed bison head in Steadman's home, drinking Jim Beam by the shotful.

The story was simple: Kellogg had devised a scheme to get around Federal Election Commission contribution limits. Using the American investors of Pemenex as the conduit, $1 million in $25,000 portions was delivered to party headquarters.

That was courtesy of Congress's ability to screw the public through complexity. The party used the cash for campaigns, just avoiding the name of the candidate. As if people didn't know who was running for President. Who were they kidding?

The third leg of intelligence on Pemenex came from contacts in Bavaria, specifically a German investment group that had installed Treulich as chairman of the mining company. (It had cost Rafferty $10,000 "talking money.")

That final key to the scheme incriminated candidate Champ Billings, who had arranged to profit personally through a clever subterfuge. He'd lay out the scam in detail to Charlie, who could use it to chop Billings off at the political knees. Schuyler smilingly took another drink to celebrate that idea.

Charlie's campaign surely needed a shot of adrenaline. The sex tapes had taken their toll. Each time he saw a new poll, Charlie's numbers were a little lower. The last CNN numbers showed Charlie with only 26 percent, Billings with 37, and Steadman with 33. Eleven points was too large a spread to close rapidly—unless.

"Charles, this is Sky," he called to the candidate in a hotel in Atlanta where he was campaigning. "I'd like you to come up here for a day beginning tomorrow. Ask George to cancel everything for twenty-four hours. I have something very important to talk over, in person. Take my jet and bill it to the campaign. It's kosher. What's it about? Charlie, I'll tell you all about it over a great steak."

Charlie knew he could turn Schuyler down with impunity. And he would have if he didn't desperately need a break from the grind of campaigning.

Arrive in a town—this time Atlanta—at night, go to sleep, and start with a radio talk show at 6 A.M. drive time. Not on the phone as he'd prefer, but for the pride of the host, smack in the radio studio with a mike and cup of hot coffee. Then a morning television show, then a luncheon at the chamber of commerce, then two appointments with newsmen, then the 5 o'clock TV news, then a campaign dinner, then by Sky's jet to another town to do it all over again.

He was also being driven to distraction by the sex questions. First it was about the pregnancy and abortion. Now, courtesy of the *Tattler*, they were about his virility. He had worked up two answers: a sincere-voiced one about the poor judgment of youth, and a funny one about Mohonk. "At least I'm not impotent—yet. But six more weeks on this campaign, and I'll be so popped that I'll ask the *Tattler* for a retraction."

Now he was on his way to Montana, away from campaigning for a welcome twenty-four-hour break.

Rickie and the Sky Ranch helicopter, branded with a puff of blue clouds zapped by a lightning bolt, picked him up at the Great Falls airport. Within half an hour, it had put him down on the pad at the giant homestead.

He was traveling with one Secret Service man, a quiet, burly youngster named Mark Connolly, from Chicago, a former college runner and cop. With his girth, speed, and ever-scanning eyes, Connolly made him feel safe. Ever since that car run-down, he had occasional pangs of fear.

A second Secret Service agent, Jim Galos, was sent ahead to the ranch to oversee the security. He would be positioned at the main house while Connolly personally covered Charlie.

This second visit to Montana was different for Charlie because in the period of seventy days, Charlie felt as if he had aged seventy years. The first visit to Sky was a lark, the upshot of a young congressman's bet about political connivers. He had lost the wager, but had come out personally unscathed.

Today, he was a candidate for the presidency, with long odds of winning and with the weight, not of the world, but of the screwy American political system, on his head. Yet the media seemed more interested in orgasms than in the need to save a wracked, and wrecked, middle class and clean up the corruption of campaign financing, and with it, the American soul.

Now that he was in Montana, he could feel the tension oozing out of him. He deboarded the helicopter and spotted Jenny.

"Charles, how wonderful," she said, kissing him lightly on the lips. "Never expected our next President to have time for little old us. How're you doing?"

Jenny wasn't the type for lengthy explanations, but there was no sense lying to her. She was more sensible than she sometimes seemed.

"Not so good, Jenny. A little worn, and all the criticism has gotten me down."

"Well, you'll spend a day here and I'll try to pick you up. Besides, Daddy tells me he has something that's going to turn things right around."

Charlie registered visible surprise. What could that be? But it didn't pay to underestimate or anticipate Sky Rafferty.

"Daddy couldn't come out to greet you," Jenny added. "He's locked in his room with two phones, negotiating a deal to buy a genetics firm in Boise. He'll meet us at dinner. But if you can stand my company, why don't we do a little riding?"

Within a half hour, Charles was saddled on Bertha the pinto, the twelve-year-olds' favorite. Connolly was given a four-year-old bay, and Charlie noticed how well he handled it. The wary young agent had come well prepared. He had put a two-way walkie-talkie in the saddlebag and strapped on a .22 sharpshooter's rifle.

"What's that for?" Charlie asked. "Here in the middle of nowhere?"

Connolly just smiled in response. Charlie shrugged.

They rode from the stables into tall grass country toward a cattle-grazing area. Charlie was in the presence of two real riders, who slowed periodically so he could catch up.

He realized that the Secret Service agent was becoming too occupied with Jenny. After one stern look from Charlie, Connolly corrected himself, sticking close to the candidate. Charlie hardly thought he needed protection in the privacy of Big Sky, but that wasn't his decision.

They had traveled almost seven miles, weaving in between the herds, acknowledging the presence of the Land Rovers doing cowboy work, when Charlie called over to Jenny and Connolly.

"I think I'd like to head back. I know it's good for me, but I'm a little tired."

They turned around and trotted toward the ranch, soon out of sight of the cattle but still about two miles from home, all alone on the plateau. The silence of the long vistas was calming, and Charlie welcomed the release of tension. At this moment, he didn't care if he ever again saw a committee hearing room or a television studio, or entertained the dream of the White House.

"Look over there," Charlie said, pointing toward an interrupting roar in the tranquillity. It was a helicopter heading their way, its whine a reminder of the hurried civilization he had left behind. "Is that one of yours, Jenny?"

Jenny reined in her horse and stared skyward. "No, I don't think so. It doesn't have the Sky brand on it."

Agent Connolly joined them, watching the helicopter change altitude, dropping rapidly from about five hundred to two hundred feet in less than thirty seconds. It was headed away, but somehow Charlie got the feeling that the pilot—and a second man he spotted within—were interested in them.

Was some magazine or television program trying to photograph the presidential candidate at play?

As they stared, the helicopter whir increased in decibels. It seemed to hover like a butterfly, then change directions. It started to turn, and within a minute, it was on a beeline with the three horse riders.

"IT'S COMING RIGHT FOR US!" Jenny screamed.

Charlie could see agent Connolly quickly dismount. He reached for the radio in his saddlebag and quickly unstrapped the sharpshooter's rifle.

"DISMOUNT!" the agent shouted. "TURN YOUR HORSES TOWARD THE HELICOPTER AND HIDE BEHIND THEM! QUICK."

He turned to the walkie-talkie. "Jim. Come in. This is Connolly."

"This is Galos. What's up, kid?"

"Might be real trouble. Get your ass into Rafferty's copter. Get Rick to pilot you. Bring an automatic rifle. We're about two miles due west of the house. And hurry!"

Connolly had accurately anticipated the mayhem. The helicopter suddenly swooped down from two hundred to less than fifty feet over the grange. The copter was all-gray without any markings. In the plastic bubble up front, Charlie could see a rifle poked through a small opening. This was no inquiring reporter.

The helicopter flew over their heads with barely six feet to spare, the whoosh of its rotors frightening the horses. Almost in unison, the animals whined plaintively.

"HOLD TIGHT TO THE REINS!" Jenny called out. Even Charlie's mild-mannered pinto started to pull away.

The helicopter passed overhead, but no gun fired. They breathed more easily for a few seconds until agent Connolly called out again.

"LOOK QUICK. They're turning back for another run. Again, put your horses between the copter and you."

The helicopter began its second run, closing rapidly. This time the weapon was not silent. The copter passed rapidly overhead, the gun opening fire, punctuating the ground below with a half-dozen bullets hitting in a near straight line, digging up the turf as would a host of bad golfers.

Agent Connolly crouched behind his horse, took aim, and opened return fire with his sharpshooter.

"I THINK IT GOT HIM!" he yelled triumphantly as the second man in the copter seemed to crumple. The helicopter dipped as if to crash to the ground no more than a hundred yards from them. Then suddenly, the nose picked up.

They watched transfixed as the helicopter gained altitude and headed away from them. For a minute it increased the distance between them, then began to make a long swooping loop in the sky, eventually changing directions a full 180 degrees. Now, once again, it was headed right for them.

"They're coming back!" Charlie shouted as Connolly dug his elbows into the ground, his rifle poised to fire as soon as the helicopter came into range.

"Looks like they're loaded for bear!" the agent shouted. "Get down on the ground behind your horses. NOW!"

As the word "horse" registered, Charlie looked around him quickly. In the confusion, Bertha had bolted.

Connolly saw the problem. "Get behind me and hit the dirt!" he screamed at Charlie.

The helicopter came down to less than thirty feet off the plain, its engine accelerating, approaching rapidly at full speed.

Up front in the bubble, Charlie could make out the man that Connolly thought he had taken out. He was crouched with what looked like an automatic rifle still in hand.

Charlie dug his face into the ground and prayed. Could his quest for the Oval Office and his whole confusing existence end so unceremoniously on this forlorn Western knoll? He glanced at Connolly, whose young visage was contorted into an expression of fear and determination, his trigger finger at the ready.

Suddenly, Charlie heard a crescendo, the sound of a volley of bullets filling the pristine air. He stared up at the helicopter, waiting for it to come in for the merciless kill.

He was shocked. Instead of making another run, the gray helicopter had turned tail sharply and was heading away. He stared upward. Some two hundred feet above him was another helicopter—carrying the brand of the Sky Ranch, the sound of automatic fire coming from its nose.

Rick and agent Jim Galos had responded within minutes, and were now chasing the offending helicopter, if futilely. Rafferty's old surplus buy didn't have the power of the modern machine that had threatened them.

Connolly, Charlie, and Jenny rose from their position and waved at their rescuers in the sky. The Sky Ranch copter was now dipping low, ready to land on a flat outcropping close to them. Charlie assumed it was to pick him up.

He searched around for Bertha, then let out a sigh of lament. During the melee, the pinto had broken his grip and moved right into the line of fire. Perhaps a hundred feet from him, Bertha lay on the ground, moaning.

Jenny ran over and with her handkerchief wiped Bertha's frothing mouth. "She's been hit in the right leg," Jenny shouted, her emotions spilling over. "We'll have to put her down."

She looked up at Connolly. "Can I borrow your gun? I prefer to do this myself."

Jenny stood over the horse's head, holding the rifle tightly. "I don't want to miss," she said as her shot rang out, echoing back on the range.

"It doesn't seem possible anyone would try to kill me," Charlie said, recounting the story to Rafferty. "But it happened just as I said. We're lucky that Rick and Galos came so quickly with your copter. Agent Connolly has called the details in to Washington. I told them I'd appreciate it if the press wasn't notified."

"Why hold it back from the press?" Jenny asked, curious.

"I don't want any more attention drawn to me, good or bad. Americans tend to get distracted by personalities during elections. Our strength is our ideas, and I've got to hammer them home."

He, Jenny, and Rafferty, and agents Connolly and Galos were at dinner. Connolly had called in the helicopter's description, but it could have put down secretly anywhere within fifty miles. So far, the search had come up empty.

Washington had decided no reinforcements were needed since the candidate was returning in the morning. But they advised Charlie to stay indoors until he was ready to leave.

Rafferty listened without a word, then finally spoke.

"Charlie, there are demons out there trying to stop your movement. I can hardly believe that the political parties would try anything so crude as an assassination. Maybe like last time, some demented person is just trying to scare you out of the race. I think if whoever's behind this wanted you dead, the helicopter gunman could have managed it. Still, I suppose some politicians will do anything for power—and cash."

Charlie's interest was piqued. "Who, for instance, is looking for cash?"

"For instance your opponent, Champ Billings, chief porker of America."

"But, Sky, that's all fat for his constituents, not for him. So far his only transgressions have been slick tricks in the raising of campaign money."

"Oh, he's still at that, but this time he's gone too far. He's gotten sticky fingers."

"In what way?" Charlie was surprised.

Schuyler told of the visit to Pemenex by Kellogg and Clara. For Charlie's sake, he was going to keep Clara out of it, but now he realized that personal feelings were less important than exposing Billings. He recounted the full details of the scheme to funnel a million into the Billings campaign.

"Are you sure Clara was involved?" Charlie asked, trying to hide his disappointment.

"Absolutely, Charlie. She wasn't the ringleader but I understand she was brought along to charm Treulich, the Pemenex boss. She did such a good job that the German offered to give her his antique Mercedes touring car as a gift."

"What? Is that true?"

"Sorry to hurt you Charlie, but I got it from a horse's mouth at the Colorado plant."

Charlie was dumbstruck, seeking, but not finding, some rejoinder to Sky's accusations. Was it all just scuttlebutt? He hoped so, but Rafferty, for all of his faults, was not prone to bad reporting.

"Was there any personal quid pro quo for Billings in the million-dollar contribution?" Charlie asked.

"You bet your life. If elected Billings has promised to veto your foreign mining reform bill if it got through Congress." Schuyler paused for effect. "But Billings wasn't satisfied with just a secret arrangement for the party. I now have proof positive—an affidavit from a Pemenex executive in Germany—that he's on the take personally."

Charlie took a swig of Old Green Mountain beer and whistled.

"What's the scam?" Charlie asked.

"Simple. If Billings wins and becomes President of the United States, he's happy and becomes rich when he leaves office. But should Billings lose, he'll be out in the cold. His Senate seat was up this year. So Pemenex is setting up a booby prize—insurance for Billings in return for his cooperation if he wins. They're secretly giving him stock options that will guarantee him a $1 million profit no matter what happens. It's been under wraps because Pemenex is privately owned with roots in Singapore, Taiwan, and Germany. If not for my contacts, no one would ever know."

"Dirty, dirty, dirty. The story of American politics," Charlie wailed. "What are you going to do about it?"

"What am *I* going to do about it? Charlie, you've got it ass backwards. I'm just the messenger. You're the candidate. What are *you* going to do about it? I'd think you'd want to expose it yourself, right on television during the debate with Billings. Cut him down in front of a hundred million Americans."

"No way, Schuyler. I won't go down into the gutter to join Billings. We're going to win this on our ideas—or not at all. What you do with the information on Billings is your business, but keep me strictly out of it."

Rafferty laughed. "Charlie, you're a piece of work. Can't you just once rise above principle? I sometimes think I made a mistake with you. You belong in a university somewhere, bullshitting with your students about the corrupt world and bemoaning reality. I sure wish you'd grow up—and fast."

Charlie was proud that he didn't get angry.

"Sky, if I grew up, as you call it, I might end up like Billings. Now, you wouldn't want that, would you? If this country's ever going to get its head on straight, I think we need a few idealistic kids—maybe like me. Dontyathink?"

CHAPTER 46

"Clara, you look beautiful, as usual. What's on your schedule for today?"

Charlie had come to New York City for the great debate and had made a date with Clara for breakfast at 9 A.M. It was for the Palm Court, a faux-French island of serenity in the grand lobby of the Plaza Hotel on Fifth Avenue and Fifty-eighth Street, the nucleus of the city.

They had checked in the day before when the management offered Charlie the Presidential Suite for only $10,000 a day, a substantial cut off the regular rate. Instead, he had settled for two rooms for a total of $650.

Now seated at a small table (they were all small) in the corner of the Palm Court, he tried to appear inconspicuous. Several passersby recognized him, but didn't approach, one blessing of blasé New York.

Three Secret Service agents were at the next table, trying to look unconnected to Charlie. But there was something about gumshoes, federal or otherwise, that gave them away.

The detail had been enlarged to three because of the fracas in Montana, and a helicopter was assigned to guard Charlie in all non-city environments.

Despite the attack, Charlie's morale was high. Yesterday, he and Clara had a wonderful day together in New York. Tonight was the debate between him, Billings, and Steadman. He was eager to confront his adversaries, whom he was convinced had little to say—just warmed-over rhetoric that the public was finally catching on to.

His schedule today was full. He had editorial interviews and back-to-back lunches with the *New York Times* and the *Wall Street Journal.* Like most of the media, they still found it hard to decipher his ideological stance. No one seemed to catch on to Charlie's political secret: He had no ideology. Whatever was good for the great mass of Americans, the persecuted, tax-burdened middle class—those who worked and made between $25,000 and $100,000—was what drove him. The fact that neither political party understood that didn't seem to penetrate the talking-and-writing heads in the media.

"Charles, I have an easy day," Clara answered. "A little shopping, then I'm visiting with an old friend from my early waitress days. She now lives in a duplex in Sutton Place. I suppose you politicians call that fulfilling the American Dream."

"That's right, Clara. But you and your friends seem to have hop-scotched over the usual hurdles on the way up."

Clara laughed. Her trill never failed to please him.

"But seriously, Charles, this business of trying to harm you is getting to me. Who would try such a horrible thing? I understand they killed Jenny Rafferty's favorite horse."

"Yes, it's strange. I suppose whoever's behind it thinks that's the way to get me out of the race. But that's not going to happen." Charlie paused. "Darling, do you think anybody in the parties would be crazy enough to do something like this?"

Clara seemed taken aback, even a touch annoyed.

"Never. Tolliver is just a fat-ass political genius with a big mouth. But he's really harmless. And Norm Sobel. Well, I don't know him well, but he's a Ph.D. and so scholarly. No, there has to be another answer."

"Clara, please keep your eyes open on that. By the way, the Synergy scam backfired on them—courtesy of your tip. Thanks again."

"How'd you stop them?"

"Easy. We asked a *Barron's* columnist to warn the financial community that my opponents were trying to get me through the stock of my ex-firm. He ran a little gossip item. After that, anything they tried would have blown up in their faces."

"I'm glad, Charles. You know I'm still with the party, but I warned them. No more dirty tricks. If they did, I swore I'd bring it right to you, which I did."

"I know, sweetheart, and I appreciate it."

Now Charlie braced himself. He had asked Clara to this breakfast to iron out what really troubled him—Clara's part in the Pemenex deal.

He'd have to face her on this, and now. How could they have a decent relationship when Clara was freebooting with Tolliver and Kellogg in some campaign finance scam? In this case, it wasn't against him, but it was another standard operating piece of political corruption.

"Clara . . ." Charlie began hesitantly. "I need . . ."

"Yes, lover, what is it?" Clara purred, taking his face in her elegant long hands. "Do you need my help on something else? Anything, Mr. President-to-be. Anything your heart desires."

Charlie stared at his love, seated just where he'd want her all his life, facing him, touching him, encouraging him.

The hell with Pemenex. It had nothing to do with him anyway, and he had told Rafferty he didn't want it divulged. He would beat Billings fair and square on the issues.

"Clara, what I need is . . ."

"Yes, darling, what?"

"Just you, Clara. Always you."

CHAPTER 47

The debate was being held in Cooper Union Hall in New York, a historic building that had hosted such diverse speakers as Abe Lincoln and Norman Mailer.

Built in 1858, the cast-iron structure—the site of a Lincoln campaign speech in February 1860—had been hurriedly fitted for a giant improvised satellite dish, which looked ridiculously incompatible with the old architecture.

Inside, Don Leland was being made up. Seated next to him was co-host newsman Roscoe Sands, syndicated columnist of "Washington Eye." Both had a reputation for outspokenness, which made them natural anchors for a debate involving upstart Charlie Palmer.

Everyone talked of a three-way split in the popular vote, but Leland was more interested in the three-way split in the Electoral College. That non-college had a total of 538 votes, one for each House and Senate member, and since 1964, three for the District of Columbia. In the final accounting, the score of that handful was more important than the vox populi.

Leland knew that no one really voted for President, or Vice-President. Instead, Article II, Section 1 of the Constitution arranged for individuals called electors to be chosen in each state. These people, generally party functionaries, did the real electing. In the old days, the electors were named by the state legislatures. Now they were popularly elected.

Popular vote tallies for presidential candidates are interesting trivia, but only the electoral votes, earned state by state, really counted. To win the presidency, a candidate needed a majority of the electors, or 270 votes. Worse yet, in most states, the winner took all.

To Leland, it was a ridiculous, anti-democratic system, prompting him to recall that three men—Andy Jackson, Samuel Tilden, and Grover Cleveland—had won the popular vote but lost the presidency, although Jackson and Cleveland won it back four years later. But there it was. And it would stay that way until the Constitution was amended, as Charlie Palmer was advocating.

Meanwhile, the candidates' first goal, Leland was sure, was to win the popular vote. In the polls, splitting the undecideds, Billings was ahead with 35 percent. Steadman was close behind with 32 percent, and Charlie, having finally diverted the public's mind from the sex tapes, now had a respectable 29 percent. The remaining 4 percent went to fringe parties.

The last week of September and the first week of October leading up to the debate had been golden for Charlie. He had stumped all over the country, repeating over and over his American Manifesto, his middle-class program to "Bring America Back," as he said.

His crowds were getting larger, and the skepticism about having a freshman congressman with only six months of elective office vying for the Oval Office was beginning to wan.

From his thirty-five-item manifesto, Charlie had broken out two central themes, his "Political Bill of Rights" and his "Economic Bill of Rights." Each contained ten points, and he seemed to be alternating his pitch between them at his whistle, bus, or school stops until he, Leland—and he was sure Charlie as well—wearied of the repetition. But repetition was apparently the name of the game.

On the political front, Charlie's crusade called for cleaning up the money mess in campaigns, creating elections in which virtually everyone could be a candidate, national primaries, term limits, no retirement pay for congressmen and other politicians, total reshaping of the Cabinet.

Charlie's jabs at the status quo were bringing cheers from crowds frustrated with politicians. Leland could smell that something was in the wind, and it was blowing away from the conventional big names toward the new kid on the block.

Charlie's Economic Bill of Rights was attractive—so much so that the major party candidates were beginning to ape him. The unsure economic environment was eating away at the natural optimism of the American people, and Charlie had remedies, one after the other.

Some daily papers even compared him to FDR, and a handful, from St. Louis to Newark to San Diego, were actually endorsing him. In an apologetic mood, one Connecticut daily dropped its lifelong attachment to Republican orthodoxy and praised Charlie in an editorial headed, LET'S TAKE A CHANCE.

Defections of high-level politicians to his cause, while not massive, were becoming regular occurrences in these last weeks of the campaign. Leland had Senator Larrimore on his Sunday morning show (Charlie had turned down him, and all talk show hosts), and the venerable VP candidate had reeled off a list who were deserting their party to join Charlie's crusade: Senator Clarence Jackson of Michigan; Governor Keith Littleman of New Mexico, even the formidable conservative from South Carolina, Townsend March.

Leland had seen Charlie on C-Span the night before, speaking to a conference in Portland. Without a strong, lighter-taxed middle class, America wouldn't be America, Charlie explained. Leland agreed that the middle class was what America was all about. Every nation had its rich and more than its fair share of poor. But America had become a legend because of social mobility that had created an ever-growing middle class. And now?

In Portland, Charlie laid out his fears that like the corporation, America was getting economically downsized. The poor had the government. The rich would always survive. But it was the middle class who was paying the freight and getting kicked in the groin for their efforts.

Charlie had ticked off his Economic Bill of Rights: Close the IRS and put in a national sales tax; free trade with developed countries but no common markets with low-wage nations, which would only depress our own wages; reduce the size of all government by eliminating six million of the twenty million government workers through attrition; cut taxes across the board thirty percent over ten years; appoint a Federal Reserve Board that will stimulate growth through low interest rates; change Social Security gradually into an "individual" plan like the 401K so that people might retire as millionaires; fight corporate irresponsibility and fat-cat CEOs; give tax breaks to companies that manufacture here and penalize those who send jobs overseas; get rid of welfare and substitute FDR's WPA—jobs not babies; curb corporate welfare.

Leland now realized that Charlie wasn't a fake, but a sensible revolutionary determined to remake the system. His genius was that he gave everything a middle-class twist, and did it very comprehensively. And finally, the public seemed to be listening.

Leland didn't like politicians and he didn't like to give them credit, but he was *somewhat* impressed by the bustling young maverick. Maybe Charlie reminded him of himself—a decade ago.

"Seven minutes to airtime, Mr. Leland and Mr. Sands," an assistant called, poking his face into the makeup room.

The hosts entered the packed auditorium and took their seats on a dais. They were separated from the debaters, who were standing on a platform with front-runner Billings in the center. Charlie was on the left and Steadman on the right.

The newscaster cast a glance at Charlie, who looked confident. Though he was personally vulnerable, Palmer had proven that when it came to ideas, he was an iron man. No controversy fazed him. He even seemed more self-assured as things heated up.

Leland noticed that Billings and Steadman, the old pros, were trying to look composed, but were nervous around the edges. The Baltimore debacle had hurt party reputations, and this was a last hurrah for both candidates. If Billings lost, he'd be vacating his Senate seat. And Steadman was an ex-governor with nothing to return to except his ranch. Charlie was also vacating his congressional seat by running for President.

"Gentlemen," Leland could hear the producer, Jerry Blackman, in his earpiece. "Thirty seconds to go. Don, announce the terms of the debate, then pick it up with Billings. Steadman next, then Palmer. I'm banking on an old pro like you to keep it moving."

Leland checked the monitor to be sure his hairpiece was on straight. He breathed easier. The makeup was superbly done, giving him ten years retroactively. Even his pointed chin now seemed less prominent.

"Eight, seven, six, five, four, three, two, one, GO!"

"Ladies and gentlemen here in Cooper Union, and the hundred million people watching, welcome," Leland began. "This is the only debate of the presidential campaign, and we've kept the rules simple. The position of the candidates is no indication of their ideology. Congressman Palmer is standing on the left, yet no one has been able to place him in the political spectrum. Unless, as some say, he's far out.

"But we'll begin with the man standing in the center, Senator Champ Billings of Kentucky. Each candidate will have a three-minute opening statement, and the rest of the time will be used for questioning. And to the audience, please don't express any partiality. Now, let's begin with Senator Billings . . ."

Charlie stood at his microphone, observing as if he were a historian, not a participant.

Billings was expounding with the usual mush mix of patriotism and government economics. The Kentuckian didn't mention it, but even in the Great Depression, all government—federal, state, and local—cost only 17 cents on the dollar, 5 cents more than during the 1920s. The number had gone up to 30 cents during the JFK years and had now hit a record 40 cents—and there was no Depression. Some people, including Billings, and probably Steadman as well, thought that was quite normal.

It occurred to Charlie that the critics like himself were not the "crackpots." It was the politicians and the government who were the true crackpots, inventing mad schemes to first seduce, then screw, the public.

The three minutes of Billings's pablum was soon over, ending with his recitation of the Pledge of Allegiance. That was followed by three minutes of Arthur Steadman. Having been a governor and hewing to a budget, he made a little more sense. But still, the combination of politics as usual and a conventional mind were obvious. He finished with "of the people, by the people, for the people," and Charlie guessed that old Abe's ghost in the building must be suffering chills.

Charlie waited his turn. He had no idea what he was going to say. That had been his strength until now, and he saw no reason to change. He stared out at the audience. The lights cut down most of his vision, but he thought he saw Clara there, smiling. If he wanted to impress anyone, it was she.

"Now, we'll hear from Congressman Charles Knudsen Palmer, independent candidate for President. The mike is yours."

Charlie stood, silent for what seemed like almost a half minute.

"Congressman, please begin," he could hear Leland prompt.

He began in his style, at first slowly and hesitantly, then building to power as he went.

"I want to start by pleading political inexperience," Charlie opened frankly. "I began this voyage just six months ago. What I bring to this race is my experience as a citizen, my independence, and my instinct for good government. My first day as congressman, I cut my office budget by $400,000, or almost one-third, something no other representative has done before or since. Why? Because I didn't know I wasn't supposed to. I have been blessed with an instant identification with the American working middle class, where I came from. Of the three men on this platform, I believe I'm the only one who has a clue as to what must be done to save America. And, frankly, it needs saving."

For the next minute, Charlie laid out much of the American Manifesto, hitting about half the now-famous thirty-five points. Suddenly, he hesitated, standing at the lectern, absolutely silent for some fifteen seconds.

"Yes, Congressman. Please continue," Leland prompted. "You only have a total of three minutes for your opening remarks."

"I know . . . Mr. Leyland, but I'm thinking about whether . . ."

Charlie could hear the buzz of impatience.

"Now, Congressman, nothing is deadlier than dead air space. Why don't you just recite your name and Social Security number. Or better still, tell me something strictly between us. There are only a hundred million people listening."

Charlie came out of his near-trance. He wasn't sure he wanted to share this with the nation right now, but he had based his campaign on frankness. Why turn back now? Yes, he'd deliver his "October Surprise."

"Mr. Candidate, can you speak now?"

"I can, and I will. For some time I've criticized our political parties. Well, I'm going to go further—perhaps even alienate a number of my backers. We once needed those parties. They brought together citizens of similar views. They made up for lack of good communications. Well, that's all passe. Communications are perfect. People know as much about the issues as politicians, and the two major parties—together—represent less than 40 percent of the nation. Yet we rely on them to run our country. That no longer makes any sense."

Charlie came to a sudden halt. Not so much to gather his thoughts as to recover his breathing. He continued.

"What I'm saying is that we no longer need political parties. Why should people have to work their way up in the ranks before they run for office? Party leadership is no test of competency or patriotism. More and more, the parties have become centers of narrowness, opportunism, and self-interest—institutions which keep people out of, not bring them into, the democratic process."

"So what do you recommend, Mr. Congressman?" Leland asked.

"In a nutshell, I believe we should close all political parties and make our elections—from school board to President of the United States—into nonpartisan races where people run on their own platforms and their own merits. People can still organize as parties—it's a free country. But they'll have no place on the ballot."

Once again, Charlie halted momentarily, then began.

"I tell you this: It's the single most important change we can make if we want America to survive and grow in the twenty-first century."

The audience was stunned. They were silent and, Leland thought, contemplative. Never had they expected this. They apparently didn't know what to think. To be frank, neither did he.

"Congressman, continue. You've got another thirty seconds."

"No, I have nothing more to say at this time."

The first question was put by co-host Roscoe Sands to Senator Billings.

"What do you think of Congressman Palmer's idea of eliminating all political parties and running our elections on an individual non-partisan basis?"

Billings had turned livid with anger.

"I think he's mad. Why, without parties, there's no American democracy. They give solidity to platforms, they organize our thoughts. And how would we raise the money we need for campaigns? Palmer is not only inexperienced, as he admits, but hopelessly naive. That's not the person we need in the Oval Office."

"Congressman Palmer. What about that? Without parties, how would we raise the money for campaigns?" Sands asked.

Charlie had waited for this one. "Well, at my kickoff in Philadelphia, I laid out a plan to eliminate private money from politics. We should make it a crime to solicit any funds or spend one's own money. I want to raise all money through a voluntary organization like the Red Cross, which will distribute it equally to all candidates on a nonpartisan basis. We don't need to use tax money. And we don't need political parties for that. In fact, I can't think of any good reason why America needs them anymore. All they do is divide the nation."

Billings seemed ready to explode, but Arthur Steadman, who had been quiet during the questioning period so far, suddenly pressed his way into the debate.

"Your scheme to get rid of politicians raising money for their campaigns sounds fine and idealistic, Congressman Palmer." The ex-Governor spoke calmly into the mike. "But you've said many times there's too much money in politics and people shouldn't be able to spend their own money on their campaigns. Meanwhile, you're being backed by one of the richest men in America—to the tune of $100 million. Aren't you being hypocritical?"

Leland could see Charlie's expression turn anxious. But surely Palmer had thought this one out in advance. He wondered if the young orator could dig himself out of that hole.

"Governor Steadman. I can't stand here before the nation and say that your comment is ridiculous, because it's not," Charlie rejoined. "But I can say this: The two political parties have invented a money system that is outrageous, and they close ranks against anyone who would change it. Yes, I am backed by a billionaire, but I tell you that only someone from the outside can break the conspiracy in which money rules. Well, I'm now an independent and if I weren't well-backed I wouldn't be standing on this stage tonight promising to stop the whole corrupt campaign finance system. No, I don't think it's hypocrisy."

Leland, who was slated to ask the next question, could see that Charlie lacked no self-confidence. In fact, it was that sureness—what some called arrogance—that had turned him against Charlie in the first place. But now? Maybe this firebrand made more sense than anyone.

"But, Congressman, tell me," Leland asked. "How would this radical plan of yours work in practice. Can it be done?"

"It's simpler than the present system," Charlie responded quickly, now glad he had risked bringing it up. "There would be no more party primaries for President. They're a crazy quilt, different in every state. We'd also close the Electoral College and rely on popular vote nationwide. Anyone who got one hundred thousand signatures nationally would automatically be on a nonpartisan ballot for President in all fifty states as *individuals.* Everyone would then compete together in a series of runoffs until there was a winner with a *majority* of all the votes."

Leland sensed his interest focused. "When would we vote in your system of elections?"

"In the first one, maybe in May, everyone would compete together. Then the top five vote-getters would enter the semifinals in the summer. In November, as usual, the top two would be in the final runoff election. The winner would be the President, with no party affiliation, owing nothing to anyone except the people. We'd use the same system for Congress, but this time candidates would need only a few hundred signatures to get on the first ballot. All candidates would get an equal check from the quasi-governmental philanthropy organization. Then the top two vote-getters would go into a runoff. Not only would we eliminate political parties, but everyone elected would have a majority of all votes—unlike today. Once they got to Congress, these non-party people would choose their leaders based on merit and integrity. No more party discipline or party corruption. And with term limits and no pensions, we'll have a citizen, no-party government just as in the days of the Founding Fathers. Do you think our present party hacks could ever write our Constitution?"

Leland could see Billings's face turning beet red. His body seemed to want to levitate.

"So again, Senator Billings, what do you think of Congressman Palmer's system of running elections?"

"THE MAN IS CRAZY," Billings shouted, his anger bouncing off the ceiling. "There's no room in politics for radicals like him. I don't have to debate this man. He's exposed himself to the nation as a complete fool, an absolute disgrace."

Billings's breath was now coming irregularly. After a half minute, he quieted, regaining his composure.

"I'm sorry I lost my temper, gentlemen," Billings near-whispered, "but this man is a threat to America."

Co-host Roscoe Sands was silent, preparing to pick up the questioning. He spent a moment looking down at his notes, then rifled through what looked like a file folder.

"Senator Billings," he addressed the candidate, "I understand that you want to keep the present system. Is it because you profit so well from the party system and the status quo?"

"What does that mean? Are you impugning my integrity?"

"Well, sir, I have an affidavit here that your party, working with a prominent lobbyist, raised a million dollars in soft money from a foreign-owned mining company, which was then funneled into your campaign."

(Ah, it struck Charlie. This is where Rafferty's dirt went—to columnist Sands.)

"I know absolutely nothing about that," Billings answered, his face still florid. "If the finance people in the party are mishandling soft money, you should take that up with the Federal Elections Commission. They have remedies."

Sands looked down at his papers again. "I also have a statement that if elected, you promised these large contributors that you would veto any mining reform bill involving foreign-controlled corporations. Is that true?"

Billings's facial muscle started to quiver.

"THAT'S A DAMN LIE. WHO SAID THAT? I'LL SUE THE BASTARD!"

Quickly, he caught himself. "Sorry. I shouldn't use that language, but I never made any such pledge."

"Fine. Now, Senator, I have just one other question. Did you receive a promise of $1 million for you personally in the form of stock options from Pemenex in return for your veto pledge—as insurance should you lose the presidential election? I have an affidavit here from an executive in Germany, whose firm is part owner of the mining company in Colorado, so stating."

Billings stood at the mike immobile, his eyes glazed, his expression frozen.

"Senator, I repeat the question. Did you ask for and accept a promise—actually a bribe—of $1 million in stock options as a booby prize in case you lost the election?"

Again Billings was mute. The camera closed in on his expression, which was stiff and disdainful. His mouth seemed set in stone. Finally, he spoke.

"I don't have to answer that question. This is not a court of law and I don't have to take the Fifth. So, I simply refuse to answer."

This time no one could hold back the audience. Catcalls filled the room. People stood on chairs and booed. Bedlam overtook historic Cooper Union Hall.

Don Leland checked the studio clock. They still had a while to go, but it was obvious that the debate was in effect over, a dramatic finis shaped by the revelation about Billings—one that verified everything Palmer was talking about.

Had Charlie known about this and held his peace for decency's sake? Or had he expected it to explode during the debate through another source—in this case Roscoe Sands?

In the remaining time, the candidates fielded questions about fiscal policy and numerous failed government programs, in which ex-Governor Steadman heavily participated, debating with Charlie while a subdued Billings barely spoke at all.

Leland smiled in satisfaction. The debate had made news, which couldn't help but boot his own sagging television ratings. And as far as firebrand Charlie was concerned, things couldn't have taken a better turn. His so-called radicalism was shown, just maybe, to be simple common sense.

Leland could hear director Blackman in his earpiece. He stared into the camera, thrusting his pointed chin forward for emphasis.

"This is Don Leland, closing the dramatic proceedings at Cooper Union Hall. This ends the debate between the three presidential candidates. The next chapter is up to you, the voter, in just three weeks on Election Day.

"And now, to a commercial."

CHAPTER 48

Charlie stood at the back entrance to Cooper Union Hall, waiting for Clara to show with her Jaguar. Three Secret Service agents standing at his side would follow them to the Plaza Hotel in their own car.

The moment the chauffeured XJ-12 arrived, he jumped in.

"So what did you think, darling?" Charlie asked, anxious to get a review from the person who mattered most.

"What should I say, Charles? You were brilliant as usual. Nobody can top you when you think and talk, and Billings has been destroyed. But . . ."

Clara pulled her hand slowly away from his grasp.

"But what? This gives me a real shot at the White House. I thought you'd be pleased."

"I am, in a way. But Charles, what's this business about closing down all the political parties and switching to a nonpartisan no-contributor system? You're not serious about that, are you? I hope that was just political humbug for the crowd."

He winced. He had not taken her reaction into account. God, the party was a good part of her life.

"It's a goal, Clara, not something the nation's going to take up right away. I admit it's radical, but it solves so many problems and opens up politics to everyone."

"Maybe it's good for politics, but not for me, Charlie," she cried out shrilly, her voice straining. "You'll be destroying everything that I'm used to, and want. If you win and do what you say, there will be no more grand social life, no more party power. Washington will shrink in importance, maybe back to the small town it was before the war. It's not just a political revolution you're planning, it's a social and philosophical one as well. This will be . . . kind of a different country."

"But better, no?" Charlie felt like shrinking into the car upholstery. The daily conflict over politics that separated them had suddenly become a gulf, a chasm, a wide divide. "And I thought that maybe . . . I pray that if I win, we could get married and you'd be the First Lady of the land. You'll be a grand hostess at the White House and help me in every way."

Clara looked at him as if he were a stranger, not someone with whom she had exchanged vows of love. Her mouth became distorted, her eyes were flooded with hostility.

"MARRIAGE? DAMN IT, CHARLES. DON'T YOU UNDERSTAND?" her shriek filled the car. "I DON'T WANT TO CHANGE THINGS. I LIKE IT JUST THE WAY IT IS. I LIKE THE PARTY. I LIKE THE LOBBYISTS. I LIKE THE POWER. I LIKE THE CAMPAIGN MONEY. I LIKE THE SOCIAL LIFE. I LIKE EVERYTHING AND YOU'RE TRYING TO DESTROY IT ALL. WHY? WHY?"

He was overwhelmed with surprise. Clara had voiced these opinions before, but never with such heat, such animosity.

"But darling . . ." He never had a chance to finish. He was consumed by fear, the thought that he might lose her.

Clara slumped back into her seat, exhausted by her own outrage. She was silent, her body heaving for almost a minute. Then she turned and stared at him, suddenly warmer, tears filling her eyes.

"Charles, dear, I have everything in life I ever dreamed of—including you. Now I'm so afraid."

"Afraid of what, darling?"

"That I'll lose it all. The wonderful world of Washington, and you as well. Why can't you become President and leave everything just the way it is? America is more than two hundred years old and we've survived. Why change it now?"

He kissed Clara on her tearing eyes.

"You know why. Because if we don't, we won't have it for another two hundred years."

She sat upright. "I hate to say this, especially to you, Charles, but I really don't care about all that. I care much more about my own life. I've struggled horribly and put up with some very obnoxious men to get where I am. I don't want to lose it all just because the man I love—who may become President of the United States—has dreams that are very different from mine. Do you understand?"

He looked at Clara, at her beauty and the joy she gave him, and how she filled that constantly gnawing void in his life. And now she was threatening to take it all away if he didn't capitulate to her narrow vision of public life.

"I understand, Clara. I understand very well. And it's killing me. But I swear, there's absolutely nothing I can do about it."

CHAPTER 49

His mother's old house was the perfect place for the Election Day gathering.

Election night in Fairview would be like a family affair, Charlie decided, except for Secret Service agents who had the area staked out. The whole town would like to have peeked in on the proceedings. Who knew, maybe the small rural village would become the hometown of the next President of the United States—a boon for the local economy.

Charlie and his mother had made up the invitation list for that day—the first Tuesday after the first Monday in November, a date that Sally, a living encyclopedia of political trivia, reminded him had not been set nationally until 1845.

On that Tuesday morning, the guests had started to arrive. There were Sally Kirkland, Robbie Barnes, and two assistants. And of course George Semple. From Montana, Jenny Rafferty had made the trip. Schuyler declined, saying his heart couldn't take it if they lost. If they won, he didn't want the media all over him.

Vice presidential candidate John Larrimore was holding his own vigil in Oklahoma. Charlie had also invited Larry Lafferty, the Synergy executive running for his soon-to-be vacated House seat. Mother's oldest friend, Mildred Cole, the feisty eighty-year-old clerk at the Town Hall, and a local landmark, was there as well.

Mother Palmer had prepared a simple dinner of roast ham, cole slaw, a mixed salad, and pumpkin pie, the kind of food she had always served him and good enough, President or no president, she told Charlie. In any case, she must have done something right in raising him. That morning, Christine had also told her son she'd love him the same if he lost tonight or won, and he believed that with all his heart.

The friend who was invited but wasn't there was Clara Staples, whose absence tore at him. They had been estranged ever since that night at Cooper Union. Clara had stayed at Maison Grise while he was out stumping, covering sixteen cities in twenty-three days. He had seen her only once, at a rally at the Washington Monument, where she had come—elegant as usual—to wish him well, with only a kiss on the cheek as a sad souvenir of lost love.

He had made do without her these weeks, and would again if he had to. After all, he had twenty years of practice being alone, even when with a woman. But Clara's absence was tougher to take.

That morning, he and his mother cast their ballots at the Fairview High School. The staffers had voted in absentia the week before. Would their few votes mean anything? Would this be like the Kennedy-Nixon contest in 1960, when Kennedy had taken only 50.1 percent in winning? Or would the disclosure of Billings's graft make it a runaway—for somebody?

By early Tuesday morning, the first results came in—from Dixville Notch in New Hampshire, up near Canada. As usual, the village's thirteen votes were cast at one minute after midnight. Would it be prophetic, as it sometimes was? This time the vote was split: three for Billings; five each for Charlie and Steadman. What it did show, maybe, was Billings's weakness.

Television coverage at the house was restricted to one announcer. Although Don Leland had been offered the anchor spot at Election Central, he insisted on covering Charlie at home. Leland could be snotty, but lately he had started to come around.

There was also an AP reporter, Jimmy Haggerty, and an engineer and lighting man for Leland. Radio coverage would be taken off Leland's television signal. Outside, there was just one mobile television van with a dish feed. Mother Palmer had put her foot down. No cavalcade of vans to mar her lawn and driveway.

"The world will find out soon enough who's elected," Christine said forcefully. "The media don't need to trample on us along the way."

The press people would not socialize with the guests, she also insisted. Stick to your knittin', she told Leland, who nodded obediently. She put them in Charlie's old bedroom, not to be seen until her son agreed to an interview. She'd have liked to have parked them on the porch, but it was too chilly.

Charlie, Jenny, and Sally went for a walk into town that afternoon, accompanied by three Secret Service men. Jenny wanted to jog, but Charlie demurred. On Main Street in the three-block business area, a banner was hung—HOME OF THE NEXT PRESIDENT OF THE UNITED STATES. People stopped, yelling "Give 'em hell Charlie," a chant copied from Harry Truman's 1948 campaign.

Sally and Jenny chatted, leaving him to his thoughts. It was obvious the two women were sizing each other up. They seemed to get along. Jenny, a neophyte at politics, was being filled in by Sally, and Jenny was telling Sally of the mysteries of the West. Sally confessed that she had never been beyond the Mississippi. "You don't know what you're missing," Jenny assured her. "The *real* West is a world unto itself."

Charlie could occasionally hear his name mentioned. "Are you girls gossiping about me?" he asked, moving closer in.

"Typical of a man," Sally answered, but Charles assumed it was human nature for women this close to a potential President to have him on their minds, and tongues.

He wondered what he thought of them, both so different. Jenny was the more attractive physically and had enormous vitality. Sally was vital, but in a reflective way. Smart as a whip. Sally was more like him, a touch of the academic. Did either of them excite him? He wasn't sure, but he cared for them both, especially now that the void in his life had reopened, in spades.

The exercise had done him good and Charlie treated himself to a nap, feeling as if he had never left the homestead of Mother Christine. But he knew that no one had ever traveled so far from home so rapidly. Was that eccentric journey that had begun only six months ago going to end abruptly, or was it just gathering momentum? In about six hours, he and the world would know.

At 5 P.M., Charlie reappeared. Ten sat at the dining table ready to eat. It was, Charlie thought, a 1950s snapshot out of the *Saturday Evening Post*, with the homespun tablecloth and friendly cheer of a large family.

The core of America was still there, Charlie assured himself. It was the political class and the establishment itself that had betrayed the nation. If only they could recover this core, whether in small towns or the inner city, America would be healthy again. If elected, he had plans to stimulate that resurgence. Not a step forward, as politicians were wont to advocate, but a step back into stability and sanity. For example, this very dinner, modest, wholesome, American.

Charlie looked aside to see Leland coming halfway down the staircase, motioning for him.

"Yes, Don, can I help you?"

"Congressman, the cameraman has a small hand-held video. He'd like to take just thirty seconds of this to use later tonight. I promise you the whole thing won't take more than two minutes."

When Charlie whispered that in his mother's ear, her expression turned disdainful. "All right, but just two minutes."

At 6:30 everyone adjourned to the parlor, where Christine's old nineteen-inch Zenith set (she almost never bought a foreign product) sat on a brass table stand. Everyone gathered around on chairs, or on the old wood-framed satin settee, while Jenny and Sally crouched on the needlepoint rug.

Suddenly, the television came alive with a shot of a fanciful New York studio with a dozen monitors, bunting, abstract patriotic art, and desks filled with commentators and pundits.

"This is Election Central," the announcer was saying. "Exit polling in six states represents only 1 percent of the votes, but it shows a small trend. Champ Billings has apparently taken a sharp blow from the revelations of corruption. The standing is Billings, 26 percent; Steadman, 34 percent; and Charles Palmer, 37 percent. It's premature but still startling for an independent candidate to be ahead. We'll return shortly as some states close their polls at 7 P.M., Eastern Standard Time."

The room quieted. The faces were simultaneously tense and bright. Sally was incandescent, as was George. Charlie stared at his mother, who allowed herself a small smile. Robbie Barnes, sitting alone, viewed the television as if he were not truly involved. Overall, there was muted enthusiasm.

When Election Central returned, 10 percent of the vote had been counted. The early forecast had been accurate. Charlie was ahead in the popular vote, now 38 to Steadman's 35, with Billings dropping to 23 percent.

By 9 P.M. no electoral votes had been awarded by the network. Then suddenly there was an ironic blip. The first victories projected went to the weakest performer, Champ Billings. From his Eastern mountain area of Kentucky, he won eight electoral votes, then Tennessee with eleven, and West Virginia with five, giving Billings a total of twenty-four electoral votes, and still none for anyone else.

"Remember folks, you don't need a majority to take a state's electoral votes," Johnny Fields, the young announcer with a vast head of real blond hair, reminded television land. "All that's required is just one vote more than the next guy. And in forty-eight of the fifty states, that gets you all the electoral votes."

By 9:45, both Charlie and Steadman received their first electoral wins. New York was projected for Charlie with thirty-three votes, while Steadman took Massachusetts with twelve. Suddenly there was a flurry of victories for Steadman. The polls hadn't closed in the

West, but the exit polling was so heavy for Steadman that the network awarded him Wyoming, Montana, Colorado, and his own state of Idaho for a total of eighteen more electoral votes.

As one state after another closed its polls, the network computers projected "wins." Each time a state fell into Charlie's column, the group let out a whoop. The popular vote trend also continued unabated.

"Congressman," Sally called out, "you're up to 39 percent. My God, it looks so good."

Charlie, somewhat numbed by the early favorable results, just nodded and smiled enigmatically. Actually, he didn't know what he was thinking.

At 10:43, the network offered a summary.

"We're at the halfway mark in vote counting and our projections," said the announcer, standing in front of a giant map, with each of the candidate's colors placed on winning states. "There are a total of 538 electoral votes, and 270 are needed to win the White House. Of the fifty-five million votes counted so far, Congressman Palmer has twenty-two million, some three million more than Steadman and ten million over Senator Billings. The percentages are 40 percent for Palmer; 35 percent for Steadman; 21.5 percent for Billings and 3.5 percent for the others.

"The score in the Electoral College is more important," the announcer pointed out. "There, Palmer has 147 to Steadman's 115 and Billings's 47—a total of 309 out of 538. Palmer needs 123 more to be elected President. Thus far all trends seem to be moving in his direction, but it's far from over.

"Now, we turn to our network commentator, Washington syndicated columnist Roscoe Sands. How does it look to you, Ros?"

The newsman, looking literary in a corduroy jacket and a bow tie, stared unprofessionally into the camera eye.

"Johnny, it's too early to call the election, but this is the first time that an independent candidate has amassed more popular votes than the major party nominees. Now with 55 percent counted, it's obvious that Palmer will take some forty-five million votes, or 40 percent of all cast. That's one point more than Lincoln had in winning the election of 1860 in a four-way race.

"Whether Palmer gains the 270 electoral votes needed to be named President remains to be seen. But whatever happens, it's a political miracle of enormous dimensions. Charlie Palmer deserves a lot of credit for guts. He's also hit a deep nerve in the American psyche— a growing disenchantment with Big Brother and big political parties. The network now considers it statistically impossible for anyone to catch the congressman in the popular vote."

That last comment released the pent-up tension. "Break out the champagne!" George Sempel called. Jenny passed around the glasses and they all drank except Robbie Barnes. "Forgive me Congressman, I'm a teetotaler."

"Charlie, does that mean you're going to be President?" his mother asked as she walked over to him, seated almost immobile in an old wing chair—looking austere if not quite presidential.

"No, Mom, we shouldn't count my chickens. There are still twelve states to report. And it's the Electoral College, not the popular vote, that counts. I need a majority of those to win."

The room had a strange ambience. After that happy blowout, sobering thought seemed to dominate. Charlie had clearly beaten his rivals, but was he going to be President? Or would it be a split three-way contest with no one gaining the magic 270 electoral votes—then thrown into the House where Charlie was persona non grata several times over?

At 11:23 P.M., after four more states had reported in, Election Central brought the race up to date.

"Congressman Palmer now has a commanding lead in the Electoral College, as the map behind me shows. Only eight more states remain to be counted or projected. They're all in the West—Arizona, New Mexico, Nevada, Oregon, Washington, Alaska, Hawaii, and, of course, California. These remaining states represent ninety-six votes, of which he needs a majority to be elected President. Steadman has strength in the West, but California doesn't typically vote 'Western.' "

Not a sound registered in the parlor as everyone focused on the screen. Election Central soon projected Arizona to Steadman, then New Mexico to Charlie, then Nevada to Steadman. The polls hadn't yet closed in Alaska and Hawaii, but the network projected an easy split between Charlie and Steadman based on exit polling: Alaska to Charlie; Hawaii to Steadman. That left only the three Pacific states: Oregon, Washington, and California.

"California is the big prize, with fifty-four votes," the announcer commented. "So without California, Palmer has no chance. He now has 208 votes. To win, he needs another sixty-two. We expect to know *something* in about an hour."

Robbie Barnes walked over to Charlie, who seemed numbed, and whispered into his ear. Charlie nodded, and Barnes tip-toed upstairs, where Leland was seated on the landing. "Don, it's OK now to set up downstairs while we wait."

The media quickly invaded the Palmer parlor under the watchful eye of Mother Palmer. The engineer and lighting man moved Charlie's chair into a corner so that the others could continue to watch television.

Leland set up a picturesque little corner with Charlie in the wing chair alongside a table, with a painting of a Puritan scene over his head. Perfect Americana, Charlie thought, laughing at the creative protocols of television land. Leland seemed happy that his hunch had worked out. Instead of being stuck at Election Central, he had walked into *the* dramatic moment.

"This is Don Leland covering tonight's presidential election. Charles Palmer is now seven million votes ahead of his closest contender," he began, his voice settling into the famed baritone timbre. "We are coming to you by satellite from his mother's house in Fairview, Ohio, built around the turn of the century by her ancestors who came here from Connecticut in 1835. The home is an old Victorian with an outside wraparound porch, and is lovingly tended by Mrs. Christine Palmer, the candidate's mother. The man who hopes to be President was born here and chose to be home with his friends and family on this historic night.

"As you've been seeing, the independent candidate, once given dim odds, has walked away with the popular vote on a platform of radical reform. Far from being rebuffed by a skeptical electorate, he has handily beaten both parties, and now awaits the results in the last three states out West for him, and us, to learn if he will be the next President of the United States. And now let's turn to the candidate himself, seated right beside me in the family wing chair. Here is Congressman Palmer—very possibly our next President. So tell me, sir, what do you think of this night so far?"

Charlie had no ready answer. His head was empty of conclusions.

"I really can't say, Mr. Leland. I'm gratified that I'll win the popular vote, but the complexities of our peculiar election system—which exists nowhere else in the world—has me sort of speechless. Maybe even without a coherent thought. I suppose, like the rest of the country, I'll just have to sit here quietly and wait."

"Do you think this system makes any sense, Congressman? You've criticized it in the past."

"No, it's absolutely moronic. Since no one is going to get a popular vote majority tonight, we should all be going home, then have a runoff between me and Steadman in three weeks. Billings, the loser, should be out of it. Will that happen? Of course not."

Charlie now stared into the camera, talking directly to the American public.

"I promise you this, voters of America. If elected President, my first job in the Oval Office will be a constitutional amendment to elect all Presidents, and all members of Congress, purely by a *majority* of the popular vote. And if no one receives a majority, we'll hold a runoff of the top two candidates."

Leland quickly took over. "Now, we'll go back to Election Central. While we wait for the Pacific states, they'll show you a one-minute video of the Palmer family and his friends at dinner earlier this evening. It's a snapshot of America as the congressman, and a lot of us, remember it. Signing off for now, this is Don Leland from Ohio."

It was now 11:52 P.M.

"Charlie, dear, I'm going to sleep," Christine said, giving her son a quick hug. "Wake me up early in the morning and let me know if you're President. If so, I'll come to visit you in the White House. If not, you can take back your old job, and have Friday night dinners here, same as always."

Christine waved good night to her guests.

Jenny, approaching Charlie, said: "You look pooped. I'll make some coffee. Anybody else? We may have a while to wait."

When she returned, everyone focused back on Election Central. The crucial remaining votes were being counted in tight contests in California, Oregon, and Washington. California had fifty-four electors, Oregon seven, and Washington eleven.

The conversation hushed as the tallies in those remaining states came in, the leads moving back and forth between Charlie and Steadman, each change accompanied by cheers or disappointed sighs. In California, fewer than two thousand votes separated the candidates.

"Come on, Charlie!" Jenny cried out, suddenly breaking the tension. Everyone laughed.

Charlie looked at his watch. It was two minutes past midnight when the volume of the television suddenly picked up.

"FLASH!" The young announcer shouted, his hair seeming to bounce with the word. "WE HAVE A RESULT IN CALIFORNIA! THE NETWORK PROJECTS PALMER AS THE NARROW WINNER THERE WITH ALL THE STATE'S FIFTY-FOUR ELECTORAL VOTES. THAT GIVES HIM 262 ELECTORAL VOTES, ONLY EIGHT SHORT OF VICTORY. WE HAVE YET TO HEAR ONLY FROM OREGON AND WASHINGTON STATE."

The small room turned kinetic. Everyone was hugging, kissing, swapping hurrahs and compliments. One by one, they approached the wing chair, where Charlie sat looking stoic, experiencing a kind of out-of-body sensation. Their congratulations were now a touch deferential. No one called him Mr. President, for which Charlie was thankful. That would have ignited his growing inner anxiety into maddening sparks.

He was truly in turmoil. If he was about to become President of the United States, he had underestimated the shock of that discovery.

If not, the whole spectacle was needless and too punishing. What had he done to himself?

He sat motionless, his eyes on the television set in front of him. It wasn't long in coming.

"ANOTHER FLASH. WE HAVE JUST PROJECTED CONGRESSMAN CHARLES PALMER THE WINNER IN OREGON, WITH AN ADDITIONAL SEVEN ELECTORAL VOTES. THAT BRINGS HIM TO 269—ONE SHORT OF A MAJORITY. IT ALL NOW RESTS ON WASHINGTON STATE. IF HE WINS THAT, WE HAVE A NEW PRESIDENT OF THE UNITED STATES."

Leland didn't approach Charlie, who sat immobile, in something approaching a trance. He sat silently, alone in a room of tense admirers, knowing that the next few minutes were unprecedented in his or anyone's life. A state in the Northwest corner of America, in the Union only because of a compromise with the British in 1854, would determine the remainder of his life, and deeply affect the lives of all Americans. Why?

There was no answer for that, but the resolution was quick in coming.

"Ladies and gentlemen," the anchor almost whispered into the camera, as if his news was confidential. His nervousness was obvious, mirroring that of much of America. "I've just been handed a bulletin. By a mere fifteen hundred votes, it appears that Arthur Steadman, former governor of nearby Idaho, has won the eleven electoral votes of the state of Washington. Charles Palmer, one vote short of an electoral majority, has not won the presidency of the United States. *I repeat, Palmer has lost the state of Washington and he will not win the presidency of the United States tonight.* Nor will anyone else. For that analysis, we shift to Don Leland, in the home of the failed independent candidate."

Leland moved a dining chair into a quiet corner. He spoke to America, accentuating each word as if it were to be buried in a time capsule.

"This is Don Leland, in the eye of the hurricane, not twenty feet from the man who just narrowly failed to win the presidency of the United States. What happens now? Well, the Twelfth Amendment to the Constitution, passed in 1804, spells it out. Folks, it's a strange system, but it's the only one we have. First the electors must meet in their home states, then send their state by state results to Washington, to the senator pro tem, the working head of the U.S. Senate, who will determine that no one has a majority. Then with great dispatch, the House of Representatives will convene to choose a President from among the top three contenders—which includes all three candidates. The House can choose any one of them regardless of the number of votes they received tonight. It's a whole new ballgame."

Leland leaned back and drew a breath before continuing.

"However, according to the Constitution, the choice of Vice President will not be made by the House. That will be done by the U.S. Senate. This time it will be between only the top two contenders—Senator John Larrimore on the independent ticket, and Senator Jason Hollingsworth of North Dakota on the Steadman ticket, leaving open the distinct possibility that we could have a President and Vice President from two different parties. Now, I will approach Congressman Palmer, who has been sitting in that same wing chair since the announcement of his loss of the presidency was made."

Charlie felt as if he were the director of a play, and the script was being written by a Brechtian-like playwright as they went along, a kind of ad lib scenario. What was he feeling? He really had no idea. It was all too much to handle at one time.

He could see Leland approach, followed by the cameraman.

"Congressman, I won't ask you how you feel. Obviously disappointed. But I would like to ask you what you think your chances are of being named President of the United States by the House according to the Twelfth Amendment. How many votes do you think you'll receive from the 435 members?"

Charlie waited, a kind of kaleidoscope of images passing before his eyes. Clara. The convention. Larrimore. Sally. Rafferty. His mother. The attempts on his life. The debate. The vote counting tonight. The future was a blur, an amorphous mass that he couldn't get into focus.

"How many votes? Well, Don, first, the Constitution—Sally, my assistant, has told me—only gives one vote to each state in the House in such a case. So California has the same single vote as Rhode Island. The Founding Fathers hadn't anticipated such great spreads in population. So there will be only fifty votes all told in the House, with twenty-six needed to win the presidency. How many votes will I get?"

Charlie had repeated himself, and was finding it hard to speak.

"I suppose I'll get the vote of the Ohio delegation. So that makes one. And I guess that's all. The forty-five million votes that I received tonight from Americans will just go down the drain."

As he finished the last sentence Charlie turned away from the camera, his sign that the interview, and probably his political career, was over.

CHAPTER 50

"I didn't call you to cry over spilled milk," Rafferty said, waking Charlie at 7 A.M. in Ohio the morning after his defeat. "You're going to get enough of that. I called because I have a plan."

"A plan?" Charlie asked. "Don't you ever give up, Sky? We lost the Electoral College by one vote. And what are our chances in the House? About as good as my making $6 billion. I'm not going to be President, so go back to your business, and I'll go back to computers. OK?"

"No, it's not OK. Who says you lost the Electoral College majority? A couple of television computer fellows?"

"Do you mean their count is wrong?" Charlie was confused.

"No, they're good at that crap. But that's if all goes according to Hoyle. It doesn't have to you know."

"What does that mean?"

"What it means, Charlie boy, is that the Constitution doesn't bind the electors. In most states they can vote for whomever they please for President no matter who they're pledged to. It's happened before and it can happen again—especially if we make it happen."

"What the hell does that mean?" Charlie's voice betrayed his frustration. He supposed he was taking it out on Rafferty. It was just four hours since he'd fallen asleep following that disastrous night. "How do we make it happen?"

"Simple, Charlie. There are 269 electors who voted for Billings and Steadman. If I know human nature, you could call up any six of them this morning and make an offer—say secretary of commerce or agriculture in your Cabinet. *Voila!* At least one will go along and switch to you. You now have your 270th Electoral College vote. Suddenly, you're President-elect of these United States and they're playing 'Hail to the Chief' when you walk into the room.''

Charlie listened, awestruck at Rafferty's gall.

"You know, these electors didn't vote for President yesterday," Rafferty continued. "They were just elected themselves. According to the Constitution, and I checked it all out, they meet in their state-houses on the Monday following the second Wednesday in December. Only then do they cast their votes for President. So we've got plenty of time."

Charlie was entranced. There was no stopping Rafferty.

"The state tallies are then sent on to the U.S. Senate, where they're opened on January 6 before a joint session of Congress," Sky explained. "If no one has a majority, like now, *then* the House will choose the new President. But that's all a formality. As soon as one smart cookie accepts your offer, we tell the press that you now have 270 electoral votes and you're the President-elect, all made formal on January 6. And we'd be right."

No wonder this guy is one of the richest men in the world, Charlie figured. Not only does he either know everything, or find a way to learn it, but he turns everything into some kind of a deal. His conniving mind continually puts his spin on life. He makes his own reality and everyone has to buy it. But not necessarily Charlie Palmer.

"Sky, I hear you, loud and clear. You're right in one way. If I get on the horn and make promises to some greedy elector, we'll have one more vote, by simple bribery. We'll have bought the presidency. Not with cash—I hope you're not suggesting that—but with the promise of power. But it's just as sneaky. We'd be taking advantage of a stupid constitutional loophole. The newspapers would know about it the next day, and my name would be mud. I didn't come into this to become like the slimeballs."

Charlie could hear Sky sigh on the other end.

"So it's all finished. Right? Charlie, grow up. I know why Jenny loves you, and why I love you in spite of myself. It's because you're a schmuck, a charming, brilliant schmuck—what I call an almost winner. You'll have enormous potential all your life, but never quite make it. You know what I mean?"

Charlie couldn't help but laugh.

"For a schmuck, I've come pretty far my way, right? If I'd acted the role you're writing, I don't think you would have laid $100 million on my nose. No, Sky, I'm going into the House and ask for the presidency because I deserve it. If I get it, it'll be a miracle. If not, it shows that politics in America really stinks to high heaven. We'll do it my way, OK?"

"Charlie, I have no choice. But I must tell you, I'd looked forward to sleeping just one night in the Lincoln Room. That's the least I could get for my hundred million bucks."

"Sky, this is also my last hurrah. If you want a night's lodging in the White House, you'll have to talk to Billings or Steadman. I'm sure they'll make a deal for the right price."

Rafferty burst out into raucous laughter. "Charlie, you really are historic. So do it your way. Go into that House and give them what for."

That morning was a test of his will. Rafferty wanted a deal where he could buy out the opposition. Now Charlie got another phone call—this time to sell out.

It was from Andy Tolliver, who had survived the Leland exposure. Despite a tarnished reputation, he was still the guru of the Washington combat zone.

"Congressman, this is Tolliver. I must tell you that you are a miracle politician. You came out of nowhere and almost made it to the White House. I congratulate you. And I mean that sincerely."

"I think you really do, Andy. But my methods are different from yours. I put my faith in the people, not in gimmicks."

"To each his own. But I don't want your fantastic effort to go down the drain. I was talking to Senator Billings and he thinks you're an invaluable public servant. Instead of your going home to Ohio to some crappy computer company, he'd like to see you in his Cabinet—either as secretary of state or secretary of defense."

"That's gracious of him. And what does he want in return?"

"Please don't put it so crudely, Mr. Congressman. But he would appreciate a detente. You have only the Ohio vote in the House, but you've got great public backing. All he asks is your endorsement of him in the House runoff for President. Plus, of course, Ohio's vote. That will put him over on the first ballot. Why waste what you've done?"

Charlie never had a chance to weigh the offer. His temper took over.

"Tolliver. I wouldn't join with Billings if we were the last two men on the deck of the *Titanic*. He's an abomination and so are you. Go fuck yourself, you political pimp!"

With that, Charlie hung up, loud and hard. But the second he did, he felt ashamed. Not by the force of what he'd said, but by its vulgarity. If Tolliver and Billings could make him do that, he'd better get out of the Beltway.

He'd just stay to play out the runoffs in the House, then head back to Ohio with George, lickety split.

CHAPTER 51

On the second Monday in December, Charlie sat quietly on the aisle on a back bench of the House of Representatives, trying to look as inconspicuous as possible. And failing in the attempt.

Press photographers and television cameramen had followed him almost into the chamber. Though he would be leaving Congress in less than a month, Charlie was on everyone's minds and lips.

Time, Newsweek, and *U.S. News* had pictured him on their covers the week after Election Day. Now, heads swiveled toward him as he sat there, hunched low in his seat. People in the packed galleries were pointing him out to their children as the man who *almost* became President of the United States.

Many members either shot daggers of disdain at him or avoided Charlie altogether. But he was surprised by the friendliness of some in the two parties he had soundly beaten. "Good show, Charlie," Dave Jordan of Delaware, chairman of the Rules Committee, said as he approached the aisle seat. "It turned out the country loved you more than they loved us. But better luck next time."

Charlie smiled in appreciation. "Thanks, but there won't be a next time."

The House Chamber, built in 1859, accommodated about six hundred people in its ten rows of benches on either side of the center aisle, and eight curved rows at each end. Today, it was packed. It was six weeks after Election Day and the President of the Senate—actually the senator pro tem, the third in line for the presidency—was presiding over a joint session of Congress, all 535 members of the House and Senate. He had just begun to read the tally of the Electoral College vote for President of the United States.

"In accordance with Article I, Section 2 in the Constitution, as amended by the Twelfth Amendment of 1804," the presiding officer of the Senate called out, his raspy voice carrying up to the visitors' and press galleries with the whole historic spectacle covered on C-Span, "I hereby certify the results of the presidential electors, each having been counted in their various states, as follows:

"Of the total 538 Electoral College members, the votes are:

"269 for Congressman Charles K. Palmer of Ohio.

"222 for former Governor Arthur Steadman of Idaho.

"47 for Senator Champ Billings of Kentucky.

"A majority of 270 electoral votes is required for the election of the President. Since no one has achieved that majority, I hereby declare that the office of the President-elect of the United States has not been filled. According to the Constitution, the members of this House must select a President from these top three candidates. In this balloting, the Constitution directs that each state delegation shall vote as a bloc, with only one vote per state regardless of its population. The candidate who first receives twenty-six votes shall be declared President of the United States."

He looked to the area where the senators were seated.

"Senators should now return to their own chamber where, according to the Constitution, you will choose the new Vice President of the United States from only the top two candidates—Senators John Larrimore of Oklahoma and Jason Hollingsworth of North Dakota."

Charlie listened, thinking of the timing of the House vote. In 1934, when the Twentieth Amendment changed Inauguration Day from March 4 to January 20, Congress set up the December meeting date for the Electors and the formal counting of their votes on January 6.

Since no had failed to receive an electoral majority since 1824, that was all theory. Now it was happening again, but there was a problem. What about the transition? Could they count the votes on January 6 as usual, vote for the President and give him enough time to form an administration by January 20?

Right after the election, Congress heatedly debated the problem. Article II, Section 1 gave Congress the right to set the dates for the Electors to meet and vote in their state, then to have their votes tallied in Washington. They could easily move the House vote for President back to December so that there could be more time for the transition. But then the *old* House, not the newly-elected members, would chose the new President. Would that be fair?

What to do? What was more important—the composition of the

House or the time needed to form a new administration? Charlie purposely kept out of the debate. He was one of three candidates and he didn't have many votes among the two-party representatives, new, or old, anyway.

Finally, Congress decided to stay with the January date. Whoever was named President would have to move quickly for two weeks, the shortest transition in history.

That chilly January morning, the Electoral College vote turned out as Charlie figured. No one broke his pledge, and electors voted as the television pundits had projected. The result was that there was no majority and no one was elected as the new President. That was now the job of the House.

Once the senators had left, the Speaker took over and rapped his gavel for order.

The whole process would be over in twenty minutes, Charlie was sure. He had spoken to several members, and it looked like Billings—whom he had swamped in the popular vote—had twenty-six states in his pocket. Steadman seemed to have twenty-three, with a strong Western base.

And Charlie? He had a firm pledge from Vince Salerno, the head of the Ohio delegation. Score one state for Palmer.

What the hell? He'd sit there and watch it play out.

The first time no one had achieved a majority was in 1800 when Jefferson and Aaron Burr tied in the Electoral College. The contest went to the House, where after a long series of votes, Jefferson won, ten states to four. According to the old rule, Burr became his Vice President.

In 1824, when it happened again, there was a four-way race for President among Andrew Jackson, John Quincy Adams, William Crawford, and Henry Clay. The final voting for President had been in the old House chamber, now the Statuary Hall off the Rotunda. Jackson had gotten the most popular votes, Adams second, Crawford third, and Clay fourth.

Clay was out of the race. According to the Constitution, only the top three were eligible. But when Clay threw his support to Adams, it took only one ballot for Adams—who had come in second in the popular vote—to get a majority of fourteen states. Andy Jackson, the popular vote winner, had lost the presidency. Clay was rewarded by being named secretary of state by Adams, a deal that went down in history as the "Corrupt Bargain."

Charlie smiled at the thought. Tolliver had offered him the same deal. If he had gone along, it would probably be remembered as the "Royal Screwing" of the American public.

The two desks at the third row off the center aisle, usually reserved for party people leading a debate, had been turned over to the managers of the presidential candidates, who were already standing at their posts.

"Congressman Canfield of Kentucky. I understand that you will be managing the vote for Senator Billings."

"That's correct, Mr. Speaker."

"And Congressman Jeffries of Idaho, I understand you will be managing the vote for former Governor Steadman."

"Yes, sir."

"Good." The Speaker turned and squinted up at the top row of the chamber.

"Is Congressman Palmer, the third candidate for President, present?"

Charlie rose from his seat. "Yes, Mr. Speaker."

"Who will manage your vote?"

"I think I can handle it by myself, Mr. Speaker. Especially considering the volume."

The gallery roared. The Speaker banged his gavel.

"Please, no comments from the gallery or I will clear the chamber of nonmembers." The gallery hushed.

"All right, then we'll begin the voting. The state delegations will have fifteen minutes to caucus. Remember, each state has only one vote no matter how many members in your delegation. Do your tallies, then name someone to announce your choice for President of the United States to the Clerk when polled."

Charlie listened, simultaneously impressed and galled. They were scrupulously following the Constitution, but it troubled him that he had won forty-five million popular votes—seven million more than Steadman and thirteen million over Billings—yet here he was sucking hind tit in the House election. Something really was rotten in the Beltway.

During the ten-minute hiatus, the representatives gathered in clusters, chatting away and counting their score. Vince Salerno, the head of the Ohio delegation, walked up the long flight of steps and approached Charlie at his rear seat.

"Charlie, we have a unanimous front on Ohio, but it looks like we're alone. Still, there's a small groundwell for you from some mavericks. In Massachusetts, you picked up four votes in their delegation, even though they were in the minority and don't count. The same in Florida, about six."

"Who does it look like, Vince?"

"Right now I'd say Billings has twenty-six states, Steadman twenty-three, and you one. But who the hell knows for sure? I've got to hurry back. They're ready to go."

The Speaker banged the gavel. "Please return to your seats. Clerk, begin the roll call."

"Alaska, how do you vote for President of the United States?" the clerk called out in a courtlike monotone.

A representative from Fairbanks rose. "The great state of Alaska, the Last Frontier, casts its vote for Arthur Steadman for President."

The roll call continued, alphabetically, with no surprises. By the time they came to Ohio, tension controlled the room.

"Ohio, how do you vote for President of the United States."

Vince Salerno, wearing a carnation in his lapel, rose to his feet.

"Mr. Speaker, members of the House, ladies and gentlemen in the gallery, members of the media, and all America watching on C-Span," Salerno began. "We may be following the Constitution, but you're still witnessing the emasculation of democracy. A member of my delegation, Congressman Charles Palmer, the independent candidate for President, won an enormous plurality on Election Day. As you listen to the roll call, you'll see his overwhelming mandate being wiped out by politics as usual, by party above country, by party above the people. It may be constitutional, but it's still a travesty."

Salerno paused. "Ohio, the home of the Ohio State Buckeyes and the Scarlet Carnation, proudly casts its one vote for the man who *should be* President of the United States, Charles Knudsen Palmer."

The gallery went wild. Charlie looked up, shocked and touched. Makeshift signs on paper appeared from people's pockets and pocketbooks. PALMER IS THE REAL PRESIDENT—DON'T STEAL THE PEOPLE'S ELECTION. The catcalls and whistling overwhelmed the speaker's frantic gaveling.

"ORDER IN THE GALLERY. ANY MORE NOISE AND I'LL HAVE IT EMPTIED."

Still the noise continued, a spontaneous citizen filibuster against the proceedings. The Speaker gaveled again, some half-dozen times. Realizing the futility, he sat down and waited. His threat to close the gallery had been a bluff.

After five minutes, the visitors quieted somewhat. Immediately, the Speaker jumped to his feet and banged the gavel.

"Now, Clerk, please continue the roll call."

The polling quickly went through Oklahoma, Oregon, Pennsylvania, Rhode Island, South Carolina, South Dakota, and Tennessee, all voting for either Billings or Steadman.

On the back of an envelope, Charlie scribbled the tally, which was now twenty-two for Billings, nineteen for Steadman, and one for him. Of the remaining eight states—Texas, Utah, Vermont, Virginia, Washington, West Virginia, Wisconsin, and Wyoming—pundits had predicted a four-four split. If that happened, Billings would be named President on the first ballot with twenty-six votes.

"God help us," Charlie muttered a little loudly, as a few heads next to him turned. Many representatives had been curt, but here and there, some smiled encouragement. Every small sign was heart-warming, if futile.

"TEXAS. HOW DO YOU VOTE FOR PRESIDENT?" the Clerk called.

The head of the delegation, Mollie Downs, chief of the House women's caucus, rose from her seat. Charlie smiled because she was wearing the same blue silk dress she had on at the convention in July. She stood erect, looking much like a lady cowpuncher in finery.

"TEXAS, HOME OF THE DALLAS COWBOYS, HOME TO PEOPLE WHO'VE LIVED UNDER SIX FLAGS AND WHO KNOW THE BLESSINGS OF DEMOCRACY, HAVING CAU-CUSED OUR DELEGATION OF THIRTY REPRESENTATIVES, UNANIMOUSLY CASTS ITS ONE VOTE FOR PRESIDENT FOR . . . ."

Mollie turned and stared up at the rear bench of the House.

"FOR THAT INDEPENDENT VOICE, WHO DESPITE OVERWHELMING ODDS WON THE POPULAR VOTE OF THE PEOPLE ON ELECTION DAY, CONGRESSMAN CHARLES KNUDSEN PALMER."

Bedlam broke out everywhere, even in the blasé press gallery, where laptops started to hum. The gallery began chanting "Charlie, Charlie." The Speaker gave the gavel a halfhearted bang as if to do his duty, then sat down, shrugging his shoulders.

This time, a dozen maverick congressmen from throughout the chamber spontaneously left their seats and began one of the strangest pilgrimages in House history. One by one, they formed a line and walked up the center aisle toward Charlie's seat at the rear.

Without saying a word, each shook his hand, turned, and went back down.

Charlie was overwhelmed. He could feel tears welling up, but he quickly checked it. The C-Span camera would record his emotions, and in his mind's eye, he saw a quick snapshot of Ed Muskie losing the presidential nomination in 1972 because of tears shed in the New Hampshire primary. Instead, Charlie grasped each hand with warmth, muttering only "Thank you. Thank you."

When the members had returned to their seats and the bedlam in the gallery had subsided, the roll call continued.

When it was finished, it was clear that Mollie Downs and Texas had blocked Billings' first ballot victory. The tally was twenty-five to twenty-three to two. No one had the required twenty-six votes. America still had no new President.

The roll calls continued, one after the other. Each took about fif-teen minutes, and still no one garnered the needed twenty-six votes. As Billings failed to win, Charlie's last-ditch stand was gathering some momentum. On the ninth ballot, the Clerk called out the results, which had been shifting since Mollie Downs's surprise.

"The recorded tally of the ninth ballot is as follows," the clerk called out, sounding more like a bailiff in court. "Billings, twenty-two votes; Steadman, eighteen votes; and Palmer, ten votes."

The speaker rose to his feet. "I believe we need a short break so that representatives may consult with one another. I hereby adjourn these proceedings for one hour. We will return at 1:30 P.M. and continue the balloting until we have a President."

The exodus was rapid. Congressmen flowed out onto the halls, most heading for the Members' Dining Room at H-1800, a taxpayer-subsidized restaurant with inexpensive fare. At 12:30, and until 1:30, only congressmen and their guests could eat there, giving them a chance to gossip, swap stories, and persuade each other.

Vince Salerno waved to Charlie, who joined him on the House floor. With several members of the Ohio delegation, they adjourned to the dining room at the end of the hall.

"Congressman, keep fighting," Dave Jordan of the Rules Committee said as they waited to be seated. "The old boys won't let go easily, so keep grinding away. I'm working on my Delaware delegation. One more switched vote, and you'll have my state in your column. I hope you didn't pack the gallery because that's what's influencing a lot of members."

Charlie was beginning to come out of his funk. He now had ten states on his side, which was little short of a miracle. He had no idea how he could get others, but so far he and Mollie had blocked Billings from taking the White House. Steadman was the better bet for the country, anyway. A decent man, if not spectacular, and if too tied to the status quo.

Before taking a seat, Charlie left his Ohio friends and sought out Mollie Downs, eating with some Texas friends.

"Ms. Downs, I want to thank you for your support. You've kept the competition alive."

Mollie looked up from her food, the slightest bit perturbed.

"Congressman, don't flatter yourself. Let me tell you right out. I don't want you as President. But obviously the people do, and that's who we're supposed to represent. If I had my druthers, you wouldn't even be on the ballot. I believe strictly in the two-party system. But the people, God help them, voted for you on Election Day, and naming anyone else as President would be a distortion of democracy."

With that, Mollie turned back to her food without so much as a goodbye.

Charlie examined his thoughts. He wasn't offended. The woman was pure courage.

He returned to his Ohio colleagues. Some representatives from other states were dispatching stares that could kill, but others came over to shake Charlie's hand. Instead of routine, it was turning out to be an exciting, and unexpected, morning.

Suddenly, Salerno poked Charlie's shoulder. "Look who's coming in the door. It's Steadman and the Idaho House delegation—all two of them."

Steadman made a beeline for the Ohio table. Charlie and the others rose in deference.

"No, no. I just wanted to thank you," Steadman said.

"For what?"

"For your Ohio delegation helping to stop Billings on the first vote," Steadman answered in his Western drawl, taking his time on each word. "And of course for somehow influencing Mollie Downs. You and she have kept this thing going, giving both of us a shot at it."

"To tell you the truth, Arthur, I never said a word to Mollie. She brought Texas along all by her lonesome. Says she wasn't doing it for me—I don't even think she likes me—but for all those who voted for me. A most surprising woman."

"That's good news. Sorry I can't join you on the floor, but my fellow Idahoan, Congressman Jake Jeffries, will carry the ball. Good luck to both of us."

After lunch, the 435 members of the House reconvened at 1:30.

"We will continue the vote," the Speaker said, gaveling for order. "Clerk, please call the roll for the tenth ballot."

That ballot produced the same result as the ninth. But on the eleventh, Steadman started to slip. Most of his strength was being picked up by Charlie, and some by Billings. By the fifteenth ballot, the vote stood at a crucial point.

"The votes having been counted, the poll for President is as follows," the Clerk called out. "Thirteen each for Palmer and Steadman, and twenty-four for Billings."

Charlie had mixed feelings. He was still in it, courtesy of Steadman's growing weakness. But Billings was now within two votes of taking the presidency.

The Speaker stood, ready to order the sixteenth ballot, one which would surely put the Oval Office in Billings's hands, when suddenly he paused. Out loud, the speaker read a message delivered by a young page.

"Congressman Jeffries of Idaho, manager of the Steadman vote," he called out.

"Yes, Mr. Speaker."

"You have an urgent message to meet with Governor Steadman outside the chamber door. We'll reconvene in five minutes."

Steadman? Charlie wondered why this sudden recess at the sixteenth ballot.

Jeffries returned soon after and asked for recognition.

"Yes, Congressman, what is it?" the Speaker asked.

"I'd like permission to read a note from Governor Steadman."

"Go ahead."

"It reads: 'As one of the three candidates for the presidency today, I had high hopes. But I believe my support is slipping and that on this ballot the winner will be Senator Champ Billings of Kentucky. Rather than see that outcome, I am dropping out of the contest.' "

Jeffries nervously shifted his weight, then continued reading Steadman's note.

" 'I urge all my supporters in this great chamber to vote in as President the man who overwhelmingly won the popular vote of the people, Congressman Charles Palmer. There is no quid pro quo involved and the Congressman knows nothing of this. That's all I have to say, except God bless America.' "

With that, Jeffries sat down, disappointment etched into his face.

The room hushed, down to a reverent hum. The Speaker's rap of the gavel was redundant.

"Clerk," he ordered, "begin the sixteenth ballot."

The vote went rapidly. When it was completed, the Clerk handed the Speaker a quickly written note. He rose to the microphone and read it slowly to the assembled room. There was not a decibel of other sound.

"The sixteenth ballot having been completed, the results are as follows: Senator Billings of Kentucky, twenty-four votes. Congressman Palmer of Ohio, twenty-six votes. In my capacity as Speaker of the House," he blared, his voice rising, "I HEREBY NAME CONGRESSMAN CHARLES KNUDSEN PALMER AS THE NEXT PRESIDENT OF THE UNITED STATES!"

Charlie audibly gasped, then felt a sharp pain in his chest. He rose from his seat and stood motionless as every head in the room turned toward him. No one moved except for four Secret Service men, who had been waiting in the wings.

Suddenly, the agents walked briskly out onto the House floor and up the aisle toward Charlie. Reaching the top row, they waited until he walked out into the tight space, then quickly surrounded him.

"Follow us, Mr. President-elect," said the lead agent. "We'll leave by the side door. We have a car waiting outside to take you to Blair House."

The small group descended the aisle and reached the House floor. As Charlie walked across it, the members rose en masse, as did the

visitors and the press in the galleries above. A quiet, respectful applause greeted each step the new President made.

As he walked solemnly, Charlie's mind was a whirl of conflicting
thoughts. Then he caught himself. This was no time to think at all.
It was a time to begin the journey of what was apparently his destiny.

Like it or not.

BOOK THREE

THE THREAT
TO THE
PRESIDENCY

CHAPTER 52

The President-elect had taken an instant liking to Mr. Blair's home.

Temporarily, they had moved Charlie into Blair House, the elegant residence for dignitaries, which was also the traditional pit stop for incoming chief executives just before inauguration.

But Charlie had two weeks of transition time left until January 20, and unlike most newly elected Presidents, he had no decent place of his own. He hated hotel life, and his one-bedroom place in Jenkins Hill Apartments was dreary.

He decided to create a precedent by moving into Blair House, lock, stock, and books, making it his home for the entire transition right up to the day of the investiture.

To Charlie, it was the nicest house he'd lived in since the old Victorian in Fairview. Not only did he have a personal apartment and an office, but he had a small study where he could think in peace, and without much Secret Service interference. Still, he cast an occasional glance out the window, reassured to see uniformed Capitol police standing watch.

Just diagonally across from the White House, this quadruple set of brick mansions had been purchased by the government during World War II from two prominent old American families. Francis Preston Blair, a member of Jackson's "kitchen cabinet" and the founder of the *Congressional Record*, had bought the original Blair House in 1836. His country home, Silver Spring, gave that name to the modern Washington suburb. So influential was he that it was in the parlor of Blair House that, under Lincoln's instructions,

Robert E. Lee was offered the command of the Union army, which he turned down.

Next door was the Lee House, occupied by Robert E. Lee's cousin, who married Elizabeth Blair, the girl next door. Unlike Robert Lee, Sam Phillips Lee threw his lot in with Lincoln and served as an admiral in the Union navy.

After both houses were bought as residences for visiting dignitaries, doorways were cut to connect the mansions, and today the complex had over one hundred rooms. During the renovation of the White House from 1948 to 1952, President Truman and his family lived there, and it was at Blair House that an attempt was made on his life.

Once Charlie had settled in, he quickly started his transition team working.

The only event that marred his sense of victory was the defeat of his running mate, Senator Larrimore, for the office of Vice President. Angered by Larrimore's defection from the party, the Senate had voted for Steadman's partner, Senator Jason Hollingsworth of North Dakota, who was named VP on the first ballot.

Charlie had immediately offered Larrimore the post of secretary of state in his new cabinet, but he had refused, preferring to remain in the Senate.

"Mr. President," Larrimore had responded. "You'll need someone in the upper house to get your American Manifesto through. I hope to be your point man."

This morning, a relatively warm and sunny January day, he and George Sempel, now his chief of staff, and Sally Kirkland, the deputy staff chief, were set to discuss his new Cabinet. Since his inside group was small, he'd have to dip into major party ranks as well as the private sector to get exceptional people.

"Mr. President, here's the trial Cabinet list that we've worked up," George said as the maid served coffee and croissants. George had brought along a few bagels, picked up at a street stand on Pennsylvania Avenue.

"The available candidates for the Cabinet will have to be carefully cherry-picked," Sempel warned the President-elect. "We can't afford to make the mistakes that have plagued many administrations, saddled with unqualified people and a few crooks. We're going to be under a special microscope from the press."

Charlie, dressed in a sport shirt and sweater, nodded agreement, but then winced. "George, I worked for you for twenty years. Forget that 'Mr. President' crap."

"No, Mr. President, no more 'Charlie.' When you finish your eight years and I'm still around, we'll see then."

Charlie laughed. "OK, George, do it your way. On the Cabinet, we have to shock the Beltway by making every one a gem. I want to announce my choices on the first business day of my administration. That will show the people that this will be an open government. We have nothing to hide, and we want that impression to register early on."

The President smiled, a touch proudly. "The two people I insist on having in the Cabinet are Mollie Downs and Arthur Steadman. Neither of them expected any reward, but both have shown enormous courage, actually statesmanlike behavior, and they should be rewarded. I only hope they'll agree to join us. They have excellent reputations, and their appointments will show we intend to do business with both parties—if they'll do business with us."

"Do you think Steadman will join your Cabinet? After all, he was your closest opponent in the race," George said.

"I hope so. I'd like to see him as secretary of interior. He's very well liked in the West, both by environmentalists and by people who seek more development. I spoke to him about my idea of returning much of the West—except for national parks and military installations—to the states. Washington owns over 40 percent of California, which is crazy. Steadman likes my idea, so I hope he'll come aboard."

The three-way discussion continued for over an hour, with everyone suggesting names.

"For education chief," George said, "I propose the commissioner of education of New Jersey. He's already brought in better teachers from outside the failed establishment. He calls it 'alternate certification,' and allows for a young summa cum laude in history from Harvard to teach in our public schools—where he's now excluded because he's not 'certified' in education. That makes no sense."

"Sounds good, George. Have him come down to Blair House and we'll talk."

The conversation ranged over all the Cabinet posts, and they concluded with a tentative list. If the candidates accepted, they would be checked out by the FBI and submitted for confirmation to the Senate right after inauguration.

"Give the FBI tough orders, George," the President-elect stressed. "No more half-assed investigations of Cabinet candidates that came back to haunt other administrations. I want them all picked over with a fine-tooth comb, back to kindergarten. And I want the FBI checks—with all the possible dirt unearthed—finished before I take the oath. The media are like sharks after blood and I don't want to feed them unless I have to. So warn the FBI that if they don't do their job, I'll fire anybody involved, up to the top."

Charlie leaned back, a smile of partial satisfaction on his face. He was encouraged by the sensation that he knew what he was doing.

Suddenly, he rose, a sign to both Sally and George that the meeting was over—that he needed a few minutes of quiet time for himself.

Clara. Clara.

The name jabbed constantly into his consciousness, even his unconscious as he slept. It was not just her beauty. He missed her vitality, her joie de vivre, her humor, her cleverness. Sometimes her lifestyle bordered on fantasy, and her values were not always sound. But he loved her, he thought maybe desperately. Yet she had disappeared the night of the Cooper Union debate, never to return. Or even call.

His only contact with her, in a ghostly way, was through the Style section of the *Washington Post*, where Clara's elegant presence graced the inked pages, smiling here and there, opening museums and charity balls. He was ashamed that occasionally he became angry, or jealous, or both, at the thought. How could she be so vital, so self-assured that she could live her life without him? And only by her standards? Didn't she respect his commitment to America? How could she be so selfish?

Charlie caught himself up cold. His self-righteousness—that only his values and lifestyle counted—was what had ruptured their relationship in the first place. And probably killed whatever love she had for him. He had shown his intolerance for her ways. Shallow, he had subtly told her. But she could have just as easily answered— compulsive, fanatic. In fact, she had. In any case, he missed her terribly.

Sally was the only woman around him now, day to day. In some ways he loved her as well. Dedicated, intelligent, attractive, her character was based on solid values. She did give him pleasure even though they had no sexual contact of any kind. The same was true of Jenny Rafferty, on the few occasions he saw her.

But Clara. There was only Clara.

To divert his mind, Charlie picked up a copy of the Churchill autobiography, and turned to a marked page, reading about the old bulldog's fight with Neville Chamberlain and his appeasement of Hitler. The President-elect swore to himself that he'd never appease his political enemies, including those in the august establishments that had let the people down.

In the midst of his reading, the phone rang. It was the Blair House operator.

"Mr. President-elect, there's a man on the phone who insists he knows you. His name is Mr. Fairview. Says you'll remember him from some California incident a long time ago and a fire in your Town Hall. Shall I tell him to write you?"

Charlie took the message, trying to decipher it clearly. Obviously, it was meant to be cryptic. Mr. Fairview referred to his hometown. But the California incident? And the fire? Who was trying to rake over his remote past? And why?

"I'll take the call, Miss McKinley. But please transfer it to my secure red phone in my office. Tell him to hold on while I go there."

Charlie walked deliberately the few feet to his office, his mind trying to absorb this new wrinkle in his already complicated life. What did this man from nowhere want from him?

In the office, he picked up the red phone, which the Secret Service had guaranteed was untapped and untappable, even by the FBI.

"Yes, this is President-elect Palmer. Who is this?"

"Sir, I don't mean to intrude on you. I know how important and busy you are. But there is the little matter of what happened in California and its consequences, and the fire in Fairview. Both going back many years. Am I right?"

"I can't really say, but what does that have to do with me?"

"Well, you see, I'm an investigator and I find out things about people for other people. Sometimes I find I can sell the information to the subjects and do better than by giving it solely to my client. Do you get my meaning?"

"In general terms, yes. But again, what does that have to do with me?"

"Oh, everything. Now that you've achieved such high office, there are surely things you don't want revealed to your adoring public. Some have already come out, and I'm proud that most of it came from my investigations. But there are a few more pieces of information the public knows nothing about. In fact, I learned about them by accident. So it occurred to me that we might strike a business bargain. One that would reimburse me $100,000 for all my work. Do you understand now?"

Charlie had to slow down to think. He now knew what Mr. Fairview was talking about. It was blackmail. So far, he had successfully, and he thought honorably, protected that part of his life that was nobody's business but his loved one's. Now he was being blackmailed for his efforts. Delay was his best response until he could evaluate what to do.

"Mr. Fairview. I have a suggestion. This is no time for me to respond. I'm preparing for my new administration. I'd prefer to postpone the whole thing just two weeks, right after the inauguration. I suggest you call me there my first day in office and we can set something up. I'm sure we can come to some kind of arrangement."

The phone was silent at the other end.

"Mr. Fairview?"

"Yes, I'm here. Just thinking. Give me the number of your secure phone in the White House. I'll call you at 5 P.M. on your first day there, January 20, and we can set something up for the next evening. But that's as far as I'll postpone it. Otherwise, I'll go right to the press. The tabloids will pay me as much as I've asked from you, or more. Do we have a deal?"

Charlie sat in silence, feeling numb. His mind delved back into his past once again. Each time he had tried to do the reasonable thing, the press and his enemies had turned it on its head. That would surely happen again. But this time he was not the only one who would suffer.

What a horrible intervention in his plans.

Delaying the inevitable by buying time was surely the best bargain he could get. Perhaps with two weeks' grace, he could come up with an alternative.

"All right," the President-elect finally said. "The number of my secure phone at the White House is 202-555-9933. Tell the White House operator that you're Mr. Fairview, and I'll have her put the call through."

For a moment there was a punishing silence at the other end of the call.

"Are you still there, Mr. Fairview?" Charlie asked after an impatient half minute.

"Yes, Mr. President-elect. I'm just thinking. It's vital that you come alone, and to my place. I'll give you the time and address when I call back in two weeks."

Charlie was stunned by the man's bravado. "That's impossible. I'm accompanied by the Secret Service wherever I go."

"Not in this case. You'll just have to find a way to shake them. If you're not alone, the deal's off and I'll sell the information."

Charlie mused, then yielded, fearful that he had little choice. His options appeared closed.

"All right. We'll speak again in two weeks."

"Good, Mr. President-elect. I can tell you'll make a fine President."

CHAPTER 53

The morning of January 20, Charlie woke at 5 A.M. in the Blair House, unable to sleep. He lay in bed, his eyes focused on the elaborate ceiling moldings while he pondered what was expected of him this first day as President of the United States.

At 10 A.M., the presidential bubble-top limousine bearing the outgoing President and his wife would arrive at Blair House to pick him up. He had no spouse, so it would be a solo voyage, from private citizen (his congressional seat had expired on January 3), to a man who swore to uphold the Constitution—if anyone any longer knew what that meant.

Only ten pages long, the Constitution had been so interpreted and overinterpreted by the Supreme Court that Charlie feared that, in practice, the document had lost much of its genius. Be that as it may, he would willingly pledge on a Holy Bible his intent to uphold it.

The day's activities had already been laid out by Sally on an typed itinerary, which he kept on the night table beside him.

After the swearing in by the Chief Justice, he would make his inaugural address. He had written it, rewritten it, memorized it, and no longer had any idea if it was any good, or just more words to pile on the mountain of rhetoric politicians had constructed over the years.

It had one unique aspect: It was short. He hoped it was not so short that, like Lincoln's Gettysburg Address, it was over before anyone took it in, and only became immortal after the fact. Fortunately, modern electronics made the hearing not only possible, but inescap-

able. People would definitely know what he said. Whether they liked
it was another matter.

Then there would be the inaugural parade, a tradition in which
everyone from the Elks Lodge of Fairview to the 182nd Airborne
Division would pass in review. Fortunately, the weather augured
well. He had received the weather bureau's report, which promised
a sunny, brisk day, changing dramatically to a near-blizzard snowstorm tomorrow.

He supposed the gods, with their unique strategy, were looking
out for him, though they regularly seemed to change their minds.
For every reward they granted, they extracted an equal number of
mini-tortures.

Take his phone appointment at 5 P.M. later today with the blackmailer, Mr. Fairview. It sent shudders through him. He was in the
clutches of someone who could bleed him dry, not just financially,
but with the threat of exposure.

If it came out, what would be the result? Possibly a sharp drop in
popularity. That he could handle. But it might also mean an end to
his hope of national political reform, which would be punishing.
More important was the irreparable damage to others close to him.
That he could not tolerate. Before the phone call, he'd talk to George
and seek his advice.

He decided to eat breakfast. Could he order this early? He called
down for his usual of scrambled egg whites, toast, and hot water and
lemon, and was surprised by the cook, who not only was up but
promised delivery in fifteen minutes.

Like most Americans, he was into health and longevity. Ever since
he had read that Mormons outlived "gentiles," as they called both
other Christians and Jews, he had forsworn coffee, tea, and caffeine,
as they did.

Of course, some madman out there could instantly cut his longevity down to zero anyway. That had happened with the assassination
of four Presidents: Lincoln, Garfield, McKinley, and Kennedy, not to
mention attempts on the lives of Teddy Roosevelt, FDR, Truman,
Ford, and Reagan, with both Reagan and Teddy Roosevelt actually
having been shot.

He looked for the newspaper to read with his breakfast. He opened
the outside door and picked it up, nodding to the agent twenty feet
away. It was filled with chatter about his upcoming presidential address, with excerpts from other inaugural speeches. There was speculation about what he would say, and one op-ed page piece filled with
snide comments, calling him "a wild fanatic."

He quickly moved to Roscoe Sands's column, "Washington Eye,"
which had been more favorable lately.

The head read: CITIZEN PRESIDENT TO BE SWORN IN TODAY REMINDS US OF ANDY JACKSON AND HARRY TRUMAN.

He blushed at the thought that he was a "Citizen President," yet that's exactly what he thought. Over these months, he had tried to figure out why politicians had dropped so low in people's opinion, and he believed he had the answer.

F. Scott Fitzgerald's comment that the rich were different was true. Charlie believed the same of politicians. They started out as "citizens" with the vested interests of everyone else—whether the price of gasoline, the fear of losing one's job, or what movie to take in on Saturday night.

But once elevated to Congress (or the presidency), they entered a new world of fantasy, mainly unrelated to normal society. They worried about the "scoring" of the Congressional Budget Office on bills totaling a trillion dollars, or the perks of their jobs, or the definition of endangered species such as kangaroo rats, or the need to raise some $2,000 a day—$11,000 a day for senators—just to get reelected.

(Or at least they believed they had to. People like former Senator William Proxmire and former House Appropriations chief Hatcher never raised a nickel, yet always won big.)

Politicians were subject to the whims of party leaders, contributors, pressure groups, and the media. As modern "celebrities," they suffered all the moral and philosophical distortions of that class, too often taken with their own inflated personas on radio and television.

Their vested interest now became the government, with its taxes and bureaucrats, schemes and false solutions. They were no longer citizens, but exiles in the Wonderland of the Beltway, doomed to a baroque, undiagnosed type of mental instability that often rendered them less able than those they had sworn to serve.

Would that happen to him? Would he betray the people?

He was sure it would not. It had all happened so fast that the memory of being a citizen was quite fresh in his mind. Besides, he had absolutely no identification with Washington or the government or the bureaucrats. To him it was all not unlike the backstage at a magic show. And not only did the emperor have no clothes, but Charlie sometimes believed that there was no emperor.

Sands seemed to have caught that about him. Again he read the columnist's conclusion. "President-elect Charlie Palmer doesn't need to think about what he should do for the people. He *is* the people."

He felt lifted, if only for a moment. Further back, he noticed a small item that irritated him. It was headlined: LEAKS INDICATE PRESIDENT-ELECT HAS MADE ALL CABINET CHOICES.

The article, quoting an "unidentified source in Blair House," accurately listed all his firmed-up Cabinet choices, including Admiral Russell Irvington, vice chairman of the Joint chiefs, as defense secretary. He intended to release that list on his second day in office. Now the punch had been taken out of his appointments. Obviously there was a spy on his staff. But who?

That troubled him on the eve of his inauguration. But what truly plagued him was his inner debate about succumbing to blackmail. Every few hours, he changed his mind, wavering between paying and fighting.

But he kept returning to his original position—to defend what he knew was decent but which his enemies would seize upon to destroy him and his.

He had no choice but to give in to Mr. Fairview.

CHAPTER 54

The swearing-in seemed like a reenactment of an old newsreel he had seen as a boy in a darkened theater. It was all done on a wooden grandstand, as expected, with his mother, George, Sally, friends, the outgoing President, and his wife, and the old Cabinet members attending, all eager to be part of this historic moment.

The setting and ceremony were awesome, yet to Charlie it seemed like a dream sequence, one that left him self-conscious, even a touch embarrassed. Raising his right hand and swearing on his mother's Bible, he felt almost ectoplasmic as the Chief Justice intoned the oath to uphold the Constitution, and he had answered, "I do, so help me God."

Never had he meant anything so fervently. But under his breath he took a separate vow—to build the strength of the Union by slicing away the intolerable burden of bad government, a distortion of what the Founding Fathers had intended.

After the inaugural parade, Charlie returned to the White House about 4 o'clock and asked George to meet him in the family quarters. There was that 5 o'clock call coming from the blackmailer. He wanted Sempel to be in on the entire event. Besides, he desperately needed his help.

"George, it may seem out of place on Inauguration Day, but I have something to confide in you, something you can never speak of to anyone, at any time. May I?" Charlie began.

"Mr. President, anything, any time. Shoot away."

"You remember the incident in California and the fire at our Town Hall, all of which happened years before we met?"

"Sure, you told me all about that. Lousy affair. Why?"

"Well, it's coming back to haunt me. A private eye who was collecting dirt on me came across it and—I hate to say this—but it's a case of sheer blackmail. He wants $100,000 tomorrow night or else he'll go to the tabloid press. Says they'll pay him as much, and I believe it."

"Are you serious, Charlie?" Sempel caught himself up. "I mean Mr. President. Do you intend to pay him? Isn't it better to let it get out and be over with it?"

"No, George. It may have bad political ramifications, but that isn't what bothers me. There are other people to think of. You know what I mean."

"Mr. President, sometimes you're too sensitive for your own good, especially for someone in politics. But I understand. I suppose from your point of view, you have no other course. What can I do to help?"

"A lot, George. I need the $100,000. I have only $15,000 in the bank. My money is in the Synergy pension fund and in Synergy stock, which I've put in a blind trust. Can you help me? I'll wait awhile, then take some out of the trust and repay you. Or I can get it from my salary. I'm paid $250,000 a year, and I'm lucky if I spend $1,000 a month, mostly on my mother. What do you say?"

Sempel rose and gave the President a fatherly hug. "Of course. I've won $100,000 from Ladbrooke's on your election alone. When do you need it?"

"I'll know exactly very soon. Mr. Fairview—that's what he calls himself—is going to call on my secure phone at 5 P.M. I want you to listen in."

While they waited, they talked about the inauguration, and Charlie asked about his address.

"First-rate, Mr. President. Succinct but powerful. Nobody can doubt that you intend to remake the Washington landscape. I particularly liked your appeal to the two parties to join with you. I think if the parties don't play ball, they risk losing the whole game."

Charlie nodded. "I hope you're right. We'll see how the media handles it on the news tonight."

He looked at his watch. Exactly at 5, the secure phone rang. The White House operator, on instruction, put the caller through.

"Hello, Mr. President, this is Mr. Fairview. I'm honored to talk with you," the voice said. "I'm calling as we planned. Please bring the money in hundred-dollar bills, unmarked and in a sturdy suitcase. We'll meet at my house tomorrow evening on Massachusetts Avenue, near the end of the District, close to Chevy Chase. The time is 11:30. Do you have a pencil? Write down the details."

Charlie scribbled the address and the time as the man spoke and George listened.

"Yes, I have it. Tomorrow night at 11:30, in the 4700 block of Massachusetts Avenue. I'm to bring the $100,000. Any other instructions?"

"Tell no one about this. Find a way to shake your Secret Service people and come alone. If you're with anyone, and I'll have someone checking, then the deal is off."

"I understand you want me to come alone, but I'm learning that it's impossible. There's always a Secret Service detail with me. Can't I send an emissary, someone who can represent me and close the deal?"

"I'm afraid not. If you're accompanied or trailed, by the Secret Service or anyone, I'll go right to the tabloids with the information. And I'll have someone checking to see that you are really alone. Do you understand?"

Charlie could see he had no leeway. "Yes, Mr. Fairview, I do. I'll come alone."

Suddenly, Charlie thought of a key problem.

"When I pay you the $100,000, what assurance do I have that you won't ask me for more money later on? How do I know that I can trust you?" Charlie asked, realizing his vulnerability.

"You can't. You'll have to rely on my word."

"I guess I have no choice."

"Good, and again, Mr. President, it's been an honor speaking with you. I've never talked to a President before. And by the way, I liked your inaugural address."

With that, Mr. Fairview hung up.

The rest of the evening went off without a hitch, except for the festering wound of Clara's absence.

He had sent her an invitation to the main inaugural ball at the Willard Hotel, but she hadn't come. From the dais, he had scoured the ballroom, but it was futile. Besides, if she were there he'd have known it instinctively.

Of course, he could have personally called to invite her, but he was not willing to bend that much. She had left him. She could return—if she wanted to.

There had been only three inaugural balls that night instead of the usual dozen or more. He was frankly prejudiced against the appearance of presidential "royalty." Nor did he want to raise money for the celebration, or take a nickel more from Rafferty.

He was trying an experiment. As he had pledged in his inaugural address, for the first three years of his administration, he would do absolutely no fund-raising. Either Congress would adopt his plan of "no money" politics or he'd wait until the fourth year to raise what he needed. If the public appreciated his work as President, the money would be forthcoming. If not, he wouldn't run for reelection anyway.

Finally, at 1 A.M., after he had danced with Sally and Jenny at the main ball, they and George and Sky returned to the White House, where they were all invited to stay over.

Rest didn't come easy for the new President that night. Once again, he rose at 5 A.M., when it was still dark outside and the predicted snowstorm was howling. It occurred to him that as President, he had never been in the Oval Office. The first day had been too crammed with official functions.

He quickly dressed in casual clothes and a windbreaker. "I'm going to the West Wing for a moment," he told the agent outside his door. He didn't know how closely he had to keep them informed, but he thought it polite.

He went down the private elevator to the first floor, then across the covered portico to the Executive West Wing, where he nodded to the agent in front of the Oval Office.

Slowly, he opened the door. He used the dimmer to only partially illuminate the room. Standing on the threshold of the historic office, he was immobilized by awe. He stood there for minutes, his eyes exploring the room, democracy's sanctum sanctorum. Ennobled in national mythology, its occupants were the high priests of the New Jerusalem on the Potomac.

He took in the detail of the chamber: its marble Adams fireplace, the scalloped niches in the walls filled with bric-a-brac, the French doors to the Rose Garden, the carefully chosen American antiques. In the center of the room was a rug with the federal eagle woven into its design. For a moment he imagined that the proud bird was staring him down, quizzically seeking out his intentions.

He liked what he saw. Other Presidents had ordered massive redecoration of the office, but he decided that it would stay just as it was without his spending a nickel. His mind was working like a cash register. At least another half million saved.

Charlie continued to stand at the threshold, spellbound, when suddenly the historic ghosts of the room rose in near unison, parading before his mind's eye—Jack Kennedy, enthused with power, chomping on a cigar and moving to and fro in his padded rocker; Teddy Roosevelt energetically striding across the room as if on a forced march, enthusiastically greeting foreign ambassadors; Lyndon Johnson, his arms encircling the shoulders of a frightened congressman, pressing the flesh as he extracted a promise of his vote; Franklin Roosevelt, cigarette in his mouth, wheeling about the room, talking, always talking; Richard Nixon, the determination creasing his face, intently dictating.

Was he an interloper? Did he belong in the great continuum of leaders who had enhanced, even sometimes abused, the sacred office?

Hesitantly, he took those first few steps. Slowly, he started a circle tour of the oval, his fingers tentatively touching pieces of furniture as he went, the contact like a child's compulsion, making the room seem more real.

Finally, he arrived at the chair behind the desk. The leather back was higher than he had expected. Was the extra foot or so the democratic approximation of a throne? He brushed aside the idea and lowered himself into the enveloping chair.

Slowly, unexpectedly, his head dropped down toward the desk until the bottom of his chin rested on the smooth wooden surface. He sat there in the half dark, his eyes sweeping the office. His thoughts wandered until they were abruptly broken.

"Mr. President. It's me."

He looked up to see Sally standing in front of the desk, dressed in her bathrobe, casually covered with an open polo coat.

"What in heavens are you doing down here so early in the morning?" he asked, abruptly lifting his head.

"I couldn't sleep either. Too much excitement and jubilation. Then I heard you walking down the hall so I thought I'd join you. Do you mind?"

Charlie didn't mind; he was just surprised.

"No, not at all, Sally. I remembered that I hadn't been in the Oval Office since I was inaugurated. Suppose I just wanted to make sure it really was mine."

She smiled warmly. "Don't worry, it's all yours. Frankly, I wanted to be alone with you, to tell you how much I admire you, and how wonderful it's been these months, starting out in our little hole in the Longworth Building and ending—well, here in this room. I just think . . ."

Sally seemed close to tears as she came around the desk and leaned over him. "This is for everything, Mr. President," she said as she kissed him on the cheek.

Charlie didn't know what to do. His instincts, starved by the work and the absence of a woman's love, seemed to overtake him. He reached up and took Sally's face in his hands, then kissed her full on the lips, gently but passionately.

"That, Sally, is thanks from me."

CHAPTER 55

"Ladies and gentlemen of the press, I give you the President of the United States."

With those words, Robbie Barnes introduced Charlie Palmer and moved off to the side.

It was 9 A.M. on the morning of January 21. The more than one hundred press people assembled in the White House press room sat with curious expressions on their faces. They had no idea why the President had so broken with tradition as to call a nationally televised press confab on the very first business day of his administration.

"I hope I've surprised you, and I hope to surprise you even more," Charlie began. "I have chosen my Cabinet officers in full, and I'm here to introduce them to the nation—all nine of them."

Charlie could see them squirm a bit, touching pen to paper.

"The reason I say nine instead of fourteen—the number of Cabinet officials in the last administration—is that I am consolidating, compressing, and changing the outmoded executive branch arrangement by Executive Order. I expect Congress to confirm my move by appropriately reducing the budget. If not, I won't sign the budget and I believe the people will back me.

"Let me show you in the form of the people I have nominated to do this job. All are experienced public servants, all have been thoroughly investigated by the FBI, and I expect confirmation of my entire slate by the Senate within ten days, without any opposition."

Charlie waved to Robbie, who then ushered ten people onto the stage, headed by VP Jason Hollingsworth.

"You all know Vice President Hollingsworth, who has been gracious enough to join us for a group picture. Now let me introduce my new Cabinet, one by one. No applause please. Instead, I'll expect fair appraisal in your media, and not just gossip and carping. These people are all exemplary and deserve your praise."

The President began with Arthur Steadman.

"Governor Steadman will head the new Department of Natural Resources, which will combine Interior, the Forest Service, Energy, and a scaled-back Agriculture Department minus its subsidies."

An excited buzz filled the room as the television cameras zoomed in for a close-up on Steadman.

The next Cabinet chief introduced by the President was Congresswoman Mollie Downs of Texas, looking as perky and determined as usual.

"Ms. Downs will head the new Department of Human Resources, which will include the eliminated Department of Housing and Urban Development, and the eighty-one welfare programs now in six different cabinet agencies, all reorganized with one computer in a subagency of Welfare. Most of those programs—except for the blind and disabled—will be closed, and I'm proposing to Congress that we restart FDR's WPA and provide jobs for everyone now on welfare. She will also handle the remaining duties of the eliminated Department of Education, which will now concentrate on expanded student loans which will be paid back by an IRS check-off, saving billions in defaults. I may remind you that not long ago we gave out $109 million in new loans to students who defaulted on their old ones."

Charlie went down the line, having each Cabinet nominee step forward, and offering a digest of his or her duties.

The next Cabinet chief was Jack Riordan, former head of the AFL-CIO, who would take over the new Department of Industry and Labor, combining the former Commerce, Transportation and Labor departments. Dr. Mary Lamont would head the new Department of Health, which would assume the medical responsibility—including Medicare, Medicaid, and public health—of the closed Department of Health and Human Services.

When the President was done, he had them all step forward at the same time.

"Here you have it," he said, "a piece of magic—nine where there once were fourteen."

The press seemed entertained, and impressed, by his presentation. But there seemed to be only one public relations cog in his smooth machine. That was Vice President Hollingsworth, who sternly posed for pictures with the President and the new Cabinet. The tall Midwesterner, with features as craggy as the Dakota badlands from where he had come, seemed determined to hold back even the promise of a smile.

After several questions from the press on the Cabinet reorganization, Shirley Townsend, senior member of the press corps and famed for her long skirts and lack of diplomacy, raised her hand.

"Yes, Shirl," the President immediately acknowledged her.

"This is the first time since 1800, when Aaron Burr lost to Jefferson in the House and became Vice President under the old system, that the President and the Vice President are of two different parties. Can you and Mr. Hollingsworth work together?"

"I hope so," the President improvised. "This situation was dictated by the Senate, which rejected my running mate, Senator Larrimore—I suppose because he left his party, as I did. But I'm hopeful that Vice President Hollingsworth will tolerate me. What do you say, Jason?"

The Vice President's face gave away nothing.

"We'll give it a try," Hollingsworth answered, finally smiling weakly. "I'll be meeting with the President tomorrow, and I may have more to say then."

The President winced.

With that, Robbie Barnes took the microphone.

"I'm sorry, but the President has a busy first business day. This press conference is over."

Judging from the television follow-ups, the Cabinet conference was a stunning hit with the press, with commentators praising his choices, stressing that "cronyism" seemed to have disappeared as a criterion, a first in many years at the White House.

The rest of the day went smoothly. Charlie even managed to *almost* push tonight's dreaded rendezvous out of his mind.

But it was soon 6 P.M., and reality had to be faced. He had a meeting with George coming up to prepare for the nightmare adventure on Massachusetts Avenue. He knew he shouldn't be going, but he had failed to come up with an alternative.

"Sally, I'm tired after the long hours yesterday and today," the President told his deputy chief of staff. "I'm going to my family quarters to rest. I'll have a BLT sent up. Call me only if it's a real emergency."

In his White House apartment, Charlie put on a simple sweat suit. Within minutes, Sempel arrived carrying a hard-shell piece of luggage, twice the size of an attache case.

"It's all in here, Mr. President," George said, placing the case on top of a table. "Glad you told the Secret Service it was top secret. They didn't search it."

Almost ritually, Sempel opened the case. "Take a look."

Inside were piles of $100 bills, ten stacks of one hundred each—the $100,000 ransom Mr. Fairview was demanding for his silence.

"Thanks, George. I can always rely on you. Do you want me to sign a promissory note?"

Sempel waved him off. "Don't be silly. I'm only worried whether you're doing the right thing. In any case, I hope this will shut the lousy blackmailer up. Mr. President, you'll have to leave a little before 10:30 to make the 11:30 appointment on Massachusetts Avenue. Will you be able to get out of the White House without anyone seeing you?"

"I think so. As I told you, I'll change into the Air Force colonel's uniform and walk out as if I were he. For me, leaving Fort White House is as hard as it is for others to get in. Thank God for the snowstorm. That'll obscure a lot of the gate. Besides, I'm about the same height and weight as Colonel Lescomb. Until it's time to go, I'll put the case in the closet and take a nap."

"George?"

"Yes, Mr. President."

"Wish me luck. In four hours, I'm going on the strangest adventure of my young life."

Later that evening, a half hour after midnight, the President returned to the White House on the floor of the back of Larry Dunn's car, shaken. The adventure had ended in an unforeseen catastrophe, and it was hard to think of anything else.

Firstly, there was the danger of being exposed. Disguised as his air attache, he had successfully sneaked out of the White House at 10:30 P.M.

He had followed "Fairview's" instructions, driving by taxi through the blinding snowstorm to almost the end of Massachusetts Avenue, to the simple little house on a rise in the 4700 block. He had been punctual, arriving at 11:30 P.M.

Never had he expected what he found—the short, red-haired blackmailer facedown on a bloodstained rug in the bedroom, a large kitchen knife protruding from his back. Panic nearly overtook him, especially when he realized someone else was in the room, aiming a gun at him.

Fortunately, he had not evaded the Secret Service as well as he thought. Larry Dunn, the night supervisory agent, had followed him. His self-possession was gone, but Dunn quickly took over, simulating a break-and-enter robbery.

Just before they left, he had spotted Fairview's briefcase half-hidden by a bedpost. He had asked Dunn to wait outside while he removed the blackmailer's file marked "Fairview," which was now secure in his closet safe. Dunn had also comforted Charlie, assuring him that he knew he was innocent of the killing. As a former Boston homicide detective, Dunn could tell that the man had been dead about an hour. He had arrived there only five minutes after the President.

On the way back, Dunn had informed the District Police of the murder by pay phone, then smuggled the President into the White House on the floor of the car's backseat.

Now in an armchair in the family quarters, resting his frayed nerves, the President was overwhelmed by shame and fear. Had he been foolhardy to take such a risk? Surely. But the facts of his life history were now secure and the blackmailer was dead.

Fairview's death presented a new dilemma. The blackmail was over, but the President had secretly been at the scene of a murder, a fact known only to Larry Dunn. Without being asked, Dunn had covered for him and was now the only person who could prove the President's innocence.

What to do? He hadn't the slightest idea. Destiny, which had brought him this far, would have to provide that answer as well.

CHAPTER 56

Detective One Sam Lemoine—still called Sergeant despite a District Police reorganization—poked his head through the broken glass French door and mumbled something inaudible.

"Whatdyasay, Sarge?" asked Al Dennis, his Detective Two assistant. "Sometimes your accent throws me."

"Don't get sassy with me, Al. It'll cost you."

In the early hours of January 22, the police had arrived at the small house on upper Massachusetts Avenue. An anonymous phone call to 911 had alerted them that someone had been killed at that address. A squad car with Detective Dennis from District Two headquarters on Idaho Avenue, which covered the affluent Northwest area, arrived promptly. Lemoine of homicide followed soon after.

When it served his purpose, the black senior officer spoke in Southern patois. But he lashed out in the King's English when he sensed a failure of respect, or because of an omission in homicide protocol. His compulsions were legendary, including an obsessive twirling of an unlit cigar, but so was his temper. That was described by some as "bombastic." Others less awed saw it as the ravings of a "crazy son of a bitch."

A thin man of medium height with prematurely white hair and a matching mustache, Sam was particularly quiet this morning, nosing around the crime scene, apparently aimlessly. He had already examined the corpse, a short man with kinky red hair and an oversize head, who had been stabbed in the back with a large kitchen knife. Now Lemoine was slowly pacing the room.

"Looks open and shut, right, Sarge?" Dennis offered.

"Now what does that mean, Al?"

"That it looks like thousands of D.C. breaking and entering cases with a little murder thrown in for good measure. His wallet was empty, and from the looks of the room, it seems like the victim put up a struggle before someone took him down."

Lemoine continued his pacing. "Anyone get the corpse's name, address and occupation?" he asked.

"There was no ID on him. We took a set of fingerprints and sent them to the FBI print headquarters in West Virginia. Word just came in. His name was Arnold Reichmann and he was a licensed private investigator from Columbus, Ohio. I spoke to the owner of this house—Reichmann had rented it for two months, furnished."

"Anybody know why he was in Washington?" Lemoine asked. "Was he on a case?"

"Nobody knows. His phone service in Columbus says he was a one-man operation. Not even a secretary." Dennis paused. "Everything points to a break-in. Right?"

Lemoine walked back to the glass door, then mumbled.

"Whatdyasay?" asked Dennis.

"I didn't."

Lemoine reapproached the body, which the coroners were about to remove. He leaned down, stared at the entry point of the knife, then got on his knees to peer in the corpse's face.

"What did you find in that brown briefcase?"

"Just the usual junk and his telephone address book crammed with numbers," his assistant responded.

"Good. Have our computer people put it on a disk, then give me a printout by area code with numbers and names."

"OK."

"What did the coroner say about time of death?"

"Says he figures about 10:30 to 11:30 last night. God, the thief could be anywhere, now."

Lemoine mumbled again.

"Whatdyasay?" Dennis asked again.

"No, Al, I didn't say anything. Not yet, anyway."

"Well, what are you thinking?"

"What I'm thinking is that it's a perfect B&E, just like you said. The glass falls right from the outside in. The money is gone and the room is the picture of someone defending his life."

"Just like I said, right?"

"That's what bothers me. It looks picture perfect. Like someone who knows his business staged it. But there's one flaw. The corpse has a knife in his back, but his clothes are not ripped and his face doesn't have a scratch on it." He paused. "Still could be the way it looks, but I don't know."

Lemoine paused, then started to circle the room again, mumbling as he went.

"Whatdyasay, Sarge?"

"Nothing, Dennis. Just ask the medical examiner if there's any signs of internal injury. And keep in touch with Columbus. Maybe they'll learn something more about our Mr. Reichmann. Meanwhile, Al, do me a favor.

"What's that Sarge?"

"Try not to say 'whatdyasay.' OK?"

Detective Lemoine sat in his Idaho Avenue office, studying the list of phone numbers taken out of Reichmann's book.

The list would be worthless if it was a routine break and entry by a local thug. But if the killer was someone that Reichmann knew, the phone book could connect the victim to a potential killer anywhere in the nation.

The bulk of the numbers were from the 614 area code covering Columbus, Ohio, and environs. The others were scattered, a mixture of clients, police leads, his family and friends. Reichmann was unmarried and no one knew if he had a steady girl friend.

Of the list, one number—555-9933—stood out. It had no area code number. Lemoine felt stymied. There were over a hundred area codes in the nation, and he didn't feel like asking anyone to try each one.

He called the most logical one, in the 614 area. A record came on. "The number you have dialed is not a working number in this area code."

Suddenly, an idea struck him. Why not try the number in the Washington area, 202?

Lemoine dialed 555-9933 directly and waited. The phone rang, then was answered by an authoritative female voice.

"Hello, can I help you?" she asked.

"Who have I reached? This is Detective Sergeant Sam Lemoine of the District Police."

"Well, what number did you want?"

"555-9933."

"Yes, you've reached that number. What can I do for you?"

"All I want to know is whose phone this is."

"I'm sorry, Sergeant, that's not public information. If you don't know who you're calling, you shouldn't be calling here at all." With that she hung up.

What in the hell was that all about? Lemoine leaned back and toyed with his mustache. He'd call the local phone company, the

Chesapeake and Potomac, and see if they could do a reverse check and give him the name on the listing.

He dialed the main office of the phone company and asked for security. Lemoine quickly identified himself.

"I want a check made of the listing of 202-555-9933," he said in his most officious voice. "This is police business, a homicide investigation."

The security officer asked him to wait, then finally returned to the phone. "I'm sorry, Sergeant. That's an unlisted number."

"I assumed as much, miss. That's why I'm asking you who it belongs to. If necessary, I'll go through the usual rigmarole and get a court subpoena."

"No, that's not the problem here."

Lemoine was surprised. "Then what is?"

"That number is one of the top security phones in the federal government. Even I don't have access to its owner. I'm sorry, Sergeant, but I can't help you."

Once again a phone was hung up in his ear, this one with a definitive, if not angry, stroke. This investigation was becoming hazardous to his hearing.

Top security? Top secret? What could Reichmann, a small-time PI, have to do with that—if the phone number was actually in the 202 area code, which now seemed less probable?

Perhaps, Lemoine thought, there was another avenue, one which he hated to lean on. But he'd try. Jake Mintz, former detective lieutenant in the District, was now a chief security officer at the Chesapeake and Potomac. Jake owed him a few.

"Jake, this is Sam. Yeah, Sam Lemoine. I'm checking out a homicide on Massachusetts Avenue. The victim's phone book was full of numbers, but one of them might be in the District. Could you help me out, sort of private like? The phone number is 555-9933. I'd like to know who it belongs to. If you insist, I'll get a subpoena from a district court."

Lemoine waited for a response, but the phone seemed dead.

"Jake, are you still there?"

"Yeah, I'm here, Sam."

"So who does the number belong to? What's the mystery?"

Jake cleared his throat, then was silent again for fifteen seconds.

"Take my word for it, Sam," he finally said. "You don't want to know."

"What the hell does that mean? I don't want to know? I want to know real bad. Especially now that everyone is so closemouthed."

"Sorry, Sam, we're old buddies in the street wars, but this one goes beyond friendship, or even court subpoenas. And like I said, you don't want to know."

Sam didn't know how to reply. He waited through the silence, which lasted almost a half minute, then heard the receiver click off.

Even his old buddy Jake Mintz had hung up on him. What in the world was going on? Arnie Reichmann, dead nonhero, had suddenly come to life in a posthumous intrigue that was driving Lemoine crazy.

CHAPTER 57

"The Vice President is here to see you, Mr. President," his reception-ist, Margaret Kingsley, called on the intercom. "Shall I have him come in?"

"Yes, please."

Charlie had invited Hollingsworth in hopes of finding some common ground, perhaps even calling upon him, as an ex-senator, to be a liaison with Congress. He also wanted to enlist Hollingsworth in his plan to cut the fat out of the executive branch.

He wasn't too optimistic, for obvious reasons.

Hollingsworth seemed to be the Beltway incarnate, open to all kinds of lobbyist and perk temptations. The *New Republic* article on congressional perks had awarded him the title "King of the Freeload-ers" for taking a slew of taxpayer-paid junkets around the world, from Tahiti to Paris to Sydney on supposed "fact-finding missions." The cost? A half-million dollars to taxpayers.

Of course, if he couldn't find a compromise, he'd make sure Jason wasn't on his ticket the second time around—if he decided to run himself. Four years was a lifetime, considering he had been in politics for only nine months.

As Hollingsworth approached, Charlie politely waved him to one of the two colonial armchairs in front of the fireplace.

"Well, Jason, we have a lot to talk about," Charlie began. "But I thought that today we might concentrate on our own staffs."

"Yes, Mr. President, whatever you think."

"Well, to put it up front—I'd like to see both of us cut our staffs in half. JFK only had 385 people in the White House besides the budget group. Now I've inherited eleven hundred people, which is ridiculous. There's been a lot of talk about cutting the president's staff by 25 percent, but they just played musical chairs and sent people back to their original agencies. The whole thing ended up with a 5 percent cut, maybe. Well, now I'm cutting back to six hundred people, and I'd like you to follow suit proportionately."

Hollingsworth seemed taken aback. "I don't follow you, Mr. President. I have only sixty-five employees. Where can I cut? I don't think that's sensible."

Charlie got up and began pacing, his substitute for losing his temper. Suddenly, he swiveled.

"Jason, let me give it to you straight. Harry Truman had a hole-in-the-wall office in the Senate when he was VP, and only four clerks. He lived in a two-bedroom apartment on Connecticut Avenue and paid the $140-a-month rent out of his own $12,000 salary. But you? Damn it, you live like a crown prince even though your only official duty is to occasionally preside over the Senate. Otherwise, you're just waiting for me to die or get impeached. You make $175,000 a year, which is too much for what you do. You've got a mansion on the Naval Observatory ground which the government has spent $3.5 million fixing up—$275,000 just for the 'verandah,' which I suppose is Southern for porch.

"You've got sixty-five people on your staff. Your wife alone has a bigger staff than Truman had. And where does she come off having more than one—a social secretary? You've got a $50,000-a-year housekeeper, a navy crew to take care of the grounds and house, and, damn it, a $90,000 entertainment allowance. And don't forget your motorcade of cars, and three drivers, and your Boeing 707 jet, Air Force Two."

The President paused and took a quick swig of water, as if to quench his anger.

"And you've got five offices—four more than me. One in the White House, one in the Senate, another in the Old Executive Office Building, another in your navy mansion, and I understand you're opening one in your home state of North Dakota. Now, that's indecent."

"So?" Jason asked, his smile a masterpiece of condescension.

"So, I want it changed, and now. I want to save at least $3 million a year on your operation."

"What about you? If I'm a prince, you live like a damn king, as do a lot of the people around you."

Charlie was called up short.

"You're dead right, Jason. I inherited that mess and I'm going to disinherit it. I'm not only reducing my staff, I'm cutting the White House residence employees from eighty-seven to fifty. Can you imagine, two full-time florists? I've got twenty-nine limos that were used by those pretentious high-and-mighty White House staffers. I'm selling most of them right away."

"What about the Eighty-ninth Airlift at Andrews Air Force Base—the 'Airline of the VIPs,' they call it? You've got a real boondoggle there."

"You're right again. I can't give up the two Air Force Ones—those flying palaces with gold faucets. But I am getting rid of eighteen of the twenty-three fancy airliners that fly members of Congress, generals, and big-shot bureaucrats around the country and the world. The planes sit on the ground 80 percent of the time. That's pure waste."

The President returned to his armchair and sat facing Hollingsworth, pushing his face within two feet of the Vice President's.

"So, how about it, Jason? Will you help me by cutting your operation proportionately as much as I cut mine? The television magazine shows will play it up big. Your prestige will skyrocket. Will you do it?"

Hollingsworth slowly rose from his chair and looked down on the President, hostility written across his face.

"The answer, Mr. President, is that I'll do absolutely nothing you ask. I like it just the way it is. If you think that you can get Congress to cut my operation, you're sadly mistaken. I'd been a senator for twenty years and even with your popularity, I think I have more muscle with them than you do. So my final answer is . . ." Hollingsworth paused.

"Yes, Jason?"

"The answer is that you can shove your reforms up you know where."

With that, the Vice President turned and strode confidently out of the Oval Office.

Charlie sat, lowering his chin onto the desk, apparently his new way of handling excess stress or disappointment.

Hollingsworth might, or might not, have the power he believed. Besides, as a week-old president, Charlie felt that his message was gaining popularity and his Cabinet appointments had received praise. Now if he could defeat the likes of Hollingsworth, Billings, Tolliver, et al., there could be a revival of the nation's spirit and faith in the government. But who knew?

Meanwhile, he'd play his own game. Truman complained that FDR had met with him only twice. He'd see if he couldn't break that record when it came to Vice President Jason Mills Hollingsworth.

CHAPTER 58

"Sam, I've got a goodie. A real goodie."

Al Dennis had just barged into Sergeant Lemoine's office, enthusiastically waving a piece of paper.

"Here it is. We got an anonymous phone tip just a few hours ago. From the background noise it sounded like a street box somewhere. The tipster said it was about the Arnie Reichmann killing. He had read about it in the paper, and said if I wanted a lead, I should call the Alliance Insurance Investigative Agency in Columbus, Ohio. Then he hung up."

"Was it a man or woman?" Sam asked.

"Strangest thing, I couldn't tell. The voice was funny. Could have been either one."

"So did you call Alliance in Columbus?" Lemoine's senses were coming alive.

"Oh, yeah, Sarge. They just called me back, then faxed the stuff. It's startling, Sam. Real startling."

Lemoine toyed with his immaculate white mustache as he read the report, dated back in June.

"We were asked by an anonymous source who wired our fee through a Cayman Islands bank to conduct a private background check of a local in Fairview, Ohio, ostensibly as part of a large life insurance application—firm not mentioned. We asked Arnie Reichmann, a licensed private investigator in Ohio, to do the work. Fee was $500 a day, and if he found any evidence of moral turpitude, he was to receive a $5,000 bonus, which he did. We don't know the name of our client, but we can tell you that the subject was a computer executive who had recently been elected to a seat in Congress. His name is Charles Knudsen Palmer."

Lemoine closed his eyes for an instant.

"Palmer! What in the hell," he shouted. "That must be President Palmer. He's from Fairview."

He rose and paced fully around the room, his steps resolute.

"Al, I know it sounds crazy, but I've got nothing to lose. What was that phone number without an area code we found in Reichmann's book?"

"555-9933."

"Good, I'll try it again, in the District. It's a long shot, but what the heck."

He leaned over and dialed the number.

"Hello, can I help you?" a woman answered.

It was the same authoritative female voice as before. He summoned his courage, a lot more than needed to handle the local punks.

"Yes, thank you. This is Detective Sergeant Sam Lemoine of District Two homicide." Having gone this far, he knew he couldn't retreat under his own pressure. "May I please speak to President Palmer?" he asked.

"I'm sorry, the President is in conference. But if you'll leave your number, I can have a member of his staff call you back."

Lemoine stood immobile, silent, the receiver dangling in his hand, still unsure of what had happened, and fearful of its implications.

Poor ass Arnie Reichmann, thoroughly dead private eye—and the President of the United States? What in the hell was going on?

He smiled to himself and slowly lowered the phone without answering. Now it was his turn to hang up.

CHAPTER 59

On his very first day in the White House, press secretary Robbie Barnes had a piece of luck he could hardly believe.

Early that morning, he had experienced a touch of serendipity that fit in perfectly with his goals. Barnes was seated at his desk in his West Wing office when his leg collided with something underneath. He got down on his hands and knees and peeked into the kneehole. It was just a buzzer, somewhat like a doorbell. He pressed it, but nothing seemed to happen.

An odd thought captured him. In his readings about the Nixon White House, he recalled that a secret button in the Oval Office had set the now-famous tape recording system into motion. Could there be a similar setup in this White House, perhaps one installed by a prior administration?

He immediately approached Pat McNulty, the Secret Service operational chief.

"Pat, is there a system for taping conversations in the White House? And is it working?" Barnes asked.

"Yes, there is one in place, but as far as I know, it hasn't been active for years. Thanks for reminding me. I'll talk to the President or Mr. Sempel about whether they'd like to get it running or not. If I had my way, I'd rip it out. Look at the trouble it caused Mr. Nixon. In any case, the house electrician knows more about it than I do."

Barnes walked to the White House basement and talked to the electrician, using an easy ruse.

"I understand there's a recording system in the White House,"

Barnes commented casually. "I might be able to use something like that for press conferences. How does it work?"

The electrician pointed to a bright blue box against the wall. "Its control is right over there. Simple as pie. It's not working now—hasn't been for years—but you can turn it on by throwing the black switch. It works off recorders in three places: the press room, the Oval Office, and the family quarters."

"I suppose the whole system ends up in a tape bank in the Oval Office." Barnes was guessing his way through.

"That's right," the electrician confirmed. "There's a turn-on in each area. Looks either like a switch, or a buzzer. The press room one is under your desk. In the Oval Office, the buzzer is in a drawer of the President's desk, on the bottom left. The switch in the family quarters is on the wall of the sitting room, right below those for the lights near the exit door. Each of them starts the audio bank in the Oval Office going. That's in the closet next to the fireplace. By recording at very slow speeds it gets six hours of audio on a T-120, two-hour VHS videocassette. It's the best way to get a lot of audio recorded in a small space. It's no good for music, only for speech. But it's not working now anyway."

Barnes thanked him and left. He waited an hour, then returned to the basement. No one was in sight. Quickly, he opened the blue monitor box and threw the switch, activating the entire system. Back in his office, he pressed the buzzer, then approached the microphone on the stage of the press room.

"Testing this mike: six, five, four, three, two, one."

The riskiest part of the operation was checking out the tape bank in the Oval Office, which was impossible right now. But he'd try to activate the recorder in the family quarters, the likeliest place for confidential conversations.

Pleading a bad cold, he told George Sempel—who was handling the inauguration—that he wouldn't be joining them this morning. He could sit it out in the White House and watch the ceremony on television. His real motivation was simple: he wanted to be here the minute the President returned that afternoon after the address and the parade. The sooner he got the audio recording system activated the better.

At 4 P.M., the President returned to the White House. Barnes gave him about fifteen minutes to get settled, then took the elevator up to the Family Quarters.

"I'm Robbie Barnes, the President's Press Secretary," he told the agent standing stiffly at the door. "I need to speak to him about the Inaugural Ball. Very important."

The agent nodded. "I know who you are, Mr. Barnes. Wait a minute. I'll let the President know you're here."

The agent moved to a desk, where he used the phone—Barnes guessed to call the President. He returned a moment later.

"He said to come right in. He's in his bedroom."

As Barnes entered, he cast a quick glance at the light switches alongside the door. Below a set of four, there was a single one. Surely, the audio activator.

"Come in Robbie, and what's it all about?" the President called from his bedroom.

As Barnes walked in, he could see that the President was relaxing. He had donned a sweatsuit and was on the bed, feet up, his head against a pillow, reading the newspaper.

"Well, sir, it might sound like a small matter but that's what press relations are made of. They're images that people gain about you, and they're cumulative. One of the first social ones you'll make to-night are at the Inaugural Ball. People will be looking for cues that have nothing to do with your politics. It's a matter of what kind of person you'll be in the White House."

"So, what can I do to help you make me look more human? Is that what you're getting at?"

Barnes sighed with relief. "Exactly, sir. The danger in your public image is that you sometimes come across a little too cerebral."

"You mean like Woodrow Wilson?"

Barnes couldn't help but laugh a touch. The President did have a good sense of humor, even if it wasn't exercised enough.

"No, not that bad. And not Calvin Coolidge either," Barnes retorted. "But I would like you to loosen up at the Ball—you know dance with several ladies, and not more than twice with anyone. We don't want to start any rumors. You've had enough of that, you know."

"Well, I'm not much of a dancer, but I can manage a fox trot or two. Good advice Robbie, as usual. I'll do what I can. You'll be there to check up on me, won't you?"

"No, sir. But thanks anyway. I can't dance, and I have to nurse a miserable cold. I'll watch it on television."

The President smiled and moved to pick up his newspaper, a sign that the short meeting was over.

Barnes walked back toward the exit door and stood in front of the light switches. He turned and stared at the bedroom. Good, he was out of the President's line of sight. Quickly, he flipped the audio recording switch on, then exited the door.

"Thanks," he muttered to the Secret Service agent and moved toward the elevator.

He was proud of his dissembling. Everything now said by the President in his private apartment, along with phone conversations, was being duly recorded. As Justinian, all he had to do was wait, then collect any taped evidence for his allies—or if need be, for the press.

Barnes was proud that he had pulled off a few espionage miracles as Justinian, but he had failed in his main goal—to stop Charlie Palmer and his obsessive revolution. The man seemed to have nine political lives. Now, things might be different.

Fortunately, Justinian's spying hadn't aroused suspicion from either Sempel or the President, or even Andy Tolliver, who had no idea of the identity, or even the gender, of his informer. In fact, the childish curiosity of Sally's intern, Maggie Swanson, who had stolen a peek at the Green Book, had fortuitously thrown suspicion away from him.

Despite some setbacks, Barnes's confidence in his labors on behalf of the Republic was unshaken. Maintaining national stability was worth all the sacrifice and subterfuge. And he had unseen allies, people like Tolliver and Sobel, and Billings, Hollingsworth, Berry, Kellogg, and sometimes even Clara Staples—those who understood that the status quo was what held this diverse nation of competing forces together.

The two-party system was that glue, and whoever opposed it was, ipso facto, the enemy of the people. He had lived through his own radical days, but they had proven fruitless. He had now come to believe that the system had to be maintained at all costs, lest new radicals, in the guise of reformers, upset the national balance.

God and government had come together in America, and although he was no longer a seminarian, he had a priestly role to play. He was willing to use his considerable personal fortune, his reputation, even—if need be—his life, to defend it.

"Mr. President, things are going swimmingly. The press would love to clobber you but they smell success," Barnes was telling the President in the Oval Office some ten days after the Inauguration. "The Gallup-CNN poll shows you with a 70 percent approval rating, topping even President Reagan in his early days."

"And the downside, Robbie? What are they saying bad about me?"

"Well, the stodgier media are still harping on the abortion and the sex tapes. But those blemishes are fading away as radical budget cutting ideas gain attention. The press likes action, and you're giving them plenty of that."

"That sounds like you have some reservations yourself, Robbie. Do you?" the President asked.

"Well, not really, but I do wish you'd be a little more circumspect."

"For example?"

"For instance, the Vice President. After he left the White House, he was besieged by reporters asking about the meeting. He became nasty and just said: 'We agreed to disagree.' The television news plastered that everywhere. It'd be best if you cooled it a little, Mr. President. I don't want to see you hurt."

"I appreciate that, Robbie, but I'm beginning to think that the more heat between me and status quo people like Hollingsworth, the more popular I'll become. The American people are pissed, and I don't blame them. But aside from that, I must compliment you. You're a truly dedicated press secretary."

The President paused, searching through a pile of papers.

"Ah here it is, the speech and your press release on my Social Security address at John Hopkins tonight. You know, we've got to change that system before it becomes just another welfare program with minimum benefits. I want a real invested pension plan for the aged, like most state employees and teachers and others with 401-Ks have, and I'm going to lay it all out in Baltimore tonight."

The President rose. "I've got to go now, Robbie, the helicopter's waiting. Please follow up on the press."

Barnes walked out alongside the President.

Good timing. The Oval Office would be empty tonight. His impatience was gnawing at him. What would he find when he became privy to President Palmer's confidential conversations?

It was almost 9 P.M. and the White House was quiet. Barnes pretended to be busy so that his late stay wouldn't seem suspicious.

At one point, the night shift Secret Service agent in charge, Larry Dunn, poked his head in.

"Grinding out the propaganda, I see," said Dunn, a tall beefy agent, obviously Irish in coloring, with a full head of hair that had turned white though he was probably under forty-five.

"Yes, this President has a lot of ideas, so I've got to keep up—if that's possible."

Barnes waited until 9, then picked up a long report he had been preparing. Taking out a classification stamp, he pushed it into the purple ink pad, and pressed: FOR THE PRESIDENT'S EYES ONLY.

It was an exaggeration, but it should serve as his passport into the Oval Office after hours.

He walked into the main area of the Executive West Wing, then down the corridor to the Oval Office. Dunn was holding down the presidential fort.

"Larry, I need to hand deliver this secret report to the President. He's in Baltimore tonight, so I'll just leave it on his desk. I also have to find the old one I left this morning. It's been amended. Should take me only a couple of minutes."

Dunn glanced at the cover notation and waved Barnes on. Robbie opened the door and put on the light. Closing the door gingerly behind him, he quickly skirted across the room to the closet on the far wall next to the fireplace. Holding his breath, he opened it.

There it was, the tape bank with three sets of VHS cassettes used as audio only. The top one was marked "Oval Office." He could ignore that. Too much routine business. The second bank held the few feet of his own test in the press room. The third was surely the recording from the family quarters.

He looked into the window of the cassette and saw that it was only three-fourths finished. Removing that cassette, he shoved it into his pocket, replacing it with a fresh one he had brought along in his jacket.

Moving to the President's desk, he checked to see if everything was in place. He left nothing behind. Instead, he moved back toward the door with the same report—FOR THE PRESIDENT'S EYES ONLY—still in his hand.

He shut off the light and opened the door.

"Thanks a lot, Larry. That didn't take long, did it? I just exchanged the new one for this." Quickly, he flashed the supposed secret report in front of Dunn. "Now, I think it's time for me to get home," he said, unable to repress a smile.

CHAPTER 60

Lemoine prided himself on a clear head, but this time it was clouded.

At first sight, he had what looked like a simple B&E. The victim, a private eye from Ohio, had been murdered with a kitchen knife in the back. And now he had evidence that Reichmann's phone book contained the private number of the President of the United States. It made no sense.

Obviously, he'd have to visit the President and seek out the connection. But before he made that risky move, he needed to pin down his routine work. Reichmann's place had already been fingerprint dusted, but maybe someone had slipped up. "ASS-U-ME" was too often the operative word.

"Al, come in," Lemoine called loudly for Dennis, his voice tinged with annoyance, his perfectionist stock-in-trade. The unlit cigar twirling began.

"Tell me, once again, how you handled the fingerprint search," Sam asked the nervous younger detective.

"I had them dust all the ashtrays, the furniture, even the lamp bases. We picked up Reichmann's prints all over. The knife handle was clean and so were the doorknobs."

"What happened to the briefcase with the phone book?"

"Well, you know. We entered the numbers into the computer. That's how you got the White House phone."

"I know that. What I'm asking is—did you find any fingerprints on the briefcase?"

Dennis drew in his mouth. "The briefcase?"

"That's right. You know, the thing made out of leather with an opening at the top. Did you dust it for fingerprints before you put your clammy hands all over it?"

Lemoine's legendary temper was surfacing. Dennis shifted from one leg to the other. "Oh, shit, boss. We did dust the briefcase. Most of the prints were Reichmann's and the others were all different. It had four airline tags on it, so I figured that the other prints were from the baggage handlers."

"You figured? That's an oxymoron. So what did you do with the other prints?"

"I'm sorry, Sam, I didn't do a damn thing. They were never sent for ID and we don't have them anymore."

Lemoine walked around Dennis, his eyes at only his assistant's neck level. Each step was an indictment.

"So where is the briefcase? You haven't sold it, I hope?"

"No, Sam. I put it in a large envelope, and it's in the evidence closet." He smiled vapidly. "Should I get it for you?"

"No, I don't want to see the damn thing. Al, I pray for your sake that no one wiped it clean. Take it over to print ID. And I don't mean after lunch. Get your big ass moving. That is, if you want to save it."

CHAPTER 61

For Patriot, events were most discouraging.

The cause was President Charles K. Palmer. The new chief executive had not only been superactive, but had already subjected Vice President Hollingsworth to a tongue-lashing.

He was convinced that Palmer was the incarnation of political evil, someone whose intention was to bring Washington back to the way it was fifty years ago. In the VP's case, that meant emasculating his office of people and perks and returning to the Neanderthal era of Harry Truman, when the capital was a small, ineffective, and unsophisticated town. Naturally, Hollingsworth had rejected the idea.

Now there was the President's latest insult to public intelligence. Executive Order No. 1 had eliminated all consultants, except scientists, from government. The last four administrations had budgeted about $4 billion a year on consultants, money well spent, especially on the best K Street lawyers for up to $600 an hour.

In making his banal announcement, Palmer had pointed out that the government had fourteen thousand underused lawyers on its own payroll. Yes, but who—even the government—would want to use civil service attorneys for serious legal work? His order had far-reaching consequences. It would destroy the prosperity of many of his friends, a top-echelon class that gave Washington so much of its elan. They were the ones who patronized the best restaurants and cultural affairs, and kept real estate values up.

Though things were getting out of hand, there was one saving grace. The unusual election had ended up with a President and Vice

President with differing views of the nation. A simple thought overtook him: With Palmer out of the way, Hollingsworth would become President. All would be saved.

Too many Loyalists were falsely optimistic about Charlie's expected failure. First, they said he wouldn't win the popular vote. Then they were sure Palmer had no chance in the House after no one gained an Electoral College majority. Now they were predicting his imminent burnout. Congress would even find the guts to fight back.

Nonsense. The President was on a roll. Patriot envisioned four years of increased presidential power and a steady shift of funds and prestige away from the likes of him toward the great unwashed. If things were not checked, the "booboisie," that enormous middle class of hard-working dullards that H.L. Mencken warned about, would soon be running the country.

That he could not tolerate. The time for less talk had arrived. He would have to contact Stony, his own man of action.

CHAPTER 62

Robbie Barnes rode the Washington Metro—fare free for government employees—with his fingers pressed against the White House VHS cassette in his coat pocket. The contact filled him with anticipation. What, if anything, was on the President's tape?

He got off at the station next to the Hill, just three blocks from his townhouse apartment in the renovated Southeast quadrant. Never had he been so pleased to get back to his cramped one-bedroom layout. (The place was a sign that he was not abusing his family's wealth.)

Seconds after walking through the door, Barnes took out the cassette. Though he publicly posed as a teetotaler, he poured himself a Drambuie for fortification, then rushed to the video player and pressed in the VHS tape. There was no video on it, but the audio quality was reasonable.

Slowly savoring the drink, Barnes listened. Too impatient to hear all its six-hour capacity, he caught pieces, then fast forwarded and reversed if he thought he had missed something.

At first he was disappointed. Most of it was banal conversation between the President and the White House operator for orders of BLTs, the President's favorite. There were also business calls, including several to Barnes himself. But there was nothing of value to his allies.

Suddenly, as he fast-forwarded and stopped, he found himself in the middle of an off-phone recording. A visitor in the President's family quarters was speaking. Barnes backed up the tape, took a sip of Drambuie and listened—hard.

The President was talking to a man. He recognized the voice. It was George Sempel, the President's oldest friend. He turned up the volume, tolerating the scratchiness to get the gist of the conversation.

The President was first to speak.

"George, it may seem out of place on Inauguration Day, but I have something to confide in you, something you can never speak of to anyone, at any time . . . You remember the incident in California and the fire at our Town Hall . . . Well, it's coming back to haunt me."

Barnes's enthusiasm rose as he picked up on each word. The President was explaining that he was being blackmailed for $100,000. If he didn't pay, the blackmailer would go to the tabloids with the whole story—whatever that was.

He raised the volume a notch. Sempel was agreeing to loan Palmer the money. Soon after, the phone rang in the family quarters. The tape recorded only the President's voice. He was repeating the details of a rendezvous, surely with the blackmailer. The place was near the end of Massachusetts Avenue, in the 4700 block. The time was 11:30 P.M. Most astonishing, the President was to go there alone, after somehow shaking his Secret Service guard.

Barnes's head reeled in astonishment. Never had he expected such a rich vein of intelligence. A true coup. But what in the world was the President being blackmailed for?

He continued to listen. There was a gap, filled with phone orders for food. Then the conversation picked up again, with the same voice—George Sempel's.

"It's all in here, Mr. President," Sempel was saying. "Glad you told the Secret Service it was top secret. They didn't search it."

They continued to talk, then Sempel asked the President:

"Will you be able to get out of the White House without anyone seeing you?"

"I think so," the President answered. "As I told you, I'll . . ."

The tape halted abruptly. The conversation was replaced by crackling noise. It had run out at a crucial point.

What was "all in here?" Was it the $100,000 blackmail money? How did he intend to shake the Secret Service and leave the White House unaccompanied and unseen?

The questions tumbled out of Barnes's surprised brain one after the other. He had no answers, but one thing was clear. This was information that he—Justinian—had to get to Andy Tolliver, and from him, he supposed, to Sobel and the others.

The two-week old reign of Charles Knudsen Palmer was now in imminent danger of exploding before his very eyes. And he would have provided the detonator.

CHAPTER 63

"Lemoine, this is your lucky day."

Dave Stanton, ID chief at Idaho Avenue headquarters, stood at the sergeant's desk, a smile dominating his face.

"We redid the briefcase prints and found nine besides Reichmann's. Five were smudged and no damn good. But we got four, photographed them same size, then blew them up eight times. I sent them to the FBI criminal ID section—they've got twenty-seven million prints on file—and one came back with an ID. It was a baggage handler in Columbus, an ex-con."

"Well, that's no help, Dave."

"I know it Sam, but hold your water. I also asked the FBI to check their noncriminal files. They've got eighty million prints there—servicemen, veterans, government employees, you name it. Their complex formula screens the prints by the number of loops and other things. Now they've even got an optical scanning system."

"So? So what did they find, Dave? You're making me nervous."

"Well, one of the prints were those of an ex-serviceman, a sergeant serving in Frankfurt, Germany, about twenty years ago. They think that one of the three unidentified prints is his."

"Come on, Dave, stop being so cute. Who is this mystery man?"

"Hold on to your cigar, Sam. The print belongs to none other than former U.S. Army Sergeant Charles Knudsen Palmer. If I'm not mistaken the gentleman is now the President of the United States."

*   *   *

Sam Lemoine was now more confident and more confused than ever before.

From the fingerprint, he had confirmation that the phone number in Reichmann's telephone book was actually that of the President's private line. And more important, that—at some time—the President had touched Reichmann's briefcase, undoubtedly in his house.

But when? Before or after his death? Or maybe—during?

And why? Why would the President have anything to do with a punk private eye, even one from his home area in Ohio?

Obviously, his next move had to be an interrogation of the President. But how did a lowly detective accomplish that? Would he first have to clear it with the police commissioner, or the Department of Justice. Or what?

Pacing became his stimulus for thought. The jigsaw pieces of crime were best laid out in his head, where he could rearrange the few facts into a pattern of reason. In this case, the confusion came from the disparity in social class, education, and power between the two men.

What in the hell, he pondered, was the hidden link between Arnie Reichmann and President Palmer?

Party boss Andy Tolliver was at home at 7 A.M.

He had just finished reading his daily allotment of eight newspapers, everything from the *New York Times* to the *Chicago Tribune*. Daily he also reevaluated the state of his defeat to date. How popular was the new President? And how destructive was Palmer to his own bread and butter?

The media response was mixed. They couldn't avoid reporting Charlie's reforms and cuts. Nor could they avoid the fact that Palmer had a 70 percent approval rating.

But the media talked out of two sides of their word processors. Charlie's restructuring was generally good, they said. But they were afraid of "radicalism," and "extremism," whether of the left, the right, or, in Palmer's case, the middle. The talking heads, in effect, had come out four-square for absolutely nothing.

But Tolliver knew that his side couldn't afford the luxury of waffling, or waiting. Since the President was steadily moving ahead, how could the Loyalist cause recoup? The best way was not straight political opposition. In that game, President Charlie Fanatico held almost all the cards. The only way to stop the President was to further defame him personally.

So far the exposures had put some doubt in the public mind, but not enough to thwart their enthusiasm for Charlie. Now he had to find something for the kill.

Tolliver was pondering his next move (he probably needed an assist from Clara Staples, who had inexcusably been out of contact with her former lover, the President) when suddenly the phone rang.

"Hello, who do you want?" he asked brusquely. His unlisted number had been floating around media circles.

"I'd like to speak to Andy Tolliver. This is Justinian."

Tolliver immediately recognized the squeaky unisex voice.

"Hold it a second." Tolliver reached over and grabbed a pen and paper. "Go ahead, what have you got for me this time?"

"It's a shame I don't need or want the money, Mr. Tolliver, because this revelation about our President is priceless. And invaluable to our cause."

Tolliver became excited, quickly lowering himself into a chair. "Tell me. What is it?"

"I have documented evidence that the President is being blackmailed, to the tune of $100,000."

The party honcho started to quiver. His usually uncertain equilibrium became shakier. Fearing he would even fall off his oversize chair, he pulled the phone cord to its limit and lay his massive body down on his bed, faceup.

"Wonderful. What's he being blackmailed for?"

"I don't know. But I do know that the night after his inauguration, he left the White House by somehow avoiding the Secret Service. All alone, he took the $100,000 in a suitcase to a house in the 4700 block of Massachusetts Avenue, to meet a private eye called Mr. Fairview, who was blackmailing him."

"And?"

"And that's it. Now you have to find out who Mr. Fairview is. Reach him, and the whole thing will break open."

"But I know Mr. Fairview."

"You what? Tell me."

"Sorry, I can't, Justinian. But thanks. This sounds like what we needed. A miracle from the political gods."

Tolliver paused. "Tell me, Justinian. Who are you? How are you privy to all this information? And besides, are you a man or a woman?"

"Sorry," the voice answered, then clicked off.

"THANKS ANYWAY. YOU'RE AN AMERICAN HERO!" Tolliver shouted exuberantly into a dead phone.

Yes, he knew Mr. Fairview, a short redhead with an oversize head. They had met at the Watergate restaurant when Fairview relieved him of $50,000, which bought something worth every penny: the Leland exposure of Cocksucker Charlie.

But this? Anyone willing to pay $100,000 in hush-up money had considerably more to hide. How in the world could he reach Fairview? Tolliver supposed he could contact his party people in Ohio to try to locate him—if he was still alive.

Why had he thought Fairview might be dead?

He didn't know. Was it a wild speculation or some unconscious reasoning? Then he remembered. A clip he had seen the other day in the newspaper might have made the connection in his head. Justinian had said the President had gone to the 4700 block on Mass Avenue with the $100,000. Hadn't he seen a report of a murder of a private investigator at that same location?

Tolliver eased himself out of bed and waddled to his three-foot high stack of copies of the dailies piled against the wall, his approximation of a filing system. He remembered that it was a couple or three weeks ago, on a Sunday.

He pulled out three Sunday copies and rifled through the Metro sections. There it was in the first one—a two-inch clip at the bottom right of a back page.

OHIO PRIVATE INVESTIGATOR KILLED ON MASS AVENUE;
POLICE BELIEVE WAS A BREAK AND ENTER ROBBERY.

"Hallelujah! We are saved," he shrieked to no one in particular, but to all his political gods-at-large.

CHAPTER 64

Detective Sam Lemoine picked up his pacing.

Why would the President stoop to visit a private eye, whose reputation, he had since learned, was less than impeccable? In fact, Reichmann was known as an inveterate scam artist, selling information to a second party that had already been paid for by one client.

"Sergeant, a phone call," Dennis said, interrupting both the pacing and the cigar twirling.

"Who is it?"

"A man, but he won't say—anonymous."

"I don't talk to Mr. Anonymous. That's your category. Get out of here."

"Sorry, boss, but you'll talk to this one. It's about the Reichmann murder."

Lemoine grabbed the phone. "Yes, this is Detective Lemoine. Who are you and what do you have to tell me?"

"I'm nobody, but I do have important information."

"Yes, I'm listening."

"Well, that private eye murder on Massachusetts Avenue has a strange twist that I've just learned about from a reliable source."

"Yes, what is it?" Lemoine was expectant, but kept his voice neutral.

"My source says that the night Mr. Reichmann was killed, he was visited by none other than the President of the United States."

Lemoine gasped, his attention instantly focused. He was obviously talking to an authentic informer. No one knew that the President was connected to Reichmann. This confirmed what he already suspected, plus new information that the President's visit was on the very evening of the murder. But he had to be sure not to sound overly interested.

"Sure, and I suppose Prince Charles was with him at the time," Lemoine said, perfecting his sarcasm.

"Don't be facetious, Detective. It doesn't become you."

"So if you believe this ridiculous story, Mr. Anonymous, pray tell—why would the President be visiting a private eye miles from the White House, and on the second day of his administration? Now come off it with your bullshit."

"The reason, Mr. Detective, is that the President was being blackmailed for $100,000 by the dead man, a private eye who called himself Mr. Fairview. The papers said his real name was Arnold Reichmann. The night of the murder the President came to his place with a suitcase full of money to pay him off."

Lemoine was astonished. Blackmail? That put another piece of the puzzle in place. He was impressed by the precision of the information. Was this anonymous tipster a member of the White House staff? A renegade employee? Whatever, he had to keep him talking. He cupped his hand over the phone.

"DENNIS. TRACE THIS CALL, NOW!"

Quickly, he returned to his informer. "Mr. Anonymous. If your fairy tale is true, tell me this. How did the President escape from his Secret Service guard, or did they accompany him to the scene of a murder?"

He tried laughing to show how outrageous it all seemed—even if he was now almost sure the tale was true.

"That I don't know."

"What about the timing? Since you've created such an intricate story, tell me this: At what time was the President supposed to be doing his blackmail payoff?"

Lemoine waited impatiently. The time of Reichmann's death had never been released to the press.

"I do know that, Detective. His rendezvous with Arnie Reichmann—or Mr. Fairview—was at 11:30 P.M. So I suppose the President left the White House by 10:30. Good luck, Sergeant. I've got to go."

With that, the phone went dead.

"*Did you trace it, Al?*" Lemoine shouted.

Dennis walked sheepishly into the room. "Sorry, boss, he didn't talk long enough. We missed it."

Lemoine's momentary disappointment vanished quickly. He was on the verge of a homicide coup, with the President as a material witness, and probably a suspect as well. His cigar started moving at a frenzied pace.

"Hot dog! I think we've got something big by the tail. Nothing less than the President of the United States pegged at the scene of a major crime. How often does that happen in this, the quiet little murder capital of the world?"

As soon as he hung up, Tolliver evaluated his call to the police. He was pleased.

Despite the detective's seeming skepticism, Tolliver sensed that Lemoine believed him. His story probably checked out with other things they knew. Would the police release anything he told them to the press? Since it involved the President, he doubted it. That was now his job.

He dialed the *Washington Weekly,* a well-read tabloid filled with news and gossip. Not quite a sensational periodical, it filled a niche somewhere between the *National Enquirer* and the *Washington Post.* Just last week he had lunch with a real pusher, Barbara Banner, a reporter and gossip columnist on the make. An attractive girl besides. Why not invite her to another lunch, and tantalize her with this, the biggest story of the decade?

"Hello, this is Andy Tolliver. May I please speak with Barbara Banner?"

She got on the line immediately. "Andy, I hope you don't mind my calling you that. You're such a friendly guy. What can I do for you?"

"The opposite, Barbara. It's what I can do for you. I've got a Pulitzer in my hand, just waiting for you to claim it. Bigger than *All the President's Men.*"

"Stop puling my leg. You politicos know how to excite a girl. Is your story—I assume you have one—exclusive?"

"Not just exclusive, but an explosive, earth-shaking, world-rattling exposé that will shiver your bloomers."

"When and how do I get this great tale?"

"Meet me tomorrow at noon at Antoine's for lunch."

There was momentary silence. "Thanks, but I can't, Andy. I've got an eat-in meeting of the national desk staff tomorrow."

"Just miss it, Barbara. Mine will be the lunch of your lifetime. But don't tell your friends. They'll be jealous. See you then, OK?"

The silence was short. "OK," Banner responded, as he knew she would. "But it'd better be a good story."

"Don't worry, we'll make history together."

If there was one thing he could recognize it was Washington reporters on the make. And this story would not only make Barbara Banner, it could be the undoing of Charlie, boy President.

CHAPTER 65

Detective Sergeant Sam Lemoine was afraid that not only was he in uncharted waters, but that he was in over his head.

Investigating a murder in which the President was the sole suspect—at least so far—gave him the professional willies. Before he talked to headquarters or to the attorney general, he'd need stronger grounding for his suspicion.

So far he had the President's fingerprints on the victim's briefcase and an anonymous, but apparently accurate, phone tip that the President had visited Reichmann's place to deliver blackmail money the night of the murder.

Should he take a deposition from the President? Maybe, but he'd better get some corroboration first.

The logical place was the White House. Not to interview the President, but to check the movement in and out of the mansion between, say, 10 P.M. and midnight the evening of January 21. It was less than a month ago, and memories might be fresh, especially since it was the first full day after the inauguration and the night of the giant snowstorm.

He made a courtesy phone call to White House Secret Service chief Pat McNulty, quickly inventing a cover story.

"Agent McNulty, I'm investigating a carjacking that took place a few weeks ago close to the Pennsylvania Avenue entrance. I'd like to question the guardhouse cops who were on duty that evening. Will that be OK?"

"OK, Lemoine. That would be the Northwest Gate. I'll issue a memo that you'll be in touch. Happy hunting."

*　　*　　*

"Patrolman Carbone, could we go over the details of that night one more time?"

"Sure, Sergeant Lemoine. What more do you want to know?"

The White House policeman on duty at that exit, John Carbone, confirmed that he had been working the 7 P.M. to 3 A.M. shift the night in question.

"Did you see the President personally leave through your gate?" Lemoine asked.

"No, I've never even met the President. His motorcade usually goes in and out at the South Gate. It's too crowded with tourists here."

"Do you remember if it was snowing that night?"

"Oh yes. A big snowstorm. Blowing like hell, with a cold wind. Not a good night to be out."

"How was the visibility?"

"Lousy. But I kept a sharp look at all the people who left by my gate. Most of the traffic was Secret Service cars."

"So the President never came through your gate that night?"

"No, sir, he didn't."

"And who did?"

The questioning was being done in the small guardhouse, the heater fighting the February cold. In response to his last question, Carbone checked through his records and rattled off a number of names. Lemoine held a list from the previous shift, showing those who exited from the same gate.

"Did you just say that Air Force Colonel Tim Lescomb was one of those who left here late at night?"

"That's right, Sergeant. He walked out at exactly 10:29. I marked it down, and I remember because I marked that he was working late."

"And you're sure it was Colonel Lescomb?"

"Why, yeah. He didn't pass exactly by the guardhouse. He walked up to the exit gate and I buzzed him out."

"Did you see his face?"

"Well . . ." Carbone seemed to be reconstructing that snowy night in his mind. "Not exactly. His collar was pushed up around his face against the cold. But it sure looked like him—his figure and all. And he was wearing a colonel's air force uniform, just like Lescomb's. It sure seemed like him. Why do you ask, Sergeant?"

"Because on the list of people who left on the prior shift, there's the name of Colonel Lescomb. He checked out at ten minutes before 6 P.M."

"I'll be damned."

Lemoine's next stop was in the West Wing itself. Maybe Colonel Tim Lescomb could explain the discrepancy of being checked out of the White House twice in one evening.

The sergeant walked through the West Wing, not far from the Oval Office, experiencing a sinking feeling that sometime soon he'd have to interview the President. Now he was headed to the small office of the air attache.

"Tell me, Colonel," Lemoine said after he flashed his police ID, "what time did you actually leave the White House on January 21, the second day of the administration. I'm getting two conflicting reports."

"Hold off, Sergeant. What's this all about?" Lescomb asked. "Am I suspected of doing anything except contributing to a large defense budget?"

Lemoine smiled, then pushed the unlit cigar into his mouth.

"No, nothing like that. I'm just checking movement at the Northwest Gate. Something to do with a carjacking."

"I remember that night distinctly," the colonel answered. "It was miserably cold and snowy. I usually leave at 6 P.M., but I left ten minutes early to beat the traffic a little."

"Did you come back to the White House that evening, maybe to do some more business?"

"Come back? Not on your life. Once I got home, the storm got worse. I was happy in front of the fireplace. I didn't return to the White House until the next morning. You can check with my wife and kids."

If it wasn't Lescomb leaving at 10:30, then who? Now he was onto the first break in the accepted scenario: the possibility that the second "Colonel Lescomb," the one of the 10:30 exit, was actually someone else, perhaps even the President.

"I presume you've met the President?" he asked.

"Oh, yes. Even before he was inaugurated he came into my office and introduced himself. As if I didn't know who he was. He's a former army sergeant you know. So we shot the breeze about the service. He even asked about my uniform."

"He what?" Lemoine's voice betrayed excitement.

"That's right. He asked if I kept a spare uniform around and I told him I did. I keep it in my closet. Here, I'll show you."

Lescomb went to the closet. The uniform was set on four different hangers. The jacket and pants were on one; the shirt and tie on another; and the two overcoats were hanging separately alongside.

The colonel thumbed through, then stopped abruptly.

"That's strange," he said.

"What's that?" Lemoine asked, his antennae alerted.

"Well, the shirt is creased, like someone wore it. It was neatly starched and pressed when I left it there. And look there at the bottom of the trouser legs. It's not pressed anymore. Looks like it went through water, or snow. I go for knifelike creases in my uniforms."

"What are you saying, Colonel Lescomb? That someone borrowed the uniform and wore it outside—without asking you?"

"I'm no detective. I'll leave that to you. But it sure in hell looks that way."

"Tell me, Colonel. Do you think that in the dark, the President could be taken for you? I mean, if he was wearing your uniform, cap, and coat. Just for theory's sake, that is?"

The air force officer stared quizzically at the detective.

"That's a strange question, Sergeant Lemoine. But now that you mention it, we're both about the same height and weight. Why do you ask?"

CHAPTER 66

Sally was on the intercom.

"Mr. President, you have a full day laid out, but Secret Service agent Larry Dunn insists on seeing you. Shall I have Ms. McKinley show him in?"

The name Dunn conjured up two images. First, he was the man who had showed ingenuity in following him to Massachusetts Avenue just a few weeks ago. (It seemed like years.) And as an ex-homicide detective, he could testify to Charlie's innocence, if it ever came to that. But whenever he saw Dunn his mind also flashed a gory snapshot of the short, redheaded corpse on the rug, the knife protruding from his back.

Never had he expected such a cataclysmic side effect to blackmail. He had read that District Police were following up the case. Nothing would please him more than for them to find the killer.

Who had killed Reichmann and why? It could have been retribution by a smeared victim. As another blackmail subject, had he just stumbled into the script by coincidence?

Or—and the second thought cut like a razor—could Reichmann's murder have been a setup arranged by his political enemies to pin the crime on him? If they somehow knew he was on his way to the Mass Avenue house, could they have killed the private eye as part of a frame-up? The police would surely believe he had a motive: to silence the blackmailer.

Had that danger vanished, or were the District Police coming closer to confronting him?

If he wanted an effective presidency, he'd have to push the incident out of his consciousness. Some nights he woke prematurely, the harrowing image of the bloodstained rug engraved on his mind. Would the police find the link between him and Reichmann? If it finally led to the White House, how would he explain it?

People who worked with Charlie mistakenly saw him as invulnerable. "Steel Nerves Charlie," they privately said. Baloney. If they only knew how he talked to himself, how he carefully shielded his vulnerability from the world. No one except George knew of the blackmail and the rendezvous with Mr. Fairview, but he had confessed other fears to Sally over these months. Clara, of course, had known about his vulnerability from the day they met. Even Jenny had clues to his frailties.

His secretary, Miss McKinley, interrupted his thoughts as she led Larry Dunn into the Oval Office.

"Larry, pleasure to see you," Charlie said, motioning him to a chair. "How's security at the White House?"

"Good, Mr. President," the beefy agent answered, still standing. "That's why I'm here. I have something that will help ensure it."

The President relaxed. At least Dunn was not carrying news of the Reichmann case. Surely, he would have raised it immediately.

"Something? What could that be, Larry? A bronzed .38 Smith & Wesson?"

"No, sir, I've brought along a defensive device. We've gotten several leads about dangerous crackpots out for you."

"Really?" Charlie was surprised. "Judging from the polls, I thought my televised speech Tuesday night on reducing the ranks of government employees by 650,000 through attrition was a big hit. You know, it costs $85,000 a year in cash for each employee—salary, benefits, and pension. We can save $50 billion annually plus even more in overhead and not fire anyone. I'm not surprised the nation is pleased."

"That's the problem, Mr. President. For every citizen who's pleased, there are others who are resentful about cutting back. Your idea about closing the Government Printing Office, for instance, because it's cheaper to use private shops. Well, just this morning, we intercepted a threat from one of its employees."

"Anything serious?" Charlie didn't suffer great physical fear, but neither was it something to dismiss.

"Oh, yes, sir. Someone watching your speech with a fellow worker heard him say: 'I'd like to kill that bastard.' Most people are just blowing off steam, but we found a loaded Uzi in this guy's apartment. Remember, it was a disappointed office seeker who gunned down President Garfield in 1881. So I want you to take extra precautions."

"Haven't you fellows got me surrounded enough? You're probably even watching me have sex—which is not going to keep you busy these days."

Dunn laughed, enjoying the president's lack of pretension. He opened a briefcase and extracted what looked like a sweater.

"This is what I brought, the latest in bullet-proof vests. It's an Armitron, and gives full coverage from your neck to your . . ." Dunn smiled. "To your genitals. We can't protect that because the bulge is a giveaway. It's a tough target anyway."

Charlie opened the vest and held the Armitron against him. "Are you telling me this little thing is going to stop an assassin's bullet?"

"Oh, yes, Mr. President. A .38 fired from seven feet away will knock you on your ass—excuse the expression. It'll make a bruise, maybe even break a rib, but the bullet won't go through the mesh. It's made of Kevlar plastic, which is stronger than steel. Weighs only three and a half pounds and is one-quarter inch thick. If President Reagan had been wearing one, he could have walked away from Hinckley's attack."

Dunn got off his chair and approached the President. "Here, put it on. It goes over your undershirt and under your outer clothes."

The reference to President Reagan, who had taken a bullet in his lung, reached him. "You mean right now?"

"Yes, sir. I want you to wear it everywhere outside the White House. I'm on my way to Chicago to clear the way for your appearance there. You should wear it on that whole trip."

Charlie obediently took off his jacket, removed his shirt and tie, and was standing in his undershirt when Sally walked in.

"Oh, excuse me," she said, starting to laugh. "Why in the world are you getting undressed in the Oval Office?"

Charlie tried to grin in response, but he was too embarrassed. "Sally, I'm being made bullet-proof by my worried friend here."

He put on the front and back pieces and Dunn helped to connect them at his sides. The President then redressed.

"How does it feel?" Sally asked.

"Not too bad. But when I began this business, I didn't think I'd be fitted for a straightjacket so early in my administration."

CHAPTER 67

Lemoine's head was spinning with theory.

The fingerprints verified that the President had probably been in Reichmann's place. He also had to assume that Lescomb's uniform had been worn by the President as a disguise to sneak out of the White House, the most elegant prison on earth. The anonymous call claimed that the President was being blackmailed by Reichmann, to the tune of $100,000—probably a down payment on a lifelong extortion. The motive for murder was surely there, in a flush of spades.

He believed Mr. Anonymous that the President was delivering the blackmail money the evening of the murder. Otherwise he wouldn't have known the time of death. Still, Lemoine wanted more confirmation.

How would the President, wearing the air force uniform, have gotten there that snowy night? He would hardly have used a White House car. The most logical way was by taxi. Quickly, Lemoine got on the phone to the security people at the District hack bureau.

"I want the names of every cabbie who delivered anyone to upper Massachusetts Avenue, anywhere near the 4700 block, between 10 P.M. and midnight the night of January 21," he told the taxi bureaucrat. "Remember, that was in the middle of the big snow storm."

The response was not long in coming: four dropoffs in the area during the time were reported by cab companies. Lemoine had all the drivers report to his Idaho Avenue headquarters.

The men sat around his desk, listening as he described the trip: from somewhere near the White House to the last few blocks on Massachusetts Avenue before Chevy Chase.

"The most important thing," Lemoine told the cabbies, holding back the key clue for last, "is that the fare was an air force colonel."

A Haitian driver enthusiastically shot his hand in the air.

"I had that fare," he shouted. "I picked heem up near ze Willard Hotel and dropped him off at the 4400 block. He was carrying a suitcase. And . . ."

"And what?" Lemoine asked.

"And I remember zat officer exactly."

"Why is that?" Lemoine asked.

"Because he pay me with a $100 bill he pulled from a case. Ze colonel even gave me a $20 tip."

"Did you ever see him before?"

"No."

Lemoine pulled a photo off his desk.

"Did he look like this?" he asked, handing the cabbie the picture.

"His face was half covered by ze coat, but yes . . . I think this is the man. Who is he?"

"Only the President of the United States."

"Mon Dieu!"

Lemoine's next step was obvious. He had to return to the White House. Could there have been an eyewitness to the President's arrival at Reichmann's place? Someone on the staff, or perhaps a Secret Service agent?

Officer Carbone had mentioned that several Secret Service cars had come through his gate that fateful night. Obviously, he'd have to reinterview Carbone.

Lemoine returned to the Pennsylvania Avenue guardhouse that night at 9 P.M. "Regarding those cars that came in and out of the White House grounds on the 21st. Were there any about midnight?" he asked Carbone.

"Yes, but I don't recall who was driving."

Lemoine's disappointment showed.

"But I can find out," Carbone quickly added. "I log in every car with the time. Give me a minute."

Carbone returned, log in hand. "Here it is. I show the movement of four cars that night. One came through my gate at ten minutes after midnight. That same car had left the White House at 10:32."

"And whose car was it?"

"Well, it belonged to the night Secret Service supervisor, agent Larry Dunn."

"Was he alone both times?"

"Oh, yes. If he weren't I'd have made a special entry."

*   *   *

"Agent McNulty, I have another request." Sergeant Lemoine had called the White House security office.

"Yes, Sergeant, what is it? Always happy to help the District Police."

"Well, sir, I'd like to interview agent Larry Dunn."

"Happy to cooperate—if I know what it's all about. Don't usually like to have my agents interrogated. They might inadvertently give out security info."

"No danger of that. It's a confidential investigation."

"The carjacking you talked about?"

"No, this is something different. It has to do with a murder a few weeks ago, out on Mass Avenue."

"Is Dunn a suspect?"

"No, but he might be a material witness. I really have to see him."

"I don't know, Lemoine. But you'll have to wait anyway. He's in Chicago and won't be back for several days. I'll let you know then."

Lemoine might have to wait for Dunn, but the case couldn't. Did he have enough information to question the President? Should he clear his actions with the police commissioner, or perhaps the Justice Department? Otherwise, he'd be risking his neck. He had only one year to go for retirement—he hoped back to Kitty Hawk in North Carolina where he had been raised.

But if anyone else entered the investigation, it could frighten the President away, even force him to go silent. One thing he didn't know how to do was subpoena a President.

No, he decided, the best way was an interview ambush. See the President and ask him outright: Did you kill Arnie Reichmann? He had nothing to lose. Except his job.

"What's it all about, Sergeant?" Sally asked. "Why get the President of the United States involved in something that happened outside the White House? What could he possibly know that would help you?"

"I'm sorry, miss, I can't tell you anything. I just want to see the President. Tell him it's about Mr. Fairview on Massachusetts Avenue."

"Will he know what you're talking about?"

"Oh, yes, miss, of that I'm sure."

The following afternoon, he received a call at the Idaho Avenue headquarters. It was Ms. Kirkland.

"The President will see you at 7:30 A.M. tomorrow morning in his family quarters. Come by the Northwest Gate. They'll have orders to escort you in. He can give you only fifteen minutes."

That morning, Lemoine could hardly believe he was on his way to interrogate the President. What if he found he was guilty? What next? Wouldn't it be better for the country if he could prove the President innocent? He tussled within himself. The President was just a man like everyone else. If he was guilty, it was his sworn duty to try to have him indicted. But he was getting ahead of himself. He didn't even know what the President would say.

Lemoine arrived by Metro and announced himself at the gate.

"I'm Sergeant Lemoine of the District Police. I have an appointment with President Palmer in his family quarters," he told the guard, who glanced at him suspiciously.

"You what?"

"That's right, Officer," Lemoine repeated, "and here's my badge and credentials."

Quickly, the guard consulted his roster, then double-checked Lemoine's ID and photo.

"Well, I'll be an SOB. Sergeant, you're right. Wait here. A couple of plainclothes agents will be along to escort you in." The guard turned to his superior officer. "Well, I'll be damned."

Sandwiched between two burly agents, Lemoine walked, almost solemnly, down the path toward the White House. Suddenly, his aplomb vanished as he realized the enormity of what he was doing. Who the hell was he—without official authorization—to question the President?

That thought was soon replaced by one of awe. Embarrassed, he pressed his unlit cigar into his pocket. They entered the White House by the North Portico, past marines in dress uniform standing at attention. One Secret Service man peeled off as the other escorted him to the private elevator. As he progressed, he took in the finery of a place where Jefferson and Lincoln and FDR had walked. And now he was there himself. But he hoped he wouldn't be making history by branding a President as a murderer. But, then again, if so, let it be.

The small private elevator took him up to the second floor, where he exited, then walked another fifty feet past more elegant appointments, to a double door. Inside, he presumed, was the living quarters of the President. He had heard he was a bachelor, so he'd probably be alone in a large apartment. The door opened, and there, staring him in the face was the same man he had seen on television the other night—the President.

Seated in an armchair, he rose as Lemoine entered the room. When he spoke, the sergeant recognized the firm baritone, one of President's trademarks.

"Come in, Sergeant. We meet again."

Lemoine was amazed that the President remembered. This was actually the third time they had come together.

"Have a seat and tell me what's on your mind," the President said, gesturing to a chair facing him.

"Thank you, sir. I must tell you how bad I feel about barging in— when you have such a big job to do."

"No, Sergeant. All jobs are important, especially law enforcement. I wouldn't have accepted your invitation if I didn't want to talk to you."

Lemoine was feeling queasy. He now realized he should have gone through channels, but there was no turning back.

"Mr. President, we're investigating the murder of someone named Arnold Reichmann, a private eye who also called himself Mr. Fairview. I understand that Fairview is the name of your hometown. Did you know Reichmann?"

Lemoine hesitated. "Before you answer, Mr. President, I should tell you that we found your fingerprints on Reichmann's briefcase."

He could see that the President was surprised, even a touch flushed.

"Sergeant, could you tell me if this is an official investigation, or just an informal one?"

"I don't exactly know how to answer that, Mr. President. I don't have permission from my superiors if that's what you mean. So in that light, I suppose it's informal. But anything you tell me will go into a report. If headquarters wants to go further, it could be used against you."

"Am I suspected of any serious crime, Sergeant?"

Lemoine could feel his confidence being sapped. The President obviously wanted everything spelled out, but Lemoine wanted to avoid a legal morass. His answers had to be circumspect.

"Well, I wouldn't say suspect, Mr. President, but so far you're the only one we've been able to place at Reichmann's house. We also have an anonymous tip that you were there the night he was killed, and confirmation from a cabbie that he dropped someone who looked like you off a few blocks from the murder scene during the possible time of the crime. There is also unconfirmed scuttlebutt that you were being blackmailed by Reichmann for $100,000. Is that all true?"

Lemoine could see that the President was becoming agitated. He shifted in his chair and repeatedly touched his nose.

"Before I answer you, Sergeant, I'd like you to fill me in on everything you know about this matter, and how you came to know it. Then we can move forward on equal terms."

It wasn't Lemoine's style to divulge what he knew to anyone, let alone to a suspect. But he could see that if he wanted the President's cooperation, he'd have to go along. Without that, things could get very sticky. The thought of his upcoming retirement flashed into his mind. Don't do anything to jeopardize Kitty Hawk, he prompted himself.

Lemoine told the President everything he knew in a succinct narrative, including the anonymous tip and the news of his and Dunn's movements that fateful night.

"So, if you don't mind Mr. President, I'll try to recreate what *could* have happened that night."

"Go ahead, Sergeant. I'm curious myself."

"Well, you left the White House at about 10:30 P.M., disguised as Colonel Lescomb, having taken his spare uniform out of the closet. You were carrying a case containing the $100,000 in blackmail money—for what I don't know, and right now, I don't care. You picked up a taxi, driven by a Haitian, not far from the Willard Hotel. You paid the fare with a $100 bill, and gave him a $20 tip. He dropped you off at the 4400 block on Massachusetts Avenue, and you walked the three blocks to Reichmann's house. There you confronted the man, known to you as Mr. Fairview, who had learned something damaging about you during his investigation in Ohio. You started to hand over the $100,000, but he refused to give up the information you wanted—maybe a file of some kind. He also told you that the $100,000 was only a down payment, that he expected more money on a regular basis. You lost your temper and grabbed a kitchen knife, then stabbed him when his back was turned. Then you searched his briefcase for the file. Being an amateur, you left prints."

The President listened, his face now drawn. "And where does Larry Dunn figure in your theory, Sergeant?"

"Well, according to the log, he left the White House by the Pennsylvania exit just five minutes after Lescomb—or really you—did. He followed you there by car, and after the murder, he pitched in by making it look like a breaking and entering case."

The President heard him out, then responded.

"Why would Dunn cooperate in a murder? He had nothing to gain."

Lemoine knew that was the big hole in his carefully delineated story.

"To be honest with you, I don't know that. Maybe instead he followed you out there because he guessed that what looked like Lescomb was actually you. When he got there and saw that you had killed Reichmann, he helped you to cover up. That makes more sense—that he wasn't part of the original murder, just the cover-up. You know, the Secret Service sense of loyalty."

"And you really believe that, Sergeant Lemoine?" the President asked, his eyes staring down the detective.

"I don't believe anything. I'm just looking for the truth."

"Well, would you like me to tell you exactly what happened?"

"Absolutely. Go ahead, Mr. President."

"First, I want to congratulate you. You have a lot of it right. There's only one mistake—and a big one. I didn't kill Reichmann. I took the $100,000 out to him, but when I arrived, he was already dead. I was about to get out of there when Dunn suddenly arrived. He had been following me because he knew Lescomb had left the White House hours before. He had a hunch it was me. He did stage the breaking and entering look of the room. While he waited for me outside, I took the Fairview file out of Reichmann's briefcase. That's when I left my prints. On our way back to the White House in Dunn's car he stopped and called the District police on a pay phone to let them know of the murder. Does that clear it up?"

Lemoine kept nodding as the President spoke. "And how did you get back into the White House afterward?"

"Simple. I lay down on the floor of the backseat in Dunn's car. The guards never inspect the Secret Service vehicles. The most important thing is that I have Dunn to prove my innocence. He's a former homicide detective. When he felt Reichmann's body, he said he had been dead for an hour or so. He was just five minutes behind me so he knew I couldn't have done it."

The President was now breathing harder. "Besides, Sergeant Lemoine, it's not my style. And when agent Dunn returns from Chicago, I'll make sure he signs an affidavit about what actually happened. I presume that will totally clear me."

Lemoine relaxed. He had secretly hoped for such a conclusion—if it was true.

"And one last thing, Sergeant," the President said as he rose. "I want you to proceed with this through channels. But I'd like your pledge that you'll keep it all confidential. I wouldn't want to see anything I've told you in the newspapers."

"You have my word on that, Mr. President. Only two people in my office know of it, and I can control them."

Lemoine left, his mind somewhat clearer. But of course the truth of the President's version of the murder depended entirely on the sworn testimony of one man—Secret Service agent Larry Dunn. He'd wait and see.

CHAPTER 68

The President woke at 5:30 A.M. in his bedroom and nibbled on the graham crackers he had left at his bedside the night before.

It struck him how lonely he had become. The absence of Clara, at first a prickly annoyance, was now a constant ache. Sally was some compensation. No one was as truthful and reliable as she, and they shared an interest in good government.

Occasionally, he looked at her as a woman, not as his deputy chief of staff. Perhaps he should woo her and gain her as an intimate companion, perhaps even as his wife. She had given hints that she would be receptive.

Just as the work of being President was elevating, so the loneliness was draining him. He didn't think that anyone except Clara could change things, but she had left him flat over politics. He smiled at the thought. That had also been the fate of his first marriage, though then it was a case of disinterest, not disagreement.

Even were he to seek Clara out—and he was determined not to—who said she would return? And if she did, wouldn't his reform work as President trigger the same hostility? The truth was that he needed her, desperately. But apparently she didn't need him. There might be solutions to government problems, but there were few in personal life. At least in his.

He would start to socialize with Sally and see if the chemistry was there. If so, he might regain some of his manliness, in and out of bed, and perhaps even experience personal happiness.

There was one favorable event: Getting the dicey matter of Reichmann's murder off his chest had been somewhat cathartic. In Chicago, he would tell Dunn to give an affidavit to Lemoine about that night immediately on his return.

Dunn's testimony should clear him of the ridiculous criminal suspicion. The political damage would depend on whether the press got wind of anything. One plus was that he might never have to reveal the personal secret that had gotten him into this morass of deceit in the first place.

He opened the door of the family quarters and said good morning to the agent on duty, who handed him the early copy of the daily newspaper, along with a copy of *Washington Weekly*. He found he either enjoyed the gossip or found it an illuminating insight into the peculiar capital scenario.

In the daily, the lead story was about his new budget, with projections George had leaked to the press. It showed a freeze for next year, a real 3 percent cut after inflation—something no President had attempted in recent years. The reporter doubted it could be done, but at least the journalist had accurately laid out the plan.

Again, his political life was surprisingly the easiest to handle. But he still had to influence Congress to come along. He was developing friends there, but it was a hostile body more influenced by Vice President Jason Hollingsworth than by him. America had never had an independent president, and if Congress had its way, he'd be the last.

But he had a secret weapon—the public card. His approval rating had now reached 80 percent and representatives and senators alike were afraid he'd use his inventory of goodwill to clobber them at the polls. And he had no hesitation doing just that.

He then picked up the semi-sensational *Weekly* tabloid. Thumbing through it, his eyes came to rest on the "Washington Chatter" column signed by Barbara Banner. He scanned through it, until his eyes halted as if at a stop sign. There was his name—PRESIDENT CHARLES KNUDSEN PALMER. Following it, the words BLACKMAIL and MURDER came off the page like verbal volcanoes.

He read the item, slowly, painfully:

If rumors are true, Prez Charles Knudsen Palmer is in hot water. Unbelievably, one major party mouthpiece is saying that President Palmer is being blackmailed for $100,000 for some unknown indiscretion. Worse yet, he shook his Secret Service boys to deliver the 100Gs. Want more scuttlebutt? New rumor is that the blackmailer was killed—yes killed—in his upper Mass Avenue house, the same area where the President delivered the $100G. Killer in the White House? Sounds crazy, doesn't it? But this party chief thinks this could be the magic bullet to destroy Crusader Charlie. In any case, Hercule Poirot, where are you when we need you? Signing off: your friendly rumormonger, Barbara Banner.

Charlie couldn't believe it. Every secret fear was being aired not on the front page of the daily, but in a cheap gossip column. Lemoine had promised confidentially. If he was not the tattler, then who? Surely the unknown spy in the White House. He'd have to act immediately by calling in McNulty, even the FBI, to find the worm.

His body was quivering like a swimmer's in winter. What was he going to do? Surely, this was only the beginning of media madness over the blackmail, even the crazy talk of murder. It could wreck his administration. Should he call Dunn to come back today? Even cancel his Chicago trip?

No, that would play into the hands of Tolliver and Sobel, surely the conniving sponsors of the White House spy. He'd just have to brave it through. Brave? That might be his middle name when it came to issues, but today he felt like a man who had just undergone surgery without an anesthetic.

His head was soon back on the pillow, as if to quiet his frantic mind. He had gotten up too early and this was his reward. He tossed for a minute, but within a moment, he was mercifully asleep.

"I'd like to see the President," she said, walking up to the policeman outside the Pennsylvania Avenue gate early that same morning.

"So would I, lady. Now just move on. This is a pedestrian mall, but we don't like people bothering us needlessly."

"No, I'm quite serious. I'm an old friend of the President's. Please call George Sempel, the chief of staff. He knows me as well."

"Really? And who shall I say is calling? Margaret Thatcher?" the guard asked, straining to sound sophisticated.

"No, use my name. Tell him it's Clara Staples, and that I want to see the President. And right now."

Something about her definitive matter must have impressed the policeman. "OK, lady, I'll call Mr. Sempel. But if he doesn't know you, I'd appreciate it if you'd move on. We're careful about security these days."

Clara just smiled as he exited to make the call. When he returned, the policeman's head was shaking, as if in disbelief.

"Yes, Ms. Staples. Mr. Sempel says he'll meet you in the White House lobby and take you right up to the President. Said he's glad you've come calling today, of all days. This Secret Service agent will escort you," the policeman said, pointing to a young man with a crew cut and a bulging jacket. "And please give the President my regards. I think he's doing a great job."

CHAPTER 69

Robbie Barnes waited while the President had left for Chicago, then hummed an old tune, smiling at his sudden euphoria. He now had an easy shot at checking out the audio bank in the Oval Office.

It had been a while since he'd tapped the system, so he expected a reasonably large take. He was especially curious about the visit of that detective, which had taken place in the president's sitting room. What could they possibly have talked about? Did it have anything to do with the blackmail attempt?

He walked from the press room to the Oval Office, his hands filled with copies of press materials that he had sent along to Chicago. He would be joining the President there tomorrow to orchestrate press coverage of the speech.

"Oh, Ben," he addressed the agent guarding the door. "I promised the President a copy of the Chicago press kit. OK if I go in?"

Ben shrugged. "Why not? You seem to spend half your time in there anyway."

He crossed the threshold, then started to close the door, hoping it would not raise suspicion. Now in the privacy of the Oval Office, Barnes glided immediately to the cabinet that held the recording equipment.

He had rehearsed this movement for speed, fearful that someone might suddenly open the door. He removed the family quarters tape, then quickly took a blank cassette from his pocket and inserted it. Instantly, he made his exit. Only ninety seconds had elapsed.

"Thanks, Ben," Barnes said, moving back toward the press room.

It was decision time. He could find an excuse to return to his apartment in the middle of the day, or, drawn by curiosity, he could risk playing it now. Barnes decided he couldn't wait. He closed his door, and with the sound at the lowest level, listened as Lemoine and President Palmer dissected the events of that fateful night.

My God. It was not just blackmail. The private eye had been murdered and Lemoine suspected the president! The motive—to silence Reichmann—was obvious. As the tape in the cassette rolled, Dunn's name came up. Apparently the Secret Service agent's testimony would be crucial. If the President was right, the burly Irishman could clear him.

Did he want the President cleared? Barnes pressed his conscience. No, he didn't. It might seem cruel to punish someone who might be innocent, but the nation's sanctity was more important.

He had to transmit this information immediately, but it was too dangerous to use a White House phone. Barnes grabbed his coat and raced for the Northwest Gate.

"Mr. Barnes. First time I've seen you leave in the middle of the day," Jack Crimmins, the uniformed officer, remarked. "Can we expect you back?"

"Sure. Just have to run an errand."

He walked three blocks then entered a drugstore, where he made a beeline for a pay phone. He dialed Tolliver's office on M Street and asked for the party boss.

"I'm sorry, I can't help you. Mr. Tolliver is in conference with his staff. Leave your number and he'll call back."

"No, that won't do. Interrupt the meeting. Just tell him it's Justinian. He'll take the call."

The receptionist was shocked, but after two minutes, Tolliver's gravel voice came on.

"Justinian. I'm here for you anytime. What's the scoop?"

"Only that the police suspect the President of murder."

"I know that, Justinian. Haven't you seen Barbara Banner's column?"

"Yes, but what you don't know is that President Palmer has admitted to Detective Lemoine that he was at Mr. Fairview's house, where he claims he found him already dead. But the police don't fully believe him. They think he had the perfect motive to kill the blackmailer. The President says that agent Larry Dunn, who's now in Chicago handling security, was there and can clear him. Please get this to every Loyalist. We may have a bona fide killer at the helm of our nation."

"Hot dawg, Justinian. Man or woman, I love ya!"

CHAPTER 70

Patriot had no time to waste. Yet he was stymied—by a failure in communications.

The information had come to him through Justinian, one step removed. It was startling news: The President might be charged with murder, just as he had planned. And only one witness, Secret Service agent Larry Dunn, could clear him. The possibility was tantalizing, with no end of ramifications.

But there was a seemingly insurmountable problem. The President's speech in Chicago was scheduled for 9 P.M. tomorrow, less than thirty-three hours from now. Not only hadn't he reached Stony, he feared there wasn't time to execute the plan. A day later and it would become a toothless conspiracy.

The last time he and Stony had met at the deserted Anacostia pier was the result of a usual notice from Patriot in the personal section of the paper. Now he had no time for the slowest of all media—the print press.

What was the alternative? There was only one possibility: the Internet, the World Wide Web. He would insert the words STONY-PATRIOT on a dozen sites, on established bulletin boards having to do with casino gambling, billiards, horse racing, dog racing, Jai-Lai, guns, Cayman Islands, even Swiss banks.

Though no expert, he was familiar enough with cyberspace. If friends of Stony saw it (it was not a common name) they might call him. Surely Stony would understand that it was a signal for an immediate confab. Usual place. Usual time.

That night, he prepared for the journey by withdrawing $250,000 in cash from his emergency hoard. Placing it in two carry-ons with "Prodigy" emblazoned on their sides, he dressed in old clothes and picked up the subway at Metro Center at Twelfth and G. At 9:45 P.M., he descended into the government-subsidized cavern and bought a $2.20 round-trip farecard. He rode the Red Line for a couple of minutes to the Gallery Place station at F and Ninth, where he descended one level and picked up the Green Line to the Anacostia stop.

The whole trip took fifteen minutes, but he had to conclude his business—if there was any—before 11. The last train out of Anacostia was at 11:30, and the entire system shut down at midnight. He sometimes laughed at the provincial nature of Washington, which, because of its enormous influx of tax money, assumed it was such a cosmopolitan city. Nonsense.

He looked a little conspicuous on the train with the two bags filled to the brim. As a drunk, smelling atrociously, approached his seat, he tightened his grip on the Prodigy satchels. It would be an unexpected haul for some petty thief.

"I see you're a fellow computer freak," the drunk slurred. "So am I."

Picking up the bags, Patriot moved farther down the car. Was this risky adventure a waste of time? What were the chances that Stony would show?

After he reached the station, he half-dragged the money-laden bags and walked haltingly the five blocks to the darkened dock. Standing at his appointed position at the edge of the river, he stared out onto the slip. The night was biting cold, but the visibility was good. No one was there. He waited, hoping that someone—if not Stony himself—had seen the notice on the Web.

The appointment was for the usual time, 10:30 P.M. Twenty minutes passed slowly and still no Stony. The meeting had obviously been too hastily conceived. He decided to call it off and return to central city. The heavy bags had been lifted when suddenly a shadow, clothed in a black pea jacket—Stony's usual—and a black woolen pullover hat, sidled by him without a word and moved quickly out to the end of the slip.

Desperately, he tried to catch a glance of his face, but it was a blur on the move.

"Stony," he called out a moment later in the stage whisper perfected for these contacts. "How did you get the message?"

"It came from all over. A half-dozen guys called me, especially those who read the casino and horse racing pages on the Internet. I got here as quickly as I could, if a little late. What can I do for you, Patriot?"

"The big one I mentioned last time is needed right now. I've brought along bags containing $250,00 for the down payment. If you can do it, I'll leave them where I'm standing now."

"What and when?"

"The what is the ultimate action. But it's more complicated than that. Detailed instructions are in the top of one of the bags. The when is the big problem. It's tomorrow night, at about 10:30 P.M."

"Where?"

"In Chicago. The President is speaking at the Ambassador Hotel. A meeting of university professors."

The silence was compounded by a lack of response.

"Stony?'

"Yes, I'm thinking."

"And?"

"And this type of speed raises the ante, a lot. It'll be a million if we fail, and $2 million if we succeed. I'll take the $250,000 now, and expect full payment in a week. If not—well, you know that routine."

He didn't exactly, but he could imagine.

"OK, Stony. It's a deal. Please carry it out *exactly* as described. No innovation, even though you might not understand the rationale for the actions."

"Patriot, don't worry. We couldn't care less why you want to do anything. That's not our bag. Understand?"

"Only too well, Stony. Good luck."

CHAPTER 71

"All right, Mr. President, the motorcade is ready to leave," agent Larry Dunn whispered as they left the Ambassador Hotel. Local Chicago police were holding back two sets of citizens, shouting invective at one another behind wooden barricades.

It was 10:30 P.M. Charlie had arrived at 8 and met for cocktails (he had one glass of white wine) with the officers of the university association. Afterward, he had spoken to some five hundred faculty members about academic freedom.

Clara was now at his side under the hotel canopy, looking exquisite and holding on to him tightly. He was sure she had miraculously materialized to rescue him from the darkness of his life, just as she had eons ago after the Leland show.

That morning, she had appeared unannounced at the family quarters of the White House, a small surprise arranged by George. His second sleep had been interrupted by a sharp knock at the door.

"Who is it?" he asked, getting up, still dressed in pajamas.

"It's me."

Hearing a woman's voice, he once again assumed it was Sally. When he opened the door and saw Clara's face, he wasted no time on preliminaries. Clara spread her arms and he fell into her embrace like a child lost at a mall.

"Darling, why have you tortured me for three months?" he asked plaintively.

"Charles, do you think I wanted to seem like a shameless hussy, playing for the hand of the most popular President in decades? No,

I had to wait until you needed me. When I saw that miserable gossip about murder in the morning paper, I figured I could play Florence Nightingale again. How do you feel?"

"I could use a bit of sympathy."

Clara broke out in her tremulous laugh. "And still in your pajamas? You haven't grown up a day since I met you."

Again he embraced her, kissing her softly on the lips, in the style of an appreciative husband.

"Darling President, may I come in? And will you please tell me all—and I mean all."

She sat with him in the drawing room of the family quarters as he related the story of the blackmail and murder, up through the police investigation and Dunn's crucial role in trying to prove his innocence.

"And what about the $100,000?"

"I gave that back to George."

"I assumed that. What I mean is—what was it for? What crime did you commit to have to pay such a king's ransom?"

"I assure you it probably wasn't worth $100,000, except to my oversensitive soul. I can't tell you now. Just give me a little time."

"Surely, darling. Now, what's next?"

"Well, I'll get dressed. We'll have some lunch, then we're off to Chicago by Air Force One so I can speak to a group of academics, God bless their ignorant souls."

"We?"

"Of course. Do you think that I'm going to let you go again? Nonsense. Sit here while I get decent."

Now, in Chicago, with Clara—stunning in a green cocktail dress and a black cape—by his side, he felt his faith in his star had been redeemed. She had listened to him as he addressed the university faculty people from across the nation.

He had warned them of both McCarthyism and Political Correctness, reminding them of the independent tradition of the medieval universities from which they sprang. It was one of separation from the popular culture, of removal from the whims and passions of the mob, so they could think honestly and clearly. But he feared they were becoming fashionable, he told them, mouthing the opinions of others in dangerously popular and predictable ways.

Now that the Chicago meeting was over, he was anxious to get back to Washington, where he would ask Clara the all-important question. What would be her response? All he could do was pray.

"OK, Mr. President, here's your limo coming up," Larry Dunn said. "In a few seconds you and Ms. Staples will be in the safety of a bullet-proof vehicle."

Charlie took Clara's hand and was about to enter the car when he suddenly changed his mind. "Larry, I'm going over to talk to those people. Right now." He dashed away from Dunn's grasp and moved to the police barricade.

On one side was an excited crowd carrying placards: CHARLIE, WE LOVE YOU. KEEP GIVING THEM HELL! Before Dunn could stop him, the President moved toward the protest section, where they were chanting: "PAY ANY MORE BLACKMAIL TODAY? WHAT ARE YOU HIDING, MR. KILLER?"

The President stood in front of the protesters, and like a drill master, called out loudly:

"THAT'S RIDICULOUS! STUPID RUMORS STARTED BY THOSE WHO LOVE BAD GOVERNMENT!"

Dunn was turning apoplectic. "MR. PRESIDENT. GET INTO THE CAR! RIGHT NOW!" he shouted, his Boston-accented voice carrying above the noise. Dunn rushed toward Charlie, his arms waving wildly in the direction of the limousine.

"GET IN THE—" he called out, then gasped.

Dunn hadn't finished his warning when it happened.

Two shots crackled in the cold air. Dunn and the President both fell to the ground in an instant. Dunn, with a bullet between his eyes, was mute, his eyes looking skyward, his hand still twisted in the gesture of warning.

"DUNN AND THE PRESIDENT HAVE BEEN SHOT!" Pat McNulty cried out.

Quickly he raced over to Dunn's fallen body and felt his pulse. "Dunn's dead," he called out. "Everyone get back! Pick up the President and put him in the limo. Let's get to the University Hospital!"

"WAIT!" The presidential physician, Dr. Gordon, who had been in a limo, suddenly appeared, shouting. "Don't move him yet," he said, kneeling where the President lay, seemingly unconscious. The doctor's hands moved quickly to the President's pulse.

"Is he dead?" Clara screamed.

Through the fog, Charlie could hear her question.

"No, I'm not dead, Clara," the President whispered, his eyes opening slowly. "It knocked the breath out of me, but I'm OK." He gestured toward his upper chest, where the bullet had torn away his suit. He could feel his breath coming in labored halts. He turned to McNulty. "Take me back into the hotel!"

"But Mr. President," McNulty balked. "We've got to get you to a hospital."

"Don't give me any *buts*," Charlie whispered. "Doctor, just get me into a bed. This is a presidential order. Now move."

The doctor quickly rechecked Charlie and nodded his approval.

Three agents gingerly lifted Charlie onto a stretcher, which an agent had brought from the trunk of a limo.

"Everyone back," McNulty ordered. "Make room for the President."

The hotel manager met them in the lobby and frantically ordered his staff to bring the President to the hotel's best suite. Within a minute, the elevator had arrived at the floor and the President was carried gingerly to a bed. Clara stood alongside, holding his hand.

"Back everyone. You too, Ms. Staples," McNulty ordered. "Let the doctor take a look."

As an agent took off Charlie's jacket, shirt, and tie, the reason for the President's insistence became clear. He was wearing his bullet-proof vest, which was also removed.

"So you listened to Dunn," McNulty commented. "Smart move."

Dr. Gordon applied a stethoscope to the President's heart. About three inches to the right and above, the skin had turned black and blue in an ugly large bruise. The doctor felt softly at the spot. "Does it hurt?"

"Mezzo, mezzo. Just some pain, and I feel chilled."

"Here it is!" McNulty called out. "A .22 caliber sharpshooter's bullet. Buried right in the vest."

"We're lucky, everyone," Dr. Gordon explained. "The bullet missed the heart and never penetrated the skin because of the vest. I think there's only one broken rib. I'll tape the President up, then examine him at Walter Reed Hospital when we get home."

Charlie, who had been prone, lifted himself up.

"McNulty, did anyone else get hurt?" Charlie asked.

The security chief gazed downward. "Yes, sir, Dunn was killed instantly. A shot between his eyes."

A second chill now coursed through his body. He felt weakened by the sad fact of Dunn's death in the line of duty. Then his mind turned to the other consequence.

The dead agent had been the only witness to his innocence, his only defense against the charge of murder.

CHAPTER 72

"Jake, can we actually indict a President for murder?" Lemoine asked Jacob Freund, assistant U.S. attorney. "Or is he immune to criminal prosecution unless, and until, he's impeached from office? Here, take a look at this."

Lemoine smiled at the confused look on Freund's face. The thirty-year-old was one of 250 prosecutors in the U.S. attorney's office on Fourth Street in Washington, responsible for crimes in the District of Columbia the same way local D.A.'s are in other communities.

Freund thumbed through the six-page murder warrant, scanning the details. Then he shot out of his chair.

"Are you out of your cotton-pickin' Carolina mind?" he shouted. "You've done some wild things in your time, Lemoine, but this takes the prize. You come here with a cockamamie story about a private eye being killed and who do you want to arrest for his murder? THE PRESIDENT OF THE UNITED STATES."

Freund drew in a breath. "Now get out of here before I send for the boys in white coats."

With that, Freund threw the draft warrant in Lemoine's direction—barely missing him—and sat down at his desk, deflated.

"Off your chest? Feeling better, Jake? Now, let's start over. Like the warrant says, I've got a good case—mostly circumstantial, but with the hard evidence of the President's fingerprints on Reichmann's briefcase."

Lemoine then went through the story of his whole investigation, including the $100,000 blackmail, the borrowed uniform, and the President's movements that night.

"OK, I'll talk to you even though you're nuts," Freund relented. "But what in the hell does the President say about all this? Have you spoken to him?"

"Yes, he admits the blackmail and going there that night to deliver the 100Gs. So he's got the motive, in spades. But he swears that Reichmann was dead when he arrived."

"Does he have any witnesses?" Freund was still looking skeptically at Lemoine, but the prosecutor's curiosity was aroused.

"Yes. He says that the night Secret Service guy, Larry Dunn, followed him and arrived just five minutes later. Dunn was a homicide dick in Boston, and he supposedly told the President that the body was at least an hour cold."

"What does the coroner say about the time of death?"

"He gives it an hour-and-a-half span, but it could have been as late as 11:30, the time the President says he was there."

"But isn't Dunn's testimony enough to clear the President? He should qualify as an expert witness. Talk to him."

"Easier said than done, Jake. I was supposed to see him this morning, and take a statement. But the assassination attempt in Chicago had only one casualty—an unfortunate one."

"Dunn?"

"Exactly. He was the agent who was shot right between the eyes. Died instantly. And with him went President Palmer's alibi. Now please give me an answer to my first question. Can we indict a President, or is he immune while he's in office?"

Lemoine was now standing right over Freund, twirling his omnipresent unlit cigar. The young prosecutor was pale.

"Geez, Sam. I'm only an assistant U.S. attorney, not a damn constitutional scholar. But I don't know of any exclusion for criminal acts in the Constitution. Article II, Section 2 says the President can pardon anybody for any federal crime, but that doesn't include himself. So I suppose *theoretically* he could be indicted for murder."

Freund got out of his chair, his agitation showing.

"But, damn it, that's just fucking theory! Sam, the real answer is that you must be nuts if you think anybody can walk into the Oval Office and slap a murder indictment on the President. That's a fairy tale. There's tradition, and precedent, and common sense. No one has ever arrested, or tried to arrest, a President. The U.S. Attorney for the District would have to approve such an indictment. And guess who appoints him to office? That's right, the President of the United States. And he can be fired by the prez for any reason. And the same is true of me. We all work for Charlie Palmer. And you want us to indict him for murder? Sam, you're crazier than they say you are."

"So, are you saying you'll do nothing about it?"

"No, I didn't say that, Sam. What I'm saying is that I'm going to play pass the buck—right up to a higher authority."

"Who's that?"

"Just follow me, madman. We're going to see McIlheny, chief of the homicide unit. He or his deputy has to sign on a warrant before we can even show it to a superior judge, who, incidentally, is also named by the President."

Frank McIlheny, a tall, white-haired man with a U.S. Marine crew cut, had the beefy face and corpulent physique of an out-of-shape football coach. He was standing looking out his office window, his desk flanked by flags of the Justice Department and the United States when Lemoine and Freund walked in. Behind him was an auto-graphed picture of President Charles K. Palmer.

"Oh, no! Sam Lemoine, the terror of assistant D.A.'s," McIlheny greeted the veteran detective. "Who do you want us to indict now? Remember that congressman who slapped around the whore? You wanted to get him on a felony—what was it? Attempted murder? Any more congressmen you want to put in the slammer?"

"No, Fred, no congressmen. But I do have this arrest warrant I need you to sign. Then we can get the green light from a superior court judge for a preliminary hearing and an indictment."

"So what's it this time, Sam? A senator who's trying to kill a political opponent on the floor of the chamber?" McIlheny laughed at his little joke.

"No, Fred. No senator. Just the guy in the picture behind you," Lemoine said softly, pointing to the wall.

McIlheny swiveled about and stared at the official portrait. Confusion covered his face. "I don't get it, Sam. That's the President of the United States."

"Nobody less, Fred. The boss of bosses. The American capo di capi. That's who the arrest warrant is for."

McIlheny's face drained of color. He sat down at his chair, his expression showing total bafflement.

"You're pulling my leg, you old son of a bitch. Am I right?"

Jake Freund, who had been silent, moved toward the desk.

"No, boss. This is for real. Sam's got something that's too hot for me to touch, so I'm passing it on to you, bureaucratic-like. OK?"

Freund laid the draft of the murder arrest warrant down on his chief's desk, and stepped back, his expression as sheepish as an errant student's.

McIlheny said nothing. He put on his reading glasses and went slowly through the document. To Lemoine, it looked as if he were doing it a word at a time, his lips visibly moving, his concentration intense. Finally, he closed the file and looked up.

"Lemoine, the work is mostly circumstantial but it looks solid. But that doesn't make you—or Jake—any less crazy. Do you know what you have here? Since the murder took place on local, not federal, grounds, this is not a case for the U.S. court system. It's an ordinary local case. That means we would have to bring the President in, maybe in handcuffs, to the courthouse on Indiana Avenue, along with the pimps and whores and druggies. Then we have to book and process him, with mug shots and all. From there he goes into the can until a superior court judge can see him and set up a preliminary hearing. And *only* then can we release him on bail. So he can go back to where? TO THE OVAL OFFICE, YOU CRAZY BASTARDS."

McIlheny got up and stomped around his office, the sound of his shoe leather reverberating.

"And then what do you think will happen next?" he said, the sarcasm dripping. "Well, that's easy. First the country will go out of its head, and thousands of press will swoop down on our crappy little office, and we'll be put under a microscope, and studied, and attacked, and shit on. Remember, the people like this President! Then, we'll all be fired in one fell swoop, that's what. The U.S. Attorney, and Jake, and me, will be pounding the pavement looking for a new job. We all serve at the discretion of the President—who, you say, is *your damn murderer.* You, Lemoine, what do you give a shit? You're civil service, so you'll escape. But tell me one thing, Sam."

"What's that Fred?"

"Why didn't you retire to Kitty Hawk last year instead of next year and spare me this angina?"

The room was filled with silence for almost a minute. "So are you going to sign the warrant?" Jake Freund finally asked.

"No, I'm going to do just what you did—pass the buck. In five minutes, I'm going to hand deliver this wired time bomb personally to the U.S. Attorney for the District and let him sweat a little. Then I'll tell you what's going to happen after that."

"What's that, boss?"

"He's going to do the same as me. He's going to drive his free government car—which the President is about to take away to save money—over to the Justice Department at Ninth and Pennsylvania. There's he going to personally hand it over to Attorney General Homer Frazier himself. From there on, it's anybody's guess."

"Are you telling me I'm out of this?" Lemoine asked.

"Heaven forbid, Sam. No one is going to stop your wonderful wheels of justice. We're just going to slow them down a little. Meanwhile, God have mercy on us all. Now that Dunn's dead, maybe the President— or you, Sam—will come up with a miracle, some new evidence that will prove that he didn't pull off that stupid murder to begin with."

CHAPTER 73

"What a glorious spot," Clara said as she sat in Aspen Lodge at Camp David with the President, staring out the picture window at the landscape. "I hope you're feeling better."

After Chicago, Charlie had taken off a few days under the orders of Dr. Gordon and was renewing himself in the Catoctin mountains of Maryland. Camp David was barely two hours from Washington by car, and only a fifteen-minute helicopter ride in Marine One. Yet it was in a time zone of its own. He calculated that each day in the Oval Office was a twenty-four-hour playlet that would fill months of ordinary time, whether measured at Camp David or at home in Fairview.

"Yes, I feel somewhat better. My broken rib hurts, but if the bullet had been a few inches lower and I hadn't worn the vest, Jason Hollingsworth would now be President. Now that I think about it, I feel a whole lot better."

"I hear they caught the assassin—Dunn's murderer that is," Clara said.

"Yes, McNulty had the good sense to keep men on the roofs. The gunman was using a Steyr sniper rifle and was beyond the security range, but they nabbed him as he scaled down the last building. The FBI is questioning him now."

"Who was it?"

"Some punk named Stony Marcal, a one-time hit man who had gone into brokering murder," the President explained. "But the pay-off was so large, he decided to do this one himself. Obviously, he was out of practice."

"Who was behind the contract?" Clara asked. "I hope it wasn't anyone in the party."

"We don't know. Stony refuses to talk—a matter of criminal honor."

"It's a shame about Dunn," Clara added. "He was only trying to save your life."

"Actually, he did, by forcing me to wear that bullet-proof vest. And now that he's gone, I no longer have a witness to my innocence."

Clara and Charles had been at Camp David for two days and were slated to return to Washington that evening. They had come up alone, and in that short period, the President—and Clara—had discovered enormous peace in the camp's pristine beauty.

Built during FDR's administration, the camp had been named Shangri-La after that fictional land of contentment. Ike had renamed it Camp David in honor of his grandson.

Charlie thought Shangri-La was more appropriate. It seemed to provide the only relief from the cauldron of Washington. Seven miles uphill from the small town of Thurmont, Maryland, the 143-acre camp-resort was protected by the marines and staffed by navy personnel, including stewards for the President. Except for the presidential lodge, Aspen, the decor was starkly simple. Someone had labeled it New Deal Rustic—but every amenity was available.

Camp David could hold up to fifty guests, but this day Clara and Charlie were alone. So far, it had been a miraculous balm, both for Charlie's wounded chest and for his injured psyche. They had even experimented with sex. No great volcano, but they had managed some intimacy, celebrating their reunion.

He was convinced that having Clara back was healing him. Their walks through the woods, on the paths trod by American Presidents and foreign leaders, going back to Roosevelt and Churchill, were romantic interludes, as if he were not President but a retired millionaire on his own estate.

Charlie was happy, except when he thought of the attack on his reputation. Barbara Banner's item had assumed a life of its own. The tabloids even had artist's renditions picturing Reichmann as a helpless dwarf and Charlie as a mad knife-wielding monster.

Other publications were speculating about the reason for the $100,000 blackmail, ranging from stories that he'd sired an illegitimate child with a thirteen-year-old in Ohio, to stories that he had AIDS. From unbridled heterosexuality to homosexuality.

If only he could clear up the miserable suspicion that he was a murderer. Again, he asked himself the question: What was Lemoine doing now that Dunn was not here to clear his name?

That news wasn't long in coming. "Charles, there's a phone call for you," Clara informed him that afternoon, gently waking him from a nap. "The operator says it's important."

The President raised himself and walked slowly to the phone, a bit annoyed that reality was impinging on his short respite.

"Yes, this is President Palmer. Who is this?" He waited. "Oh, Attorney General Frazier. What's up, Homer?"

What was up, he learned, was not what he wanted to hear.

"Mr. President, I have in my hand a warrant for your arrest for murder. Fortunately, it hasn't yet been signed by the U.S. Attorney for the District. Everyone's afraid if it, as they should be. They passed it up to me. I've read the details, and I'm sure they'll all correct, except for the conclusion. I can hardly believe that you've killed anyone."

"You're absolutely right, Homer. I killed no one, but I did a stupid thing by leaving the White House that night. And like an idiot, I put my fingerprints on the dead man's briefcase. Agent Larry Dunn was my alibi, but now he's gone."

Charles could feel his broken rib sticking as his breath involuntarily quickened.

"So, Homer, what do you suggest we do?"

"Well, first thing, I'll hold this warrant up for a while. Next, I'll get the FBI into the act. We have a great snooper in the District office, a Jim Buchanan. I'll put him on the case right away. Do you have any suggestions?"

"Yes, please, don't leave Sergeant Lemoine out of the loop. The Reichmann killing is in his jurisdiction. Maybe between the two of them, they'll find the real killer. And, Homer . . ."

"Yes, Mr. President?"

"Let's keep it out of the newspapers. We don't want the people to know there's a warrant pending for my arrest, no matter how false it is. The truth will never catch up with the gossip."

He could hear a sigh on the other end. "Mr. President, I'll try, but that's the hardest part of my job. When it comes to gossip, everyone in Washington is an Olympic competitor."

Clara, who was listening, came over and spontaneously kissed Charlie on the cheek.

"Bravo. And keep up the spirit. You'll lick it."

They sat together on facing chairs. "Clara, I want to ask you something that has been on my mind these months."

"Shoot, Mr. President."

"When we first met, were you assigned to spy on me?"

He could see that Clara was taken aback.

"Charles, that's not a fair question from a lover, but I'll answer anyway. It was partially the reason."

"What does that mean—partially?"

"It means that I wanted to meet you. I was attracted by the courage you showed. You know, simple hero worship, a woman's Achilles' heel. But at the same time, I was afraid you'd clobber the party. So, I combined the two motives and we met—and I think fell in love. As to my spying, maybe I would have been good if I was better motivated. But I never told them anything more damaging than that you snored in your sleep."

Charlie's face lit. "Does that mean that you've come to love the message as much as the messenger?"

"Well, don't go too far, Charles. At least I'm no longer totally against it. I am impressed by what you're doing, and how much the public loves it, and you. But I'll wait and see how it all plays out—if it's worth destroying my party over it."

"So you're taking me on approval. Is that it?"

"You might say that, Charles. I think that's why you love me, because I'm a challenge. Am I right?"

"No way, Clara. I love you solely because you've got an absolutely gorgeous body. I assure you, it's pure lust."

Clara screwed up her face and approached Charlie with a certain look in her eye.

"You SOB. I'll get you for that."

She reached his chair, bent down, and planted a kiss on his lips. "So there." They laughed like teenagers.

"Seriously, though, Mr. President, if I didn't spy on you—and I didn't—who's passing on all the information to Tolliver? He told me he gets regular calls from someone in the White House who refers to himself, or herself, as Justinian."

"I don't know, but I have the FBI working on it."

"Well, now that I'm back, I think I'll do a little spying on my own," Clara said. "This time it'll be for you."

CHAPTER **7 4**

Clara knew she had her work cut out for her.

She wasn't living in the White House; too much risk of press gossip. She stayed at home in Maison Grise, but was spending a good deal of time in the family quarters, much of it nursing the President.

The rib was slow to heal because, as Dr. Gordon believed, the President was pushing himself too hard now that he had returned to work. He had a low fever, but was at least listening obediently to Mother Clara, who was prescribing aspirin and ordering chicken soup from the White House kitchen.

In the family quarters, Charlie and Clara rehashed his conversation with Attorney General Frazier about holding up the arrest warrant while he put the FBI sleuth on the case to help Lemoine.

"Charles, is there anything you can do to pressure Frazier to quash the warrant completely?" Clara asked. "This thing is getting too serious, and I'm getting worried."

"I am too, Clara, but I'm innocent. And besides, anything I do as President to slow down the wheels of justice will only make me look guilty. Remember—when Nixon carried out his 'Saturday Night Massacre' it only moved him closer to impeachment. We just have to have faith that the truth will come out."

Clara nodded and gave him a motherly kiss on the cheek.

"You're brave, Charlie. More guts than I'll ever have."

In her spare time, Clara was determined to help the President. The first task she assigned herself was to find Justinian. The spying, from what she garnered from Tolliver, included some intimate items, such as Charles's $100,000 blackmail. Unless the spy was Sally or George, the inside informer wouldn't be privy to such confidential conversations and would have had to rely on taping.

Which staff member could be Justinian?

The first suspect was Maggie Swanson, who had been caught reading the Green Book, which had later turned up at Tolliver's headquarters. When questioned, she pleaded simple curiosity. McNulty had assigned an agent to watch her, but there were no further transgressions.

One day, when Clara and the President were alone in his bedroom, while he worked at a small antique desk, she asked him:

"What are those switches on the wall over there?"

"The top series are for lights throughout the apartment."

"And this one at the bottom?"

"I haven't the slightest idea. Try it."

"I have, and it appears to do nothing." She hesitated for a moment. "Charles, do you have a recording system here or in the Oval Office, as Nixon did?"

"I sure hope not. That's nothing but a troublemaker. Nixon was worried about history. Not me. I'm just into survival. Why not ask the engineer in the basement? Tell them I said it was OK."

Clara removed her high heels and slipped into moccasins. Once down in the utility basement, she questioned the staff electrician.

"Excuse me, Mr. . . . I'm Clara Staples. The President sent me."

"Jansen, Otto Jansen, Ms. Staples. I know who you are. How can I help?"

"Well, President Palmer wanted to know if there is a recording system in the White House, like the one President Nixon had?"

"Yes, there is, but it hasn't been in operation for some time. Here I'll show you."

Jansen walked across the room and opened the blue metal box.

"My gosh. The main switch has been thrown by somebody—but not me," he exclaimed. "That means that the recording terminals are working at all three sites."

"Which are those?" Clara asked, now excited by the chase.

"The family quarters, the press office, and the Oval Office. In the family room, it works off a turn-on below the light switches in the sitting room. In the other two, there are buttons under the main desks. When it's working, everything being said is taken down on magnetic tape at the central audio bank."

"And where's that?"

"In the Oval Office, in a small built-in closet next to the fireplace."

Clara went back up, and moved toward the West Wing.

"Sally," she said, walking unannounced into the deputy chief's office. "I have something to ask you."

Sally's expression was blank, even a touch hostile.

"Yes, Clara, how can I help you?"

"Well, I'm on kind of a mission for the President. You know there's been a spy in the White House, and it occurred to me that someone might be taping the President. Now it appears there's a recording system in the Oval Office. Come, I'll show you."

Sally seemed befuddled by Clara's involvement.

"Are you sure the President authorized this?" Sally asked, the tension oozing from her every syllable.

"Oh, yes. If you'd like, call him. He's in the family quarters working. He still has a fever and some pain, but he's coming along."

When it came to the rivalry for love, Clara knew she was a master. Sally probably knew it as well, and the regrets were written on her face. Sally was obviously in love with Charles and didn't know how to handle Clara's reappearance. Clara sympathized with Sally, but that didn't mean she would forgo an iota of her supremacy in Charlie's affections.

"No, that's not necessary," Sally responded. "Let's go look. I'm just as curious as you."

As they entered the honored room, Clara made a direct line to a small cabinet next to the fireplace. "Just like the electrician said. It's a triple bank, one for each of the recording sites." She looked at Sally, hoping her attempt to protect Charles would drain some of the tension.

"Don't you think we should set up a sting?" Clara asked. "See who comes to remove the tapes. That would be Justinian, the spy."

"Yes, that sounds like a good idea. Why don't you discuss it with the President?" Sally's voice was cool.

"Shouldn't you be doing that, Sally? After all, it is an official act."

"Really? Why didn't you think about that before?"

Clara was stung again. This was probably a good time for a reality check on their relationship.

"You hate me, don't you?" Clara asked.

"No, not really. In fact, I admire you. You're the kind of woman who always gets what she wants. You're exciting, smart, and beautiful. I can't compete with that. I may not be a librarian, but I'm not exciting. Just steadfast and reliable. But that can be a curse in a woman. You have no such problems."

"Is that how you see me—as unreliable?"

"Absolutely. The President is not very mature when it comes to women. He doesn't know it, but the truth, dear beautiful Clara, is that you're the worst possible person for him. In fact, I don't think you're good for any man."

Clara was hurt, but she was not about to argue. History, so far, had supported Sally's charge.

"Don't you think people can change? I do love Charles, as I know you do. I make him very happy. Isn't that something?"

"Oh, yes. But for how long? Now, he's President of the United States. Who wouldn't want to be the First Lady? But what about ten years from now, when he's gained twenty pounds and is playing too much golf? Will you still love him? And how much?"

Again, Clara felt a stab. Sally had come even closer to the truth.

"What you don't understand, Sally, is that Charles is my first love. I'm thirty-nine and I've never felt like this before. People can and do change, and I intend to."

"You know, Clara, you sound like the twelve-step oath at Alcoholics Anonymous, when all you're waiting for is another high on money and power. I don't believe you know yourself."

"And I suppose you believe that you could love him truer, and forever—more than me?"

Sally laughed. "Well, of course. Old reliable Sally would always be there for him. But I can see that's a pipe dream. No woman can compete with you. But anyway, since you started this Sherlock Holmes chase for the spy, please keep on with it. I'm only happy about one thing, Clara."

"What's that?"

"That the spy is not you. I was convinced you were Justinian."

"Charles, that's the way it looks," Clara reported to the President. "Justinian has to be someone close to you, otherwise he or she wouldn't be able to get into the Oval Office to retrieve the tapes."

"You're right. I'll have McNulty monitor the Oval Office continuously by closed-circuit television—when I'm not there. I don't want anyone watching while I'm working."

Charles paused, then changed the subject. "Sally tells me you and she were chatting. How are you two getting along?"

Clara was not about to reveal all that was said, but this was a chance to gauge his emotions.

"You know, Charles, I think that woman is wonderful. And I believe she loves you. Not just because you're President. She has true, deep affection. Did you know that?"

"Yes, I suspected as much."

"And how about you, Mr. President? What are your intentions toward Sally Kirkland?"

"Clara, you sound like a mother-in-law. I have no intentions. But if you hadn't returned when you did, I might now be in her arms. She's a fine woman, and I couldn't stay loveless forever. The loneliness was killing me."

"And now?" Clara asked.

"And now I'm the happiest man in the world. I have my work

and I have you—I hope. What more could I want, except to get this ridiculous murder charge off my back."

"Speaking of that, Charles, I hope you now trust me enough to explain what that blackmail was all about. The media have you involved in all kinds of evil plots."

"I know. In retrospect, I probably should have followed George's advice and told all. It really had little to do with me. I was just trying to protect two people I love and admire."

Clara was startled. "And who are they?"

"My mother and her lifelong friend, Mildred Cole, the clerk at the Fairview Town Hall. It's a long story, but I'll tell you the outlines if you'd like."

"Please do, Charles. The curiosity has been killing me."

"Well, everyone in town, including me, was told that my father had been an army officer killed in the Korean War. He went overseas before I was born. My mother had been working in Los Angeles when they met and married. After he went overseas, she came back to Fairview, pregnant. Two months later, in 1954, I was born. All my childhood that's what I was told. My father's name was Captain James R. Palmer, and we even had a picture of him in uniform, with medal, ribbons, and all, in a silver frame. After I was born, she was informed that he had been killed in action."

"So what's there to be ashamed of?" Clara asked, confused. "You should be proud having a father who was a hero."

"Yes, Clara, but the trouble is that a good part of the story is a blatant lie."

"You mean your father wasn't a war hero?"

"No, that part of the story is completely true. He was a decorated veteran of the Korean War—received the Silver Star for action near the Yalu River. But the rest of it was made up by my mother. It's really a sordid tale, Clara. Are you sure you want to hear it all?"

"Oh, absolutely. It's gotten you into a lot of trouble. I'd like to know why."

"Well, the full truth, as I later learned, is quite different. My mother had been away in Los Angeles during the Korean War, working in a company that made radar equipment for the army. There she met Captain Palmer, a Signal Corps officer who had returned from Korea, wounded and decorated, but quite alive. He was assigned to the firm as army liaison, to oversee the radar work. They weren't too different in age. She was twenty-eight and he was thirty-two. They dated, but for some reason, my mother didn't want to get too close to him. But he was in love with her, or so he claimed. Well, one night, actually Christmas Eve at a company party, the captain got crazy drunk and started to paw my mother. She resisted him, and he started to rape her, right on a desk in a back storeroom."

As Charlie spoke, his voice broke.

"Are you sure you want to go on, Charles dear?" Clara asked. "I've heard enough to know it's heartbreaking."

"Yes, I'd like to talk it out. The only other person who I've told is George, and he's kept my secret all these years. Well, Captain Palmer actually did rape her. But my mother is feisty. While he was assaulting her, she reached over and grabbed a letter opener off the desk and stabbed him right in the throat. He died a few minutes later."

"Oh, my God!" Clara shrieked. "No wonder you wanted it kept secret. I don't blame you for protecting your mother. Did she go to jail?"

"No, thank God. While it was happening, a fellow worker left the party and went to look for something in the storeroom. She walked in just as my mother stabbed the captain. A coroner's inquest was held, but she was released immediately. A case of pure self-defense."

"So if not Captain Palmer, who is your father?"

"He was my father. My mother is religious and refused an abortion. She came back to Fairview in her eighth month and told the whole story to Mildred Cole, the town clerk and her good friend. When I was born Mildred made up a birth certificate indicating that my mother and the captain were married, all legal-like. No one in Fairview, except her and then George, have any idea what actually happened."

Clara listened, drained by Charlie's recounting.

"Does your mother know that you know?" she asked.

"Oh, absolutely not. I think that might kill her. That's why I was willing to risk everything, even my presidency, to keep it quiet."

Charlie halted for a moment to regain his composure. "So my mother and father not only were never married, but they came together in ultimate violence and I'm the product. I'm what they now call an out-of-wedlock child. I suppose I'm the bastard your party always said I was."

Clara was shaken, unable to take it in her stride.

"How did you learn about all this?" she asked.

"When I went into the army after college, they shipped me to Germany. I was curious about my father and I asked them to check out his death in Korea in 1952. They came back to me and said sorry, that Captain James Raleigh Palmer had served in Korea and was wounded and decorated, but that he died in Los Angeles and not in action. They didn't tell me how, so on my return to the States, I went to Los Angeles and checked the newspapers for that whole year. There it was, an article on a Captain James R. Palmer, thirty-two, who was killed during an attempted rape. My mother's name was not mentioned. The authorities withheld it from the public. The big shock was that the picture of him in uniform in the paper was the same one we had at home. Obviously, he had given it to my mother when they were dating. I give my mother credit. She's been covering all these years, which takes stamina and courage. I know because it's torn me up and I'm much less involved."

"How does Mildred Cole come into it?"

"Well, when I became executive VP of Synergy, a lot of papers were doing profiles and they approached Mildred at the Town Hall. She didn't want them to have info on my father—not even his full name—so she did a silly thing. She started a fire in the basement and burned my birth certificate, then several others from 1953 and 1954 as a cover. Later on, when I learned what had happened, she confessed everything to me, and swore me to secrecy. Especially I was not to tell my mother that I knew. So now you know it all. I've been protecting both of them all these years—and right or wrong I was willing to pay blackmail to continue."

Clara watched as the President got off his chair and started to pace aimlessly about the sitting room, obviously in painful thought.

"Then Reichmann found out about it—I think through the new mayor, who had been courting Mildred's daughter—and he blackmailed me," Charlie continued. "I didn't give a damn for myself. It's no shame for me, but my mother struggled to build a good life in Fairview. You know how small towns are. I couldn't stand to see her reputation destroyed, especially at her age. So I went along."

Clara was moved.

"Do you think this is the time to tell her now?"

Charlie contemplated. "I thought of that. But no, she's seventy-two and I think she should live out her life without public humiliation—although she really has nothing to be ashamed of. She killed in self-defense. Maybe I am wrong not to tell her. Maybe I'm underestimating her. She's one tough cookie, but I'd rather not risk it."

"How about the political damage to you if it came out? Did you care about that?"

"It might have bothered me during the Leland period. But no more. If people don't like it, they can lump it. I'm growing up, you know."

Clara bent over the President, who was seated at his desk, and kissed him on the head.

"Charles, I've always admired you. You know that. But this makes you tops in any book. When a child shows such regard for a parent, it goes far beyond any impact you'll make on history—and I believe you'll score there as well."

"Thanks, Clara, I appreciate that. But I think my place in history is now up for grabs. In fact, it's all up to the FBI and Sergeant Sam Lemoine."

CHAPTER 75

Sam Lemoine woke in a sweat.

"Deborah!"

"Yes, Sam, what is it?" his wife asked nervously. "Did you know you were babbling in your sleep?"

"No, I didn't, but I was only half asleep—turning the damn case of the President over and over. I thought it was a nightmare."

"And?"

"And I'd better get dressed. It's past 6 in the morning."

Debbie watched, astonished, as Detective Sam Lemoine, who usually fussed over his appearance, threw his clothes on hastily, strapped on the shoulder harness for his 9-mm Beretta, and blew her a quick kiss as he exited the door of their small home on Cathedral Place.

He drove the unmarked District vehicle at the edge of the speed limit to the Idaho Avenue office, where he arrived an hour before his regular shift.

"Early bird catches a President!" the departing night shift chief chanted as he came in.

He had become a controversial figure at headquarters. Some colleagues considered the Reichmann case a coup, but others were convinced that Lemoine was pursuing the case against the President for celebrity points.

They were off base, completely, but he never tried to explain. He had turned down radio shows and press interviews, and had not returned persistent calls from television tabloid magazines. He was more tortured than proud or cocky. In his mind, he had tried to handle it as a routine case. Someone had been killed and he thought he had the murderer, and procedure had been followed.

Bullshit. He now realized that he was fooling himself. He had taken on too much responsibility in accusing the President. His draft arrest warrant had gone up into the judicial stratosphere. Jake Freund had told him it was sitting on the desk of the attorney general of the United States.

And leaks in what should have been a super-confidential case had popped up, outside his control. There were leakers in the police department, in the U.S. attorney's office, and apparently in the White House itself. What he had fantasized as a sensitive, confidential case now threatened to explode and take the country with it.

At his desk, he poured himself a coffee, black, put aside his cigar, and thumbed through the paper.

Damn it. There it was again. More revelations. In "Washington Chatter" was the latest, right up to the minute.

Under a short headline: PREZ PREDICAMENT PARALYZES PROSECUTORS, Barbara Banner had provided some uncanny insights—or fictional inventions—to conversations between the attorney general and the President from Camp David. How in the hell could she know that? The regular dailies, he was pleased, hadn't written a word about this, watching for some official confirmation from Justice—or he. But he had refused to talk to anyone.

Banner, though, was unrestrained. She wrote:

> We hear that the attorney general has held up further action on a murder one arrest warrant against the President in the $100,000 blackmail murder case. Meanwhile the AG has ordered the G-men to work with Sam Lemoine of the local homicide squad. Watch this column for news of the mad killer. In the Oval Office? Unreal!

God. What had he gotten himself into?

The FBI lead was true. Jim Buchanan of the Washington office had been assigned to the case, and they were meeting at the J. Edgar Hoover Building on Ninth and Pennsylvania in two days, on Buchanan's return from Idaho.

Meanwhile, he had to convert his nightmare into action. It had come to him when he was half awake at 4 this morning, when like clockwork of late, he rose to pee. Not so bad, really. It gave him a chance to think without interruption.

And think he did. The idea was born instantly, as with those cartoon characters with an electric light over their heads. Why didn't he get it sooner?

The only way to test his theory was to visit Stony Marcal, the man who had killed Dunn. Where was he being held? Jake Freund would know. He called him at 8:30 A..M.

"Jake, this is Sam Lemoine. I need your help. First, where are they holding Stony?"

"He's in Joliet, the federal pen outside Chicago. Why?"

"Do an old gumshoe a favor and arrange an interview for me with the hit man. I've got a theory."

"Anything to do with the arrest warrant for the President?" Freund asked, some excitement in his voice.

"Could be. Please arrange it and call me back. I want to go there today, ASAP."

Joliet was forty-five miles southwest of Chicago. He made O'Hare airport by noon, and by rented car arrived at the massive federal pen by 1:15.

Everything had been arranged for him to interview the killer in a small private room. Marcal was of middle height, a touch stocky, and with a strange milk-white, almost transparent, skin. He spoke in low decibels, but not like Brando's Mafia hoarseness. Still, Lemoine had to lean forward to catch his drift.

"I understand they have an open-and-shut case against you," Lemoine began. "They have your gun. The bullets match. You were caught climbing off the roof. I suppose all that's missing is your patron, the man who paid for it all."

Marcol shook his head as if in agreement. "Yes, but I have a fool-proof defense."

"What's that?"

"Insanity. Who in his right mind would attempt such an outright killing? I've hired the best defense attorneys, and they think I'll go the Hinckley way, which is the truth. If I was sane, I would have kept the $250,000 fee and hired others. And they're watching me closely here. I've become as mad as a bedbug. Besides, why would I try to kill a President who I think is doing a swell job?"

Lemoine listened, entertained.

"That's why I came here, Stony. Did you really intend to kill the President?"

"What does that mean?"

"Well, I understand you were once the best marksman in the mob. You hit Dunn between the eyes at 275 yards, yet you only hit the President near the shoulder, and he was wearing a vest, which you would have figured out. If you wanted to ice him, you'd have given him the Dunn treatment—right between the eyes. Right?"

Marcal suddenly broke up, laughing raucously.

"Lemoine, I'll tell you nothing. But it is true that Stony Marcal could take out anybody anytime, anywhere. See you in court, Mr. Detective."

"Just one more thing, Marcal. Who paid you the money?"

"You want the hundred percent truth?"

"Sure."

"I haven't the slightest idea. I've done business with the guy several times, and never met him. All I know is that he calls himself Patriot."

"How did he reach you and make the deal?"

"Come on, Lemoine, you're kidding. Right?"

"All right, just answer this last one. Did this same guy, whoever he was, hire you to get professionals to do the other jobs—like killing Reichmann, or trying to kill or frighten the President in a car run-down, or later in a helicopter shoot-down? Or wipe out Boxley, the reporter?"

"Now, Mr. Detective, you're getting real nosy. See you in court."

Lemoine's confidence in his theory was growing. Everyone assumed Marcal missed the fatal shot at the President. Unlikely. With his Steyr sharpshooter he had hit Dunn right between the eyes. Yet the President, who was the same distance away, only got a bullet that knocked him on his ass.

If Stony had come there to kill the President, why would he kill Dunn at all? It was superfluous, yet it was the first shot out of his gun. The truth was now as clear as spring water. Stony hadn't come to Chicago to assassinate the President. His true target was Larry Dunn.

Why? Because Dunn was the only person who could clear the President of murder. Whoever was behind the plot wanted the President besmirched, ruined, impeached, imprisoned—but not dead.

CHAPTER 76

"Mr. President, I hope you weren't sleeping, but I thought you'd like to know right away."

Charlie shook himself and sat upright. He had been awakened by the phone call. What could be so important to rouse him at 1:30 A..M.? Was there a national emergency?

"Who is this?" he barked.

"This is Pat McNulty. Mr. President, we caught him red-handed in the Oval Office just ten minutes ago, rifling through the audio bank. What I'm saying is that we've finally got the in-house spy. Ms. Staples had the right lead."

Now the President was fully awake, his mind suddenly clear.

"Who is the damn spy?"

"Mr. President, it's Robbie Barnes, your press secretary. We've got him here in the Oval Office. We'll be questioning him, but we'll wait if you want to come down."

"Barnes? That son of a bitch. And to think how much I trusted him. Give me ten minutes."

The thought of being betrayed by Barnes, a neurotic surely, but a dedicated worker, was most depressing. The presidency was complex enough without worrying whether every sentence he uttered was being dispatched to his enemies.

But why? He'd soon find out. He put on his bathrobe, then an overcoat, and shuffled downstairs, then across the portico, the chill reminding him of that unfortunate night.

As he entered the Oval Office, Barnes turned his face away. The

President decided he'd be a passive observer. "Go ahead, Pat. I'll just listen in."

McNulty did a professional job of probing. The actual situation was worse than the President thought. Barnes had been privy to everything—the blackmail, his trip to Massachusetts Avenue, up through his recent chat with Clara about the attorney general's phone call at Aspen Lodge.

"Robbie, who did this information go to?" the President asked, his curiosity overcoming him.

"Tolliver." Barnes looked down, never making eye contact with the President. "I spoke only to Andy Tolliver. I don't know what he did with it, but I guess it was disseminated to your enemies. They called themselves the Loyalists."

"Does Tolliver know who you are?" McNulty asked.

"No, I used the name Justinian, and spoke with a high voice. He doesn't even know if I'm a man or woman."

"But Robbie, why?" the President interjected. "Didn't I treat you well? Do you have anything against me personally?"

Barnes turned his head ninety degrees from the President's line of sight.

"Personally? No. You're flawed, but I think that as an individual I admire you."

"Why then?"

"Because you're a radical determined to upset the political system. I was once a radical—at seminary and Berkeley—and I also wanted to remake everything. But I learned I was wrong. Our system is two hundred years old and it's worked pretty well so far. I'm convinced that to survive we have to leave it strictly alone. It doesn't need tampering with. Radicals can be dangerous, and from what I can see, sir, you're the most dangerous one of all."

"But, Robbie, I know you admire Jefferson. Do you think he'd be happy with the state of democracy in America today?"

"That's beside the point. I FEAR POLITICAL CHANGE. It invites instability. I'm not sorry for an instant about what I did. It was for my country."

Charlie could see further discussion was useless.

"I leave him in your hands, Pat. But I do have a suggestion.".

"Yes, sir?"

"Please ask Sergeant Lemoine to interview Barnes. There might be a connection with the Reichmann murder—somehow."

"I've already thought of that, Mr. President. He'll be here in a few minutes."

Lemoine had come as requested, his sleep for the night aborted. Fortunately, he didn't have to confront the President. That would be embarrassing, and premature, at this point.

It was now 2:30 in the morning, and he had just begun his interrogation of Robbie Barnes in the Oval Office.

His first question was direct:

"What do you know about the Reichmann murder?"

"Nothing, Sergeant, except what I overheard in the White House. I didn't even know the name Reichmann until I saw it in the paper. Here, the blackmailer was called Mr. Fairview."

As Lemoine continued, Barnes provided a short political education about the Loyalists, their distaste for the President, and the hope that he would be replaced by one of their own, Vice President Hollingsworth.

"How?" Lemoine asked.

"That wasn't up to me," Barnes answered. "I don't have the stomach for mayhem. I just passed the information on to Tolliver. Just doing that took more strength than I normally have."

The man was pitiful, wailing out his disappointment in himself. It was obvious Barnes was no murderer. He couldn't even handle the revelation of his odious role.

Tolliver was the key, still another sign that politics was at the crux of it all. Lemoine had to decide when to see the party boss. If he went home now, sleep would be impossible. Why not bust Tolliver's chops? He'd wake him and maybe shake him up.

Was Tolliver "Patriot," the person who had dispatched Stony on several missions? Was it all part of a larger conspiracy to get rid of the President, preferably by a frame-up, a trap he himself had fallen into (finally, he was admitting it to himself) then replace him with Hollingsworth?

Lemoine lamented that he had been a little blind, a little too cocksure, the occupational disease of veteran detectives, especially just before their retirement.

He leaned on the concierge's desk, flashing his District Police badge.

"Keep pressing the buzzer," the detective instructed. "I don't care if he's sleeping."

The concierge smiled weakly. "But, sir, it's only 3:30 in the morning. I'll get hell for this."

"You'll get worse if you don't lean on that bell until he answers. Such a big shot should already be up and working. Look at me. I had only two hours' sleep this morning."

Suddenly, Lemoine could hear a thud coming over the phone line.

"Hello, who in the fuck is this? You startled me so that I fell out of the bed. What in the hell is going on down there?"

"Mr. Tolliver. It's the police, a detective sergeant from homicide. He says it's urgent he see you—right now."

"Ask the motherfucker if he has a warrant."

"Sergeant, Mr. Tolliver wants to know if you have a warrant?"

"Warrant, is it? Tell his nibs that if I get a warrant, it'll be a search warrant, and three of us from Idaho Avenue will rip his place apart looking for a murder weapon. OK?"

The concierge had cleverly placed the phone so that every word had been transmitted up to Penthouse B, Tolliver's sanctum.

"I HEAR, GOD DAMN IT. THE LAW IS LAWLESS. SEND THE MOTHER UP!"

Lemione laughed. He enjoyed stripping privilege from the privileged. All Justinian's info had gone to Tolliver. From there, had Tolliver been a conduit to Stony, directly or indirectly? Or was he the mastermind himself?

He rang the bell just once before Tolliver answered the door. His appearance was surprising. A rotund three-hundred-plus pounds, the party chief had several chins, all of which were now on nighttime parade. He was wearing pajamas, and with his wisps of uncombed hair, he looked monumental and disorderly.

"What can I do for you, Detective?" Tolliver asked, his manner now more subdued. "I'd ask you to sit down, but the chairs are all filled with the castoffs of my life."

Suddenly he spotted Lemoine's cigar, twirling slowly in his hand.

"Would you like a light?" Tolliver asked. Lemoine shook his head.

"Oh, here's a telephone stool you can sit on. Now, why a man from homicide? Who was I supposed to have killed?"

A smartass, he could see.

"Well, Mr. Tolliver, you may know that I've been investigating the Reichmann murder—the private eye who got killed on Massachusetts Avenue, the man who was blackmailing the President."

"Oh, yes, I know all about that. I understand that our President is the killer."

Lemoine ignored the comment.

"Did you know that Justinian in the White House has been apprehended and has told all? I just left him."

"Him? Who was it?" Tolliver's pink complexion flushed even brighter.

"Robbie Barnes, the press man."

"Son of a gun! Good American. Barnes gave us fine intelligence, all very damaging to the President."

"You fellows play hard."

"Oh, yes, Sergeant. This is the biggest chess game in the world."

"Do any of the chess pieces commit murder?"

"Come now, Detective. Do I look like a killer? All I did was take

Justinian's information and pass it on to Loyalists who hate the President as much as I do."

"Enough to kill him?"

"Who knows? Not me. I'm a coward. But Charlie Fanatic dead—say of natural causes? That would be nice."

Lemione, who considered himself unshockable, was shocked.

"If you didn't do it, who do you think killed Reichmann and Larry Dunn?"

"How should I know? But I thought the President killed Reichmann to stop the blackmail. No?"

Lemoine again ignored the comment.

"Sergeant, all I did was pass on juicy tidbits. If you remember, I passed some to you—the poop about the President being at Reichmann's house that night. It came directly from Barnes to me, then to you, all within minutes."

"That was you—Mr. Anonymous?"

"None other."

"So who are the Loyalists, the brand of patriots who you kept informed?"

"Well, naturally yours truly, *primus unter pares.* Then the first line of defense includes Vice President Jason Hollingsworth, then Norm Sobel, the campaign chief of the other party, then former presidential candidate Champ Billings, then Senator Harry Berry, who ran for Vice President, then Karl 'King' Kellogg, the master lobbyist."

"Do you think they were involved in any murders?"

"Now, Sergeant, don't be silly. These are all upstanding Americans."

"Did you pass Justinian's information on to anyone else?"

"Well, I've also kept Barbara Banner up to date. Have you seen her excellent pieces?"

Lemoine nodded. "Tell me, Mr. Tolliver, have you ever used the name Patriot and do you know anyone who has?"

"No, not really. I'm a patriot, but that's with a small 'p.' I hope you are too. So you now know everything I do."

Lemoine sensed he had met his match, but that didn't mean that Tolliver was not a prime suspect, now one of six. He got off the stool, and weaved his way through the detritus toward the door.

"Tolliver, don't leave the District. We may need you."

"Don't worry, Mr. Sergeant. I go outside the District as little as possible. This is the Promised Land, you know."

As Lemoine left, he was already formulating a way to connect with Patriot, the final, deadly point of Tolliver's network.

CHAPTER 77

"Charlie, what in the hell is going on in Washington? There's such a ruckus that we hear all about it even in Montana. Blackmail and murder. Come on kid, that's not your style."

He hadn't heard that voice, still tinged with Brooklyn, for over a week. He didn't know if he wanted to talk it out with Sky, but he had no choice.

"Sky, it's a holy mess. The blackmail is true, but the murder charge is crazy. I just tried to keep private something that would have hurt my family and a friend. And now it's all come back to haunt me."

"Private? Such as? I thought my elves found out everything about you?"

"No, Sky, your spies missed this one. It's something I've shared with no one except George, and that was years ago."

"So what's it all about?"

"I can't tell you what I was willing to pay blackmail to keep secret. But I can fill you in on the Washington end of things."

"Please do, Charlie. I'm dying of curiosity, and I'm also afraid that this time they may clobber us."

Charlie told him the story of the trip to Massachusetts Avenue, the murder, the fingerprints, the involvement of the attorney general and the investigation of Sergeant Lemoine.

"Don't say another word, Mr. President. Jenny and I will be in Washington first thing tonight."

Before Charlie could respond, the line went dead.

Now, he and Rafferty were relaxing in front of the fireplace in the Oval Office that night. Charlie had poured Sky an Irish whiskey, and he was nursing a light beer.

"Charlie, this stupid murder charge must be killing you. That's why I left paradise to come to this madhouse—to see how you're doing. Are you holding up?"

"Best as can be expected."

"Any new developments?" Rafferty asked. "Everyone with brains knows you're innocent, but that circle of smart Americans is getting smaller every day. That's why I'm worried."

"There's some news," Charlie tried to reassure him. "Lemoine is working with Jim Buchanan of the FBI. Jim tells me Lemoine is having second thoughts—even coming around to believe that Reichmann's murder and Dunn's are connected, all part of a plot to frame me. Together they've cooked up something to get Stony Marcal to help find the mastermind—someone who calls himself Patriot. Stony swears he has no idea who he is, and they believe him."

"Good. Charlie, it'd be a shame if something as outrageous as a frame-up kills all your work so far. And . . ."

"And what, Sky?"

"And wastes my $100 million."

Rafferty laughed and took another drink but Charlie wasn't so sure he was kidding.

"Charlie, we've also came to this capital of rhetoric and waste because my daughter, Jenny, is in love with you. You must know that."

The President smiled. "Well, she's young and impressionable, and she is a wonderful girl. But you know, I'm back with Clara and . . ."

"You don't have to apologize. I told her you're almost old enough to be her father. But if you have a chance, let's all dine together tonight. That'll make her happy."

"Of course, Sky, anytime."

"Good. Now on to more important matters. Aside from that Reichmann madness, how is the politics going? Are you accomplishing everything you wanted?"

Charlie was pleased that another topic could occupy his mind.

"Yes, as a matter of fact, my replacement in the House, Larry Lafferty, is co-sponsoring my constitutional amendments, the Twenty-eighth and Twenty-ninth. They will totally remake our elections and lousy campaign finance system. Senator Larrimore is carrying the ball in the Senate."

"A comprehensive change?"

"Oh, yes, Rafferty. And all in one package. We're closing the Electoral College, going by popular vote only. No more Presidents without a majority, and the same for Congress. The top two vote-getters will finish in a runoff, like most civilized countries. No more spoilers. Independents will have the same shot as the regular parties at making the top two spots. We want a small number of signatures for all nominations so ordinary people outside the parties can throw their hat in—like the congressional primary ballot in Ohio."

"What about all that 'legal bribery,' as you call it, the millions in cash flowing into politics every day?"

"That'll all be gone. No more peddling for money, not from PACs or anybody. And not that phony campaign finance reform Congress is pushing. Under my amendment, it'll be illegal to raise even $1 from any source. Candidates won't be able to spend their own money on their campaigns either, no matter how rich they are. No more using taxpayer funds, either. We'll have a quasi-public philanthropic group collecting money from everyone without any limit and dispensing it equally among all candidates for each office. No more soft money crap either for the parties. They'll get their hunk from the same fund. So in one fell swoop we'll have cleaned up legal bribery, two-party domination, most corruption, scrounging for money, the power of special interests and lobbyists, and Presidents and congressmen elected without a majority—and God knows what else is now going on."

"Good, except—"

"Except what?"

"Except that'll stop billionaires like me from influencing elections."

"You bet your ass it will, Sky. You did your job—one time and the nation is thankful. I hope that's all we'll ever need to set things straight."

Schuyler laughed. "Mr. President, you're a piece of work, and that's why I love ya."

Rafferty downed his whiskey tumbler in one swallow.

"What about your 'no-party' idea?"

"We'll do that in stages as independents gain power. Can't push the people too quickly. First we have to clean up what we have."

"What are the chances of passing this Boy Scout amendment?"

"If that damn murder suspicion wasn't hanging around me like an albatross, we'd be in like Flynn. But my 80 percent approval is down to 50 percent. The people are just waiting for more news, and so is Congress. If I get cleared, they'll be afraid to buck me. If not—well, at best, it's back to Ohio."

Rafferty got up, went to the silent butler, and poured himself another drink.

"Objectively, I'm worried about you, young man. But you still strike me as a solid investment. Like I've always said, you've got destiny written all over your face."

CHAPTER 78

"Do you think Patriot will show?"

Lemoine stood alongside the questioner, Jim Buchanan of the FBI. Both men peered intently out the window of a deserted warehouse overlooking the pier on the muddy Anacostia River.

It was 10:30 P.M. They had been waiting since 10, before Stony himself had arrived. It was close to the time of his usual rendezvous with Patriot. Standing, even for a half hour, was wearing on Lemione, but he was happy he was still able to handle a stakeout at age fifty-five. The smallest arthritic pain invaded his legs, but he couldn't afford to sit. He diverted himself by thinking of retirement to his small place near the ocean at Kitty Hawk.

The two law enforcement men, outfitted with infrared night binoculars, stared out toward the slip, where Stony now stood, unaware of their presence, garbed in his usual dark pea jacket. The full moon shone on his strange milk-white skin, now half-covered with his disguise of a mustache and beard.

On the other side of the old pier, its weathered planks advertising their age, a team of FBI and Secret Service agents were ensconced in another deserted warehouse. The night sights of their sniper rifles were aimed at the land portion of the pier where Patriot would be standing—if he arrived.

"Would you show if you were Patriot?" Lemoine asked.

"Figure it this way," the FBI agent responded, "I owe the guy maybe another million and a half bucks. But he's damaged goods—supposedly an escapee from Joliet. So if I ice him, there's nothing lost and I'm that much ahead. Maybe Patriot doesn't usually use his hands, but this is tempting."

"And what happens if he doesn't show?" Lemoine pressed.

Buchanan had a ready answer. "Then since Stony is a 'free man,' or so he and Patriot both think, Stony will go to the ends of the earth to find and kill him."

"We'll see in a few minutes," Lemoine responded.

The FBI and Secret Service had met and collaborated on this rendezvous, an idea developed in exquisite detail by Lemoine. He was determined to clear the President, even though the only available evidence still pointed to him. He was now convinced that President Palmer was the victim of a frame-up.

Lemoine knew that only Stony "free" could set up the sting to ensnare Patriot. The next step took place at Joliet. An undercover FBI man made contact with Stony through another family member in the pen. An amazingly realistic toy gun, plus a survival kit of a fake mustache and beard, plus a new ID, along with $5,000, was delivered to Stony through the prison underground. Guards were told to let Stony "escape" as soon as he threatened them with the "gun." A new Mercury was waiting outside the gate.

In the car, driven by an ex-con, now an FBI informer, was a new set of clothes. His friends in the family had arranged it all, the driver explained. Where did Stony want to go?

"Washington, D.C. Anacostia to be exact."

They had driven an hour from Joliet when Stony broke the silence. "I'll need a piece. Do you have one?"

They had anticipated the request. It held potential danger, but Lemoine knew they couldn't refuse. Stony could always buy a gun in the thriving Washington black market, anyway. The driver handed him a Beretta 9-mm and two magazines of ammunition.

It was vital that Stony not know his escape had been stage-managed. If he felt free, he would surely arrange to collect the million or more due from Patriot, leading them to the man who was behind all the mayhem. Who knew how Stony would react otherwise?

A team of four undercover men were assigned to follow him. They settled in motels, separately, not far from where Stony rented a room in Anacostia. His disguise, which included nose putty, was well executed.

For a few days, Stony spent most of his time watching television. Then one day, he left and took the Metro to the newspaper building in downtown Washington. He entered the classified ad room and scribbled a personal, paying for it with a $100 bill.

The FBI tail waited until he had left. "Miss, could I please have a copy of that ad?" he said, flashing his identification. "It's important government business."

The ad was simple: PATRIOT. STONY NEEDS TO SEE YOU SOONEST. RESPOND.

Lemoine and Buchanan watched the personals every day. Almost a week went by without response. Then on a Tuesday morning, there it was. STONY. PATRIOT ADMIRES YOU.

The response was ambiguous, but contact had been made. So Patriot admired him? Did that mean he would show with the money, or was that just his way of kissing Stony Marcal goodbye?

The FBI tails had followed Marcal everywhere that day. At 9:40 P.M., he had walked from his room down toward the river and was now standing on the pier, waiting.

Lemoine stared out at the wooden slip. The full moon changed the melancholy landscape into one of drama, with light hitting the creaky wooden pier at odd angles. He checked his watch: 10:35. It was getting late.

Maybe his conviction that Patriot would show was wrong. The second Lemoine thought that, a man suddenly appeared on foot at the edge of the land carrying two large bags. He half-dragged them until he reached the edge of the pier. Lemoine stared at the new arrival but he couldn't make out his face. The moon was shining on the man's back.

The two were now some thirty feet apart.

"Stony, this is Patriot. How are you? Heard you escaped from Joliet."

"Yeah, I have good friends. Do you have the money?"

"Of course. I know better than to stiff you. I'll leave it here at the edge of the slip, and you can come get it. I'd like to say hello to you personally. Taking out Dunn was a real coup. I think that will finally sink the President."

"Sure, I can say hello. No need to hide my face anymore. It's plastered on wanted posters all over the country. As far as the President, I couldn't care less. You know that with me, it's strictly business."

Lemoine watched transfixed as the two men approached. They stood face-to-face and shook hands. The expression on Stony's face was nondescript. It was obvious he didn't recognize his patron.

Stony leaned down to pick up the bags and as he did, he froze. Patriot had taken his hand out of his pocket. He brandished a pistol, pressing it against the side of Stony's head.

"Don't, Patriot. Don't shoot. You can keep the money. Please . . ."

Several shots suddenly exploded in the night. Lemoine squinted through the infrared binoculars. Stony had slumped over, onto the boards. Patriot, standing over him, walked a step further into the pier, then collapsed, the sound reverberating.

Lemoine ran out of the warehouse toward the pier. Several agents reached the spot at the same time.

He stood there as Stony rose up from the boards, his face covered with confusion. Stony had defensively dropped to the boards when he heard the shots, and was unhurt.

"What happened? Who are you guys?" Stony shouted.

"FBI. You're lucky we arrived in time. We got Patriot just as he was about to finish you."

Lemoine and two agents then rushed over to Patriot, who was lying facedown, his blood smearing the pier.

They turned him over. "He's dead. Anybody know who this is?" Buchanan called out.

Lemoine bent down and stared at the face.

"Yes. I know him. I interviewed him months ago when someone tried to run down President Palmer with a car when he was a Congressman. Part of a hate list Palmer gave me. This is King Kellogg, a top Washington lobbyist. Strange, the man impressed me as an intellectual, not a killer. But you never know when someone is consumed by hatred."

Lemoine walked over and opened one of the two duffel bags Kellogg had dragged in, pulling out a fistful of $100 bills. King had come to pay off his debt, or kill his man, whichever seemed more feasible. In the end, he had accomplished neither.

The detective moved out onto the old planks and walked toward the end of the pier, to the spot where Stony had been.

It had been a roundabout investigation, but as he stood in the solitude, Lemoine reflected that he had done his best, and in the end, it had worked out. He knew nothing about American politics, but one thing he had learned. It was too rough a game for the likes of him.

CHAPTER 79

Detective Sergeant Sam Lemoine shifted uneasily in the old wing chair in the Oval Office, waiting for the President. He still felt somewhat sheepish, but confident that at last he had unraveled the most difficult case of his career.

The President entered from his small study next door and walked directly to Lemoine, who rose as he approached.

"No need, Sergeant. Please sit down. Tell me, what's up?"

"Mr. President, I have good news. Stony has talked—under the threat of a District prosecution on top of the federal one. We now have all the details on the Reichmann murder and the other crimes. I've asked the U.S. Attorney for the District to tear up the draft arrest warrant against you."

"Well, that is good news." Charlie could feel his breath release, as if it had been stifled all these months. This was the first assurance that he was fully cleared.

"How did Kellogg arrange all of this?" the President asked. "It's a shame such a good mind was put to such perverse use. And he must have spent a fortune on this mad adventure."

"Yes, he started out by paying Stony to investigate you. When his gumshoes learned that Reichmann was doing that same job, and much better, they followed him around Ohio in a white Ford Taurus. From the new mayor, they found that Reichmann had hit paydirt, although they weren't sure what it was. Stony's people followed Reichmann from Ohio to Washington, D.C., where Reichmann set up shop on Massachusetts Avenue."

The President leaned forward, intrigued. "How did they know that I was coming there that night?"

"Easy. Stony had Reichmann's phone tapped, and when he learned that the private eye was blackmailing you, he reported that to Patriot—Kellogg—who developed the plot to frame you. They knew you were coming at 11:30. At 10:30, Stony's hit man forced his way in with a gun, then stabbed Reichmann in the back. He made sure nothing was disturbed so it wouldn't look like a simple robbery. Since you'd be there shortly, Kellogg figured it was a perfect setup. And of course, you helped by leaving your fingerprints on Reichmann's briefcase."

"Was Patriot behind everything that happened?"

"Oh, yes, sir. Justinian was feeding the information to Tolliver, who passed it along to his group, including Kellogg. Tolliver didn't know anything about the violence, but he was an ally against you, as was Norm Sobel. They put aside their differences when it came to you. The seeming attempts on your life—the run-down by the Taurus and the helicopter attack—were just Kellogg's way of scaring the shit out of you, hoping you'd quit and go back to Ohio before the election."

Lemoine paused nervously. "I'm sorry, Mr. President. Excuse the language. Comes from working the Washington streets."

"That's all right, Sergeant. I've been known to use a few four-letter words now and then."

"Kellogg also had that reporter, Boxley, killed. A contact in the Caymans picked up cash by informing Kellogg that Boxley was checking on him and Tolliver. Kellogg had Boxley followed to the Baltimore diner and was hoping to find the tape of the Tolliver-Sobel meeting. When Stony's people couldn't find it in Boxley's house, Kellogg decided to shut him up permanently. It was lucky Boxley's wife tracked down the tape and gave it to Leland. Then Kellogg ordered you and Ms. Staples recorded at Mohonk, part of the plan to discredit you with the public."

"How about the Chicago assassination attempt?" the President asked, trying to keep up with the details of the plot. "How come Stony missed me and killed Dunn instead?"

"Actually, he didn't miss you. They had no intention of killing you. If Stony had wanted to, I'm afraid you wouldn't be here now. No, their target was only Dunn. Kellogg was afraid that with you dead, you'd become a martyr and Senator Larrimore would pick up your mantle and continue the reform work. No, he just wanted to discredit you—get you convicted of murder or be forced to resign because of public pressure. Then his boy, Vice President Hollingsworth, would become President. The final kill, the murder of Dunn, was an important part of the plot. If Dunn had lived even one more day, his affidavit would have cleared you."

"So is everything now settled?"

"Yes, sir. Except for one thing."

"What's that, Sergeant?"

"I owe you an apology—for not seeing through their frame-up sooner."

"No, Sam, if I may call you that. You did a thorough job and all evidence did point to me, and no one else. I helped it along by going out alone to see Reichmann, then leaving my fingerprints. And that same thoroughness of yours finally broke open what could have been a continuous blackmail plot against me in the White House. Now the secret stays with me. And it's not anything the country need know anyway. No, you're to be congratulated."

The President rose and shook Lemoine's hand.

"Thank you for that, Mr. President. And I've learned one thing from all this."

"What's that, Sergeant?"

"That I've got a tough job, but it's still a dream compared to yours."

"George, this madness of King Kellogg is a symptom of the break-down of civil democracy. When people's ideology and emotions run so high that they connive, scheme, even kill to get their way, we're in big trouble."

The President was in the Oval Office just an hour later, seated with Sempel and Clara.

"The whole idea of democracy is to be able to lose graciously, grin and bear it, and come back and argue your position for the next time," Charlie said. "I'm afraid we're losing that precious concept. Instead, we're poisoning the system with self-interest. I may not agree with my opposition, but either my view or theirs wins out. That's what our Founding Fathers believed. Maybe we'd better go back and study them."

"Mr. President, you're right," Sempel concurred. "It leads to people like Tolliver with their dirty tricks, then to Kellogg, who was so consumed by hatred of your reforms that he actually became mad. I think had he lived, he could have successfully pleaded insanity. But it's a shame that politics can lead to such excess."

"So, George, now that I'm cleared and my program is on track, what will you do?"

"I told you when I joined up that I'd only be here as long as necessary. Well, now Synergy and Ohio call. I'm on my way back tomorrow. I think you'd be wise to appoint Sally as chief of staff. She knows the job as well as, or better than, I do."

As the President nodded agreement, Sempel rose from the wing chair and walked toward him.

"I think this last time I can become familiar," Sempel said, placing his arm around the President's shoulder. "Charlie, it's been a thrill serving you and the country. I hope you stay in office eight years. But if not, your job will be waiting—if an ex-President could manage to live in Fairview. But after all, Truman returned to Independence, and he's stood up well in history. I think you will too."

Sempel then said his goodbyes to Clara, and left the Oval Office.

Charlie and Clara, the two protagonists in their on-and-off love affair, now sat across from each other, smiles crossing their faces.

"So, Clara, it's just me and you. How do we stand?"

"What does that mean, Charles. I'm here, aren't I?"

"Yes, but for how long? What I mean is—will you marry me and switch from being Miss Gotrocks of the Political World to the First Lady of America?"

Clara flirtatiously cocked her head.

"Well, let's give it a month or so and see. I'm getting accustomed to your politics. Not as much fun as mine, but it makes me feel good about myself, which is saying something."

"So is the answer yes or no?"

"Darling, Charles, the answer is maybe. But I think if you play your cards right, we could soon be America's First Couple."

Charlie looked quizzically at this elusive woman, then reached over and hugged her warmly.

It had been an extraordinary adventure, but travail and all, he had to confess that, God help him, he absolutely loved the political fray. Especially when every once in a while he could hear the glorious strains of "Hail to the Chief."

Besides, he was now convinced that it was, ultimately, his destiny. And perhaps a better one for America as well.

Martin L. Gross has established a nationwide reputation as a critic of wasteful and corrupt government. He has written a series of nonfiction political critiques, three of which have become *New York Times* bestsellers.

His first, *The Government Racket: Washington Waste from A to Z*, reached number three on the *Times* list and triggered a widespread debate on government spending and the need for reform. He has testified before the U.S. Congress five times, and has received praise from both sides of the aisle and from the White House. His other bestsellers are *A Call for Revolution: How Washington is Strangling America* and *The Tax Racket.*

Other nonfiction works by Mr. Gross include *The Brain Watchers, The Doctors,* and *The Psychological Society*—critiques of personality testing, medical care, and psychology and psychiatry, respectively—all of which aroused considerable controversy within those professions.

Mr. Gross has appeared on numerous national television programs, including "Larry King Live," "20/20," "Good Morning America," "Prime Time Live," and "CBS This Morning," as well as on CNN, the Fox News Network, PBS, and C-Span. The former editor-in-chief of *Book Digest,* he is an experienced Washington reporter, whose syndicated column, "The Social Critic," appeared in newspapers throughout the country, from the *Los Angeles Times* to the *Chicago Sun-Times* to *Newsday.*

Mr. Gross has served on the faculty of the New School for Social Research and has been Adjunct Associate Professor of Social Science at New York University. He lives and works in Connecticut.